Fred Nicholls was born in a village near Canterbury, Kent, and has had a lifelong interest in the sea and ships. Serving at sea in sail is part of his family's history, and he himself served at sea in the Royal Navy for three years, ending up as a watch-keeping officer in a fleet sweeper. In addition to this, he has been a cub reporter, a farm labourer and an Oxford student, before settling down as a teacher of English, and doing some small-boat sailing off the Welsh coast in his spare time.

Fred Nicholls' love of writing has also been practically lifelong, and this is his seventh published book; he has also written often for country and yachting magazines, and for sound radio. He and his wife Ann now live in Newport, Pembrokeshire - the fictional home of many of the characters in this book.

ALSO BY FRED NICHOLLS

Published by Starborn Books
MASTER UNDER GOD

Published by Wm Heinemann Ltd.
THE LOG OF THE SARDIS
THE FREE TRADERS
HONEST THIEVES (NON-FICTION)

Published by Tynron Press
THE LOBSTER PIRATES
INTO THE FIRE

Fred Nicholls

THE DARK OCEAN AND THE LIGHT

Starborn Books

THE DARK OCEAN AND THE LIGHT
Fred Nicholls

First published in 2009
by Starborn Books

ISBN 978 1 899530 33 5

e-mail: sales@starbornbooks.co.uk
website: www.starbornbooks.co.uk

Printed in Great Britain by the MPG Books Group,
Bodmin and King's Lynn

FOREWORD

'The Dark Ocean and the Light' is a wonderful sequel to Fred Nicholls' 'Master under God' - both absolutely thrilling books. Yet I have to admit that in this book I sorely miss the presence of the testy, pugnacious, but very human Jacob Roberts, late captain of the now wrecked barque 'Figaro', and the original Master under God.

I had no idea about - no interest even in - life aboard old sailing-ships in the company of men. Yet I found this book utterly compelling, because of the writer's descriptions of the merciless and savage sea, and the lifeboat which manages to stay afloat only through the unyielding dedication of her crew, who risk their lives constantly, performing superhuman feats of strength and courage in order to keep their creaking, flapping, frail wooden craft afloat in the grip of nature's most powerful forces.

Fred Nicholls' descriptive writing is breathtaking, and heartbreaking too: he portrays the characters of the men - so brave and strong, and yet so limited, so bound by their educations and the station in life in which they find themselves trapped, the limited opportunities offered to them, and their stunted emotional intelligence which often leaves them as their own worst enemies.

No less impressive is the fastidious and painstaking historical research which must have gone into the preparation of this book, giving the reader a real opportunity to be transported aboard a 19th century working sailing vessel.

Then of course there is Eleanor, who is a catalyst of so much that happens - strong, opinionated, spirited, clever, sexy - no wonder sailors say that having a woman on board a ship is unlucky (but lucky for Raven!) Fred Nicholls' description of the roughness of the men and their struggles with the ship, juxtaposed with his insights into the lively mind of a captain's daughter and her awakening passion is a credit to the breadth of his writing style.

I can only recommend this book to all readers, regardless of whether or not they have an interest in ships and sailing.

Atinuke Sears
Short-listed children's book writer
and traditional story-teller

ACKNOWLEDGEMENTS

To Ann, for her careful reading and corrections to the typescript.
To Professor Alastair Couper for background advice about maritime law and the Pacific Islands.
To my wife's cousin, Sylvia Lawer and the late John Butterman for invaluable help with research on the topography of Auckland Islands, when all other sources had failed.
To Rhiannon and Simon for their IT expertise.
To my grandson Tom for his guidance on Southern Ocean fish species.
To my friends Liz and Elvet for their corrections to my often faulty Welsh grammar. Diolch yn fawr iawn i chi!
To my friend and distant relative Kiran Malik for his advice on late Victorian dollar exchange rates.

To my wife Ann for her help and support, and to the large number of my Newport friends and neighbours, whose appreciation of my previous book MASTER UNDER GOD has been a huge encouragement and an incentive to follow it with this one.

THE DARK OCEAN AND THE LIGHT

'I saw also that there was an ocean of darkness and death, but an infinite ocean of light and love, which flowed over the ocean of darkness.'

George Fox (1624-1691), English founder
of the Society of Friends (Quakers)

The Auckland Archipelago

PROLOGUE

You, my friend, are looking, with your mind's eye, across miles of sea at the coast of a desert island - desert in the sense that nobody lives on it, or would want to. Decades ago, some hardy - perhaps foolhardy - people tried to make a home of this cold, wet, windy place, but failed, defeated by the wretched monotony of the climate. For you are not looking at long white beaches, waving coconut palms or coral reefs - you are a very long way from those. Instead you see one of the grimmer parts of the planet; the backcloth to the scene in front of you is a twenty-five-mile line of high black cliffs - five hundred feet or more high - of basalt rock. You're seeing the west coast of the sub-Antarctic Auckland Island in fifty degrees of south latitude, three hundred miles south of New Zealand's South Island. The nearest human dwellings are at Invercargill, the nearest ships at Bluff Cove, across a great deal of very dangerous water.

It is not long after dawn on a relatively fine morning; it's late September - early spring here, but the brisk westerly wind is still keen. A great, tireless albatross rides easily on it. The huge grey swells you see have rolled here, unhindered by any land, all the way from Cape Horn, many thousands of miles to the west. Ceaselessly, the swells batter at the base of those black cliffs. From this far off you see only a white fringe that comes and goes, spreads and shrinks, but if you were nearer you would hear the regular dull, ponderous thuds as the moving mountains of water explode, sending sheets of spray a good fifty feet up the cliffs. The scene is typical of so much of the world's cold extremities - savage, primeval, desolate, devoid of human life, or any sign of Man's existence.

And yet - look there! Under that high black peak! Look, there are three specks of white moving steadily north in front of that gloomy wall. Get your glasses focused on them. Now you can see better what they are: three ship's lifeboats, each with a small lugsail that's set into a hard concave by the brisk wind. Each boat keeps appearing and disappearing as the swells raise it and plunge it down, till only the extreme sharp peak of its sail shows. The boats are tiny, puny things, yet brave, persistent and buoyant, and evidently skilfully piloted, for they keep in the formation of line ahead, following steadily in the leader's wake. This far off, they seem to crawl, but through your glasses you can see each one ploughing steadily towards the north end of the island, leaning away from you, the fleck of foam at its bows showing that it's making a decent speed - six knots or so, by the look of it.

The lifeboats are full of clustered sailors, who must have been a crew once, must also be escaping from some lost ship, but what wreck, and where? Foundered below this grey lonely sea? No. Train your glasses to your right - no, further, further... Now do you see it? There's little enough to see, it's true. Keep going right, past that little skerry of rocks on which the swells dash themselves in fury - Sugar Loaf Rocks, they call those - a nice homely, cosy name, isn't it, for a dreary death-trap for ships? Now then, under that high peak - must be fifteen hundred feet or more, that one - do you see, sticking up out of the sea, right under the cliffs, a small yellow mast, white tipped, with a loose sail flapping from it?

That is all that's left to see of the Welsh barque 'Figaro' of Cardiff, a ship of three thousand tons, registered A1 at Lloyds. She had three other, much bigger masts spreading forty thousand square feet of sail, but they, like the ship herself, are now in ruins; she's been forced, stuffed, rammed by the remorseless swells into a huge cave - can you see the mouth of it now, blacker even than the cliffs themselves? She was trapped by fog and a treacherous flat calm, you see, a calm that made her a great lifeless, unmanageable log. Impossible, you say? Well, yes, but then with thousands of ships plying the seas for centuries, all over the globe in all weathers, sailed by all manner of men, sometimes the impossible is bound to happen. Shakespeare's 'Tempest' was based on an impossible escape from destruction (in the Bermudas, wasn't it?) and what about the 'Mary Celeste'? No-one's ever been able to work out what happened to her. Anyway, you can see for yourself - it's happened, impossible or not.

What you're seeing now is her aftermost mast, the jigger mizzen; the sail that flaps uselessly in the wind is her triangular jigger topsail. Inside the cave, where no-one now will ever see, the ship's strong, beautiful steel hull, stoutly riveted, is being ground to pieces, torn apart by the heaving sea and sharp spikes of rock jutting from the cave floor, her complex geometrical web of masts, yards, stays, halyards, braces, lifts, backstays and shrouds now a meaningless, horrible tangle. Soon the three thousand tons of good bright coal that she loaded in Newcastle, New South Wales, to take to Valparaiso in Chile will pave blackly that thundering dark hell which was her graveyard.

And graveyard it is, too, for, lying under a fallen spar, fixed forever at the break of the poop, the place from which he'd piloted his ship thousands of miles from Penarth, is the body of the only casualty of the wreck, her captain, Jacob Roberts of Ty Coch Isaf, Newport in Pembrokeshire. Driven by centuries of tradition, he'd insisted on being the last to leave her. Then, as he lingered, dazed and overcome with grief at the loss of the ship he'd come to love, her heavy mizen t'gallant yard fell on him, and there he, or his bones, will be forever. Perhaps, deep down, he had no wish to leave: perhaps he felt too deeply the shame, the cruel burden of responsibility for the loss of a huge, brand-new windjammer while he was her master - her master under God, as he used to say some-times. Now, his friends would say, may that same God rest him, for he was a good man, for all his faults.

Come left now with your glasses, back to those boats in close, strict formation, like naval cruisers. That was the order of the man steering the leading boat, a man not to be trifled with, Simon Grant, mate of the barque. No, that was in the past. Now, though he does not yet know it, for his was the first boat to leave the wreck, he will have to become captain of 'Figaro's' crew of homeless distressed seamen; distressed indeed, for all their humble possessions are now lost but for the clothes they sit in - thick jerseys and trousers, stiff oilskins and sou'wester hats that shadow grim, drawn faces.

Grant's attention is on his steering, for the sharp westerly wind has raised a short choppy sea on top of the huge, sliding, whale-backed swells. His twenty-foot lifeboat is clinker-built of overlapping planks, and, as she crunches into the steep little waves it sounds as if she were hitting successive heaps of gravel. But at the back of Grant's mind must be worries about what lies ahead on the island - even fears perhaps, though he is a man - tough, squarely-built, athletic, auburn-haired with light-blue, very intense eyes that make people uneasy when he fixes them with a stare - a man, then, who's not easily frightened by anything.

His crew sits, huddled together, in a line on the windward side of the boat to balance the pressure of the lugsail, which the wind has set in a steely, beautiful hollow mould. They are a mixed lot: youngish, mostly Welsh seamen, some fresh-faced apprentices not yet twenty - more like overgrown schoolboys - and in the bow, in dignified solitude as befits his status, a stout, grizzled black cook from Jamaica with a name more impressive than any other in the boat - Wellington Jones.

The next boat in the procession is steered by an oldish man, long-chinned, leathery and mahogany-coloured of face, also absorbed in the effort to keep station on his leader and - much more important - to make sure that his boat doesn't heel to the point of capsize, for in this icy sea that would be the finish of them. He's Reuben Mathias, bosun, the chief of the lower deck and the ship's carpenter too, for, like many in the crew and like his dead captain, he's a countryman from Pembrokeshire, and, like most countrymen, he's almost infinitely versatile with his hands and his knowledge - sailor, carpenter, rigger, boat-builder, farmer, horseman, mason - the list is impressive.

Now what of the last boat of the little flotilla? Train your glasses on her. At first she's like the others, her men in glistening oilskins lined close together on the port side, some even perched up on the gunwale - the boat's top plank. But look at her helmsman at the tiller - do you see something different there? He's younger than the other boat-skippers - better-looking too: dark-eyed and dark-skinned with an almost Spanish look, and suitably enough his name is Raven - John Raven. He was the windjammer's second mate, only recently promoted from being the senior apprentice, but his captain's death has promoted him again, so he is now the mate, though only twenty years old.

But while the other steerers sit clear of the rest of their crew, he steers with his right hand while his left arm embraces the figure that leans tightly against his left side, its bowed head resting on his left breast, so close that from this distance they form one unified shape. Now that you didn't expect, did you?

It is, of course, a woman, the ship's only passenger, though now dressed in the same rough, stiff garb as all the rest. She's Eleanor Roberts, only nineteen - Nelli, her father used to call her, but he will not call her again, for she is the dead captain's daughter. Only half an hour ago she was waiting in the boat as it heaved and sank and heaved again under the stern of the stricken ship, waiting, desperate with anxiety, for him to come down the ladder from the poop. But, as we know, he never did leave his ship, so now she is an orphan, for her mother - a passenger too - died of typhus two months ago on the long voyage from the River Plate to Australia; she died of her own goodness, for she spent many hours tending the two men down with that deadly fever. They recovered but she did not, so now Eleanor has only the lover on whom she now - in every sense - leans. It was he who, in the ship's last moments, went back to find her father and bring him to the boat, but found him trapped and at the point of death. He it was who heard the Old Man's last words - words that Raven will carry to his grave: 'I know I'm finished... Listen, boy, I can't look after Nelli any more, can I? You're not a bad young fellow, even if you are English. I know I've been no friend of yours sometimes, but that's all in the past, isn't it? You will look after her, won't you? And love her? And be faithful to her, for my sake and for her dear mother's sake, God rest her? So now leave me, for I don't want you to get drowned in this miserable hole that I put you all in.' Then he'd begun to pray in his native tongue, but after only a few words - silence.

So, while all the men in the three boats have their minds fixed on the present danger and possible future hardships and dangers on a desolate, damp, windy island at the end of the world, hundreds of miles from human aid, Eleanor is sunk deep, deep, in the present agony of her loss, the final obliteration of all she knew and held dear - mother, father, ship, and even her old home back in Newport, Ty Coch Isaf, the warm comfortable pink cottage on the north flank of the little mountain called Carn Ingli - the Cairn of the Angels, for that, she knows, has passed into a stranger's hands.

Only John Raven is left to her; she has loved him, with all the reckless, fiery passion of a nineteen-year-old, for some months now. She ignored all her parents' warnings about Raven's reputation as a notorious womanizer in every port of call. She has many times in the night watches abandoned all caution and all the principles of her strong Christian faith, and gone secretly to his cabin, and lain naked with him in his bunk, drunk with the feverish ecstasy of deep kisses and frantic, unbridled fondling of each other's bodies. Yet she has never taken him into her own body, for her faith forbade that, and she is strong-willed and determined to save that final sacrament to her passion for some far-off future when they, with her church's blessing, will be man and wife, and have endless time and freedom to be lovers, to be secret, hasty and furtive no longer. As for Raven, his passion for her - the first he's ever experienced - has changed him forever. So he accepts the desperate aching frustration she imposes; he will wait too. He can't now believe his former shallow obsession with the shabbiness of hasty commercial sex, with his brief couplings with poor, painted, sweaty whores, and the resultant (as he now sees) pathetic and ridiculous swaggering and boasting among his fellows in the half-deck - the lair of the young apprentices aboard ship.

For now, of course, none of these fleshly matters is in the lovers' minds. She is plunged into tears, sobs that shake her body, agony at the memory of the final parting with her father when, half-demented by his shame and guilt at his ship's disaster, he curtly, harshly, ordered her into the lifeboat. As for Raven, like the other boat coxswains he is absorbed in his steering, for there is now an ugly lop of small steep seas on top of the massive swells, and, because one of the lifeboats was destroyed in the cave, his boat, like the others, is overloaded. He must keep a sharp eye open ahead and to port for bigger waves; when they come, he must ease his pull on the tiller and let the boat luff up a little to meet the menace head-on. But at the back of his mind he's sharing Nelli's grief. The captain - old Jake, they used to call him behind his back - had been enraged when he found out about the mutual love between himself and Nelli, and had let Raven feel the full weight of his fury, yet their final tragic parting on the foundering ship had wiped out that enmity, and he remembered him as a proper captain - rock-like, stern, yet sometimes with a fatherly kindness and humour too.

Unlike many captains, he'd been their conscientious schoolmaster, had taken the time and trouble to teach them their trade.

The future worries him too; he is prepared to take his chance about the general problems of a safe landing and survival on this horrible island, for he has seen from the chart that its eastern, sheltered shore abounds in deep, fjord-like inlets, but he foresees problems, especially if their stay on it should be a long one, with safeguarding Nelli. Having one beautiful young woman on an island with twenty or more seamen, themselves mostly young, and starved of any contact with women for weeks now - that wasn't a good situation. He glances for'ard at the men in the boat, and especially at the one furthest from him - Billy John Ffynnongroes, the other Welshmen call him; a smart, intelligent sailor, but one with a grudge, it seemed, against the whole world, and particularly English officers. He and his fellow-malcontent, Jimmy Protheroe, the noted sea-lawyer - they especially might be trouble. No doubt they deeply envied him for his relationship with Nelli, quite apart from the lust they might have for her anyway. They'd need watching.

Slowly the black cliffs slide past, the wind holds and the North Cape of the main island is where it should be, broad on the starboard bow. The boats have sailed well, and will weather that craggy point safely. Grant hands the tiller to Jac-y-Bont, the ship's sailmaker, and studies the small sketch-map of the islands - five altogether. His face is still set in lines of worry. Once the cape's past they will be able to come off the wind, be able to turn down-wind and sail more easily, but the sound between the main island and Enderby Island might have some ugly tide-rips in it. Still, by then they'll be only two miles from the mouth of the so-called Port Ross, a long fjord-like inlet cutting west into the island; from there it'd be only another two miles of - presumably - sheltered water to the place marked 'Camp' on his map. These lifeboats were not too good at tacking straight into the wind, and on the lee side of the high ground there might not be any wind, so they might have to row the last miles, but what of that? It'd warm the men up a bit, and give them something to do.

Almost despite himself, he felt his spirits rising. They'd been lucky so far today with wind and weather - the elements that the day and night before had so cruelly destroyed their ship. Things might be a lot worse: the main island was a bit like a huge comb - its west side high, straightish and totally without harbours, but on the east side, he could see, from his sketch-map, as Raven had, that the coast was broken by long inlets, fingers of safe water where ships could anchor or boats be beached, away from the rage of the west wind. Besides, he'd read in the New Zealand Pilot, the captain's bible for these waters, that on the leeward side of the island there was thick scrub forest, and hence plenty of fire-wood for cooking and keeping warm.

Still, it was a cold, harsh place to be stuck in, so many miles from any other human being. The Pilot said that New Zealand government steamers called here regularly to check for castaways, but the ship's copy of that publication had been years out of date; what if they'd stopped coming here now? Who else would come to such a God-forsaken place? No, he said to himself: what's the use of thinking like this? Be a bit more positive; start thinking like a man with guts and a big job to do. They all had a chance of coming through this safely, and by God they would - somehow! Had the Old Man got away from the barque, and was he now back in command of himself again? If not, then you, Simon Grant, will have to be the captain. What a prospect! So for God's sake, start thinking like a captain.

CHAPTER ONE

For the twentieth time Grant took Nelli's sketch-map out of his oilskin coat pocket and laid it flat on his knee. Thank God he'd thought of getting it copied in time; it had taken the poor girl's mind off the disaster of the wreck for a bit, and she'd made an excellent job of it, carefully labelling all the points, headlands and rocky islets. Thanks to her, he could be sure that the high cape abeam, a mile or so off, was North Cape, because he could see at its foot a tiny skerry of rocks on which the swells smashed in white fury. So far, so good then; they'd sailed more than ten miles against a strong tide. He pulled out his grandfather's silver watch. Half-past nine, nearly - they'd been under way about two hours then - good going for such a heavy lubberly tub as this quarter-boat, with its single crude lugsail. His father's beautiful thirty-ton ketch - how she'd have stormed along in this breeze! She'd have been over the horizon by now.

Never mind, they were all alive, and she hadn't shipped much water, and now things could get a bit more peaceful. He saw the island's north coast opening out beyond the cape as a long vista of bare vertical headlands stretching away to the east. Good, now they could come off the wind and sail faster and more easily. It would be quite a bit warmer too, with the wind astern. That might cheer the crowd up a bit; so far they'd sat there lifeless, like a lot of cold, glum, stuffed dummies.

'There we are, boys - round the first corner. That's the North-west Cape to leeward there. We can free the sheet now, and be a bit more comfortable.'

Up spoke the predictable complainer, Jimmy Protheroe, the ship's champion sea-lawyer: 'Jesus! Comfortable? Sitting here freezing our arses off in this bloody tub!'

Grant mastered his irritation: 'All right, my friend - not so uncomfortable, then. Our Jimmy always looks on the bright side, doesn't he, boys?'

He was glad to hear the short rumble of gruff laughter, and even gladder to hear the familiar cockney voice of Curly Kellock, the old AB from the Navy, weighing in with an old lower-deck jibe: 'Thass right, mister. They used to call him laughing boy; nah they calls him drippin' bastard.'

This time they all laughed outright. Kellock had struck just the right note; a bit of crude foc'sle banter might shut Protheroe up, and distract them from their plight - which was chancy, to say the least. Grant looked at Kellock and grinned; there was something almost distinguished about the old boy - he was no ordinary shellback. He was built stocky, solid, almost fat, you could say, and his speech was that of the mean streets of the Isle of Dogs, yet behind that broad-cheeked, weathered face there was a depth and an intelligence beyond the common. In the dog-watches aboard the windjammer - the seamen's leisure time of the day - while others loafed about or sang or smoked and gossiped you'd see him reading - and reading serious books and pamphlets too, not the pornographic rubbish that some of them liked. Pity, though, it was all political stuff, by people like that rabid lunatic Karl Marx. Grant had heard him lecturing the other hands sometimes, and they used to call him 'Curly Karl'. His lectures however seemed to fall on stony ground and the 'Curly' nickname was a bit cruel, since the old boy was as bald as a coot. Still, he was a good steady character and a good seaman, if a bit too keen on standing up for his rights, as he put it. But he wasn't a rebel or a whiner or a shirker, and he never stirred up trouble.

Right, that was far enough on this course - plenty of clear water between boat and cape. It was time to come off the wind and turn the corner. He spoke to the man holding the mainsheet, the rope controlling the angle of the taut sail to the wind, Jones of the starboard watch; they'd had two other Joneses, not counting the cook, Wellington Jones, aboard the windjammer - why couldn't the Welsh think of a few more surnames, for God's sake? This chap's name was Iorwerth, and he came, Grant had gathered, from some bit of Cardiff called Splott, so he was called Yorry Splott. He wasn't the brightest or handiest of the crowd, but decent and quiet. 'All right, Jones, pay out your mainsheet. Hey! Who the hell told you to take two turns with it round the thwart? (The thwart was one of the seats that went across the boat.) That could have been dangerous, man, if we'd had a sudden heavy squall.'

'Sorry, sir. I done it to save my hands. That sheet was pulling real hard, isn't it?'

'All right, then. Only next time for God's sake ask me before you do anything like that. If you'd just taken it under the thwart that would have saved you a lot of the pull.' Inwardly he was cursing himself. He should have noticed that the idiot had taken a round turn round the thwart. That would have been hard to free in a hurry; that could have capsized them. He ground his teeth: Come on, old son: if you reckon to be the skipper of this boat, you've got to remember you're responsible for everything, even if one of your men does something totally stupid. So keep your bloody wits about you!

'Got it free now, Jones? Right, pay it out...more... more... Well, that'll do. Now that doesn't pull so much does it? So damn well *hold* it, and don't be such a cack-handed sojer!' Soldiers were - rather unfairly - scorned for their nautical ignorance by seamen, so 'sojer' was a serious insult to a foc'sle hand.

They'd turned nearly ninety degrees from the wind, so now the sail lay out wide on the starboard side and the jagged seesaw motion of the boat turned into a rolling, swaying, headlong rush through the waves that now rose steeply behind them and passed under their keel with a satisfying roar, the boat surfing for a moment on the face of every wave. The mood of the men changed too; they began to talk, to chaff, to look about them at the coast to starboard. Like many Welsh ships, 'Figaro' had had a mainly Welsh crowd, many of them from the same county as their late captain, the rocky-shored, windy county of Pembrokeshire. They felt almost at home, with those green, grassy, fern-clad sloping cliffs, white with seabirds in places, with black headlands and a jagged, rock-strewn shoreline edging a wild sea.

Three miles of easier sailing brought them to another headland, this time with a deep sheltered inlet on its far side. Perkins, the senior apprentice, was the man nearest to Grant, and with the sharp eyes of youth, was first to spot the inlet. 'Look, sir - just left of the point - a decent bit of shelter. Is that...?'

'No, that's marked "North Harbour" on the chart. No good going in there - no-one would find us there. Port Ross is where we need to be - another six miles or so - nearly all down-wind, though.'

He spoke easily, confidently, but, looking ahead, he

felt inward twinges of unease and doubt. 'Take the tiller for a bit, Perkins. Keep her steady as she goes. Watch she doesn't yaw about. There's quite a strong tide against us, and there may be some swirls and tide-rips.' He pointed ahead to a treacherously flat calm patch in the dark, wind-ruffled water. 'Be careful about those calm bits; the water's boiling straight up from the bottom there, so you'll find the tiller goes dead in your hand at times. Just try to keep her on course through it. Right?' Perkins nodded confidently. 'Carry on, then, because I need to have a good look at the map.' His worry came from the fact that, though the course along the north coast was due east, dead before the wind now, there was what looked like a solid wall of black cliff ahead. They seemed to be sailing into a dead end, and a dead lee shore as well, instead of having a free run round the northernmost point of the main island. If they were, it'd be no fun clawing off a lee shore in this tub - no headsail, no keel.

Come on, come on, man, he said to himself. The map's all you've got - you have to believe it or chuck it overboard. You have to trust that Eleanor traced it right. He shook his head to clear it. Now take a good look ahead, man, keep on the course - and stop panicking, for God's sake.

The grim wall of rock was spread right across his course, but - yes - there was a lower bit in the middle of it; if Nelli's map was right, that must be Rose Island, right in the middle of the sound between the main island and Enderby Island. And that - Enderby Island - must be the high ground on the extreme left. Must be. When they got further on they'd see the gap where they'd need to make another right-angled turn to starboard to get into the haven they wanted, Port Ross. He'd have to trust the map and his own eyes and intelligence; after all, what looked clear and simple on a map often looked very different when you actually got there and saw it. The trouble was, in most places nowadays there'd be buoys, lights, landmarks to help you, but here - nothing but Nature at her rawest!

Still, it was a fine sunny day now, and the wind was in a favourable quarter, if a bit strong for their little craft. With that good following breeze he could steer where he liked; if he were to keep the boat going to the north-east, slanting away from the land, he'd soon see the gap and the corner they needed. He took the tiller back from Perkins and let the boat's head come up a bit to port, and as she drew away from the land he heard - as he knew he would - mutinous mutterings from the hands including, from Jimmy Protheroe, of course, an audible: 'Where the fuck's he going now, then? Valparaiso?' The grousing made Grant realize how much things had changed: aboard the windjammer all decisions were made on the poop, an upper deck right aft, away from the crowd, who'd usually have no idea where they were, or where they were heading; and even if they grumbled, officers on the poop wouldn't hear them. Now these chaps could see just as much as he could, and also see exactly what he was doing, and they were all sitting only a few feet from him, and on the same level.

So perhaps, he thought, it'd be sensible to say something: 'All right, you can stow that growling. I'm just getting a bit of an offing so that I can see the gap between Rose Island - that bit of low land dead ahead - and the mainland. And once we're through that, boys, we're home and dry in Port Ross.'

Even as the growls subsided in a grudging truce, another problem dawned on Grant: once he saw the gap, he'd have to come right round to starboard to go through it, and that meant gybing her, and that'd be no picnic. Gybing meant bringing the boat's stern across the eye of the wind, and letting the sail come right across to spread out on the other side of the boat. In a stiff breeze like this you had to be careful that the sail didn't slam across hard; that could cause a sudden violent heel to port. In this wind and sea the gybe would need to be done damn well, otherwise - a capsize; all of them soaked and frozen, maybe drowned, and all the food stores they were carrying lost.

'Now listen, all of you,' he said urgently, 'to get through the gap, as you can all see now, I'll have to gybe her. So when I give the word, you, Jones, will have to bring the sheet in tight; the rest of you get ready to get across to the starboard side, and pretty damn quick, too, to sit her level on the new tack. Don't want to see any silly bugger floundering about in the bottom of the boat. Got that?'

He glanced astern at the two white boats, rolling and swaying faithfully behind him; good, Raven and bosun understood what he was at, and would also be getting ready to gybe, for they'd also got copies of Nelli's sketch-map. And....Yes! There it was - the gap! As they approached you could see the separate bits of land slide apart, one behind the other, like stage scenery. His good Zeiss glasses would be handy now, but like everything else he owned, they were now five fathoms down in that horrible cave.

'See the gap, boys? That's where we're going. Stand by to gybe. In with that sheet, Jones ...right in ...Well, that'll do. Ready all? Gybe-oh!' He drew the tiller up towards him, swinging the boat's stern across the wind, and slipped round it to take it in his left hand for the new tack. As the boat came up level the men came off the port gunwale where they'd been perching and made for the starboard one. Then, with a fearful wham, the lug-sail slammed across to port, full of wind, Jones, in his new perch, hanging on desperately to the bar-taut sheet. Over and over the boat heeled to port, so far that the sea began to lip over the port gunwale. Some of the men, caught unawares, fell clumsily into the boat's bilge, and their heavy cargo of tins of bully beef and biscuit started to slide too.

Grant screamed at the top of his voice: 'Pay out that sheet, Jones, you bloody lunatic! Let it go right out or she'll be over!' His heart nearly burst with panic and rage, but just in time Yorry Splott freed the sheet, and with the fierce pressure of the wind reduced, the longboat came staggering back up into the wind, so that she slowed almost to a halt, lurching dangerously to starboard, while the released sail flogged thunderously in the wind, shaking the whole boat and everything in it. Grant hauled the tiller savagely towards him, forcing the stern round with repeated sawing, frantic heaves, and as the boat, wallowing like a dead thing in the waves, began to sag back onto her course, he said: 'Perkins, take the sheet off that stupid Welsh lubber, for God's sake. Bring it in till the sail fills, to get some way on her again. You, Jones, get up for'ard out of my sight, before I knock your bloody teeth in!'

Jones wasn't sorry to get away from the sodding English bucko, but he didn't go without a protest: 'How was I to know I'd got to free the sheet, mister? You never said nothing about that, did he, boys? The last thing you said when you give me a bollocking about taking a turn with the sheet was "Just bloody hold it, and don't be a cack-handed sojer". Them was his very words, wasn't they, mates?' There were some murmurs of sympathetic agreement, but most of the hands were too shaken by the near-disaster and too depressed about the future to make much of it.

As for Grant, he made no reply to the man's grouse; he was much more concerned with cursing himself for making such a monumental cock-up of a simple everyday sailing manoeuvre. He glanced astern and gritted his teeth in chagrin as first the bosun's boat and then Raven's executed the gybe smartly, with no loss of speed and not much of a heel. Because of his lubberly balls-up they were a lot closer now. They must have seen everything, and he could just imagine the roars of derisive laughter there must have been, once they saw that Grant's boat was safe again. Why the hell hadn't he given the sheet to Perkins in the first place? In his time at nautical college in Conway he'd have done hours, days, weeks of small-boat sailing. He'd have known without being told that when the sail comes across in a gybe you let the sheet run well out under control to soften the jar. Instead, without thinking, he'd given it to a pretty thick chap from the crowd, who'd probably never sailed in a small boat in his life. Christ, they might all have been drowned! They'd certainly have lost all the bully and biscuit - and who knew if there'd be any of that ashore?

That hadn't done much for his credit with anyone, in this boat or the others. He was galled to see that Raven and the bosun were both spilling the wind from their sails, so as to politely fall back into their stations. It was time for a grand gesture of apology to the crowd, no matter how much it hurt his pride and dignity. 'That was a near one, eh, lads? We nearly got a wet arse and no fish, as they say! And to be fair, it was my fault as much as Yorry's. No-one's perfect. Eh?'

Kellock spoke up, reasonably but firmly: 'No, mister, they ain't. Yorry's dad was a Cardiff milkman; Yorry shipped aboard in Cardiff because he couldn't find no decent job ashore. Green as grass he was then. Me and the others and the two old mates we had then showed him the ropes. He got to be a useful hand on board, knew his job, like. But what's he supposed to know about farting around in small boats under sail? None of us lot knows much about that because we ain't been taught. We ain't idiots; if someone shows us summat, we'll learn it, same as you must have had to once.'

There was a low growl of agreement from the other hands. Grant ground his teeth in silence; in his calm, almost fatherly way, Kellock was being insubordinate, but on the other hand - damn him! - he was right, so no point in prolonging the row: 'Aye aye, but never mind that now. We're alive and afloat, and that island over there is Rose Island, and that' - he pointed ahead, to where the cliffs fell away sharply to the south-west - 'that, my boys, is Port Ross, and if you feel religious, you can thank that God of yours that we got here. And, to be fair, you can thank Miss Roberts too for making us a damn good map.'

*

After the bluster, the hurly-burly of the rough wind, and the quick, jarring, pitching and rolling of the quarter-boat, there was an almost eerie quiet and calm on the waters of the deep inlet. The wind had gone, blocked off by the high land to the west, and gone too was the high, cruel black wall of basalt cliffs. The water was flat calm, and the cliffs here were green, low, sloping, studded with outcrops of rock and dense patches of ferns, and white here and there with the crowds of nesting seabirds - albatrosses and petrels. A cloud of birds rose, wheeling and screaming at the boat's intrusion into their sanctuary. On the shore of a little rocky cove a group of seals lay basking like huge shiny black slugs, for all the world like the somnolent, paunchy members of a London gentlemen's club after a very good lunch; a few of them lifted whiskered headss to glance indifferently as the passing boats before resuming their doze.

'Here we are then, boys - Port Ross - home for a bit - not too long, I hope. Some nice calm water too, for a change, but no wind, so it looks as if we'll have to ship the rowlocks and out oars, and row the rest of the way. Not far, though - good chance to warm yourselves up, eh? Up for'ard there, someone let go the halyard and get the sail down.'

There was more sullen muttering, and Protheroe - unheard by Grant this time - grumbled to his mate: 'Here we go again, boys! Poor old Jack does all the work while the bucko just sits there shouting at us.' But the men, stiff from hours of sitting in a cramped boat, were not really sorry to be lifting the heavy ash oars and fitting them into the rowlocks. Lewis, a cheerful character from the south of Pembrokeshire, commented out loud: 'Damn, this is like being home, b'ys! All wind and rain and rocks! That island back there could have been Skomer, and this here place don't half remind me of Milford Haven. Decent old harbour, this is.'

'Aye,' said his neighbour, 'but wild beyond, though. Don't look as if anyone's ever set foot on the place.'

'Could do with some houses, and a pub or two,' said another man. 'And some place to sleep, and all. A few tarts'd come in handy, too.'

There were some rueful laughs before Grant cut in: 'Come on, give way together, boys. *There...there...there!* That's the way; get her shifting. Get yourselves loosened up. Not long now, eh? And the sun's come out for us.' There were some ironical cheers as the men settled into a steady rhythm with the oars. The fresh chilly breeze that had brought them here was almost totally gone, deflected by the high ground above, only the smallest fluky puffs of it betrayed by little dark patches on the glassy waters of the inlet. The silence was deathly, strange, after the hellish booms of the great swells on the cliffs where the ship had met her end, and the dull roar and bluster of the wind in their ears during their rough boat journey. The only sound now was the screaming protests of the clouds of seabirds that rose, disturbed by the steady clunk-clunk of the oars in the metal rowlocks - a sound echoing back from the lonely shores. Grant, his spirits rising now, murmured to Perkins: 'This reminds me of old Coleridge. "We were the first that ever burst into that silent sea".'

'Never liked English lessons much, sir, but I do remember that bit - it's good, isn't it?'

'Not just good, the best, my boy, the best.'

Looking astern, the rowers could see the bosun's boat lowering sail and shipping oars, and, beyond that, Raven's boat still ghosting in on the last of the breeze. Looking ahead from his seat in the stern-sheets, Grant could see a long inlet of quiet water; it was a good two miles wide here, but now he could see clearly that it gradually narrowed and curved to the right between low rocky shorelines. He pulled out the sketch-map again; well done, Nelli - that was exactly what it showed. She'd done a good job, considering the uproar around her, and the sense of impending, inevitable disaster. He had a mental picture of her in 'Figaro's' warm, mahogany-pannelled chartroom, bent over a table where the chart was spread out under the bright oil-lamp, the tip of her tongue just slightly out as she concentrated on her tracing. It was as if she was enjoying some footling hobby - until you saw how she from time to time gave her cheeks a quick brush with her hand to wipe away her tears - tears at the forth-coming ruin of the ship and (probably) her father's career. She was new to the deep sea, but she must have understood the horrible dangers and desolation that lay ahead for all of them. A chip off the old block, she was. God, even in those stiff, ugly black oilskins she was so beautiful - dark-haired, dark-eyed, tanned by wind and sun on the long voyage. Young Raven was a lucky devil! Why couldn't he himself find someone? Why could he never commit himself to... He shook his head as if to clear it. Good God, what was the point in letting your mind ramble on about your disastrous love-life at a time like this? For God's sake get a grip on yourself!

But Nelli now: she was a real problem, or might be, no mistake. It was no fault of hers - she couldn't help being here, or being beautiful, but she might cause a lot of trouble for him - one girl stuck here on an island with lots of mostly young and pretty randy sailors. He'd have to...He shook his head again and shut off that thought too. 'Sufficient unto the day is the evil thereof', as the good book said. No time for worrying about Eleanor now. Got to find this place marked 'camp' on the map, and hope to God to find something there worth finding. Keep scanning the shore - don't want to go past it.

The shore, now that he could see it clearly and closely, consisted of tongues of low rocks jutting out between small coves with beaches of black shingle at the mouths of little valleys, where no doubt streams came down from the high ground. Above those there were patches of flattish land that were riots of wild growth - tall rough grass, huge stiff ferns, little scrubby bushes. Above those again the island sloped up, the slopes thick with a seeming impenetrable scrub forest - small trees, their young leaves beginning to show a pale green, trees so impossibly crammed together that their tops formed an almost solid surface. It looked from the boat as if you could walk across those tree-tops. Good - no shortage of wood for fires, and, the forest being so thick, there was bound to be a lot of dead wood lying about, maybe, even dry dead wood. He tapped his pocket to reassure himself - yes, he'd got his box of matches. Wouldn't need to start rubbing two sticks together! He spoke to one of the passengers in the stern, Isaac Hughes, steward: 'Plenty of wood, steward, for a decent fire to cook on.'

'Aye, but what about sleeping? It'll be cold beyond here at night, won't it? Where are we going to get blankets from? We should have brought some from the ship, isn't it?'

Grant gritted his teeth; was there ever such a bloody whiner as this chap? 'Jesus, man, there was no time for that. We were lucky to get away ourselves with a bit of grub - you must remember what it was like back there.

Let's hope the government store will have some blankets - and some more grub too. We might be here a long time.'

'Don't count on nothing, mister, even if there is a store, and even if we find it. The sealers might have been here. This is the sort of island where they come to hunt.'

'And what if they have?'

'Those sealing schooners are manned by the scum of the Pacific - bums and scallywags from every port. They'd murder their grannies for tuppence. I've seen them when I was in Frisco once, a dirty, disgusting rabble they were - damn savages! I've heard of survivors finding these stores looted - every blessed thing gone.'

The man's glum pessimism struck cold fear into Grant's heart. That hadn't occurred to him, though, now he thought about it, he had heard similar stories. They might just find an empty shed. He dismissed the thought angrily: for God's sake don't start thinking like this stupid old woman Hughes. You don't know yet whether the Old Man got away safely in Raven's boat - the boats had been too far apart for him to see; if he didn't, then you're the captain of twenty-nine assorted souls now; you've got to be the one to give them heart and hope, or else we'll all slide into chaos and disaster. You mustn't let the others see your own worries. Old Will Shakespeare was right as usual - 'Uneasy is the head that wears the crown'. He said, shortly: 'Let's not moan and groan, Hughes, until we've got cause to. We shan't...'

He was interrupted by a yell from the other passenger, the tubby, grey-haired Wellington Jones, cook, in the bow: 'Hey, look at that, mister!'

'Look at what?'

'See, above the shore there. Big patch of tidy grass,

nice short green grass - and look, a track leading from it up through the bush.'

'Yes, I see, but....'

'But nothing, mister! You educated man - bin to college, eh? Just think: no people here - right? So what trimmed that grass and made that track? Not nature, not the Almighty. Got to be animals, ain't it? Goats, sheep, cattle - something that grazes. Ain't that so?'

'Damn, yes! Well spotted, doctor...' - windjammer cooks were always called 'doctor' - '... yes, I remember now, it said in the Pilot that cattle, goats and pigs were running wild here, left by settlers years ago.'

'Settlers?' said Perkins incredulously. 'In a god-forsaken hole like this! They must have been off their chumps to try living here.'

From the rowing thwarts came ironical ragged cheers, followed by derisive orders to the cook: 'Right, that'll be rump steak for supper tonight, Welly, and it'd better not be tough, mind!'

'Yeah, same for me. And for breakfast tomorrow I'll have two decent rashers of bacon and a couple of them birds' eggs.'

The cook was irritated: 'Arl right, you lot. Don't you worry none about the food. You fellas can run up and down the rigging and I can't, but you couldn't cook hot water, not to save your lives, you couldn't. I fed you good aboard the old hooker outa that salt workhouse junk the company gave me, didn't I? A few fried sea-gulls' eggs won't hurt you, eh? And I bet I could get some decent steaks outa one of them seals we saw back there.'

'Gull's eggs?' cried another rower. 'I've tried them

once - too bloody fishy for me.'

Wellington Jones was not the man to be a timid victim of this baiting: 'Go and stay in a posh hotel then, if you can find one. I cook you food - right? First one that grumbles gets a good smack in the mouth from me - right? If you don' like what I cook, you can stick it up your jacksie and eat hard-tack for a month - I don't care.'

Then the hoary old foc'sle joke had to come - from, of course, the cocky Jimmy Protheroe: 'Who called the cookie a bastard?' and from further down the boat came the dutiful reply: 'Who called the bastard a cook?'

Grant felt his spirits rise again. The crowd was, as usual, needling the doctor, but that was better than despair - a lot. Still, he was in charge here, and might, for all he knew, even be captain now, so it was time to brace them up a bit: 'All right, all right. Stow that row and save your breath for rowing. Put your backs into it or we'll be sculling about in this tub all day. Keep her going - not long now.'

He steered the boat in, close to the northern shore to starboard, looking for the place laconically labelled 'camp' on the sketch-map, keeping an eye open for outlying rocks that might wreck their boat, but all the time scanning the shore for some sign of a building - a shed, a store, anything - or for a sign of a landing-place and a track leading up from the shore. If I were a praying man and not a heathen atheist, he thought, I'd be down on my knees, praying that the New Zealand government ship does still call now and then. That's what it said in the Pilot, but maybe the ship's copy had been published years ago? Maybe the visits were things of the past, and there wasn't a shelter any longer? Maybe, even if there was, some lousy bunch of sealers had been here to loot the stuff that's meant for poor buggers like us?

CHAPTER TWO

Once again Grant's officer's brain cut in sharply: For God's sake stop your miserable worrying and deal with what's here and now! You need to look for a sheltered spot where a steamer could anchor safely, handy to a decent beach where her boats could... *There!* Just off the starboard bow, past that jagged point, there was a small bay and - yes - some sort of track going up from it. It was very overgrown, but still a beaten grassy path leading up from the beach, winding up between outcrops of basalt rock, and disappearing into the thick low forest of small stunted, twisted trees. Grant tried to think his way into the mind of the imaginary New Zealand steamer's captain (if there was one, of course!). He'd have looked for an anchorage and a landing-place near the north end of the island. After all, wrecks were most likely to happen on the savage windward west coast. Any survivors from a wreck would take the first chance of shelter, so they'd probably be found at either the north or the south end of the east coast. The north end was the nearest to his New Zealand base, so he'd call here first. Glancing at his little map, he saw that there was a big sheltered inlet in the south called Carnley Harbour, but that was another thirty-five miles away, so this place - Port Ross on the map ('port' was surely a rather flattering title!) - this would be the place where the captain would search first, and therefore the best place to locate a shelter.

Now then, where would he build that hut, shed, whatever it was? Not on the beach - too bleak and exposed, but not far from the beach, because his chaps would have to manhandle all the timber - planks, rafters, roofing - to the site. There was still no sign of anything man-made, although they were now almost alongside the beach, but then -yes - it would make sense to put the hut in among the forest to give shelter; there must be streams coming down off the grim, bald, flat top of the island - God knows there was plenty of water landing on that - so the skipper would try to find - or make - a small clearing in the tangled bush in the valley of a stream, so that the survivors would at least have shelter from the almost ceaseless wind, and good supplies of water and firewood handy. Right, this was the spot to land - *must* be, had *got* to be.

He called cheerfully: 'I think we're there, boys. I'm going to beach her in that bay just ahead, so bend your backs, there's only another twenty strokes to go, and then we can stretch our legs and have a leak. I don't know about you, but I'm dying for one myself. I haven't even had enough time to piss in the baler.' He thought it was best not to be too dignified, too aloof; better to cheer them up, make them feel some hope and companionship coming from him, not just cold orders. Thrown suddenly out of the closed, disciplined world of the windjammer, he felt somehow naked, diffident for the first time in his adult life. Here they were, all dressed the same, all (literally) in the same boat, no more separate quarters - foc'sle and poop - to symbolize their difference of status in the hierarchy. Why should they obey him? He'd said a lot of tough words before the ship sank - I'm still an officer and you're still my crew, and I'm going to have discipline, and so on and so on. But what if they...? He shook his head and clamped his jaw for the umpteenth time: stop worrying like an old woman! Get on with your bloody job - don't be so feeble! The Old Man might be in Raven's boat; he went to pieces when they hit the cliff, but he might be all right again now. He could take over when he got here. But in the meantime…

He looked around; the water was strangely still, like a placid reach of the Thames near Marlow; the boat slipped along, the double boom of the strong strokes of the oars gently disturbing the island's silence. At last he called: 'Easy, all. Boat your oars,' and there was a gentle crunch as the steel-shod keel took the shingle. There was another cheer from the benches and a cry of: 'Thank Gawd for that! My hands is blistered to buggery' which brought a sympathetic laugh from his fellow-sufferers. Windjammer sailors were men of the sea and tough as nails, but they didn't often have to row boats, so they weren't too good at it - and incidentally most of them couldn't swim either.

Soon the other two boats grounded, and the beach was full of oil-skinned sailors walking, jogging, bending and stretching to bring life back to cold, stiffened limbs. The young apprentices, or 'brassbounders', like the overgrown schoolboys they were, scampered about, pushed each other over, brawling amicably with all the resilience of youth. They were destitute, and on the most miserable island you ever saw. What would happen now? What would they have to eat, how would they live or sleep without being frozen? Let the others, the old blokes, worry about all that! All the crew, young and old, felt, as sailors always do, the strange, uncomfortable deadness and solidity of the firm ground after the ceaseless, restless, live motion of the ship and the boats. Grant walked among them looking for the Old Man and the other two boat captains, Raven and the bosun, to discuss the next move.

He found the bosun first: 'Where's Raven, bosun - and the captain?'

'Can't say for sure, mister. I got a nasty feeling the capten didn't get into Raven's boat. Haven't seen him yet, anyway. But you'll have to ask Mr Raven. He went off down the beach there with the capten's girl.'

On top of his misgiving about the Old Man, Grant felt irritated; he didn't want the group splitting up, and neither did he want Raven's very special relationship with Eleanor to be too obvious. Mind you, gossip, especially about anything even faintly sexual, was so rife in foc'sles that probably all the crowd knew they were lovers, especially Raven's boat's crew, as she had no doubt made it obvious that she wanted him alone for comfort and company. He rapped out an order in his old bucko manner: 'Right, all of you stay exactly where you are, or God help you when I come back,' then set off down the estuary towards the sea.

He soon came across Raven standing, stretching, alone in the rocky corner of a small bay hidden from the landing beach. He greeted his subordinate with a mixture of anxiety and irritation: 'Jesus, Raven, where's the Old Man? Didn't he...?'

'No, he didn't, Simon. He's back there, five fathoms down. Tydfil Jones and I went back up on board and found him trapped under the mizen t'gallant yard - right in his favourite bit of deck by the break of the poop - remember? He was still alive, but only just. We offered to try and free him, but we both knew it would be hopeless - so did he, of course. That yard must have weighed half a ton. He just ordered us to go; the water was swilling across the deck by then. But before we left, he just, sort of, faded out. We had to go then, or we wouldn't have got off ourselves, and the boat might have been smashed too. I can tell you, it was a bloody near thing for all of us by that time.'

'I'll bet it was. So I'm skipper now, God help me. Poor old Jake.... We had our ups and downs, but he was a good captain, and a real man too. And where's Eleanor? Is she all right?'

'With all due respect, Simon, that's two damn silly questions. Where would she be, and why should she need to be on her own for a bit, after hours in a boat with a bunch of hairy-arsed matelots?'

'Yes, of course - silly question. What about my second question?'

'The second? Well, of course she's not all right, man. How the hell could she be? She's now lost everyone and everything.'

'Yes, she has. Except you.'

Raven's face was set in grim lines of misery. 'Yes, except me, for what that's worth, and that's not much. I very much doubt if she's thought about me for one second since the wreck.'

Grant put an arm awkwardly across Raven's shoulders in a comradely way; being English public school products, neither was good at showing their feelings openly, but in a strongly Welsh ship they felt themselves especially close, since much of the talk around them was in Welsh, of which they understood not one word. Good God, Grant thought: only nine months ago I was a new dog's-body of a second mate, and Raven was just a rowdy nuisance of a brassbounder. Then the first mate goes down with consumption and the captain's lost in the wreck, and here we are, captain and mate. He felt a strong bond of friendship for Raven now, rather than any feeling of superiority coming from his place in the hierarchy, so he spoke with earnest feeling: 'You're worth a hell of a lot to her, old son, believe me - a lot. How was she then, in the boat?'

'You never saw a person so…so destroyed, Simon. I really believe she'd got it in her mind to throw herself out of the boat, she was so wretched. She'd just almost seen her father killed in the most miserable circumstances. And, after all, she must have understood that the wreck was largely his fault. I'll never forget her face when Jones and I came down into the boat without him - never. By then the boat was about to be smashed up against the ship's stern and the chaps in the boat were nearly shitting themselves in panic, so I had to yell at them to start rowing, to get the stroke together, so I couldn't say a word to her or offer her any comfort then.'

'I see.'

'No, I'm not sure that you do see all of it, Simon. It wasn't just that she'd lost him. Don't you remember *how* they parted? How she wanted to stay with him to the last and he wouldn't have it? He shouted at her - very coldly and harshly - as if she was just some scrimshanking AB. The poor old chap was beside himself by then. Anyway, neither of them knew then that that would be their last moment together, did they? D'you see? It'll take a very long time for her to be anything like herself again. Of course, I needn't tell you that for me she's now the most important person in the world, and that - if she'll have me - she's the one I want to spend the rest of my life with. I can see now that I wasn't properly alive, not a proper human being, till I met Nelli and fell in love with her. She's just...everything to me now.'

Grant tightened his clumsy grasp of Raven's shoulder: 'Yes, I understand. You're a lucky young devil, old son, though no doubt that's not the way you feel at the moment. We shall all have to help her, but especially you, of course. But I've been thinking - I'll have to have a word with you - with both of you - about that.'

'About what?'

'Later, old boy...got a lot to see to now. Ah, look, here's Eleanor coming back now. Phew! I see what you mean - she looks a hell of a long way from her old self.'

Eleanor approached, her eyes cast down to where her big, incongruous leather sea-boots crunched the glistening dark shingle; her face was pale, set in a grim mask of determined stoicism. In the stern-sheets of the boat she had somehow felt alone with John, and she had let her desolate tears and her racking sobs come freely. But now, in full sunlit daylight, she must face - and be one of - the whole ship's company, and she was resolute that they should see a strong, composed woman, not a weeping wreck. Like Grant, she could see the possible dangers of being one young female among so many men, who might not now be the disciplined body they had been aboard the ship. Who knew what anarchy and mischief might happen if their stay on the island was a long one? Simon and John and the bosun would do their best, she knew - but would that be enough?

As she came close she raised her reddened eyes and gave Grant a ghost of a smile that went no further than her lips. Grant, moving out of his usual stunted range of emotions, held out both his hands and took hers in a firm, affectionate clasp. 'Eleanor, it's good to see you safe and sound ashore. But what can I say that's of any use or comfort to you? I'm more sorry than I can say.' He too now had to struggle to keep back tears. 'I'm sad beyond words myself at the loss of your father. He and I didn't always agree; sometimes I got the feeling that he was sorry he ever signed me on. But I always respected him as a man - for his seamanship and his humanity to everyone, high and low. With the loss of your mother too, fate has been very cruel to you lately. But you're a strong young woman, I know, and I also know that whatever else has gone, you still have a wonderfully staunch friend and partner in this young man - this very lucky young man - beside me. But we shall all - all of us - do our best for you.'

Eleanor nodded, with that half-smile again; she could not trust herself to speak, but in an odd, mute gesture of gratitude and affection, she lowered her head and raised her and Simon's clasped hands to brush them lightly against her lips. Then she let go of his hands and gave her head a slight shake, as if to close off this time of silent grief: 'Yes, Simon, I know you will, I know you will. Life's got to go on - for all of us. You're captain now. You must have a hundred things to do this minute.'

Simon also came to, as it were, and reverted to the old Grant - the officer, the martinet, the bucko. Briefly, furtively, brushing his eyes with the back of his hand, he said: 'Yes, by Jove, I have. Can't stop here talking any more. We'd better get back to the crowd before some half-wit decides to wander off and get lost.'

Grant was disturbed when he got back, to see the crowd - apart from the brassbounders who were still fooling about - sunk into postures of sullen despair. Blind to the wild quiet beauty of the fjord-like inlet, they slumped on rocks or grassy banks, glum, morose. They obviously felt the strangeness, the blankness of their new surroundings - no stuffy foc'sle, no bogey stove to warm them, no shipboard routine of watch on, watch off, no regular, reliable lumps of salt junk to eat, no big, safe Cardiff windjammer that, like a cocoon, had kept them secure against the naked savagery of nature.

Come on, Grant, he said to himself. Like it or not, you're their captain, so act like one! Get the buggers moving, get them started on something. Can't be sure what, but something! He spoke briskly, forcibly: 'Come on then, all of you! On your feet, quick-sharp! You've been sitting on your arses for hours, haven't you? So gather round and listen to me. First of all, don't let anyone get the idea of wandering off. We've *got* to stay together, or some of us will die. Now the next thing: for God's sake cheer up and act like men! Don't despair; there's no need to give up. We are all going to survive this disaster, and get back home alive. The captain's dead, I'm afraid, as I expect you all know by now. He left it too late, more's the pity, and one of the yards fell on him. Mr Raven and his boys would have saved him if they could, but it was hopeless. He was nearly dead when they found him. He himself ordered Mr Raven and his men to leave him with his ship. So I know I'm speaking for all of you when I offer our deepest sympathy to Miss Roberts here. She's suffered a terrible double blow, losing her father and mother in the last two months. So it's up to all of us to offer her whatever help, support and kindness we can while we're on this island.'

Even as he spoke, Grant thought: these are fine comforting words, but there's a few chaps in front of me who may be thinking of her in a very different way. By God, I hope not, but there's one or two I don't trust.

Kellock, standing in the front row of the foc'sle men, spoke up: 'Yes, miss, all of us hands from for'ard are with Mr Grant there. You've had a cruel hard time, no mistake, but we're all your friends here - ain't that so, mates?' There was an answering growl - almost like a cheer - in support, but no-one noticed that, in the rearmost ranks Billy John and Jimmy Protheroe were exchanging furtive winks and grins.

There was a long, desolate empty silence, until Grant went on: 'Yes, I can guess how you feel. A ship's like a family, isn't it? No doubt some of you had sailed with Captain Roberts for years.'

Jac-y-Bont, the old sailmaker, spoke up: 'Aye, he was one of the best, one of the old school. He was the top dog all right, and tough as nails, but he was like...like one of us. His bark was worse than his bite. He'd never do the dirty on you.'

'He knew how to handle a crew, he did,' said Curly Kellock pointedly. 'Not all boots and fists and cursing and fines. He'd been a foc'sle hand himself, y'see. That don't half make a difference.'

Grant bit his lip in irritation; the drift of Kellock's elegy was not lost on him. He forced himself to speak gently, tactfully: 'Yes, I'm with you there, boys. Well, we can't give him a proper funeral, but if you've a mind to that sort of thing, you can all say your own prayer for him. Or later, when we're more settled, you could hold your own service. I'm a bit of a heathen, I'm afraid, so I can't lead it myself, but I'll be very much with you in spirit. But now - for us - life has to go on. Now it's time to save ourselves, to find some shelter and maybe some more food.'

He was about to lead them up off the beach, when Raven said: 'What about the boats? Hadn't we better...?'

Grant thought: Thank God for Raven! Always the practical chap; got his head screwed on, as they say. Not a scrap of imagination or culture in him, but loads of common sense. He could always focus on what needed doing now and he was a sailor through and through. But *you,* you blithering idiot - you should have thought of the boats yourself. A fine start you're making to your captaincy! Wouldn't it have been wonderful to spend an hour exploring, then come back here and find the boats had all drifted off on a rising tide with all the food we've brought from the ship!

Raven went on: 'I mean, it looks as if the tide's on the ebb, but we'd better...'

'Yes, of course. All back to your boats, boys, and give them a good haul right up the beach. But watch you don't hole them on one of those sharp rocks. Then lead the painters further up the beach and make them fast to a decent big rock. One chap from each boat to stay with the boats, just to make sure they're safe.' Inwardly, he said to himself, with something like panic: that's the second bloody great bloomer today, you moron! Come on, get a grip on yourself!

Raven saw one or two of the men looking meaningfully at each other, and one shaking his head. Simon's not at his best today, Raven thought. He's slipping a bit; nearly capsized his boat in that gybe, and now this. Time to back him up. 'Right, then - up off your backsides and let's do something useful. D'you want all that biscuit and bully-beef floating off to the South Pole? I don't!' Some purpose, some work, some positive effort - that was what the crowd needed, he thought. None of them had had a wink of sleep last night; they'd all had a long, cold, rough trip in the boats, and they must all be starving - he certainly was - and the future didn't look exactly rosy, but there was no use their just feeling sorry for themselves.

A few minutes later, when he and his crew had spread themselves round their lifeboat, taking a good grip of the gunwale, he was astonished to look across and see Eleanor taking her place among the four other oil-skinned figures on the port side, ready to lift and heave with the others. He opened his mouth to protest, but was instantly silenced by a flash of sheer fury from her dark eyes. Don't start being gallant and wrapping me in cotton-wool, that look said. I don't *want* to be a 'lady'. I just want to be one of the crowd; after all, I look like one of them now. Don't start being an old-fashioned English gentleman, you idiot. Do you think I want to be marked out as a helpless female amongst all these men?

Raven nodded a silent agreement and called, in the odd traditional idiom of seamen: 'Right then, boys. Lift and larnch! All together...two-six - *hup!* Two-six...*heavy! Shift* her...O *shift* her!' With the same rhythmic, co-ordinated yells and convulsive heaves, the heavy boats came sliding and grating up over the black pebbles to safety.

Ten minutes later found the main party floundering, in single file, up a wildly overgrown track through the thickest scrub they'd ever seen. The stunted trees, their grey bark coated here and there with yellow or red-gold lichen and leathery, grey-green moss, were crowded, twisted, interlocking; they were not much more than twelve feet high, but so thick on the ground that they shut out much of the sun, so that the party plodded slowly uphill in an eerie semi-darkness. Grant and Raven, in the lead, had broken off heavy sticks and flailed them around to flatten the stiff coarse grass and ferns. The green-ness, the strangeness, the alien forms of every plant and tree made them all vaguely uneasy. Eleanor, toiling and panting behind Raven, thought: It's just as if we've somehow landed on a different planet.

She heard Jac-y-bont muttering to Kellock: 'These trees - what the hell are they? They grows like the scrub-oak back home, but look at the leaves! Nothing like oak....nor hazel...nor willow, nor nothing I've ever seen. Bloody weird place, this is.'

Despite his shortness of breath, Kellock, being a great reader and didactic by nature, took a calmer, more scientific, philosophical view: 'I dunno, me old son. You bin to Aussie, haven't you? They got kangaroos and wallabies and eucalyptus trees there, ain't they? You don't find none of them in Wales, do you? Nor yet a duck-billed platypus neither, eh? Everythink's different down here. Still, nemmine, eh, s' long as we can keep alive somehow till someone comes to pick us up in a steamer. Cheer up, me old cock-bird.'

After the first sharp slope up from the beach, the track led them down again into the valley of a fast-running mountain stream. Grant halted at a point where the path led close to the brim of a deep, dark pool that circled slowly between black rocks, clad in places with patches of thick, lush green moss. 'How about a drink, lads? I don't know about you, but I'm as dry as a bone - spitting feathers, as they say.' And then, with a feeble attempt at jocularity: 'And this one's on me, mind!'

They all knelt on the grassy bank, Eleanor shoving

unceremoniously into the bunch of clustered men; they cupped their hands and swallowed deep draughts of the clear fresh water, throwing handfuls of it over their faces to wash off the stiff film of dried salt spray. The coldness of the water made them gasp, but their spirits rose a little. At least the water was the same as in Wales, and at least they didn't have to worry about going thirsty on this island.

'Well, *chwarae teg,* boys,' said one man. 'This is a good bit better than the stale old stuff out of the casks on board.'

Only the fastidious Isaac Hughes, steward, hung back: 'O *Duw* no, I don't fancy it; it's not safe to go gulping that water down. I mean, we don't know...'

'Don't be such a bloody fussy old woman, Isaac,' said the bosun. 'It's straight from the Almighty onto the mountain, and then down this brook to here. How could that poison you? And anyway,' he added pragmatically, 'it's all there is for us to drink until we gets off this godforsaken island. Be thankful, mun, and get it down your neck for God's sake.'

Much refreshed, they all got to their feet to resume their slow upward plod through the grotesque low, chilly, damp jungle. Here, down by the stream, every rock had its fleece of green, wet, velvet moss, and every trunk and branch of every tree its many-coloured patches of lichen. Sometimes they had to push aside long horizontal branches that stretched out, thick with green moss, like bony arms clad in velvet sleeves. Everywhere, water dripped and gathered into tiny rills that trickled into the stream on their left. Johanssen, the big, phlegmatic Swede, said laconically: 'Anyvay, ve don't die of t'irst here, I t'ink.'

The genial Lewis was behind him, floundering and

slipping in the long sodden grass, and agreed with cheerful irony in his odd South Pembrokeshire English: 'Noo, b'y, we just drinks water and eats up all our bully and biscuit, and then we bliddy starves.'

Grant, at the head of the party, came to a halt; the track had divided. A path of sorts led up the stream-side, but a broader track led up to the right, up into the bush. He felt a knot of tension within him - of suppressed triumph, though, not panic. Yes, this must be the right way. If there's a shelter, we've nearly reached it. Not too far from the beach, near the stream, but high enough to be a bit drier. Concealing his excitement, he said prosaically: 'I think we'll try the track to the right, boys. It's like a damned wet sponge down here.':

There were mutterings of doubt behind him, but he *knew* - he was sure now: the depot was up this path, and not very far, either; they wouldn't carry tons of timber and stuff much farther, would they? The small hollow rushing of the stream had died away, muffled by the thick trees. The path turned left along a ledge, back towards the stream, and Grant's heart sank again as he saw, dead ahead, above the trees, a solid wall - a cliff, of the grim basalt rock. He heard an indignant voice behind him say: '*Iesu mawr, bois,* he's taking us straight into a bleeding cliff. We should have...'

He stopped, and they all halted in their tracks, for suddenly they saw the forest open out into a flat grassy glade, and on the other side of which, hunched under overhanging trees, and backing straight onto the vertical rock-face, was a hut - a rough timber hut with a rusty, sharply-peaked tin roof.

No more muttering now, but a real, heart-felt cheer

from all the hungry, weary hands, and from the rear of the party a quiet, slightly disrespectful compliment: 'Well done the bloody bucko!'

Happily ignoring the impertinence, Grant suppressed his pride, delight and triumph; he was, after all, English, and never a man for emotional displays. Instead, he said casually, with apparent calm: 'Well, here it is, boys. It's not Buckingham Palace, but this must be what we've been looking for. Now we'd better see what - if anything - is inside. Any religious blokes among you can start praying again that there *is* something worth finding.'

CHAPTER THREE

The huddle of black-clad sailors fell so silent, tense with anxiety, as Grant and Raven stepped forward to the door, that they were half-aware of birds calling and the wind sighing in the massed treetops around them. So much - maybe even life or death - hung upon what he found - or didn't find; they were dependent on the decisions of a colonial government who, of course, didn't even know if anyone would ever approach and open that rough wooden door.

Grant too licked his dry lips as he said: 'All right boys, here we go then; don't all crowd in; just wait there a sec while we see what's what.' He lifted the latch; the door opened inward, its rusty hinges squeaking, the foot of the door grating harshly on the floor. The two men stepped up onto the raised wooden floor; inside, the air was damp, musty from its being sealed off. The darkness was at first total as they stepped out of the strong sunshine of the glade, but as light came from the doorway and their eyes became accustomed to the gloom, they saw that they were in a long shed, maybe about fifteen feet wide and forty long. At the end of it was another door. Down the middle was a long table of unplaned planks, with rough benches on either side. Right along each side of the hut was a two-storey row of raised wooden bunks and - best of all - down at the far end was a round-bellied stove of black metal.

Raven whistled in astonished delight: 'Jehoshaphat, Simon, this is pretty decent, eh?'

Grant said: 'You're right, my boy. Not the Ritz, but better than I expected - a lot, especially the stove - that'll make life a sight better. It's pretty chilly here, even if it is spring.'

'Yes, and look: enough bunks for all of us, and they've even put a palliasse in each berth!'

'Ah yes, the old donkey's breakfast, as they say. Well, a straw mattress is a hell of a lot better than nothing. Hey, stand back a bit from the door, boys, you're making it dark in here. You can all have a look-round in a minute. Now, John, let's see what's through the door.' He creaked the flimsy door open into another room, smaller and darker than the bunkhouse, and whistled in delight: 'Look at this, John! A stack of biscuit and bully in tins!'

'Yes, and let's have a look at these big sacks. Yes, I guessed that: a sack of rice and two of beans.'

'Good, that'll be a nice change from all the dried peas on board. And these two are of flour - that'll be handy. I bet the doctor will be able to knock up some sort of bread from that.'

The two men were almost like children under a loaded Christmas tree. 'Gosh!' said Grant, 'look at this over here: a whole lot of tools - axes, saws, nails and a hammer.'

'Yes, and all sort of pots and pans on this shelf here - big ones, too. Three cheers for the New Zealanders! Must cost them quite a bit, this stuff - and running a steamer to bring it here.'

'I should say so. And think of the grind to unload all this onto a beach and then lug it all the way up here. Well done them!'

'Let's have a dekko inside this cupboard here. Ah, thank God for that - a great big bale of blankets! They've thought of everything, just about.'

They heard footsteps on the creaking floor and voices as, despite orders, the crowd came straggling in, looking about in the gloom, whistling in delighted surprise at the bunks and the straw mattresses. 'Not bad, eh, boys,' said Lewis. 'Bit dark and musty, like, but it smells better than the old foc'sle don't it?'

'Yeah,' said Kellock, 'but just you wait till us lot have been in here for a bit, sweating and farting and that. I fancy a bunk by the door, I do. Git some fresh air.'

'So do I,' said Lewis with a grin, 'but you'd better be in one of the bottom bunks, boy. You'd never get your big old carcass up into a top bunk, and anyway, damned if I wants to sleep underneath you - the bunks aren't built that strong. I've a-had the missis on top of me on times, and that was a bit of all right, but I don't fancy you there.'

Only the steward raised a querulous voice: 'These palliasses - I've had to sleep on them before. A lot of dust comes out of the straw, and they go dreadful hard after a bit - there's no comfort in them.'

Billy John was scornful: 'Bloody old woman, you! You've had it too cushy, you have, living down aft there among the *crachach*. Now you'll see what it's like for poor old Jack up for'ard. So will the rest of them, and serve them bloody right too.'

'Anyway, Isaac,' said Jac-y-Bont, more helpfully, 'when the mattress gets hard you just pick it up and shake it about - it goes soft again then - for a bit, anyway.'

Eleanor had edged her way through the crowd, and now joined Simon and John in the store-room. She had set herself to come out from her dark private nightmare of grief to rejoin the company in spirit as well as in body, though her face was still pale and drawn. 'Aren't we lucky?' she said, 'and aren't the New Zealanders true

Christians and good Samaritans, to think of poor people who might be marooned here, and who might be in distress? Do you think there are a lot of ships wrecked here, Simon?'

'Not many, but some, I believe. It's not altogether surprising; these islands and The Snares further north - they're right in the track of ships leaving Melbourne or Sydney or Newcastle and heading for the Horn. There's a bad current here, and, as we all know only too well, there's sometimes dangerous fogs that mean you can't get a decent fix on the chart.'

Once again, Raven was his prompter: 'Simon, don't you think we'd better start getting a meal organized? The crowd must all be starving - I am!'

'Yes, quite right, old son. We'd better all have a tuck-in. Get them all outside, will you?' Two minutes later, he was once more standing by the hut and looking at the semi-circle of his men and boys. It was time to put some heart and hope into them. 'Well, you've all had a good look round now, so you'll all know that we've been damn lucky, and I reckon we should all be grateful for the folk in New Zealand for looking after us like this.'

There was a growl of agreement from the men, though the bosun, not noted for light-heartedness, put in: 'Aye, well, we could bloody do with some good luck after what happened to us yesterday.'

'Yes, right enough, bosun, we could. But what's done is done, and here we are - all alive, all well, no-one even injured. So the first thing is to make up our minds to do our best to stay well; there's no doctors here, and not even a ship's medicine-chest. So now it's the present and the future we've got to think about, not the past. And the first thing we need is a decent dinner - right, boys?'

'Bloody right, mister,' came a voice from the back.

'Yes, but first I want to say a quick word about food. As you've seen, the steamer has left us a good supply, and of course, on top of that, there's all the stuff we brought from the ship in the boats. We'll lug that up here later on today. But you're all sensible men; you know there's nearly thirty of us here, and you can see that the stock is... limited; when that's gone there won't be any more till the next steamer comes, so two things are very important: none of it must be wasted, and all of it must be shared out fairly. So all the grub will be kept in that store-room, and no-one - *no-one* - will help himself to anything. I'm going to ask the doctor to be in charge of all the food, and he - and he alone - will decide who eats what, and when. Is that all right with you, doctor?'

Wellington Jones' eyes opened wide, and from his place to one side of the crowd he raked the assembly with a fierce, open-eyed African stare: 'You bet your life, mister. All that grub belong to me until I give it out. I seen a nice big, long carving-knife in there; any greedy bastard I finds helping himself gets that between his ribs - right? He won't pinch no more grub after that.'

Grant was pleased to hear a genuine relaxed laugh from the crowd at the comic ferocity of the cook's threat. Jones kept his dignity despite the mirth: 'Arl right, you jackasses can laugh your heads off if you like, but you just remember this: my great-grandaddy was an Ashanti warrior before they caught him and shipped him over to cut sugar-cane. None of you ain't seen me when I'm *really* mad - but you'll see! If you try your luck with me - you'll damn well see!'

This time the crowd cheered, despite the grim menace; there was a manliness, an integrity about the cook that commanded respect and liking. He knew his own worth, and he'd always done his difficult and arduous job well. The treachery of other Africans and the greed and rapacity of Arabs, Europeans and Americans had made his ancestors slaves, but no-one could ever think of him as one - they would not dare. Nor would it have even occurred to any of them to call him contemptuous names arising from his colour; he was just Welly, the doctor, and you kept on the right side of him if you were wise. Grant could not possibly have found a better guardian for the food.

Grant held up his hand for silence: 'Good for you, doctor - you tell em. Well now, it's midday, and even the doctor will agree we all need to get a bit of dinner into us. After that, why don't we all have a bit of a snooze for an hour or so? But no more than that; we've got plenty to do before it gets dark.' He turned to a chubby, fair-haired apprentice: 'Robbins, away you go at the double, down to the beach. Tell the boat-keepers they can come back up here now, if all's well down there. But you see what I mean, boys: we can all survive here; we're all going to leave this island fit and well, and get back to our homes - and our blessed owner will have to pay for our passage back, too. But we'll only do that if we're a sensible and orderly society, not a bunch of selfish, scrapping savages.'

He was about to end his address and let them fill their stomachs, when he noticed that Waters, the quietest and most studious of the young apprentices, had raised his hand like a schoolboy in a Latin class. 'Yes, Waters,' he said, with more than a trace of irritation, 'what is it now?'

'Please, sir, did you see that notice pinned to the

back of the door?'

'No, boy, what notice? I was too busy with more important things than bits of paper.'

The boy swallowed nervously, but persisted: 'Yes sir, but I think you should read it. It's about the next visit and the future food supplies. Shall I get it?'

'Oh very well, then, only be quick. We're all dying for a bite to eat.'

His impatience was echoed by groans from the crowd. Billy John grumbled: 'Bloody hell! We got to wait for some stupid English *crwt* of a brassbounder? My guts can't wait for nobody.'

Waters came scurrying back with a sheet of paper he'd unpinned from the door. Amid further groans Grant quickly scanned it, and gave a grimace of disappointment and displeasure. 'Well spotted, Waters. Yes, you're right - I should read it, and you all need to know what it says. Not good news, I'm afraid. Just listen: "These supplies are for the use of genuine castaways from shipwreck only. Those making wrongful use will be liable to severe prison sentences...." and so on. Here's the bad news for us: "Regret that the regular New Zealand rescue vessel has been damaged by accidental grounding, and will require dry-docking for extensive repairs. As no other vessel is available, the next visit is postponed for at least six weeks. To compensate for the delay, extra supplies have been left on this occasion, together with a box of fishing-lines to enable castaways to augment their food supplies." H'm... and it's signed "Lieutenant-commander Richard Travers, RN, Commanding Officer, HMS 'Halcyon'". There you are then, boys: they've wrecked their own ship, so they had to get the Navy to do their delivery for them. I didn't notice any box of fishing lines; did you, Mr Raven?'

'I saw them, sir,' said the sharp-eyed and now eager Waters. 'They were behind some tins on a shelf.'

'What a treasure you are, lad,' said Grant, with an air of resigned irritation. 'But still, well done. Well, there you are then, boys. As I said, it's not good news, I'm afraid. This is dated September the twelfth - only a week ago. It says six weeks, but we all know what dockyards are like, don't we? Once they get hold of a ship they don't hurry too much. The more they can find wrong with it, the more money they can make. Never mind, what I said is still true: it's up to us to be proper men, disciplined, using our wits and energies, and not lolling about moping and grizzling. We'll still pull through, but this news shows even more clearly how important it is to ration our food; after all there's quite a lot of us to be fed -more than usual after a wreck, I should think But in the meantime, doctor, what about opening a tin or two? I don't suppose any of these gentlemen will mind a cold lunch today, eh?'

*

About two hours later, Grant, though still exhausted, dragged first himself, then Raven and the bosun from their deep, drugged sleep: 'Come on then, gents. Time to roust out the crowd. Plenty to do before dark.'

The hands had all selected their bunks, and lay sprawled like corpses, making up for a long sleepless night of terror, toil and cold exposure in the boats. Grant noticed with passing amusement that, like cows in a cowshed, they had mechanically imposed a kind of order in their choice of berths: all 'Figaro's' port watch of seamen were on the left side of the hut, leaving the other side to the starboard watch. The only exception, he noted, was that the two malcontent cronies and trouble-makers (or, as Kellock would have called them, 'skates') of the crew were to be found together, though of opposite watches. I'll have to keep an eye on those two specimens, he thought, but he let that irksome problem go for the present.

When at last the men were outside, yawning, stretching and scratching in the spring sunshine, he made an effort to be cheerful, positive and reasonable, discarding for the moment the habitual curtness of a bucko: 'That's better, eh, lads - a bellyful and a bit of kip? But now there's some jobs to do before dark, so let's shape up and get on with them. I'd like you to split up into your watches, as you were on board. Port watch, I want you to get axes and saws from the store and go out after firewood. We're going to need a lot of that for the stove and for a cooking fire out here. I think we should keep a fire going night and day, once we get it started, so that we can dry out any wood that needs it. Go off that way,' he pointed to a thick copse dead ahead, 'and try to find some dry dead branches that will burn easily to start the fire off. Don't bring back sodden stuff that's been lying on the ground.'

As the men went for their tools, Grant said: 'Will you take charge of them, bosun? Keep the beggars at it - it'll be good for them to be doing something useful. And watch out that some halfwit doesn't decide to wander off - it's a big enough jungle for an idiot to get lost in.'

'Aye, aye, mister. We'll cut the wood off long and bring it back here for sawing in stove-lengths. They're funny old trees here - all crooked, and the branches all twisted, like, but if I can find some bits of tidy, straight poles we can soon make a saw-horse by here for that. I noticed some odd bits of rope knocking about in the store. And I'll try and stop the boys from cutting their own feet off - they're not used to axes, some of them.'

'I shouldn't worry too much about them,' said Raven, when the bosun and his party had gone. 'I know them; whatever our cheerful bosun may say, they're nearly all country boys, from small farms. They'll be pretty handy at that sort of job.'

'Let's hope so.' Then Grant raised his voice to address the ten men of the starboard watch. 'As for you lads, I want you to start bringing up the grub and any other gear from the boats. Don't try to carry too much at a time - it's a fair way up here - and don't for God's sake drop any of the tins of bully. If they get punctured by falling on a rock, and the air gets in, the meat will be ruined. Tidy up the boats too; unship the rowlocks and lay the oars on the thwarts. I think what we'll do one day soon, John, once the boats are empty, is all go down and lift them - one at a time - right up onto that bit of grass, so that they can't drift off, and can't get knocked to bits at high water by an onshore breeze.'

'Very good,' said Raven briskly. 'That sounds like a good idea - only, it's just struck me - if we're going to try fishing, hadn't we'd better leave one of them handy to the water, and keep the mast up? For now I'll see to the unloading and lugging the stuff up here. We'll put it all in the store, I suppose?'

Grant felt a stab of annoyance with himself; once again Raven had suggested something that he himself should have thought of: 'No, I want you here.' He raised his voice: 'Right then, boys - away you go, and put your backs into it.' As the starboard watch shambled off down the path, Grant put his hand on Raven's shoulder: 'I need to have a serious chat with you - and Eleanor - and there's no time like the present, while it's quiet here. I think she's still in the hut; can you ask her to come out?'

Raven found Eleanor in the store, looking somewhat more like herself. She had taken off her oilskins, and was attempting to restore some sort of order to her tangled hair, using her fingers as a crude comb. The rest, warmth and sleep had brought back some colour to her cheeks, but she was still an incongruous - almost comic - figure in her thick, oversized, high-necked seaman's jumper and baggy trousers of the same navy-blue, stuffed into the tops of her clumsy sea-boots.

Raven's heart was wrenched by a sudden vision of their first proper meeting at supper in the ship's saloon while 'Figaro' was at anchor in a bay in Chile, just after Eleanor and her mother had arrived in Caleta Buena to join the ship. His mind flashed up a picture of her dark eyes and stunningly-beautiful, regular features, tanned a little by the sunshine of her voyage out and framed by long black hair that fell silkily to her shoulders. That evening she'd worn a crisp, frilled, spotless white blouse and an immaculate long smooth grey skirt that revealed, now and then, a glimpse of white stocking and neat, soft leather boots. Another memory, which he quickly suppressed, was that of the much later nights in the semi-dark of his cabin, when a blind, hungry, mutual passion had arisen between them, and she'd come to him in a black silk nightdress of such flimsy thinness that his touch seemed to be on the warmth and smoothness of her flesh itself; How often, too, in those far-off, delicious times, he'd buried his face in the fragrance of her long tresses!

He bit his lip, as if in pain at the brutality of the change in her looks. Eleanor said: 'What's the matter, John? You look as if you're in pain.'

'No, not in pain - not in my body anyway. It's just... seeing you like this...and in this awful place.'

She took his hand lightly: 'Listen *cariad,* I know I look a complete guy - a real fright - but what does that matter? There were times on the night of the wreck when I didn't expect to see another day, but thanks to the bravery and skill of you and all the other men, we're still alive and unhurt. Now we've got to be brave... strong. We both believe in a merciful God. He will not leave us here forever. One day we'll be able to...to be as we were on those wonderful nights on board the ship. I'll wager that was what you were thinking of just now, wasn't it?' She gave a shrewd half-smile at his nod and sheepish grin, and went on: 'Yes, I thought so. Do you suppose I don't have memories like that too - memories that delight and torture me, both at the same time? One day, when my present agony of grief, and the memory of this nightmare has receded from my mind a little, one day - a very long way off, I suppose - I swear, we'll live together in a home of our own, and do whatever we please, whenever we please. Try to think of that, John, like a kind of beacon ahead of us, not back to times when we were young and reckless - and wicked, of course. And in future we'll try to behave a little more respectably, won't we?' She smiled faintly, and gave his hand a gentle squeeze.

'God, Nelli, I don't know what I've done to deserve you, I really don't. Things are going to be a bit rough for us for a time - perhaps a long time, but I agree; one day we'll be together and we'll be free to love each other like other couples.' He shook his head to bring himself back to the dreary present: 'But listen, Simon wants to see us.'

'About what?'

'Don't know. Something serious, he said. The hands have all gone off to work.'

'H'm, I think I can guess what he's going to say. Let's see if I'm right.'

'Ah, Eleanor,' said Simon with a smile as they came out. 'I hope you're feeling a bit better now?'

'Yes, in myself I suppose I am. As for the loss of Mam and Dadi, one so soon after the other in such terrible ways, I'll carry the pain of that to my grave, I expect. It was like the end of one of those Greek tragedies - you could foresee it but do nothing to prevent it. Thank you for your kindness, Simon. But now - now we've got to do whatever needs doing to survive and escape back to Wales.'

'Yes, exactly so. Now I'm going to have to talk to you both very personally, and in a way that I wouldn't dream of if we weren't in this fix. But I'm not just a friend to you both, remember; I am, for my sins, captain of this crew, so I've got to speak to you officially, as it were, in a way you may not like.'

Raven flushed like a guilty schoolboy; Eleanor frowned: 'Simon, do for pity's sake get to the point. I think I know what you're going to say - there's no need to beat about the bush like this. We're both adults, I hope.'

'Very well then, this is my point: I'm concerned, Eleanor, about your presence on this island. Firstly, I'm worried about your safety from....from insult...or assault, and I'm also concerned about the general effect of your presence on morale and discipline among the hands.'

Eleanor began, indignantly: 'I don't see…'

Grant held up his hands to arrest her protest: 'No, no, please hear me out. God knows none of this is your fault. But you are a young and extremely attractive woman, and you're marooned on an island in close company with twenty-odd men, some of them little older than yourself. Though I shall try to keep them busy, there will be much more time for idleness and mischief than there was aboard ship, and you won't be, as it were, sealed off from them as you were then. On top of that, I doubt if I command a quarter of the respect among them that your father did. There again, that can't be helped.'

Eleanor snorted impatiently: 'Good heavens, why do you men treat us women as objects to be talked about and managed - as if we were naïve halfwits with no will or intelligence of our own? D'you suppose I haven't realized all this myself? But I'm not weak and I'm not stupid. I don't need wrapping in cotton-wool.'

Raven too was nettled: 'Yes, Simon, and what do you take me for - a coward? Do you think I won't look after Nelli and see that she's safe? I'd guard her with my life! By Christ, if any of them so much as *touches* her I'll….'

Grant had begun this talk in a tone of embarrassed politeness, but now their petulant resistance to his will and guidance riled him: 'For God's sake shut up, both of you, and *listen:* John, talk sense. You can't have your eye on Eleanor all the time, and don't you see that your knight-in-shining-armour attitude could lead to just the kind of strife and violence that I'm determined to avoid if I can? Any sort of fighting and feuding among us would be a disaster. And Eleanor - surely you can see that your presence here and your… your relationship with John might give me serious problems? Don't you think I've got enough of those, without you two adding to them?'

He paused for a response from them, but both stood in sullen silence, averting their eyes to look at the gloomy forest thickets around them.'

'Huh - sulking like spoilt brats! If you two can't see the truth of what I'm saying, you're not being very bright - either of you. All right then, I'll stop being diplomatic and give you both a straight order, and you can like it or lump it, I don't care which: I'm quite sure all the hands know that you two are lovers and they will either know or guess you've been pretty intimate lovers too. Right: that is the past and can't be altered, but I'm telling you, as your commander, that from now on things are going to be very different on this island. You're not really stupid, either of you, however you may appear so now. You must see the envy that you'd stir up among the younger hands if they saw your precious love-affair going on in their midst. For God's sake, John, use your bloody wits and try to put yourself in *their* shoes! How would you like it?'

Raven said nothing but turned his back on Grant in a sullen silence.

'All right, sulk like a stupid kid if you want to. D'you think I like having to say all this? But I'm going to say it anyway: from now on, you two have got to be just two fellow-castaways - two of the bunch. There must be no signs of any special relationship between you; you will both behave towards each other exactly as you would towards the bosun or the doctor or any of the ABs. You will *not* seek each other's company, and most of all you will *not* sneak off together when I'm not looking. Now, is all that clear?'

They both gave silent, morose nods, but the look they exchanged said: We're one; nothing you say will alter that.

'Good,' said Grant coldly. 'Eleanor, there's one other thing: when the bosun comes back I'm going to get him to rig you up a berth in the store. It won't be very comfortable in there, I'm afraid, but I'm sure he'll do his best, and at least it will be safer. He and John and I will sleep next to the door of the store to see there's no funny business in the night. John, go down to the beach now and take charge of the starboard watch. But before we leave all this I'll just say one more thing to both of you: when you've cooled down and stopped hating me, just think things over for yourselves. By being so stubborn you've made all this a lot harder and more unpleasant for me - and yourselves - than was necessary. But when you've had a good think, you will see that I am right, and that what I've said was no more than my duty. Anyway, whether you do think that way or not, that's the way it's going to be, because I say so, and I'm in charge.'

Without a word, Raven turned and trudged off down the now trodden path among the high green ferns; Eleanor, in the same sullen silence, made to go back into the hut, but Grant raised his voice and called after her: 'Eleanor, will you join the cook and Davey Jones, please? They're going to set about making a fireplace for cooking on the other side of the clearing.'

She turned and fixed him with a dull, furious glare: 'O, of course, sir, of course. Anything you say. Even wretched inconvenient females are of some domestic use. After all, I've been banished to the attic like any other skivvy, so you might as well use me as a skivvy. You obviously don't want me lolling voluptuously about as a half-clad siren, displaying my female charms, and luring your poor dear sailors to their doom, do you?'

Inwardly raging, gritting his teeth, Grant said nothing, but thought: *Women!* By God, old Crusoe was lucky; he only had cannibals to worry about!

CHAPTER FOUR

'Now then,' said the doctor to his helpers, 'what we got to do is make a kind of stove - like a kind of grate that we can put pots and pans on. That little ole bogey stove in the hut ain't no manner of use for cooking. So what we gonna do is build two little walls about a foot and a half apart, and - what do you call it? - parallel, and about a foot high, and about three foot long. The tops got to be real level and the same height, so the saucepan or skillet can rest on them nice. Then all we do is get dry wood and make a fire between the walls, and when that start to burn down low you just shove in more wood from the end. You unnerstand that?'

Isaac Hughes steward wrinkled his face to show his distaste for this job. He was used to clean, light work below decks in his pantry or in the officers' saloon, and was not disposed to be helpful: 'Walls, doctor? What the devil are we going to make walls of? They haven't left us no bricks.'

'No, Isaac man, so we got to use whatever the good Lord *has* sent us. Just look around you, man! There's lots of rocks stuck in the grass, and - look, over there - a pile of rocks. I dare say the men what levelled this bit of ground slung them down there.'

Isaac would not be comforted or encouraged: 'You'll need a hell of a lot of stone for two walls that size. And these stones are all very rough; it's not my kind of work - terrible for your hands.' He shook his head and his dirge continued: 'And - *ach y fi!* - the ones in the grass will be stuck fast and covered in horrible old wet mud. And drat, it's beginning to drizzle with rain; how can we be expected to...'

'Listen, man: you want to eat cold bully and biscuit all the time and nutten else? We got to get ready to cook, rain or shine. How're the boys gonna eat rice or beans if'n we don't cook em?' He turned to Davey Jones, the small, wiry cabin-boy or peggy: 'Davey boy, fetch me that mattock from the store. That'll be handy for getting up the stones from the grass.'

Davey, a lad from the smallest, poorest and roughest of the farms on the slopes of the Preseli mountains, had none of Isaac's fastidious inhibitions: 'Right you are, Mr Jones,' he said as he sped off, returning in two minutes with the mattock - a kind of pick-axe, but with a thick blade set across, like a very stout, heavy hoe.

'Good boy,' said Jones. 'Now then, you's a bit of a shrimp to look at, but you been a farm boy, ain't you? So you'll know how to swing that thing. So you dig out the stones, then Isaac fetch them across, and me and Miss Eleanor here - we build the walls. I don't want no big stones, mind, and I don't want none like balls - you can't build nutten with them. I want them as square and flat as you can find - with some decent corners on them.'

Isaac still grumbled as he left: 'One of that foc'sle crowd could have done this - I didn't sign on for this kind of work.'

The doctor lost his patience: 'Jesus, Isaac, they ain't here and they busy with harder jobs than this. So shift your goddam arse and do like I say.' He turned to where Eleanor stood, silent and preoccupied with a chaos of conflicting thoughts: 'I'm real sorry about my language, miss, but that Isaac do rile me sometimes - he so damn picky.'

She came to, and half-smiled: 'No matter, Mr Jones, I've heard worse. And I remember my mother could never stand that man. Now, tell me what you want me to do.'

'D'you think you could help me build up these little walls? I know that's dirty work - not a lady's sort of job...'

It was the wrong thing to say to Eleanor at that moment: 'O, don't keep apologizing, for heaven's sake! I'm not a lady, I'm just a woman who happens to be here among all you men. I'm not weak, I'm not lazy, and I've lived halfway up a mountain and looked after ponies all my life, nearly. That's not clean work, I can tell you. As for dry stone-walling, I'm sure I've seen more of that than you have, up on Carn Ingli. I haven't done it myself, but I know how it's done. So let's just get started, Mr Jones.'

'Okay then, miss. Now, these walls, we got to be careful that they nice and firm - not rocking about, so they got to be fairly thick. And on the inside they got to be real straight and flush - no bits sticking out - so we can push the wood in easy. But it don't matter how rough the outsides are.'

'Yes, I see... You say they've got to be firm? So what about packing all the gaps in the courses with mud? That would make them firm, and the mud wouldn't burn, it'd just bake hard, I think.'

A broad, beaming smile spread across Jones' black, grey-grizzled face: 'Now, if that ain't the best idea I heard today, missy!'

'You agree? Right, I'm sure I saw some spades in the store - I'll go and get one and start digging some sods up.'

'There you are, Isaac,' Jones called across the clearing when she had gone. 'She got the spirit I need - she don't keep dripping on like you, but get started, cheerful-like.'

'Huh - that young madam! Just a common hoyden, she is. She gets started all right! If I was to tell you half of what I know about her and her goings-on with that cub Raven… Going off to his cabin in the middle of the night with nothing on, hardly...'

'Just shut your trap, man, and get on with what I told you to do. I don't want to hear no dirt about her from you. Ain't you got no feelings, no sympathy, in that Welsh hide of yourn? She's just lost her…' A nod and a grimace from the steward stopped him, and he turned to see Eleanor approaching with a rusty spade. 'Ah, that's the hammer, miss, just what we need. If you give it to me for a minute I'll mark out the places for the walls and level the ground off a bit. Pity we ain't got no iron bars to rest the pots on, but we'll just have to manage without.'

With the sites marked out, the building began. As the work proceeded in silence, Jones found the girl's quiet determination and absorption with her wet and dirty task deeply moving. Indifferent to the steady drizzle and chilly breeze, she plodded to and fro, building a pile of muddy clods, and then knelt to bed them in each course of stones, working like a potter to fill each crack between the stones till they lay as firm as bricks in mortar. She had tied her hair back roughly with a piece of twine, and some of the black mud from her filthy hands had got smeared across one cheek, but the old cook was stirred by her beauty and by the passion that she was putting into this rough, wet, dirty chore. She'd be a real good woman to have for a wife. That Raven - he was a lucky young bastard!

Then, working closely beside her, he saw that the mud on her cheek was caused by her brushing her face with the back of her hand; and it was not rain, but tears that she was brushing away. Words were forced from him: 'Hey, Miss Roberts, I don't like to see you at this damn wet dirty job, and I got to tell you something: I feel real sorry for what's happened to you - all the boys do too. Why don't you...?'

'For God's sake stop feeling sorry for me, man! Why can't everybody leave me *alone* to do something useful? What the devil do I care if the job's dirty, or if it's started to rain? I told you just now - that doesn't bother me. I've had enough of this from Grant - telling me what I can do and what I can't do, wrapping me up in cotton-wool! I don't *want* that!'

With an effort, Jones suppressed the resentment he felt at this furious rejection of his heart-felt concern, and said stonily: 'All right, Miss Roberts, ma'am; I just shut my big trap.'

They worked on in silence for a while, picking up the stones that the steward - also in a sullen silence - dropped nearby, and fitting them in like pieces of a jigsaw puzzle, Eleanor ramming the soft wet clods into the gaps. The simple satisfaction of seeing their structures rising, neat and firm, from the ground began to soothe Eleanor's mind, and she became deeply ashamed of her petulant and rude rejection of the cook's kindness. Good God, he was just a decent, big-hearted, fatherly man trying to offer her comfort, trying to ease her desolate loneliness by showing her that he and others cared for her. He was as alone and as far from home as she was, and she could see he was cheerfully doing his best to make life better for everyone - not grumbling selfishly, like that awful Isaac Hughes. Why on earth had she been so horrible to him?

'Mr Jones,' she said when the other two were off after stones, 'I'm sorry I was so rude to you when you were trying to be kind just now. I'm ashamed of my....'

He put his big hand on hers among the mud and stones; thanks to the mud, both hands were now of the same colour: 'Hey, don't you fret none about that, miss - and why don't you call me Welly, not Mr Jones -everyone else do?' He smiled widely: 'And your ma - she used to call you Nelli, didn't she? Welly and Nelli - we'll make a good team, eh? This place is gonna be my galley now, and I'd be real glad if you was to be my buddy here, and help with the cooking. That Davey, he's a good boy, but got no more sense than that spade you're holding. I be darned if he could boil water prop'ly.'

But his generous, sensible kindness made her tears flow again, and unconsciously she placed her other hand on his great paw and leaned against him: 'You're such a good man, Mr - I mean Welly. I don't deserve such treatment. However sad I am, I shouldn't be so cold and rude; you didn't cause my troubles - nor did anyone on this island. And yes, I'd love to have a job in your galley. I'm sick of being useless.'

'That's good, honey, that's good. Only I better tell you now that when things get busy and I'm all hot and hectic, I'm like all cooks - liable to git mean and shout a lot.'

She smiled easily: 'I can stand that, Welly; I used to get shouted at a lot in school, because I didn't always behave like young ladies should.'

'I b'lieve you, Nelli. I can see you got too much spirit to toe the line all the time. But there's another thing I got to say: you didn't ought to get too mean with Mr Grant neither. He a man with a whole lot a problems, and he trying to care for you. It ain't easy for him here, and I can tell you, I wouldn't want his job, not for a sackful of dollars.'

'No, I can see things are hard for him here - it's all such a wilderness, and it's so strange for all of us - so different from what it was like on the ship. He knew where he was there - we all did. Now he, and all the rest of us, we're so alone, and so…so naked, you might say, and with no idea of what's going to happen to us.'

'You just keep your mind on the future, gal. We gonna be off this island one day, and I'll bet my bottom dollar you gonna settle down with your man and soon have some young uns to care for - don't blush now - it's only natural. You ain't like me - I got nobody in the wide world to care for, nor to care for me. When I was young and stupid I didn't think of no-one but me myself. I left Jamaica, I left my mam and pappy, I left my gal and the baby I'd given her. I just lit out to see the world, and by God, I've seen too damn much of it now. I'm like a big ole black tree what's lost its roots; but you - - you gonna be happy one day, and be one of a family. As for me - we got an old song back home that goes like this:

Brown-skin gal, stay home and mind the baby,
Brown-skin gal, stay home and mind the baby.
I'm goin away on a sailin boat,
an if I don't come back,
Stay home and mind the baby.

And I was just exactly like that guy in the song, more's the pity.'

Eleanor gave a clap with her muddy hands: 'Welly, you've got a lovely deep bass voice. I come from Wales, so I know about singing. You should be in opera in New York!'

The cook shook his head resignedly: 'No, miss. If I turned up there they'd just say "Git your butt outa here, you ole buck niggah!"' They both laughed in a comradely way and went back to their cold, dirty task.

Over on the other side of the clearing, Isaac took a furtive, prurient look at their closeness and laughter, and muttered to Davey: 'Look at that, boy! I do believe that baggage is making eyes at the doctor now! I never saw nothing so disgusting as the way she do carry on. Just a tart - that's what she's turned into. She'd open her legs for anyone in trousers, she would. What her poor mother would say if she could see her now....'

Davey was indignant; Hughes might have been his lord and master aboard ship, but the boy had a dog-like devotion to Eleanor, and could not stand this self-righteous sneering: 'Don't you talk so nasty about her, mun. She's no bloody tart! She nursed me like a mother when I had that horrible old fever. She could have caught it off of me, couldn't she? But she was there all the time, she was, like a blinking angel, bathing that terrible mucky rash I had then. If she's sweet on Raven, and had a bit of fun with him - well, why not? It's only natural, isn't it? Doesn't hurt you or me. She's never going to fancy either of us, is she? I'm just a poor little *crwt* from off the mountain, and you're just a skinny old misery. As for the doctor, damn, he's old enough to be her father; he's just been trying to cheer her up, I reckon, so don't go thinking and talking so dirty about her. There you are - there's another bloody stone for the wall, so get on with the job and take that to the doctor.'

'*Cau dy ben,* boy! You talk to me like that, you'll get the back of my hand across your chops.'

'No I won't,' said Davey stoutly. 'I got this bloody great mattock here, ain't I.?'

Hughes snorted and trudged off with the same uneasy feeling experienced by Grant - that the old order was collapsing, and that on this island things were going to be different, and very much less pleasant, than aboard ship.

Grant came across from the hut, where he had been making a thorough check of all the provisions and equipment: 'Ah, that looks shipshape, doctor. Nearly finished?'

'Yes, mister. Got to just level the tops of the walls off neat.'

'Excellent.... yes, I see. We just poke the wood in this end to keep the heat up, and the pots and pans rest on the walls. You're a genius, doctor.'

'No sir, I ain't no genius. I've just learnt a few things by cooking all over the place, mostly out in the sticks - mining camps in California, logging camps in Oregon - all over. Even once on a cattle drive from Texas, before I took up to cooking at sea.'

'Not the Yukon? I hear they're prospecting up there.'

'No *sir!* That too damn cold for Jamaican boy, I ain't cooking up to my arse in snow - oh, sorry miss, there I go again with my rude language. I forgot you was there.'

Eleanor smiled, and, to Grant's great relief, included him in her smile: 'Don't worry, Welly. It's only a word for something we sit on, and we've all got one, haven't we?'

'Absolutely,' said Grant, returning her smile, 'and it was a good enough word for Chaucer and Shakespeare. In our polite, very respectable Victorian world it has just gone out of fashion, that's all.' It was all just casual chat, but it reminded her comfortingly of the link that had grown up between them aboard the ship - their common love of books.

Jones' mind was back to practicalities: 'This will have to do to cook on, but it would be a whole lot better if I had some iron bars to go across between the walls - be a lot handier and a lot safer too.'

'Yes, I'm sure, but....'

'No, you just hold on, mister, never mind the "buts": I just bet you there's been all kinds a folk here before us - whalers and sealers, maybe even folk trying to settle here, and they might have left all sorts a stuff lying about in the grass. You tell the boys to keep a good lookout for something handy, will you? Some bits of iron bars, f'r instance.'

A voice came from behind them; 'Gosh, look at that, Perky! Pretty neat, eh? Well done, doctor!' Smith and Perkins, the two oldest and strongest of the four brass-bounders, had arrived back with their loads of biscuit from the boats.

'Yes,' said Jones, 'well, you see now I ain't just a pretty face. But' - and he nodded towards the grimy-faced Eleanor - 'I didn't do it on my own.'

The boys gasped in astonishment, and looked at Eleanor with a new respect. She for her part grinned at them, and spread her wet, filthy hands with pride.

The cook had not finished with Grant: 'And I can see I'm gonna have another problem, mister, and that's the rain and the wind. It ain't been too bad so far today, but I can see this is a damn wet and windy place. I could do my job a whole lot better with a bit of shelter from the weather. The wind is the worst thing. How'm I gonna cook proper hot food in a damn gale? Half the heat of the fire going to blow away. And how do I keep a fire going at all in the pouring rain we get here?'

While Grant was still pondering, young Smith said, half-facetiously: 'Build a log cabin - there's lots of wood here.'

'Good for you, boy,' said Grant. That's a lot more sensible than you seem to think. I don't see why we couldn't do that, doctor.'

'Yeah, it's an idea, mister. I've seen many a one of those built in the lumber camps. You sink four big logs as uprights, and then fix smaller cross-pieces to them in a square, to make a kinda framework, and then you split lots of smaller timber to make the walls. But that's OK when you're in among big woods of pine and fir, nice straight, tall trees. The problem on this damn weird island is the kind of trees we got - all bendy and twisted - no decent straight lengths of timber. We gotta have that shelter, and we gottta use whatever there is here. Ain't no use complaining about what we ain't got. And I'll tell you, mister, what you have got here: you got a whole lot of strong country boys from off farms. They ain't professors from no college, but they got their heads screwed on good. They know how to manage and make all kinds a things. They live out in the sticks, and they ain't rich, so when they got a big job to do, they gotta use their wits, an get their neighbours round to help, else how would they ever get their harvests in, or put up a new barn? I reckon if'n you got them together you'd get some good ideas outa them.'

Grant had been aware, while the cook was talking, of a growing murmur of voices behind him, and he now turned to see Reuben's wood-cutting party straggling laboriously back along the track into the clearing, each man bending under the weight of a twisted mossy bough, or dragging a bigger branch behind him through the bushes and rough tussocks of grass. 'Ah,' he said, 'and here they are, dead on cue.'

'Noo, mister,' gasped Lewis, the Milford man, 'oon'y half-dead, sweating, and parched beyond, mun.'

'Well done, boys! Sit yourselves down for a bit and drink a drop of water. We need to have a word together.'

'Water?' cried one man scornfully. 'Couple a pints of home-brewed beer, I needs, after that bloody job.'

'Wish I had some for you, lad,' said Grant cheerfully, 'but just now I want to pick your brains about something important.'

'Pick their brains?' said the sardonic Reuben. 'That won't take you long with this crowd, mister.'

'No? Well, let's see, shall we? We've got some building to do, and I'm no sort of hand at anything like that, so I need some advice from experts.'

Simon's implied flattery produced an attentive audience. 'This is the problem, boys: the doctor needs a more or less weatherproof shelter above this cooking contraption he and the others have made. Well, we haven't got bricks or good building stone, or nice straight timber either. All we've got is what you see around you, and plenty of time, plus your ideas and your energy. So now then - what do we do? Tell me.'

The men were silent, exchanging glances; the foc'sle crowd was used to orders from officers, but not to requests for advice. Lewis, one of the brightest of them, was the first to speak: 'Well, I don't know about a roof, but making walls round it wouldn't be too hard. You just puts a decent hedge round...'

'A *hedge?'* said Grant irritably. 'How long is that going to take to grow? We need the shelter now!'

'Hang on, mister,' said Reuben. 'The boy ain't talking *twp* like you seem to think. There's hedges and hedges. You ain't been down our part of the world, have you? Down in our part of Wales a hedge is a big bank, four or five foot high, made of earth and stones, and faced with turf. Nigh on all the fields and roads and lanes in Pembrokeshire have got hedges like that, to keep the sheep and cattle in, and give the poor beasts some shelter, cos the weather back home can be just like it is here.'

'Aye,' said Jac-y-bont, 'it'll be a big job, I know, but if we build the bank up to, say, five foot, you won't have to have any walls. You can rest your roof rafters on the top of it; that'll be strong beyond, mun - last a lifetime and more!'

'And I tell you what, sir,' said Lewis, now fired up with architectural enthusiasm, 'if the doctor's gonna have a fire in there, and we can't build a chimney, one end had best be left open, to let the smoke out, like. We could put the bank round the north, west and south, and leave the east end open. That faces towards the hut, and the cliff-face behind the hut, so you won't get much wind from that quarter, I reckon, and that would make it handy to get in and out with the grub and that.'

Grant had been listening with rising spirits to the growth of a sensible, practical consensus on the design. How easy it was for middle-class, public school- and college-educated chaps like himself to under-estimate the powers of these apparently ignorant, illiterate, simple men! Probably they'd all been turned out of some village dame-school at twelve years old, just schooled enough to recite their tables, write a little and stumble through some bits of the Bible, and here they were, running rings round him, able to visualize a structure without any written instructions or drawings!

He smacked his hands together in approval: 'Excellent! Well done, boys! I'll sign up to that idea, but, by God, it's going to be a big job, and it'll take time too. There's a lot of soil to shift, and we've only got three or four spades.'

'Where there's a will there's a way,' said bosun sententiously. 'We keep half a dozen hands on fetching wood, and all the rest of us - ' he stared belligerently at the sulky steward - *'all* the rest of us works all the daylight hours to get it done. You don't have to go far for the soil; you just skims off the top foot or so all round where the banks will be, and the more stones we put in, the less soil we need.'

'Aye,' said Jac, 'and I reckon we put the chaps who know what they're doing to build the banks, while those who don't - like these blessed brassbounders - get to work fetching rocks. We'll need tons of those.'

All the apprentices were now back from the boats, and pulled faces of comic gloom at each other.

'Which leaves us,' said Grant thoughtfully, ' with the problem of the roof. Jac mentioned rafters, but you need straight timber for that, and all the wood on this island is twisted to hell - not a straight foot in it.'

'No,' said Reuben. 'Not all of it, mister. I did a bit of scouting while the boys were cutting wood. I climbed up the slopes above the trees, so I could see a long way to the south of here. I was looking down on the top of the woods, see, and the trees was so thick together, all at the same height, you'd think you could walk on the tops of them. But way off to the south - half a mile to a mile, maybe - I could see different trees - straighter, taller ones - poking up through the twisty ones. Not many, mind, but maybe enough for us to make rafters.'

'Big tall trees a mile off!' said Billy John mutinously. 'How're we poor buggers s'posed to lug them back here? You'd need a fuckin elephant for that!'

'We do it,' said Jac, red with irritation at Billy's predictable moaning, 'because we bloody *got* to do it, *twpsyn!* And by using them brains what the skipper was talking about, and what you haven't got, seemingly. What we do, mates, is this: when we've got the earth walls done, we'll know what length the rafters have got to be, and how long the ridge-pole in the middle has got to be. Then we finds these straight trees, cut off bits of the right length; I makes some timber-wedges out of hard wood; we use the flat of the mattock to tap them in and split the logs any way you like, and…'

'And Bob's yer bleedin uncle!' said Kellock with a grin. 'We just carry one split rafter at a time! See, Bill, you got a lot to do to catch up with ole Jac here. You're a clever ole sod, Jac!'

'And, speaking generally, you're a bunch of geniuses,' said Grant. 'I expected nothing less. But I can still see some other problems ahead. I can see that we can fix the bottom of each rafter by digging its end into the hedge-bank, but how the hell do we fasten its top end to a ridge-pole? And what goes on top of these rafters to keep the rain out?'

'Well, as for the fixing of the tops of the rafters, we use rope,' said another voice. Raven was now back with his load.

'Splendid idea in theory,' said Grant drily, 'but unfortunately we don't happen to have any rope.'

Smith, a burly, blunt, practical young fellow, said: 'Rope? I know where there's tons of that - and tons of canvas too, that you could use to make a roof covering.'

Grant cut in irritably: 'What on earth are you blathering on about, Smith? We're trying to make some sensible plans here.'

'I'm not blathering, sir, I'm talking about the ship's jigger mizen-mast. That never went into the cave, did it? That was still standing when we left, and the jigger tops'l was still set, and flapping in the wind. I remember looking at it as we rowed away.'

Raven joined in with enthusiasm: 'Yes, sir, I remember that too. We could sail round on a calm day, row the boat alongside the mast, and one of us could shin up and cut the sail loose from its hanks, and its sheet and tack, and lower it down into the boat. That's a big piece of cloth, and good new canvas too.'

Grant pursed his lips sceptically, and replied to their gusto with cool irony: 'H'm. A wonderful idea! You see what it's like to be young, doctor: at that age you can easily think up scores of novel ways of getting yourself killed. And anyway, my young friends, that doesn't get us any rope.'

Smith was undeterred: 'No, sir, but what about the jigger tops'l halyard - and the topping-lift?' The halyards raised and held the sail, while the topping-lift did the same for the spar on which it was spread.

'Another nice idea, boy, but you seem to have forgotten some important trifles: those ropes are secured on belaying-pins, which are now umpteen fathoms under water. You could cut the top ends free certainly, but what use is that? And even worse, if you cut the topping-lift, you might have half a ton of steel spar landing on your stupid heads!'

'Yes, I see. All right, just the halyard, then, and maybe the sheet and the tack. Those would be no problem for me, sir. I come from Cornwall, and ever since I was a nipper I've spent every summer swimming and diving. We can cut the top end of the halyard, the sheet and the tack and secure them in the boat. Then I dive, pulling myself down with one of them, and cast them all off from the pins at the bottom. Then you'd have the whole length of all three - that's a lot of rope! I used to do any amount of diving onto wrecks at home in Penzance; I can hold my breath for ages. I reckon I could manage that.'

Grant was still visibly doubtful: 'H'm..... Let's hear what the bosun thinks of your hare-brained notions.'

The bosun tilted back his cap and scratched his head thoughtfully. Grant, never the most patient of men, said: 'Well? Say something, man.' He had been expecting the bosun to scout the ideas as rapidly as he had.

But the bosun had been thinking, with the deliberate slowness of maturity: 'Well, mister, there's no doubt some canvas and those whole lengths of rope would be a godsend. Jac-y-bont could soon knock you up a bit of shelter with them - a roof, or whatever. And that young dab' - he nodded towards Smith - 'he can swim like a fish all right. Back in Chile there, when we was at anchor, he used to strip down, mother-naked, dive down off the deck, disappear, and when we thought he'd drownded hisself, up he'd come, blowing like a whale, with some shell or other off the sea-bed.'

'That's all very well, bosun; I've seen him too, but the water was a hell of a lot warmer and calmer there. And anyway, I'm responsible for these young ruffians. I've got to try to bring them back alive to their doting parents. His idea's too dangerous. He could get caught up in that God-awful tangle of ropes and spars - you saw yourself what it was like before we left. And what about the boat? With that swell running, it could get thrown against the mast and stove in. Then they'd all be in the drink, and no beggar around to fish them out. And anyway, we want ropes for lashing rafters to a ridge-pole; those halyards would be too thick for that.'

Patiently, like a sympathetic teacher with a rather slow pupil, the bosun said: 'We'd unlay the rope, mister - pull the three strands apart. Then we'd have three times the length, and each one of those strands'd be plenty strong enough to secure the top ends of the rafters. Damn, if we wanted to, we could split the ropes, right down to the rope-yarns themselves and use them as twine - that's good Manila hemp, that is. But I'm with you about the danger - he'd have to be damn careful he didn't get caffled up with all the wreckage down there.'

He paused; Smith, the subject of their debate, was, like a spectator at a tennis-match, comically switching his gaze from one senior officer to the other. Now he waited anxiously for Grant's final verdict. The bosun scratched his head again: 'It's chancy, no mistake. They'd have to put a rope round him when he goes down, in case he does get stuck. But if he's game, I can't see it's any more dangerous than furling a foresail in a Cape Horn gale, eighty foot up, with nothing but a wire to stand on. You're never very safe if you're a windjammer sailor, are you?'

Raven and Smith exchanged excited grins, but Grant was not finished yet. 'No, that's true enough, but you're not thinking straight, any of you; you say "put a rope on him", but don't you see, until he's gone down they haven't got any rope! Their scheme still doesn't make sense!'

'Hold on a bit, sir,' said Raven, 'I've been thinking. I know where there's rope we can use - the lugsail halyards from the lifeboats! If we unrove those and tied them together, they'd be plenty long enough. We could put them back afterwards. And I've been thinking about the swell too; we'll make the boat's painter fast to the mast, man the oars, and back water to keep ourselves clear of it while Smithy's making his dive.'

There was a long silence, then Grant, who felt himself helpless, cornered, said: 'All right, I'll think about it. But we'll have to have a calm spell of weather; I don't think you'll be able to do it and get back in one day. So,' he added, in a last attempt to display his authority, 'you'll go when I say, and not before. And you'd better take the whaleboat - she's a lot lighter and faster than the quarter-boats. And you'd have to be sure to take a boat compass and an anchor - you might be able to find somewhere sheltered to anchor for the night on the way back - the North Harbour, perhaps. And that reminds me, don't forget to take your copy of Eleanor's sketch-map.'

There was a whoop of delight from the brass-bounders, and they and Raven began eager discussions about details of the mission. Perkins, the senior apprentice, said in his customary sardonic way: 'If that fat idiot Smith gets himself tangled up down there, I can dive a bit too, so I might go down and fish him up - if I feel like it.'

Eleanor, ignored and silent on the fringe of the crowd, was the only one to look troubled. She knew well enough who would be the leader of this - to her - madcap enterprise, and he was now too excited about the expedition to even look at her. But she knew too that she must show no emotions, say nothing, and tell no-one of her tormenting fears. Blank-faced, under the wind-driven rain and grey clouds of a sub-Antarctic island, she offered up the bitterest, most earnest prayer of her life: Please, please, God, let him come back safe to me. Haven't I suffered enough for you already? Why do you give me more tortures? I'm not as steadfast as Job. In our prayer-books and services we worship you as a merciful God, yet you have already taken my mother and father. If I should lose John too, what is left for me to live for? Nothing...nothing... no-one.

CHAPTER FIVE

A fortnight later, on a typical Auckland Island morning of cloud and chilly wind, a silent figure, sitting hunched, clad in black oilskins on a rock on the black beach, heard the clunking sound of oars in rowlocks, stirred, and stood up, motionless as a statue, as the splash of oars in the still water once more echoed from the rocky shores of Port Ross, but this time to the accompaniment of cheerful young voices. The smart white whaler, with its crew of brassbounders, was returning in some triumph with its cargo of canvas and rope from the wreck. So successful had the lads been that the stiff folds of the thick sail-cloth stuffed into the bottom of the boat made rowing difficult, and the boat's bow was weighed down by huge coils of the best hemp rope.

The crew's high spirits arose partly from sheer relief, for the expedition had not been easy or safe. They had set off at dawn the day before on a day of weak sunshine and a rare gentle north-easterly breeze, and had straightway met head-on such a fierce tide in Rose Island Sound that they had had to anchor for hours until it slackened, and they could at last weigh anchor and make sail. Keeping well out from the shore, so as to keep the wind, they had sailed quietly in the friendly breeze past the grim, high, black wall of the west coast cliffs, until they sighted, three hours later, the forlorn yellow jigger mizen-mast right under the cliff, in the jaws of the great cave that had swallowed their ship. Reaching it at last, approaching cautiously under oars, they found the swell long and high, but fortunately not steep; Raven had realized all along that getting onto the mast, climbing up it, and cutting the sail loose was going to be difficult, and damn risky, and that therefore he must be the one to do it. He couldn't dive, but he could climb better than the others.

He called tensely to Perkins, the senior of the apprentices: 'Ship your oar, Perky, and come and take the helm. I'm going up in the bow and I'll jump from there. Right now: ease her up close, so that I can make the painter fast to the shrouds. Then hold her there, and say a little prayer for me, you horrible godless shower.' Now they were right up to the mast, the sail, although the smallest in 'Figaro's' forty thousand square feet of canvas, looked dauntingly big, and it was made of Number One quality thick stiff cloth, its edges strongly roped. It'd be quite a cargo for the whaler.

Silent, and with the sour taste of fear in his mouth, Raven stood poised in the heaving bow, waiting for the right upward swing, then leapt forward and up to clutch the topmast shrouds - the ladder of wire rope and hemp ratlines. He had rehearsed in his mind exactly how he would go about this hair-raising job, but now he was close up to it, the problems seemed worse than ever. The triangular sail was held at its three corners by ropes from the deck, led through blocks, and the sail was held close to the mast by rings called hanks; each hank was sewn tightly to the edge of the sail. All those fastenings would have to be cut, and the sheath-knife in his belt had been honed up ready for that. The fastening at the top, the halyard by which the sail was hoisted - that would have to be the last, so the worst part of the job would have to come first. He would have to straddle the spanker gaff and heave himself up its steep diagonal slope to the end to get at the sheet, the rope that held the sail's outer corner. No land-lubber could have done it, but young windjammer sailors were used to horrific jobs aloft, so up he went, inching his way carefully along the spar, until he was able to reach out and saw through the sheet. When he saw that it was about to part, he called over his shoulder: 'Catch hold of the end of this sheet-rope! We'll try and save that too - and the tack, when I get to that.' As soon as the sheet-rope was gone, the sail started to flap ponderously to and fro in the breeze, shaking the slender mast. Coming back down the slope of the shuddering gaff was horribly awkward, with the flapping sail clouting his hunched shoulders, threatening to knock him off his perch. 'Come on, old son,' he whispered to himself, 'you've got to do it. Even if it has you off, you'll only fall a few feet into the drink. This won't be the worst bit - you wait till you have to shin up and down the bloody mast.'

His years aloft had given him a monkey-like agility and strength; as soon as he felt the mast against his back, he had to twist round and get his feet back on the ratlines so as to climb further up the mast. From there, at full stretch, he was able to reach and cut through the sail's tack-rope, which held its bottom corner. Now he would have to get to the truck, the block of wood at the very top of the mast, to be able to cut the halyard, and the shrouds didn't go that far; the last fifteen feet would have to be climbed by shinning up, grasping the mast itself, and stopping every few feet to hang on one-handed while he cut the sail loose from its hanks. His mouth felt dry and sour with suppressed fear; he'd gone up this mast before, at sea, but this was different - so much depended on it now and the big triangular sail was now held only at the top, so that every now and then the loose heavy canvas swung ponderously against his body, as if trying to shove him brutally into the icy sea. But they really needed this canvas and rope, and he needed to ignore his fear and think out carefully the proper sequence he'd have to follow if they were to get both sail and halyard, as well as the sheet and tack ropes.

He yelled: 'Below there! Haul the boat right up to the mast; let go the painter from the shroud and hitch it to the halyard so it doesn't sink when I cut it at the block. Give it plenty of slack; back off a bit and then watch out when the sail comes down - it'll be damned heavy. Right, here goes.' Looking like the very cliché of a pirate, with his knife between his teeth, he began the slow, painful task, at first reaching from his perch in the shrouds to cut the lashings that held the sail to its hanks, then, clinging with legs and arms to the shiny, slippery timber, inching his way up and halting at every hank to hack the lashing free, clinging on to the mast with his left arm only. He had not realized till now just how many hanks there were!

The top at last! He rested for a moment to ease the muscular agony of his left arm by hanging on to the peak of the sail with his right hand. Then he called again: 'Stand by, there and look out! It'll come down pretty hard, and there's a lot of it. But grab it as soon as you can - don't let it sink, for Christ's sake. Ready? Right!' He sawed savagely at the rope 'Here she comes, boys! Watch your heads!'

Five minutes later the wet, heavy sail had been hauled out of the water and stuffed into the bottom of the boat, and Raven too was back in the boat, rubbing at his tortured left arm while grinning at the others; somehow this joint enterprise had temporarily wiped out the difference of rank between them. Perkins, his old rival, and not always the best of his friends, thumped him genially on the back and said: 'Well done, old boy! That looked bloody hard.'

'It was, Perky, bloody hard, especially on this arm. Right now, Smithy, it's your turn now, so get your clobber off and show us all something to amuse us.'

'All right,' said Smith, peeling off his clothes, 'give us a chance. I'm going to get frozen down there - frozen stiff.'

Raven sensed his fear; Smithy was going to take far more chances with his life than he had; quite apart from the freezing water, there must be a hideous tangle of wood and steel, rope and wire, down there. He would have to go into that nightmare web, following the cut halyard , sheet and tack, right down to where they were made fast. Raven was honest enough to admit to himself: I wouldn't do that job for all the tea in China. But the best thing to cheer poor old Smithy up was a bit of banter: 'Never mind, Smithy, old son. Now we see you in the altogether, we can see you've got plenty of blubber to keep you warm. And as for "stiff" - you're certainly not that at the moment, are you?'

The coarse, comradely raillery cheered Smith a little: 'All right, you smart-arsed cissies: anyone else feel like stripping off and coming down to help? No? Then shut your faces and get me that life-line if you want to see me again.'

Smith stood, shivering violently, white, naked, and looking very vulnerable, but with his face set in lines of grim determination. Then he said 'Here goes, chums,' took a very deep breath, sat himself on the boat's gunwale, and tumbled backwards skilfully, with little splash, into the icy water, grasping the halyard, by which he would haul himself down to its lower end on the fife-rail at the foot of the mast, among God only knew what lethal clutter and tangle there might be down there.

He was gone for a very long time - to the boys in the boat an impossible age. Young Waters sat, dry-mouthed, holding Smith's life-line, ready for the signal of two tugs to mean: Haul me up quick! But at last the rope went slack, and with a sudden burst of foam, Smith surfaced alongside, panting and heaving for breath. The whaler lurched as Raven and Robbins bent over the side to grasp Smith's arms and haul him from the water, trying hard not to scrape his bare chest and trunk on the boat's gunwale. Smith came over the side and flopped like a seal onto the bed of canvas in the boat's bilge, retching up sea-water, his chest heaving desperately. He was shuddering uncontrollably; a few more minutes in that water and he would have been dead as mutton. Leaving Waters and Robbins to dry him with one blanket, and then wrap him up in another, Raven and Perkins bent to the task of pulling up halyard, sheet and tack, fathom after fathom of good hemp rope, and coiling it neatly in the bow of the boat.

That done, Raven turned to where the diver lay, still shivering and speechless. 'Right, boys, get his togs on him if he's dry, poor bugger. Well done Smithy, well done! No-one else could have done that, old son.' Then he returned to his role as captain of this little crew and looked out to the west. 'Can't stay here any longer, boys. The sun's starting to go down, and I don't like the look of that bow of cloud over there. We're in for dirty weather, by the look of it. It's starting to breeze up a bit already, so we'll put a reef in the lugsail, I think, and then get the hell out of it. We won't get back to Port Ross tonight, so we'd better find some shelter and doss down under the sail for the night.'

Ten minutes later the whaler was on her northerly course, pitching and crunching in the choppy waves, rising and falling as the huge swells passed under her, thrashing along with a stiff beam wind from Cape Horn, Raven at the tiller, the others, including the now revived Smith, perched along the port gunwale, their feet hooked under the thwarts so that they could, like racing yachtsmen, lean their bodies back almost horizontally to balance the pull of the sail. With the exuberance of youth, they laughed, joked, and yelled as the sprays rattled on their coats; they'd undertaken a tricky job, two of them had taken a hell of a risk, and by God they'd succeeded!

They were sobered up considerably by a cold night at anchor in North Harbour, huddled together under the damp stiff sail and their blankets through a long night of wind and drizzle. First light saw them labouring at the oars to get clear of the inlet, but once outside, with a strong favourable tide in the sound, the boat tore along, and it was not long before they were dousing the sail and taking to the oars for the last short stretch back to the camp, past the portly, idly-dozing seals on the rocks. They gave a combined hoot of triumph and relief as they felt the boat's bow grate on the shingle, but Raven's exultation died abruptly as he saw the black-clad figure of Eleanor approaching, her face showing the strain of her anxiety.

He jumped nimbly out of the boat and went up the beach to meet her: 'Nelli, I didn't expect to see you down here. Nice of you to come to meet us, but I thought Grant said...'

She was tense and unsmiling: 'It wasn't my idea - Grant sent me. I've been here for hours. Of course I'm glad to see you back safely - I mean all of you - but there's possible trouble up at the hut, and he wants you up there straightaway. He says you're to leave the boys to beach the boat and bring up the gear. Come quickly now.'

'Right-o.' He turned to the boat: 'Perky, Mr Grant wants to see me. Get the boat beached, will you, and get the boys to bring up the rope and canvas.'

The two erstwhile lovers walked quickly up the beach and into the trees, Eleanor still cool, depressed, curt in her manner, answering questions only in monosyllables. Raven halted and plucked at her sleeve to stop her dogged plod: 'Listen, Nelli, I know what Grant said about us not showing our feelings in public, but we're alone now anyway for a moment. Couldn't we be like we were, talk like we did - just for a minute or two?'

'No, I don't want to - I don't want to even.... even sample normal life - life as it should be. It would make me hate this island more than I do already - so many cold, grey, misty days, so much wet black rock - hardly any sun, and that everlasting wind. We're cut off from everything that could make us feel normal, human.'

'You mean our feelings - the way we feel for each other, love each other?'

'I don't want to let myself even *think* about that sort of thing - not until we're out of this prison - worse than prison, really. I'm not allowed your company, and there's no other woman here. And I can see the way some of the men are starting to look at me - as if they're trying to picture what I'm like under all these horrible oilskins and jerseys and trousers - as if they were choosing a tart in a brothel. I'm beginning to feel like Eve must have felt.'

'Eve? Why her, for Heaven's sake?'

'Because she's always treated as the source of all of Man's troubles on earth. She's not noted for anything except being beautiful and causing disaster to mankind. Of course,' she added with vehement bitterness, 'this place is hardly Eden, and we mustn't forget that the Bible was written by men.'

Raven caught her arm: 'Nelli, don't go on like this, as if you were blaming yourself. None of this is your fault.'

He attempted to put his arm round her, but she abruptly pulled herself free. 'Please let me go, Mr Raven. I don't want to...to become normal. I don't want to have any feelings at all in this jail of a place. I told you - I'm just a messenger, and Simon needs you in a hurry, so come on and don't try to fool about with me!'

Raven felt a strong surge of anger: 'This isn't bloody fair! You're being cold and horrible to me, as if it was all my fault!'

'No, I'm not exactly angry with you, I'm just dead inside - dead and cold, and you seem too insensitive to understand that - too preoccupied with boats and sails and bits of rope. You don't even seem to remember that it was my father's mistakes that put us here in the first place. Do you think I feel happy or proud about that? I don't - I feel a deep shame, though God knows it was none of my doing. Now come on, Mr Raven, for Heaven's sake, we're wasting time.'

She strode away, leaving the weary Raven to follow. 'All right then,' he said sulkily. 'What's Grant's trouble anyway? You could surely tell me what all this panic is about.'

'It'd take too long. I'll leave him to explain. Nothing has happened yet, but Grant's been told about something which might lead to a lot of trouble. He needs to see you at once. Now just stop talking and hurry.'

*

On the morning of the previous day Grant had watched the boat row away down the harbour towards the sea with mixed feelings: satisfaction that something positive was being done to improve their lives, but with that a strong anxiety about all the hundred-and-one things that could go wrong with this youthful enterprise. Raven was a first-rate seaman and leader, but very young and green for such a risky business as this; Auckland Island was a grim and cruel place, and he himself was responsible for everyone's safety, and for the decision to commit five young lives to a chancy and difficult expedition. And he would one day have to stand to be judged about all his decisions. But there it was - he'd said they could go, and they'd gone, and now he must get on with his tasks and hope for the best.

But when he got back to the camp he felt his spirits rise; the new galley was taking shape. The solid earth walls were now finished, after many hours of back-breaking toil, and the men had started to bring in the lengths of split wood which would be the rafters. And it was good to see the hands sitting in the weak sunshine after breakfast, chatting quietly for a few moments before the day's work began, as they used to aboard the 'Figaro'. The useful, practical work had been good for them, and now it was time to find some of them other jobs that would improve their lives and stop them brooding on their misfortunes.

He took the bosun aside: 'Things are looking good, bosun - ship-shape and Bristol fashion, eh? You don't need all the hands now, do you?'

'No, not all; I needs four or five to start facing the banks with sods of turf, in case we gets hard rain. That'd wash half the soil off.'

'Yes, I see. That makes good sense. Well, what about launching another boat and sending some of the rest of them fishing? The doctor's done wonders with the food so far, but some fresh fish would be good for us, I'm sure, and it's good anyway to keep the crowd busy.'

The bosun was a marvellous craftsman, but was also of a pessimistic turn of mind, and could always see problems that hadn't occurred to others: 'Aye, not such a bad idea, mister. But what about bait? Got none of that.'

'Bits of bully-beef?'

'Not a bit of good, mister. It'd come to pieces as soon as you cast the line. But I suppose (he produced his own solution grudgingly) you could soon prise some shellfish off the rocks with a sheath-knife and use them. Then, once you'd caught your first fish you could cut that up for bait. But of course we don't know if there are any fish in this harbour worth catching.'

'Oh come on now, bosun, let's look on the bright side! When we came in we saw plenty of fat happy seals lying on the rocks; well, they wouldn't be there if there weren't any fish about, would they? Now pick me a few men who'd make the best fishing party.'

'All right, mister: well, there's Johanssen the

Swede - he used to catch a few when we was anchored sometimes; and he's got more sense than half-a-dozen of the others put together; there's Lewis from Milford - he's been a trawlerman; then there's Bryn Parry from Solva - you know, the one they call Holy Parry - he was talking to me the other day about making some lobster-pots if he could get some twine; you'd better put Jimmy Protheroe in too - that'll keep him away from Billy John Ffynnon-groes for a bit - I don't like the way those two *crwts* are shaping up; I can tell you. And then you've got to have Jac-y-bont.' His leathery face cracked in a rare smile: 'He's been the best poacher in Pembrokeshire for most of his life. *Duw,* I'd like a shilling for every salmon and sewin he's had from the Nevern River on the Llwyngwair Estate - I'd be rich, mun! The poor bloody keepers could never catch him at it.'

The whole crowd, trooping down to the beach to launch one of the big quarter-boats, also seemed happy with the change from chopping down wood, sawing it up, and lugging it about, slithering in the wet grass and ferns underfoot. The heavy job of half-lifting, half-dragging the big boat down to the water was lightened when Jimmy Protheroe, the inveterate sea-lawyer, showed another of his talents - that of a high Welsh tenor, and led the lads in a suitable shanty, the stresses on the words helping them to get their heaves exactly together, to work as one man:

I'll sing you a song of the fish of the sea,
Way down Rio,
I'll sing you a song of the fish of the sea
For we're bound for the Rio Grande.
Then a-way love a-way,

A-way down Rio.
So fare you well, my pretty young gal,
For we're bound for the Rio Grande.

The men were out of breath from heaving and from bellowing out the choruses, but they cheered as the boat finally floated free on the quiet water. Prematurely, their mouths watered at the prospect of some real fresh food at last, at the imagined delicious scent of fresh fish sizzling in Welly's big skillet.

The camp seemed strangely quiet, as both watches had gone down to launch the boat; the only sounds were the wind, bird-calls and the tinny clatter of plates as Eleanor and Davey washed up after breakfast. Grant, bosun and the doctor sat on the cut timber in an informal cabinet meeting, though the bosun had his mind elsewhere: 'Jesus, Welly, what I wouldn't give for my old pipe, and an ounce of good shag…I've had a puff of baccy all my life after breakfast - can't do without it.'

'Well, now you jus' have to, Reub, and maybe that'll be good for you; cos you used to cough your head off, man, when you lit up.'

'Got enough wood for the rafters now, bosun?' said Grant beginning the agenda.

'Aye, nearly. But we'll need a good ridge-pole as well as the rafters to spread the sail on - if we get a sail, of course. And we've got to fill in one pine-end.' Seeing Grant looking puzzled, he added didactically: 'The triangle bit at the end away from the hut, mun. And, come to think of it, I'll need to make a ladder out of some small stuff, if we're going to start roofing - so long as those damn boys manage to bring back some rope to make twine out of. Useless sons of Satan they are - the lot of them!'

'Ah, come on now, bosun, fair play, as you Welsh keep saying: those sons of Satan - especially Smith - are taking quite a chance climbing up the jigger mast and diving down on the cleats. They've got to get back too, and we all know you can't rely on the weather in this bloody place. Right: now, doctor, wouldn't a floor be handy? You're standing about in mud at the moment.'

'Well, sure, mister, but that'd be a whole lot more wood needed.'

'True, but luckily there's plenty of that, God knows, and the more work there is for the crowd the better.'

'Aye,' said bosun sententiously, 'Satan finds work for idle hands, and he's got one or two followers here, I believe.'

Late in the afternoon, the fishing party returned in triumphant mood with their catch - a sackful of fresh, gleaming hake, cod and mackerel - the latter familiar in shape, but oddly green-spotted. 'There you are, mate,' said Jac-y-bont to Jones. 'No need for us to go hungry; that harbour's bloody swarming with fish, mun. I reckon that's because a few years back, the sealers came down here and wiped out most of the seals, so that's been good for the fish.'

'Aye,' said Parry, 'they're hungry devils, seals. We got a lot of them round our bit of coast at home, Solva way. My old dad was a fisherman, and he used to curse them up in a heap, sometimes. But here - well, the fish - especially the mackerel - lining up, they were, to get hooked. We tore up an old red handkerchief of mine and hitched little bits of that to the lines, and that was enough.'

The men were filled with a boyish enthusiasm that Grant was glad to see. Lewis broke in eagerly: 'Then, once we'd got a few of them we'd got bait for the big boys, so we went trolling for them - you know, some of us rowing along gentle-like while one held the line. Look, lovely big fish; like cod they are, only a funny blue colour. And look at them hake, Welly; they'd be real nice fried - only you ain't got no fat, have you?'

'Don't you worry none about that, man; you leave that to me. If I put some slices of bully in the skillet over the fire, I'll soon get some fat outa that. But I ain't cooking them fish tonight - they're too fresh. They'd all go to bits in the skillet. And talking of fat, mister, why don't you send some of the lads out after them seals? Now the sealers don't come here no more they've come back. We saw plenty of them on the rocks when we first came in. We ain't got no rifles like the sealers have, but them seals can't move very fast, not on the land anyway, so you can get close enough to club them if you're quick and quiet - I've seen it done on the California coast. Seal steaks would be mighty good eating, I reckon - and fresh meat too. We don't know how long we gonna be on this doggone island, and this bully won't last for ever, not with so many of us eating it.'

'Good God, doctor,' said Grant, 'this is beginning to sound like a West-end restaurant!'

'Well, mister, I don't want to boast, but I ain't no slouch in a galley. I been all over and I've cooked pretty near anything you could name, one time or another - buffalo, bear, moose, turkey, salmon - anything what can walk or swim or fly. An' if'n I had me some seal blubber, I could get enough fat to fry up some dough and make some johnny-cake. Hey boys, that'd line your ribs pretty good, eh?'

'Aye,' said Jac, 'I was aboard a Yankee clipper once - Christ, a hard ship she was - but they used to eat that. Heavy old stuff, like you say, like a damn great fried pancake, but good if you're hungry. The cook there, he used to say: "Pork, beans and Johnny-cake, Make the Frenchman's stomach ache." But we used to like it - and you got some beans in that store, haven't you?'

Grant listened to the cheerful chatter with rising optimism, and reflected with amusement on the child-like nature of foc'sle hands - easily delighted by simple pleasures, and as easily enraged by disappointments. One very big disappointment, he knew, was awaiting them when they got back to Wales, but there was no need for them to know about that, and today the outlook was good - as long as the boys were successful and got back safely. All the hands were cheerful and busy about useful jobs, and the food situation had been drastically improved, a sheltered galley was taking shape, and it had even stopped raining.

*

Later, in what would have been the dog-watches on board, Jones had finished his work for the day, and he and the bosun and Curly Kellock sat together on some cut timber like a coterie of elder statesmen. A weak evening sun still shone through the haze of thin cloud, and the wind sobbed quietly in the scrub forest all round. Most of the hands were sitting or lying stretched out on their bunks after a busy day and a hearty supper. From the open door of the hut came the sounds of their chat, their bursts of laughter and their raised voices in genial argument. Only Eleanor, Isaac Hughes and Davey Jones peggy were still at work nearby, cleaning the greasy tin plates in a bucket of water which Jones had warmed for them, and taking them back to the store. The galley fire smouldered between its laboriously-made walls, made up for the night with hefty chunks of wood, and sending up the homely smell of wood-smoke - a smell that powerfully and painfully reminded the band of stranded Welshmen of their own fires in the black-leaded ranges in their stone-built cottages, snug in green valleys or on mountain-sides, on the other side of the world, or, as it seemed to some of the younger, less travelled men, existing in another world altogether.

Curly gave vent to a hearty belch, and said cheerfully: 'Pardon all, I'm sure. You know what, doctor - that wasn't half a decent cracker-hash tonight. Funny, ain't it? Now we're stuck on this island like poor ole Robinson Crusoe, we're eating a sight better than what we did on board the old hooker. Never got no bully then - only salt junk out of a barrel and Gawd knows how old - the cheapest grub the bloody owners could find. Them officers aft got all the bully; now we all get the same.' The thought pleased the Marxist in him.

The cook had made the celebrated windjammer dish, cracker-hash, by pounding the hard ship's biscuit into small pieces, adding some water to soften them, then mixing it with generous chunks of bully-beef, and heating the whole concoction so that the fat of the beef bound it into a warm, hearty, comforting coarse paste, slabs of which, served with beans, had filled hungry bellies, and brought on a pleasant torpor.

The cook, ever the professional and perfectionist, ignored the praise and said: 'That hash woulda been a whole lot better with some onions and some salt and pepper. I just bet you my bottom dollar there's vegetables growing wild on this island somewhere, left behind by the guys that lived here in years gone by, but none of you ain't found me none yet, and I ain't got time to go looking for them. Still,' he said with a complacent smile, 'it's going to be better cooking here once we get this galley finished; we ain't slamming and pitching and rolling our way round the world with the ship like a half-tide rock and the decks knee-deep in water, and my pans sliding all over the stove. And another thing: we ain't got no chance to spend a cent, and back in Cardiff our pay is mounting up while we sit about here. By the time we get back there, boy, there'll be a tidy sum for all of us.'

The bosun opened his mouth to reply, then abruptly closed it again as Curly gave him a meaning look. There was an awkward silence, and Jones, always quick and alive to the thoughts of other people, had caught that meaning look, and knew at once that something was wrong - that there was something hanging in the air between him and the other two men, something that they knew and he didn't; above all, a piece of knowledge that they didn't want to share with him. Being an alert and masterful man, he was determined to get at that knowledge.

'What? Why you look like that, the two of you? You got some damn secret? You know something I don't know? You better tell me now what it is, cos I don't like being in the dark. I'm your buddy, ain't I? This ain't fair -

not if this secret is about my pay.'

Though he was some yards off, kneeling by the washing-up bucket, Isaac Hughes, always the ship's champion eavesdropper and source of gossip, sensed that the easy atmosphere between the three friends had suddenly changed. His two helpers were away, stacking plates in the hut, and Isaac silenced the clatter of the tin dishes in his bucket and strained his ears. This could be interesting!

The cook persisted angrily: 'Come on now, you goddam shysters! Spit it out! I ain't having this!'

At length, quietly and reluctantly, Curly spoke: 'All right then, on'y for Christ's sake keep it to yourself: it's what you just said about your pay piling up.'

The cook was too indignant to speak quietly: 'Pay? What about pay?'

Bosun took in the break in the clattering of dishes; Isaac had his back to him, but that back had suddenly gone rigid, and bosun could sense the close attention the steward was giving to their talk, and was annoyed by the cook's outburst: He muttered: 'Stop hollering like that, you daft bugger! Shut up and listen. Curly, you can explain better than I can.'

Curly spoke quietly: 'All right, only mind, doctor, don't you let this go no further. This is it: you ain't got no pay mounting up - none of us ain't, not even the officers - because our job with the company finished the day the ship was lost.'

'Wha...!'

'Shut up and *listen,* I say! When we do get back to Cardiff, Grant will have to give the company - old Powell's lot - all the ship's papers, including the log - they brought that off the ship, remember. So then the company will know to the minute when the old hooker went down. So they'll pay us up to that day and no further. Not a bloody penny more!'

With a supreme effort the cook mastered his desire to shout his rage to the whole island: 'But *why,* man? There ain't no justice in that!'

'Never you mind about "justice", mate; we're talking about the capitalist system, what rules all our lives, not justice.' The crisis had brought to the surface all Curly's evangelical socialist fervour, so that he now forgot to lower his voice: 'You're forgetting, mate, that you're a wage-slave. Them what pays us makes the rules, never mind how much we suffer. All the while we was carrying coal to Valparaiso we was earning them money - right? But now we ain't carrying nothink nowhere, so they thinks: "Why should we pay the buggers for that time? They wasn't making us any money, they was just sculling about on an island."'

'But that's just wicked, man! It ain't our fault we're here. The man that put us here is dead and gone. We ain't taking no holiday, we working our arses off, just to survive. We'd rather be afloat and doing our jobs like normal.'

'Course we would, mate, but don't sound off at me about it. It ain't my idea - it's just what them owners do. Ship-owners and their shareholders have got big old houses to keep up, and servants to pay, so that they themselves can live idle and go to balls and races, and go chasing poor bleeding foxes. They can't afford to waste their money on a bunch of shipwrecked matelots, can they?'

'Christ, them damn miserable, penny-pinching

Limey bastards!'

'Never mind about "Limeys", mate. It ain't just the British - the Yankees and the Froggies and the Dutchies - they're all the same. And you just think about it: you're grumbling, but you're paid four times what the ABs get, and you ain't got no family, have you? What about a young AB with a missis and kids to support - cos all the allowances to his family will stop too? How the hell are them pore women going to manage, eh? Beg? Borrow money off of swindling money-lenders? Sell theirselves on the street? There's others a lot worse off than you, Welly.'

The cook sobered down, and there was a pause, during which Eleanor and Davey came back for more plates to stow. He said quietly: 'You boys sure about this?'

The bosun nodded: 'Quite sure, Welly. It happened to me myself once, years ago, when I was an AB in a fruit schooner. And Curly's met other chaps what have lost pay like that. Doesn't happen very often, of course, cos usually either the crew goes down with the ship or they're picked up straightaway.'

The cook was silent, taking in the news and its implications, and a fresh thought struck him: 'D'you think all the crowd knows about this?'

'No I don't,' said bosun, and for God's sake don't tell them.'

'Why not, man? That ain't fair neither!'

Curly spoke urgently: 'What good would it do to tell them? None of us can't change it. It'd just cause trouble, coming on top of what the poor buggers have suffered already. We don't want no more trouble, do we?'

The thin, whining voice of the steward cut in sharply: 'No, we don't, not if you're talking about what I think you are. Come on now, Kellock: I want the truth! It's the pay, isn't it - it's about us not getting any more once the ship's gone, isn't it? I've heard of that before, but I didn't believe it. But then there's no end to the wickedness of rich men, and today, I see, I'm not thought to be of sufficient importance to be in the confidence of you three gentlemen, for some reason.'

Hughes' sneering irritated Curly into an outburst: 'Oh, for Gawd's sake don't start your moaning, Isaac. Yes, it is true - your pay stopped when the "Figaro" went down. We just thought the fewer people know about it, the better - that's all - twasn't nothing personal. Tell you what, though, Reuben: I'm surprised our expert sea-lawyer Jimmy Protheroe don't know about this wonderful custom among ship-owners.'

Eleanor had drifted towards the group when she sensed the seriousness of their talk; her mind was quick to understand what had been revealed, and she could not contain her generous indignation: 'No pay while they're marooned - through no fault of their own? I think that's utterly disgraceful - shocking! That man Powell with his big house and that stuck-up wife of his from the so-called gentry...'

'Nah, don't pick on old Powell, miss,' said Curly, in his usual judicious way. 'He ain't no worse than the rest of them. They all do it because it saves them money, and it's what they've always done. I s'pose there ain't no law against it. There ought to be, but there ain't. But you won't say nothing, will you? Not even to...' His natural delicacy made him hesitate.

'To Mr Raven?' she said, suddenly cool and strong in her tone. 'No, of course not. As you say, what would be the use? The poor fellows will find out soon enough, if we ever get back to Cardiff.'

'Right, miss,' said Curly. Eleanor noted that, without anything being said, Kellock had become, as it were, the chairman of their small meeting. He turned to the steward: 'Nor you, Isaac? You won't say nothink?'

'They'll hear nothing from me, gentlemen.' His native paranoia added: 'In any case, I'm just a skivvy, I'm not of any importance. Who'd pay any attention to anything I said?'

'Good, then we'll leave it at that,' said Curly, 'and hope for the best. But I think I'd better mention it to Mr Grant, so he's prepared for it, if it should get out.'

Isaac, injured that his complaint about his status had been ignored, called sharply to Davey, who was sitting on a nearby rock, dozing after a hard day: 'Hey, get up, you idle *crwt*, and ditch this bucket of slops over there. Then rinse the bucket in the stream, and quick about it, mind!' His mean heart was cheered a little by still having at least one person he could bully, and at the back of his mind was growing another, darker, thought: that bloody doctor is beginning to act as if he was some sort of officer, and who does Kellock think he is? A damned common English AB from the back streets of London telling *me* what to do! Good God, the man's too ignorant to speak his own language properly! Dragged up in some slum by the London docks, I bet! And as for Grant, strutting about like a captain, when he was only a second mate a few months ago! And that puppy Raven - no more than an overgrown schoolboy really - throwing his weight about too! Now, wouldn't it be interesting to see what would happen if Billy John and Jimmy Protheroe were somehow - by accident, of course - to get to know about all this? That would give that bloody *Sais* Grant something to think about! Might take him down a peg or two. I can't, Isaac thought, tell them straight out, of course, or that damn Grant will be down on me like a ton of bricks, but there'd be ways and means, ways and means... It could all come out, just by pure accident, like, couldn't it?

CHAPTER SIX

'So there you are, mister,' said Curly. 'It's a pity it turned out like that, but that's the situation: I know, the doctor knows, bosun here knows, Miss Eleanor knows and - worse luck - Isaac Hughes knows.'

Grant, Raven, bosun and Kellock were seated next morning, hunched gloomily on rocks in the steady rain and gusty wind in a small clearing, further up the stream which the castaways had all followed on that first triumphant day, that now seemed a year ago. Most of the hands were hard at work some way off in the scrub forest, cutting short lengths of thinnish wood for the floor; a few were gathering slender, straight saplings to use for the sides and rungs of ladders; those still back at the hut were unlaying some of the newly-acquired rope to make twine. The apprentices, under the command and guidance of Jac-y-bont, were out fishing in the quarter-boat. How long, Grant thought uneasily, will a busy and orderly routine like this be possible, after this disastrous development?

He'd already had to resort to caution and subterfuge: the four men had all slipped quietly away at different times and by different routes, so that the hands wouldn't know they were meeting secretly, and wonder why.

Grant looked both worried and angry, his face set in grim lines of determination: 'Very well. I've got you up here because this could be a serious setback to progress, and because two of you are responsible for the damage done. Also because I realize that you, Kellock, and you, bosun, are much more in touch with the crowd than I am. Well, it's a bloody poor show, and I have to say that I'm disappointed with both of you. I'd always got you down for sensible chaps. Why the hell did you have to talk about this affair in front of Hughes, of all people? You know he's the biggest sneak and spy and blabbermouth in the whole bunch! What possessed you to do it?'

Kellock and the bosun exchanged sheepish looks of guilt, and bosun said: 'Well, mister, we got to apologize for that. We'd kind of forgotten he was there, and the doctor forced us to tell him, and once he heard he proper lost his rag, like, and got so worked up that he raised his voice, and that was that - you know how quick Isaac is. Back on the ship he always knew where we were going next pretty near as soon as the capten.'

'We tried hard to shut the doctor up,' said Curly, 'but once Isaac heard Welly shout "pay" he twigged what it was all about. He said he'd heard about pay stopping after a wreck, but didn't believe it. Well, he does now. Miss Eleanor didn't take long to cotton on, neither. But, like bosun says, we didn't ought to have talked about it with that steward there, and we're right sorry, sir - no excuses.'

'All right. Well, it can't be helped now. Now we've got to consider what we do - if anything, and in my judgement we start off with the premise that - from what we know of him and his character - we can't trust Hughes any further than we could throw him, no matter what he's promised. Agreed?'

All the others nodded. Bosun added: 'A proper twister - never liked him. Mind, his mother was the same; she had a shop in Eglwyswrw back home, and I remember her being up before the beak for crooked weights and scales. She got off, but only because all the deacons in her chapel said what a wonderful Christian she was. They didn't want the scandal, see.'

'Runs in the blood then,' said Curly laconically.

Grant was irritable, impatient: 'Yes, well all that doesn't help us much now, does it? Let's stick to business. It seems to me that we have two alternatives. Firstly, do nothing, in the hope that Hughes does keep his word and keeps his mouth shut; or, alternatively, hold a meeting of all hands and announce it straight out, and hope that after a lot of shouting they'll get used to the idea. In that way we'd get the business over and done with.'

'There'll be a bloody row when they do hear, no mistake,' said Curly. 'And, by the way, mister: did *you* know about this - about the pay stopping?'

'Yes, of course. I've been in this profession long enough to know about Owners and their little ways.'

'But you never told nobody else?'

'No, what would have been the point? None of us can do a damn thing about it, and all of us are in the same boat - we're all losing our pay. Surely not even the wildest hoodlum or the stupidest idiot could blame me - or us - for that?'

'No, they wouldn't,' said Curly didactically, 'not if they used their reason; but people don't always do that, do they? Half the wars we've had in history could a bin avoided by using reason and common sense. Like, f'r instance, what's the point of fighting other people cos they've got a different religion?'

'Yes, yes, I agree,' said Grant testily, 'but let's for God's sake keep to the point. Let's have some opinions about the here and now. My own view is that we do nothing. I'll keep the hands busy; there's plenty of work for them to do. We need a lot more wood cut for the galley fire, so that we can stack it to dry out. The doctor's complaining that some of it is too green to burn properly; and of course there's a lot more work needed on the galley. And there's the fishing to do as well. We'll sit tight and hope that Hughes keeps quiet.'

'The trouble with that idea,' said Curly, 'is that while we're pretending nothing's changed, Isaac may tell Billy John and Jimmy Protheroe - cos that's where he'll start - and leave them to spread the news and turn it into mischief - use it against you, p'raps. After all, Billy ain't no friend to you or Mr Raven here, is he? You've both belted the daylights out of him at different times. He ain't forgot that, I'll lay. So anything what gave you trouble would make him happy.'

'But that's mad! Trouble for me would soon turn into chaos, and that would mean trouble for everybody - including him and his precious crony.'

'Of course it's mad, but, like I say, people don't use their heads - not if they're out to settle a grudge.'

'Aye,' said bosun, 'and we all know what a mad ugly bugger Billy is. He's a clever lad, really; he's got a brain, but he don't use it much. He's always angry about something or other, and if you knew what his father was like, and what Billy suffered from him as a kid, you wouldn't be surprised at the way he's turned out. His big brother couldn't do no wrong, but Billy was beaten black and blue, he was, for every little thing he done wrong. Treated like dirt, he was.'

'H'm,' said Grant. 'That explains a lot, and we can all agree it was a damn shame to treat a nipper like that. However, we've got to deal with him as he is now. Raven, you're very quiet. Let's hear your views on this.'

Raven had been thinking hard, though discursively. He was never an intellectual, and had scraped through every examination he had ever taken, but his mind was lively and shrewd, pragmatic and practical; a century or so later he would be called 'streetwise'. He had his mother's genes to thank for that. While his father - the vicar of a parish in the poorer part of Oxford - was dry, scholarly and ineffectual, spending his time in his study and driving himself into helpless despair by reading the subversive theological tomes of Newman, Froude and Keble, and agonizing over the schismatic tendencies of the Oxford Movement, John's mother, daughter of a country grocer, devoted herself to adding to her husband's meagre stipend. He, of course, had been incapable of coaxing, campaigning, lobbying and ingratiating himself with bishops and gentry - the strategies necessary to the obtaining of a fat, comfortable country living, so it had been up to her to amend things. Driving herself and their one general servant to the limit, she had established a small private day school for the sons and daughters of prosperous tradesmen; she also read proofs for a local newspaper and contributed homely recipes and verses to ladies' magazines. She shrewdly made sure that, several times a year, her husband's dry sermons included passages on the importance of educating the young. Raven loved and admired her, for without her he would have stood no chance of becoming an officer apprentice in a good company.

'Well, there is another way,' he said, 'a kind of mixture of your two ideas, Simon. At the usual muster of the hands tomorrow morning you could announce that there'll be a meeting of all hands in the dog watches in three days' time to discuss our situation generally, and to talk about any problems that have arisen. I bet you can think of some, Curly?'

'Blinkin right I can, mister. For a start, I don't like the...'

'No, not now, for God's sake,' said Grant. 'Keep it for the meeting. John, I don't see any advantage in what you're suggesting.'

'You don't?' said Raven. 'Well, suppose Hughes *has* kept quiet. Not likely, I know, but just possible, because he's shit-scared of you, Simon. Then, in that case, we don't have to do anything or give anyone any bad news, because if he hasn't blabbed by then, I reckon he won't later. But if he has blabbed, someone - and we can all guess who - will be sure to bring it up at the meeting, hoping to floor you. You'll, as it were, flush him out into the open, and we can then, one would hope, have a general discussion, and you - and I'm sure Curly here - can talk some sense into the more half-witted chaps in the crowd who might follow Billy's lead. Wouldn't that be better than letting it all fester up among them in secret?'

Curly, always a political animal himself, smiled and was frank in his applause: 'When we git back home you oughter give up sailoring and stand for Parlyment, you should, mister. Your heart's in the right place, you got some good ideas for everyone's benefit, but you're a right crafty bugger underneath - cute as a cartload of monkeys, you are. That's what you need to be to get on in politics. What do you reckon about his idea, Mr Grant?'

Grant pursed his lips thoughtfully. Raven was a young chap, and culturally practically illiterate, but by God he had his head screwed on - a good chap in a crisis. 'Yes,' he said, 'well done, old son. That sounds like a good wheeze. If Hughes is going to spill the beans, he'll do it soon, I think, and if our legal friend Protheroe has that up his sleeve and he's got the chance to look big by addressing all hands, and making things difficult for me, I can't see him hanging back. I should think he'll play right into our hands, and give us a chance to talk some sense into the crowd. I think most of the hands will see reason - eventually.'

'Right then,' said bosun, indifferent to, and bored by, the Machiavellian tactics being discussed. 'I'd better get off down to the wood. Like enough, if I'm not there the hands will do nothing but sod about.'

'Me too, Simon,' said Raven. 'We want to start laying some short, straight lengths of wood for the galley floor this morning. I reckon we need to have a pretty level floor, so that the cooks won't trip up with their pots and pans.'

'Yes, yes, you go ahead,' said Grant dismissively. 'I'll leave all that to you. I've got a lot to think about.'

The two men made off, dead sticks crackling under their feet, leaves rustling as they forced their way through the thicket. Grant made as if to rise, but Curly sat still and said: 'Yes, mister - bloody true, you have got a lot to think about. But I ain't sure you realize yet how things have changed, nor yet how you've got to change.'

Grant flushed with a confused anger: '*I've* got to change? What the devil are you talking about, man?'

Curly spoke with a cool dignity: 'Yes, there you are - you don't see, do you? Right: well, in the first place, don't get riled with me. You yerself wanted to discuss things with me and bosun and Mr Raven, so we might as well talk calmly - right? Man to man, like, not officer and dogsbody.'

'Yes, all right then, but let's not be long about it,' said Grant irritably. 'We haven't got all day.'

Curly gave him a look of patriarchal severity: 'Mister, when something's this important, you got to give it the time it needs, nemmine how long it takes. You haven't realized yet how things have altered, I can see, so let me ask you some questions like what old Socrates used to, eh?'

Grant clenched his jaw in frustration. Good God, an old buzzard, a fat cockney AB from the back streets of Wapping, talking to him about *Socrates*! This was getting utterly impossible! He sighed and shook his head. 'Oh very well then - only let's not be all day over it.'

Curly ceremonially cleared his throat and promptly floored his commander by asking a totally unexpected question: 'Right-o, then, here we go. Back aboard the ship, why did you obey Captin Roberts?'

'What? Because he was my captain, of course.'

'Right. And why did I obey you - most of the time, anyway?'

'Because I was your superior officer.'

'Right. So we was parts of a hierarchy, wasn't we? You think about it, top to bottom: the Owners ordered the captin to take the ship here and there, and load and unload this and that. So then the captin ordered you to do something or other; you ordered the bosun to get it done, and the bosun ordered us in the crowd - right?'

'Right,' said Grant wearily. 'Kellock, where the hell is this leading us? What's the point of all this rigmarole?'

Curly ignored the petulant protest. 'Now then, speaking legal-like, why did any of us obey anyone?'

'Good God, man, you know that! Because the Owners had taken us on and agreed to pay us and feed us - after a fashion - and in return we'd agreed to carry out all lawful orders. That's all in the Crew Agreement that we all signed.'

'Ah,' said Curly, in ponderous triumph. 'The Crew Agreement! Now we're getting somewhere.'

'We are? I'm bloody sure it doesn't seem so to me.'

'That's because you ain't seen my train of thought yet.' Curly was beginning, rather complacently, to enjoy this colloquy, where he held the whip-hand over someone he'd always had to obey. 'No? Well nemmine, you'll see in a minute. Now then, this Crew Agreement: that was a contract, wasn't it?'

'A contract? Yes, I suppose so, in a way.'

'And in a contract, both the parties reckon to get summat out of it?'

'Yes - for a period of two years in this case.'

'Which ain't up yet, by no means?'

'No, not for six months or so.'

'Right, then,' said Curly confidently, 'now we get to the point I'm making.' Thank God for that, thought Grant, but said nothing. Everything he said seemed to prolong the tedium of this dialogue. Kellock's train of thought was a confoundedly long train, and a slow one too.

'Where's that contract now, eh?' said Curly, pointing an inquisitorial finger at his victim. 'We're sitting here, not lugging coal to Valparaiso, because our ship was wrecked - through no fault of our own - and they've stopped paying us because they think it's a waste of their money. So what they've done, when you come to think about it, is to tear up the contract before its final date. Nothing what that contract says means anythink no more. See what I mean? All of them obligations we signed up to are gone now.'

Grant nodded, feeling uneasily that all the old certainties by which his life had been ruled were melting under him. 'Yes,' he said soberly, 'I suppose if you look at it like that...'

'Ain't no other way of looking at it. You're just Simon Grant, I'm just Ernest Kellock and our prize skate and hoodlum is William John. We're all in the same boat. The old order is gone now, as you might say.'

'Oh, for God's sake, Kellock, don't start bringing in your Marxist politics! I'm bloody sure we don't need those. Let's stick to our situation here and now!'

Curly shook his head, more in sorrow than in anger: 'You still don't see, do you? I'm not bringing in politics - they're always present when a group of people live and work together. What we've had up to now is the politics of dictatorship, the plutocracy of some wealthy geezer and his shareholders in Cardiff. The old captin always had to dance to their tune, and aboard the ship, you - and the old captin before you - said "Jump!" and we all had to jump. Now all that's gone.'

'But bloody hell, man, the way you're talking is going to lead us into complete anarchy - every man for himself. Christ, we'll be fighting each other for tins of bully before long, at this rate!'

'Anarchy,' said Kellock in a tone of weary frustration, 'is *exactly* what I, like anyone with any sense, wants to avoid like the plague, but it's what might happen if you try to carry on as we were, like the French upper classes in the 1790's. From now on, whoever governs on this island will have to govern by the consent of all - or the majority, anyway.'

'Right; so what are you proposing? Sending Mr Raven and me to the guillotine? I'm sure the bosun could soon knock you up one of those.'

Curly could contain his anger no longer: 'Christ Almighty, man, when are you gonna stop being sarky and clever, and start facing the facts? Stop hiding yer head in the sand! You go on like this, you're gonna get real trouble.'

Grant sprang to his feet, all his cool, scoffing manner suddenly lost. 'What! Are you threatening me, Kellock? Because if you are, by God I'll...'

'Sit down, Grant, and stop being such a bleeding twat! You oughter know me by now; I ain't no bloody mutineer, I'm just the opposite; I'm trying to suggest to you how to *keep* order, not lose it, but you won't...'

He broke off as a voice behind them said: 'Simon, do you mind if I - Oh, sorry, have I interrupted something?' Raven stood there irresolute, suddenly aware of, and embarrassed by, the heavily charged atmosphere between the two men.

The accidental interruption proved a blessing; Grant realized the foolishness of his petulant rage, and Kellock was intelligent enough to realize that he had been sermonizing pompously and tediously for far too long. Grant sat down, and he and Kellock exchanged rueful grins. Nothing could have shown better their new equality than this shared feeling that they were like naughty schoolboys caught squabbling in the playground.

Grant said: 'No, it's all right, old boy. Curly and I were just having a...er... discussion about the future. Go on, man, tell young Raven here how you see things - only don't take so bloody long about it this time.'

The miraculous relaxation that Raven's arrival had

brought about was confirmed by Curly's reply: 'All right, I know I go on a bit, but you was being a bit of a thick, wasn't you? Right then, young feller-me-lad, it's like this. You better sit down, though.'

In a remarkably short time, since he had dropped his laborious technique of Socratic dialogue, he outlined his ideas for a quiet revolution, and finished by turning to Grant and saying: 'Y'see, it's like Engels said: the old order has got to wither away, slow-like. No bloodshed, no hatred, just a natural change, like these green leaves going brown and falling off in the autumn. I know we can do it.'

Grant said: 'Well, John, tell us what you think, if you've had time to take it all in.'

Raven's reply was characteristic: 'That's easy: I entirely agree with Curly, though who Engels was or is I haven't a notion. I've been thinking, ever since I heard about the pay, that things would have to change, but I hadn't thought it out so well. You should have been a professor of political history, Curly.'

'Fat chance of that, mate. We was poor as church mice after my dad got killed in the docks. No college for me - just hard graft, starting when I was only a nipper. Sweeper and general dogsbody in the Milwall Dock, I was. I only know about old Socrates because I go reg'lar to the Mechanics' Institute in Poplar when I'm ashore. They have some real brain-boxes from the university down there to talk to us poor ole proletarians.'

Raven smiled: 'Well, Curly, you're a brain-box yourself now, right enough. But, going back to where we are now, there is just an outside chance that Hughes will keep quiet, but that's so slender that we'd better assume that in three days' time some of the hands will know, and prepare for that.'

'Very well, then,' said Grant. 'I'll agree too - government by consent it is, but I don't quite see....'

Curly's libertarian socialist zeal was now unleashed, together with more than a little bureaucracy, the close companion of all left-wing movements: 'Right, then: we got to think up a new constitution; we got to have a kind of collective leadership, and we got to start writing down the things what we've decided, so we don't get in a muddle or have arguments afterwards. You've got the log-book, haven't you? And pencils and that? And I was thinking, Miss Eleanor would be just the person to have as a sort of cabinet secretary, like, being she's a well-educated young lady with a lot of sense.'

Raven said swiftly: 'And I know she'd be glad to do it. I know it depresses her to feel that she plays no part in anything but cooking and chores.'

'Right then,' said Curly, turning to Grant, 'now let's get one thing straight, mister: personally, I ain't got no interest in replacing you as a leader. I respect you for what you've done so far -getting us all off of the ship, finding the hut, getting us all organized and working, putting some heart into the lads when things was looking bad. You've been trained as a leader, and you're good at it. Same with this young feller too - and bosun. All of you have done a lot of good, one way or another, and you all deserve to be in the kind of cabinet we need to have from now on. Then there's me: I don't want to push myself, but I'm the senior hand of the foc'sle crowd, and, as you'll remember, I used to represent the lads. I reckon they'll want me there.'

Grant said with a smile: 'My dear sir, you'd have to be Prime Minister at the very least.'

But Curly had got his teeth into his vision of the future, and did not respond to the friendly jibe: 'And then there's the doctor, of course…'

'The *doctor*?' Grant's good humour evaporated in a trice. 'A black cook one of our leaders? Now you're going a damn sight too far, my friend!'

Curly also exploded in wrath: 'Black? Black? What the fuck's that got to do with it? He's a *man*, isn't he? A man what's found a way to cook for us - and bloody well too; a man what's got to plan how to keep on feeding us for Gawd knows how long! Where the hell would we have been without him, eh? Tell me that! And tell me what's wrong with him being black - it's only the colour of his skin, ain't it? Just because, years ago, various greedy bastards - black and white and brown- made his great-grandad a slave, does that make him less of a human being than you or me? Eh?'

'When you think about it, Simon,' said Raven diplomatically, 'it's not such a bad idea. He's got a lot of sense, he's worked all over the world in all sorts of situations, and he always seems to think about the welfare of all of us - not just himself. He's worked damned hard to get his galley up and running. And after all, we've no idea how long we'll be here, and it's jolly important for us all to be fit and healthy and…'

'And don't forget,' said Curly, ' you two officers were trained for work and leadership at sea, but we ain't at sea now, so everythink's different.'

'Yes, yes, all right,' said Grant, raising both hands to arrest the protests. 'The doctor, then, and yourself. But that's that, Kellock; no more after that.'

'No, that won't do,' said Curly doggedly. 'if we're

gonna have a kind of democracy, all hands have got to have some say. We got to let them elect one member outa the foc'sle to represent the junior hands.'

Grant snorted in disgust: 'Rubbish! We all know damn well who'll get himself picked - Jimmy Protheroe, sea-lawyer and trouble-maker.'

'Yeah,' said Curly, triumphantly, 'but that's good, see? That way, we'll know what he's thinking; we'll have him out in the open. And, you never know, he might get a bit more sense once he's involved in actually making decisions, and putting them into practice. He'll see that grumbling and grouching don't achieve nothink.' He added shrewdly: 'And don't forget, he won't have no real power, cos the cabinet'll be making policy by majority voting, and he'll likely be a minority of one, so any daft ideas he comes up with can soon be knocked on the head. That's the way democracy works, see?'

'You're in your element, aren't you, Curly?' said Grant with a smile. 'Mr Gladstone and Mr Disraeli rolled into one! Though what on earth our old captain would say about Protheroe being in any sort of government, I don't like to think.'

Raven said: 'But I've been thinking: you're both calling this new idea government by consent, but it isn't really democratic, is it? I mean, just sitting here now, Curly has created the whole constitution himself. The hands didn't have any say in that, did they?'

Curly was more than equal to that challenge: 'Ah, but you see, in politics it's how the public *perceive* things that counts. You give them somethink a bit more democratic than what they had before, and they *feel* a lot freer than what they really are. Like what old Bismarck said:

"Politics is the art of the possible".'

Grant said: 'H'm. But *"demos"* in Greek means the people, in our case, the crowd, so I suppose if we're going to stick to your opinions and be democratic here, we've no right to just impose a regime on them.'

Kellock again became didactic: 'Yeah, I know all that, but, like I just said, it's the art of the possible. I mean, old Abe Lincoln talked about "Government of the people, by the people, for the people"; sounds good, but "by the people" is just eyewash, ain't it? Ain't possible to have all the people voting on every damned petty thing that comes up every day. There ain't a country in the world run like that - never will be. But if the crowd can speak, and them in power will listen to them, things can be a lot better. Take you and the old captin: you had to fight him once, off South Africa there, to stop him rolling the ship under in a gale, didn't you? And then again, would *you* have gone blundering on in thick fog, when you hadn't seen the sun or the stars for days on end, and you didn't really know where the hell you were? No, you wouldn't. Then maybe we wouldn't have hit this bloody island, and we'd all be safe and sound in Valparaiso. See, rule by just one person don't work neither, cos if he's lazy or careless or ill or off his head, everybody suffers. Two or more heads is better than one, sometimes...Hello, what's this?'

The small scrawny figure of Davey Jones peggy had suddenly appeared, crashing his way hastily through the clustered trees. He was beaming and excited, and clutching a double handful of greenery. 'Hey!' he shouted, 'look, mister, at what I found further up the hill there! Look - onions! Doctor said he wanted some. I found them growing wild in a big old garden, like, back up there. They've started growing out a bit, cos it's spring here, isn't it? But the bulbs will be all right still, I reckon, if we pull them up and dry them out. Welly'll be happy now, isn't it?'

'Very well done, Davey boy,' said Grant affectionately. 'You've cheered us all up on a very difficult day - don't you think so, chaps?' Seized by a sudden spurt of fatherly affection, he stood up, took in the boy's skimpy form, his hair like jutting black straw, his thin face, usually so pale, now tanned and flushed with pride. Impulsively, he put an arm round Davey's narrow shoulders and said: 'Well done indeed! *Da iawn wir,* you say, don't you, in Welsh? Now our grub will be a lot tastier and healthier too.'

As for Davey, his soul was a turbulent mixture of pride, joy and incredulous awe. *Iesu Mawr!* The bucko giving *me* a hug! Damn, there was funny things happening on this island - things you wouldn't believe! And what are all of them doing up here, on their own, in the rain, sitting talking, secret-like, in the bushes? Never mind, I've found us all some onions now, and the doctor will be pleased beyond with me!

CHAPTER SEVEN

Despite the leaders' hopes, it took only a day for the news of the lost pay to leak out, and to leak out into the least desirable minds in the island community. And by a supreme irony, the secret was revealed to those malicious minds by Davey, the simplest, most innocent, guileless and best-natured of all the castaways; unfortunately, like all guileless people, he was totally without discretion, which is, after all, a virtuous form of guile.

Jimmy Protheroe and Billy John, like most malcontents, were not really liked by most of the crowd, who were bored and irritated by their constant grumbling and whining, and preferred to live, in the South Pembrokeshire phrase, in a 'come day, go day' mood, making the best of a grim existence and an uncertain future. Some indeed, like the staunch Baptist, Tydfil Jones, took a pious view of their fate; he had once declaimed, after a companion had complained bitterly of their bad luck: 'The Almighty has willed us to be here, boy - perhaps because of our sins. It is not for us to question His justice or His great purposes. Sooner or later He will relent, and rescue us by His divine power. All we can do is pray, repent our past carnal sins, and work to keep ourselves alive.'

So the rebels were sitting apart in the evening dogwatch, on a pile of drying logs in a far corner of the clearing. They were an odd pair, united only by an undying paranoid ill-will towards all authority - Billy the bold, warlike and reckless, Jimmy the shrewd, cunning thinker with a lurking streak of cowardice. Tonight, Protheroe was applying his talent for political insight to the morning's announcement of a meeting.

'What's he calling a special meeting for, Billy?' he said. 'Why does he want to talk to us, and let us talk to him? He's never done it before, has he? Usually he just musters us in the morning, tells us what bloody rotten jobs we got to do - and that's that. So why now? I reckon something's happened; he's been told something, or he's just thought of something. But what? And why is he giving us three days' notice of it?'

'How the hell am I supposed to know that? He's a bucko, ain't he? He does whatever he bloody likes. This meeting won't do us no good - you can count on that. Still, it'll be a chance for you to do some of your belly-aching, Jim, and get on his wick a bit. You might even get some others in this feeble crowd to give him some lip.' He raised his voice to call mockingly to the peggy, who sat nearby, whistling as he whittled aimlessly at a stick: 'Oy, what about you, Davey boy? You going to lead a nice mutiny for us, eh? We needs a big strong leader like you, isn't it?'

But Davey was still basking in his rare moment of triumph: 'No, boy, I ain't doing no mutiny. Mr Grant was nice to me yesterday morning, when I showed him the onions I'd found. He said I'd done real good. And then, when I got back to camp and give them to the doctor, he was happy too, and said I was a smart little feller.'

Protheroe was swiftly alerted: 'Just a minute; didn't you tell us you found them onions right up in the woods - higher up the stream? A long way off from here? What was you doing sculling about up there at that time of the morning, instead of working?'

'Cos bloody old Isaac upset me, talking about my family.... He called my mother a....a...something nasty. So I ran off up the stream a long way. I was crying, see, so

I didn't want none of you to see me.'

Billy too was suspicious: 'Then how come you showed your precious onions to the bucko *before* you gave them to the doctor?'

'O well, I got a bit lost up in the wood there. I was wandering about, a bit frightened, like, when I heard their voices.'

'Their voices? Whose voices?'

'O, Mr Grant, Mr Raven and Curly. They was talking and arguing, having a meeting, like.'

'What! You mean they wasn't down by the hut?' said Protheroe.

'O no, boy. They was miles away, up in the woods. Half a mile off, I reckon.'

'You see, Billy! They was up to something!' Jimmy was delighted at his own perspicacity. 'Meeting in secret one morning, arguing about something, then the next morning they say there's going to be some sort of council with all hands in three days' time. I can see right through them buggers, I can. Course, what we don't know is what they were arguing about…'

'O, I knows that, boys,' said Davey proudly. 'It was the same as what the doctor and bosun and Curly were arguing about the night before.'

Protheroe adopted a gentle, wheedling manner: 'And what was that, Davey? Be a good boy and tell us.'

'Don't know exactly, Jim. I only heard bits of it, cos I was working then. It was something about pay - about money, like. But Isaac knows, I think. He went to talk to Curly and them about it, but I didn't understand what they was on about. I got bored, see. You'll have to ask Isaac.'

Protheroe gave a short, grim laugh: 'O, we'll do that

all right, Davey, don't you worry. And thank you, you've been a good boy. Billy, go and fetch that slimy old bastard over here. Tell him he's wanted, urgent-like.'

Isaac was aggrieved to be interrupted in his evening work so unceremoniously: 'What do you two impertinent young *crwts* want, then? I got work to do...'

'*Cau dy ben,*' said Billy, 'and tell us something: what's this big secret that Grant and you and half-a-dozen others know, and we don't? Davey says it's about money...'

Isaac was rattled and became evasive: 'O, you don't want to listen to that little half-wit. What does he know about anything?'

'*You* know, Isaac,' said Protheroe. 'I can see by your face that you do. So tell us - *now!*'

'Yes,' said Billy, clenching a big fist, 'or that face will get altered a bit. Why was they arguing about pay, when we're stuck here with no bugger to pay us nothing any-way?'

'Well,' said Isaac, looking nervously all round, 'I don't know anything for certain, and I've promised Curly on my honour that I wouldn't...'

'Stuff your honour and Curly too,' said Billy. 'Stop pissing about and tell us what you do know.'

'All right then, Billy, only - fair play now - don't get angry with me if I tell you some bad news.'

Protheroe lost patience and hissed at him: 'For Christ's sake spit it out, you old fairy! We got a right to know.'

'Very well then, here it is, only don't tell nobody I told you. When we get back, the company won't pay us nothing for the time we've spent here. Our pay stopped when the ship went down. Bosun and Kellock both know that.'

Billy John exploded in impotent fury: '*Iesu Mawr!* Those Owners! Mean, cruel bastards! Did the bucko know about this?'

'How the hell should I know that, man? What difference would that make, anyhow?'

Jimmy was silent, lost in profound political speculation: 'I expect he did,' he said at length, 'and I think I knows why he never said nothing. If this is true - and I bet it is - this changes things a lot. If the company don't pay us no more, why should we obey their officers any more? Why should we say "yes sir" and "no sir" to Grant now? All his authority's gone if the pay's gone. We ain't working for them Owners no more, not if they ain't paying us.'

'Right,' said Billy urgently, 'I'll get the lads together straight away. Even this spineless lot would like to see that bucko pulled off his perch.'

'No, Bill,' said Protheroe, with infinite cunning in his look. 'No, not yet. Don't say nothing yet. Let the bucko have his meeting, thinking that we don't know nothing, and *then* we'll spring it on all of them, and I'll bet we'll get the whole crowd going then - when they hears, sudden-like, about all the money they're losing every day, and about how old Grant has been keeping it secret to suit himself. That'll put the skids under that jumped-up English bastard.'

'Right,' said Billy. 'I s'pose you knows best. Well in that case, you shove off, Isaac. You don't usually sit around chatting with us, and I don't want nobody to spot you here, and wonder what we're up to. We got to box clever now, isn't it?'

*

From the plotters' point of view, it was a pity they had not finished their interrogation of the hapless steward two minutes earlier, for then John Raven, returning from his evening wash in the stream, would not have noticed the three men on the log-pile, their heads together, their expressions dark, scowling, tense.

As it was, his immediate reaction was to go swiftly to the hut, where Grant sat alone, writing up the day's log of uneventful events. Grant yawned and stretched, not noticing his air of urgency: 'God, life's such a bore here, isn't it, in the evenings? No lamps for when it gets dark, and anyway nothing to read, not even an old newspaper or a penny dreadful. For want of anything better to do I've almost a mind to start writing a novel myself, in the back of this - Hello, what's up, old boy? You look bothered.'

'Simon, I'm virtually certain that Isaac has spilled the beans - that he's told Billy John and Protheroe about the pay - or lack of it. I've just seen the three of them talking, thick as thieves, right over on the far side of the clearing, but they were too busy talking to see me, I think. Well, you know there's no love lost between them; you never normally see them together, do you? And Isaac was looking scared witless. So I reckon the secret's out.'

'Damn and blast that nosy, spineless old toad! Now all the crowd will know in two shakes. We'd better bring the meeting forward to tomorrow night, don't you think?'

But Raven's mind was turning things over, in the devious way so much admired by Curly: 'No, I think it'd be better to sit tight and see what happens. We'll soon know if they've been told. But Protheroe is a crafty bastard. I don't think he'll tell the rest of the crowd yet. I think he'll keep mum until the meeting, and then spring it on us suddenly. That's what I'd do in his place. I don't think they saw me go by, so at present they don't know that we know that *they* know - if you see what I mean. Now I reckon that, at the meeting, it'd be better if you tell them the bad news before anyone asks. Then it doesn't look as if we've been keeping a guilty secret from them. And - yes, I know what - it'd be better still if you can work it so that Curly tells them, not you. Then it won't look as if we officers are to blame.'

Grant gave a wry smile: 'Yes, I just about see what you mean - with an effort. We make poor old Curly do the dirty work? H'm; so Jimmy's a crafty bastard, is he? Well, it takes one to know one, old son. But yes, I'll do what you suggest, that is - nothing.'

*

When the meeting began, in the cloudy twilight, the sullen clouds racing eastwards in the darkening sky, the tops of the trees bending and whipping in the everlasting stiff damp breeze, the assembly was curiously divided. Two small groups were taut, tense, waiting for the oncoming conflict, while most of the hands were bored and restless even before the proceedings began.

Grant, like any holder of office, like any complacent Chancellor of the Exchequer on Budget Day, began with an optimistic review of all that had been done under his leadership, together with tactful compliments to almost all of his subjects and a measured cheerfulness about the community's prospects. He ended: 'So, there we are, lads - that's how I see it. Now it's time for you to have your say, if you want to.'

There was a lengthy, almost embarrassing, silence. The sharp-eyed Raven saw John and Protheroe exchange glances, and saw Protheroe shake his head ever so slightly. At last Lewis, the indomitably cheerful AB from Milford, spoke up: 'What about this here rescue steamer, Mr Grant? I mean, we've a been here weeks now, and not a sign of her.'

'That's a question I can't answer, I'm afraid, Lewis, but there's no need for us to despair - to lose hope. I'm as certain as I can be that she will turn up one day quite soon. You'll remember that, unfortunately, a Navy ship called here with the supplies just before we landed up, and that the regular New Zealand steamer's next visit's going to be delayed because she's in dock for repair. Well, I'm writing the ship's log up every night, so I know that we've been here for three weeks - twenty-two days, to be exact.'

'And you got to remember,' said Kellock didactically, 'that we know we're here, but no-one else does. You got to look at it from the New Zealanders' point of view. They bin calling here reg'lar for thirty years now, ever since the "General Grant" got wrecked, and in that time I b'lieve only three or four other ships have bin wrecked here - ain't that right, Mr Grant?'

'Yes, I think so. Now, are there any other...'

But Curly had got his teeth into a theme, and was not to be put off: 'So y'see, mates, it won't seem urgent to them to get here quickly. I remember reading in the "Illustrated London News" about the "General Grant's" crowd; poor beggars, they was stuck here for a year and a half. All their clo'es wore out; they had to make clobber and shoes out a seal-skins, and...'

'Yes,' said Grant, gently stemming the flow, 'I remember hearing about it, but of course I was too young at the time to understand much. Now, is there…'

'Well, sir,' said Lewis, 'we always had a lookout on duty aboard the old hooker, didn't we? Seems to me we should have one now - down at the beach or up on the cliff somewhere - so we re sure to see the steamer when a does come, and make some kind of signal to her - light a fire or something. I mean, we'd look bliddy silly if a came, didn't see nobody, and buggered off again.'

'We should indeed, Lewis,' said Grant, pleased to hear a laugh from the crowd at even that ghastly prospect. 'An excellent idea! We'll get that organized tomorrow. Now, anything else?'

Yorry Splott overcame his congenital nerves, and blurted out abruptly: 'How far is it to the nearest port, mister?'

'To Bluff Harbour? About three hundred miles, Jones. Why do you ask?'

'Well, that ain't all that far with a decent breeze. Why don't we rig up one of the big boats, and a few of us sail there and tell them we're here? I don't mind going.'

There was a tentative rumble of agreement from the crowd, which Grant rapidly quashed: 'No, I'm going to rule that out, for the moment anyway. It'd be far too dangerous; you've all seen what the seas can be like in this latitude, and you've seen how often it blows a gale. Some of the "General Grant" survivors tried that, and were never seen again. I'm responsible for all your lives, and I can't see them thrown away like that. As I've said to you before, we've got water, wood, bully-beef, stacks of biscuit, fish to catch, seals to hunt, maybe birds' eggs to collect from the cliffs, and a roof over our heads. We'd be pretty poor specimens if we couldn't survive here for a few months if necessary. Now, anything else?'

His heart sank as he saw Curly Kellock rise to his feet with a solemn urgency. 'Yes, mister, there is, and it's shit - crap - whatever you want to call it...'

There was a spontaneous uproar of laughter as the tension was released by Curly's blunt, homely, and totally unexpected words. He remained standing, flushed with dignified irritation, and raised his hands for silence: 'All right, you can laugh like kids, and I apologize to Miss Roberts for using rude words, but I ain't joking. We got to have some rules about what they call hygiene, mister, or none of us won't get away. Anyone heard of Sir Joseph Bazalgette? No, I thought not. Well, back in London he done more for people's health than a cart-load of doctors, and he done it by digging big new drains to take all the people's turds away. Before that, people went down like flies with cholera and all sorts a gut-troubles. Well, the same will happen to us if people do their business all over the place - and I've seen lazy beggars doing just that, sometimes real close to this clearing. Well, there's flies here, same as everywhere, and they'll soon carry the filth on their feet onto our food - and then, look out! We all got to crap every day, but it's all got to go into the stream well *below* the camp, so it'll wash down into the sea, and then people have got to wash their hands above the place where they've crapped, so that...'

Grant stopped the inexhaustible flow of rhetoric by raising his hands and saying: 'Yes, Kellock, that is a very sensible warning, and I agree entirely. Thank you for bringing it up. Bosun, there's that handy pool fifty yards downstream. You could rig up some suitable privy seats there, couldn't you?' He sensed that the time had come for the crucial revelation: 'Now then, if there's nothing else,

I'm afraid I've got some rather bad news for you about money, and I'm going to ask your senior AB to explain it to you. I know you've all got a lot of faith in him - and quite rightly so, too.'

He sat down, giving Raven an almost imperceptible wink. That observant young officer had seen a quick look of astonishment exchanged between John and Protheroe. Curly rose with mixed feelings; he was always partial to addressing attentive audiences; on the other hand, he felt indignant that Grant had, without warning, landed him with the most difficult topic of the meeting, and one that was not likely to make him popular. He cleared his throat with due dignity, and began: 'Yes, mates, what I'm going to say may be a shock to some of you, but there's nothing that anyone on this island can do to change it, so there's no point in you blaming anyone here for it. Some of us older chaps have been talking, and we've realized that p'raps some of you young uns don't know that when a ship is wrecked and abandoned by her crew, that crew's pay stops. So that, for the last three weeks, and for however long it takes us to get off from here and get back home, we ain't earning nothing, not even the miserable two pound fifteen a month we usually get.'

There was a roar of scandalized rage at the injustice of the world in general, and of Cardiff ship-owners in particular. Notwithstanding the presence of a well brought-up young lady, the clearing resounded to countless loud obscenities from poor men who were about to become much poorer. Billy and Jimmy added their yelled epithets, but exchanged looks of anger and dismay. After all their scheming, they had been cheated of the opportunity to lead a small revolution. Someone had known - or guessed - that they knew, and had pulled the rug from under them.

As for Eleanor, sitting silent on the very edge of the crowd to emphasize her status as a mere passenger, she felt a profound uneasiness. Under Grant's leadership the island community had settled into a quiet, dull routine of useful domestic toil - wood-cutting, building, cleaning, cooking, hunting, fishing - the life of poor peasants everywhere since humans first trod the earth. Would these orderly workers now turn into a Paris mob, baying for blood round the guillotine? Only the three existing leaders, Grant, Raven and Curly Kellock, could prevent that, and of these, Kellock seemed by far the best hope. She saw him standing, calm, silent, still, waiting for the tumult of impotent rage to subside, saw him strengthened, empowered, roused to his full stature by the possibility of impending disaster.

At last, with superb timing, he raised both arms so high that, from where she sat, he formed a perfect letter "Y". He spoke now in a stronger, full-bodied voice, as if he felt his supreme hour had come: 'Yes, mates - you're angry, and so am I, so are all of us, the officers too. It's not right, it's not just, it's not humane, but - shame on the government - it's not illegal, and it's what all ship-owners have always done. Luckily, it doesn't often happen to seafarers, but that doesn't make it right. The only comfort is that, when we are picked up one day, mister bleeding Powell will have to pay our fares back home to Cardiff.'

The groundswell of sullen rage rose as he paused for breath, but subsided as soon as he raised his hands again: 'So now we got to face the future - here, on this godforsaken wet island, and we got to face it like *men* - not cowards and most of all, not like quarrelling animals. And that means, chums, that we still got to have leaders, and we still got to have rules, and - now that we ain't the crew of the "Figaro" no more - above all, everyone has got to have a right to speak his mind, and whatever leaders we have, have to listen to him. But what we can't have is everyone pleasing himself what he does. That way, we'd finish up fighting like...like hyenas over every tin of bully or bit of biscuit. That way, my sons, we'd be too busy fighting and guarding our bits of grub to do any building, cleaning, cooking, hunting or fishing - all the ordinary things we been doing. And that way, my sons...' he paused, and there was an awed silence, 'that way, we'd be lucky if one of us lasted long enough to see the rescue boat drop anchor. We'd all die, mates, and by God, we'd *deserve* to die.'

Strewth, thought Grant, listening in admiration, I thought Mark Antony did well with his 'Friends, Romans, countrymen' stuff, but old Kellock takes the biscuit. But now comes the difficult part; he's designed his new constitution - though they don't know that yet; and now he's got to sell it to them. That won't be easy.

Predictably, Jimmy Protheroe, sensing an opportunity at last, stood up: 'All right, Curly, you say we got to have leaders. But who they gonna be, eh? Who's gonna choose them, and how?'

Curly was equal to the challenge. 'Yes, that's the next thing to be decided. The main idea, I reckon, is that no-one from now on will decide things for himself, like the old captin did. He was a good man, but, like any of us here, he made mistakes - that's why we're stuck here.' He suddenly remembered Eleanor's presence, and said with much embarrassment, 'Sorry, miss, for me saying that about your dad. Twas nothing personal, like. I thought a lot of him, I did. I hope you don't think…'

Eleanor had felt a stab to the heart at his words, and flushed at suddenly becoming the focus of attention, but she said, as calmly as she could: 'No, don't apologize, Curly. You spoke nothing but the truth.'

'Right, miss, that's handsome of you. Now then, mates, we got to consider who's gonna lead. Well, the main thing is, there's got to be a big change. We got to have what they call a democracy - government by the people.' He paused, realizing that he had just used the Abraham Lincoln phrase on which he had recently poured such scorn. Never mind, it was a fine-sounding slogan! He went on: 'From now on, whoever leads, he ain't doing it on his own; every big decision has got to be voted on, cos two or three or more heads are better than one. Now, we can't all vote on every little thing, else we'll be sitting here on our backsides all day and every day, so what we need is a committee - what they call a cabinet, back in London. And then every big decision has got to be made by all of its members voting on it. And every one of them members has got to be ready to listen to all of you - sorry, all of us, I should say.'

Raven thought: Whoops! Careful, Curly! You nearly announced yourself as one of the cabinet already!

Curly went on: 'And another thing: after a certain time - say two months - any of the cabinet members who you think hasn't done well enough can be chucked out at a second election.'

Again, Raven was secretly amused: Two months! That's a good idea! With any luck the steamer will have called by then, so the cabinet members won't have to worry too much about being dismissed.

Grant thought: Phew! I'm glad this chap is on our side, not against us!

Curly went inexorably on: 'Nah then, a proper election like that takes time, and people who've never bin in charge of anythink will find it bloody hard at first. But - see - we need a new scheme that'll start straightaway - tomorrow, so what I reckon is this: as a temporary government - just to be going on with, like - we stick to them what have bin our leaders so far - Mr Grant, Mr Raven and bosun here...'

His voice was suddenly drowned by an uproar of anger and discontent; Billy John's voice rose, high and strident, above the others: 'Jesus, what sort of change is that? S'pose some of us don't *want* to be led by that lot no more? Bloody officers...'

Curly too was angry, and raised his voice to thunder: 'Why don't you silly buggers let me finish, instead of yelling out a lot of rubbish?' As the noise subsided to a sullen grumbling he went on: 'That's better. Now then, those three would only be *half* of the committee. There'd be three others to balance them, to represent you, so it will be a change. It won't be just the officers in the cabinet. To start with, I'm the senior foc'sle hand...'

'O, here we go, boys,' said Billy derisively. 'Old Curly's elected hisself already...'

Now Curly was seriously angry, and his cool statesmanship disappeared: 'Why don't you shut yer bloody trap, Billy? Who saved you from a damn good hiding that night in Caleta Buena? I did. Who stood up for you when you was ill? I did, and I took a chance of being fined myself for it. I've stuck my neck out and tackled the captin himself several times. And then, when we was wrecked, if I hadn't suggested rigging that boom over the stern to make the boats fast while we was loading, none of us wouldn't be here now.' He turned to where Grant sat: 'Ain't that right, mister?'

Grant nodded and said: 'That's absolutely right. I hadn't thought of doing it - though I should have done - but Curly did, and just now you heard another example of his intelligence and common sense - about our sewage, I mean. You had a laugh about it, but that might save our lives, because we've got no medicines of any kind if someone does get ill. And I may as well say this: if you think this man will be some kind of obedient lap-dog to me or anybody else, then all I can say is that you don't know him. As he says himself, he stood up to the captain and to me on your behalf, and I don't mind telling you there were times when I'd have cheerfully chucked him into the drink for his cheek. He's always fought for all of you, not just himself, so you needn't think he won't see fair play for you in this new scheme.'

He and Kellock exchanged looks, and Grant thought: Come on, chum, it's time you relieved the old boy in the speech-making department. He raised his voice: 'Now then, to show you this isn't just the after-guard taking over everything, we think that - if he's willing - the doctor ought to join our cabinet, as he's such an important person in our welfare and comfort. Where would we have been without him?'

He looked across at Welly, who, after a jump of surprise, nodded coolly like a man who knew his own worth, and replied: 'OK, mister. You want me, you got me - only, you mind now, I ain't giving you no extra helpings of nothing for that.'

He had struck the right note; the short laugh and ironic cheers lowered the tension, which diminished further when Grant added: 'And to balance it even more, we'd like to include a member from the junior part of the foc'sle. Then there'll be three officers from the ship, but three others as well. Now, would anyone like to nominate a man to be the crew member on the committee?'

There was an instant yell from the back: 'Go on, Billy, now's your chance!' But Billy shook his head and thought: We could stir up a bit of trouble for him yet. If I suggest Jimmy, old Grant will be sure to turn him down - say he's a sea-lawyer and not suitable, and all that - and then there'll be a proper hullabaloo, and *then* we can upset his apple-cart all right. So here goes: 'No,' he said, 'I ain't willing to stand, cos I know someone who'd be a lot better. I'm suggesting my friend Jimmy Protheroe, and I'm asking all of you to vote for him. He'll put some people straight, isn't it?'

There were cheers and loud cries of assent, but Billy was surprised and uneasy when Grant simply said: 'Very well. Now, are there any other nominations?' There was a pause, during which the formidable Billy looked round, daring anyone to challenge his candidate. No-one did, for many of the crowd, while not wishing for mutiny and chaos, were no friends to Grant the bucko, and took a mischievous delight in the notion of landing him with such an out-and-out rebel and rabble-rouser on his committee as Jimmy. They too were surprised when Grant said calmly: 'Right, then in the absence of any other nominations, I declare Able Seaman Protheroe to be the sixth member of the cabinet, and I very much welcome the chance to hear his views and suggestions about our situation and our plans. That then concludes this meeting. Thank you for your attention.'

There was a hearty bawling cheer for the new member, and the clearing rang with cries of 'Good old Jim....You show them, mate....Well done, boy!' and Billy thumped him cheerfully on the back, shouting: 'Good boy, Jim! Now we'll see what's what!'

But Jimmy, far from rejoicing, muttered: 'Don't be so fucking *twp*, boy! Can't you see? The whole bloody thing's gone wrong. They knew Isaac had told us, and they had the whole thing worked out beforehand, and they've pulled it off - they've got all this stupid crowd to agree to their precious scheme. I don't reckon that being in their blinking cabinet will make much difference. I'll do my best, like, to get justice for us. But if they vote for things, I'll likely be only one vote against five. And you know what? This meeting shows that it ain't really Grant what's running this island - it's bloody Curly Kellock! Able Seaman? The bugger's more like a Lord High Admiral!'

CHAPTER EIGHT

As if Nature had welcomed the new human order, Auckland Island was bathed in warm spring evening sunshine. All day the strengthening sun had shone down, and with only a gentle northerly zephyr blowing, the builders, fishers and wood-cutters had worked in rolled-up shirt-sleeves, cheerfully whistling and chaffing, feeling at last that things were improving. Summer was approaching, their food was tastier now, thanks to Davey's onions, and if the rescue steamer didn't arrive for a while it didn't seem to matter too much. They were working pretty hard, but not so hard as they had been aboard the ship, nor was the work so dangerous. Moreover, every night they had that incredible luxury for seafarers, an 'all night in' - no night watches, except for the duty look-out, no mate or bosun thundering on their foc'sle door to roust them out of their scrappy sleep to furl tops'ls, eighty feet up in a howling gale and lashing rain.

Strange birds sang their unfamiliar evening songs in the thick clustering forest around the clearing; the new galley stood four-square in the centre of the clearing, roofed over now by thick canvas, drawn taut over stout rafters, fragrant wood-smoke drifting up from the smoke-hole in the centre of its ridge. The doctor had insisted on this simple modification to Lewis's design, for cooking for twenty-nine people in there was a smoky job. If a little rain thereby landed on his head, well, that was better than choking to death!

'Middling good here now, b'ys,' said the ever-optimistic Lewis to a group around him, 'what with a bit of tidy weather, like. Apart from the girls, o' course, the oon'y thing I misses is my pipe and a bit of baccy. Pity, wasn't it, we had to leave the old hooker so bliddy quick that night?'

There were quiet, lazy grunts of agreement from his tired mates, but over on the far edge of the clearing, a very different mood was being shown by the two determined malcontents. 'Look at them all,' said Billy John in disgust. 'Loafing about, happy as pigs in shit. Forgotten about that meeting last night already, most of them, I'll bet. Don't seem to see how they've been cheated.'

'No,' said Jimmy, 'nor they don't see how Curly has gone over to the other side, neither. Him and Grant are thick as thieves now.'

'Yes, that's what I don't understand, Jim. What's changed Grant so much? I mean, back on board, he'd sooner give Curly a boot up the arse than listen to him, never mind agree with him.'

Jimmy frowned, bringing his utmost powers of political perception to bear: 'Well, Bill, don't forget, there's two other officers - bosun and Raven. Well, bosun is a good old boy - straight as a die. He just gets on with his work. He don't fill his head with a lot of scheming and that. But that Raven.... I reckon he's more than a bit crafty. Look at what happened when he got promoted third mate: he was the wildest of all them bloody young brassbounders until then, but once he went aft he turned into a bit of a bucko himself. He knocked you out cold once, remember. He even gave his old brassbounder mates a rough time. I don't trust him. I mean, to give old Grant his due, in them days you knew where you were with him. He was a hard bastard, but you knew where you were - he wasn't no schemer - just a bucko. Now, he's giving way here and changing his mind there; it's as if, just lately, someone else has been backing up Curly and getting Grant to agree with that old buzzard. Well, if it ain't bosun, it must be Raven, I reckon, and….' Protheroe suddenly had a blinding insight: 'Davey!'

'Davey? What about him? What could a half-wit like him tell us about this sort of thing?'

'Don't be so sure, boy. Let's see if he does know anything. He goes here and there; nobody pays him no attention. He don't understand nothing, but he sees and hears a lot. He told us all about the pay, and the secret meeting out there in the woods, didn't he? Well, he knew we got the truth out of Isaac that night, didn't he? And at the meeting you could see that Grant knew that we knew about the pay - right? How was that, eh? I reckon Davey might…'

Protheroe paused for a while, deep in profound thought, then went on: 'Right, Billy. Let's find out. Go and get him, but don't be rough, be real nice to him - that's the way.' The two rebels had suddenly realized Davey's value to them: like the surveillance cameras of a later century, he saw all and understood nothing. His fatal innocence and simplicity meant that, like a camera, he not only saw, but also told any enquirer what he had seen, with no notion, and therefore no heed, about the possible consequences.

However, even Davey's simple mind was puzzled as well as flattered by the way Billy and Jimmy wanted to talk to him these days - they never had before. But Billy had been so friendly, asking him over for a chat when no-one else bothered with him - except Miss Eleanor, of course. She was always nice to him, and she'd nursed him when he'd had that horrible fever. 'What do you want,

Jimmy?' he said. 'I ain't done nothing wrong, have I?'

'No, Davey - not on your life! We just wanted a chat, like - to see how you're getting on. Seems to us they're making you work too hard, boy. They're not fair on you.'

'O no, I don't mind, boys. Old Isaac made me work hard on the ship, and he was nasty with it. It's better working for Welly - he's nice to me. He got me to show Yorry where the onions were, and Yorry and I came back with two big bags full of them - and there's plenty more up there, too.'

Onions were not quite what Jimmy wanted to discuss, but he checked his irritation: 'Yes, Davey, you was a clever boy to find them. Real nice, they are... But we was wondering: you remember the other night when Billy and I got Isaac over for a chat, and asked him some questions?'

Davey groped in the drifting mists of his memory: 'O yes... And you wasn't very nice to him...'

'No, p'raps not, but never mind that now. What Bill and I are wondering is this: do you think anyone else noticed us talking to Isaac? Can you remember that?'

The boy frowned with the effort of recollecting: 'No, no-one, Jim.... O, except Raven. I think he did. I think he looked at you three. He was coming back from *Pwll Ty Bach* - you know, where we're supposed to...'

'Yeah, all right, all right. But what did he do then?'

'He.... he... can't remember, Jim.... O yes, I know! He went into the hut - to see Mr Grant, I dare say. I remember he walked fast and shut the door behind him with a bang... Made me jump, that did!'

Jimmy smiled and patted the scrawny, waif-like lad

on the back. 'Well done, Davey *bach*. You're a real good boy, and I wish I had something to give you... I will, some day, I promise.' Then, suddenly, turning from Davey and dropping his treacly, benevolent manner he said: 'There you are, Bill!' What did I tell you? It's Raven we've got to thank for all this - for all our plans for the meeting going wrong. He's the bloody schemer.'

Both of them had now forgotten Davey, who had found a strong blade of grass and, holding it between his thumbs, was attempting to blow a rasping note on it.

Billy was filled with a cold, deadly rage: 'Right, well, I'll show that bastard Raven he can't treat us like shit. Like you said, I've got a few scores to settle with him, anyway, and now's the time to do it.'

Jimmy had an attack of caution; being physically cowardly himself, he dreaded confrontation and blows, preferring furtive cunning and sedition. 'Now you want to be careful, boy. That Raven is big and tough, even if he is younger than you.'

'O, don't you worry, I could fight him easy, but I know a better way to get even with him, and that's through his nice little bint - Miss high-and-mighty Eleanor. A few punches and black eyes is nothing - he'd soon get over them. No, I wants to hurt him in a way he won't get over so quick. I've been wanting like hell to have her anyway. Kill two birds with one stone, like.'

'Christ, Bill, you don't mean...?'

'Yes, I do! I'll get my own back through his nice fancy bird. Looks so prim and proper, she does, but used to jump into Raven's bunk, Isaac said. She went to him, the randy bitch, not the other way round. That toffee-nosed English bastard knows what her fanny feels like, I'll bet, and so will I, by Christ, with a bit of luck. If he gets to know about what I've done to her, he'll suffer, and if he don't - well, I'll be one up on him anyway, and pull that trollop down off her perch too. I've just got to get her at the right time and place... Come to think of it, she must have her own *ty bach* somewhere, where she does her business and washes, and that. But we don't know where, do we?'

'O, I knows where that is, boys,' said Davey casually, over his shoulder, with the same deadly, disastrous naivety. 'She goes down there after breakfast every day, when you've all gone off to work. Welly don't say nothing; he just nods, and off she goes.'

'Yeah, she goes,' said Billy tensely, 'but *where* does she go? Do you know?'

'O yes, I knows where. I was nosey-like, one day, and bunked off after her. Wish I hadn't now.'

'Yes, but *where*, Davey? Be a good boy now, and tell us.'

'Well, you know the beach we landed on, where the boats are now? Now then, if you goes left, right to the end of that beach, there's cliffs and rocks and that, sticking out.'

'Yeah, a headland - I know.'

'Well, if the tide's real low, you can walk round the end of the rocks to another small little cove, but most of the time you got to go up over the headland by a little path, and down the other side. Like I said, I followed her over there once, and I seen her having a bath, like, in the stream. Hell, boys, it must have been cold! She had a spare blanket for a towel. I was hiding in some high reeds, so she never saw me. O, drop dead, boys, she looked so nice without no clothes on! I started to rub myself - you know, my john thomas - and that was a lovely feeling too. But then, after all the stuff came out, I felt real ashamed, to treat a nice lady like that; she's always been so good to me when nobody else was. So I ran away, crying. I'll never do that again, honest. I mean, what would my Mam have thought of me doing that?'

'No, that's right, Davey,' said Jimmy, kindly but virtuously. 'Miss Eleanor is a nice lady and you was a naughty boy, wasn't you?'

'Yes, I was.' An unease came into the boy's clouded mind. 'You two ain't gonna hurt her, are you? Nor upset her?'

'What - us?' said Billy blandly, righteously. 'No, we wouldn't dream of it, boy. She's a nice lady, like you say. Don't you worry about that, Davey. You go back to your whistling.' He turned to Jimmy and said, with quiet savagery: 'Yeah, a nice lady - very nice, but fancies a bit of dick now and then, like all of them. If Raven don't fancy her no more, I'm ready to oblige. That'll bloody show him who's who.'

Jimmy suddenly thought of the boy: 'Listen, Davey: we've had a nice chat, but you better go back to the galley, hadn't you? Welly might get cross with you.' And, as the boy strolled off, Jimmy sounded a note of caution again: 'You best be careful what you say in front of that *crwt*, Billy... You never know...'

'He's as *twp* as a pig, mun - don't understand nothing. Never mind him. He got a good eyeful, though, didn't he? Gave me a hard-on, just hearing him talk about it. Well, we'll see if she likes a bit of rough from a common Welsh AB instead of a dilly-dallying English toff. I reckon she must get a bit horny herself on times... We'll see, won't we?'

'*Duw,* Bill, you could get trouble from this, boy. *Real* trouble.'

I don't give a toss, mate. They can't hang us, can they? Can't put me in irons, nor give me fifty lashes, nor nothing.... Anyway, I don't care, so long as I get my own back on that bastard Raven, her darling lover-boy - and have a good screw into the bargain.'

'I dunno about "lover-boy", Bill. I'm not so sure about them two now. I think he's gone right off her, like - don't know why. And she's gone right off him too, for sure. Never even looks at him. And then again, she ain't much to look at now, is she? Not like back in Chile, when she had all her nice frocks and frills? And you remember how Raven carried on before she came - when we was in port? He was always off ashore looking for some crumpet, for some nice fresh greens, and a chance to dip his wick? Well, p'raps he needs someone a bit fancy-looking to get him hard? Anyway, one way or another, they've gone cold. I mean, he never takes her off into the bush for a walk, like you and I would, does he? He don't look at her, neither. Trust me, that little fling is all over.'

'Don't you believe it, Jim. Remember how he cuddled her in the boat - all the way here? He's still her bloke, I reckon, and she's his bint - only now it's all under cover.' Billy had a sudden flash of his friend's deep insight into motive: 'What if Grant's told them to act like that, eh? Maybe so that the rest of us poor sods wouldn't get too jealous?'

'Might be that, I s'pose, but I reckon he just don't fancy her no more.'

'Well, I do, Jim - I fancy her, by Christ I do! This place is driving me mad: no proper work, not getting anywhere, no going ashore for a bit of the other. Don't care what you say, I'm going to try my luck, mate.' He added, with casual brutality: 'As for her looks, you know what the English lads say - you don't look at the mantel-piece while you're poking the fire.'

'For God's sake, Bill, don't try it! She won't have you, and God knows what sort of trouble you'll get us into....'

Billy turned and looked at him with cool disdain: 'You're s'posed to be a mate of mine, but sometimes I reckon you're just a creeper and a wanker. At least if you come with me you can watch - you might enjoy seeing a proper man at work. You say she won't have me; p'raps she'll have to, like it or not. Then you'll have something to watch, won't you? We'll bunk off after breakfast tomorrow, when bosun ain't looking; no-one will notice.'

Jimmy was torn between his old loyalty to Billy - his only friend in the crew - and the fear of the dire consequences if the whole community turned on them. What might they do if Billy actually....? 'All right, I'll come, but I don't like it, Billy. Why don't we just get a good eyeful and come away without her knowing? I ain't having nothing to do with no rape - she ain't no cheap whore, whatever you say.'

'Rape?' said Billy. 'Who's talking about that? She'll like it, mun, once I get going - they all do really. Tomorrow, then, after breakfast.'

*

Eleanor had christened her private space on the island '*Cilfach Dawel* - the quiet cove - and loved it for being her very own place, known only - as she thought - to no-one else but Raven and Grant, who had been with her there on that very first morning. They, she knew, would never intrude.

Practically, it was her lavatory and bathroom, for she had not needed Curly's orations on hygiene. More importantly - spiritually - it had taken shape in her soul as a kind of shrine for private thoughts, and as a place in which to remember her parents. It looked out onto a broad reach of the long winding harbour, and she could imagine her father bringing a fine big barque up to anchor there. If she turned the other way, she took in the grassy, rock-strewn cliff slopes, the narrow valley snaking back to the great bare hills, the small stream that wound its way through the wide reed-bed to gurgle down the beach - a prospect compellingly like a score of such coves in her - and her parents' - beloved county of Pembrokeshire, at the end of Wales. She felt both their presences in *Cilfach Dawel*; neither had an earthly grave, which she could visit and decorate with fresh flowers, so with that she must be content. She had visions too of rare sunlit days in her childhood, when Dadi was home from the sea, and borrowed a neighbour's trap to take Mam and herself to Pwllgwaelod - just such a cove as this - so that she and her friend Bethan could play on the sand under Mam's watchful eye, for her father sometimes strayed across to the little stone-built inn, the 'Sailor's Safety', and sat outside on a bench in the warm sun with a glass of the local brew, chatting and laughing with old friends who had walked down from Dinas or Henllan.

Her eyes filled with tears as she remembered those distant golden days, but she tried, too, to recover that lost happiness, that feeling of total security - the feeling that this settled certainty of existence would go on forever. When, later, at school, she discovered Wordsworth, she found that he, in his own matchless way, expressed her own visions of such moments, when:

The earth, and every common sight,
To me did seem
Apparelled in celestial light,
The glory and the freshness of a dream.

Cilfach Dawel was emphatically no biblical Eden; it was lonely - with no Adam - desolate, generally grey, windy and chilly, but it was the nearest she would have to a paradise on this gloomy island; she did not, alas, know that her Eden had been betrayed by the inevitable fatal serpent - a serpent of total innocence and goodness, but nevertheless a betrayer.

Naked to the waist, she knelt by the brook's side, gasping as she splashed the icy water onto her face, her arms, her breasts, to wash away the stale, sweaty reek of her unwashed shirt. She had never before suffered the squalor of dirty clothes, and so welcomed the sting of cold clean water on her flesh. Then, as she dried herself, she hummed a tune she had heard so many times in Ebeneser Chapel - *Calon Lan* (A Pure Heart). Its simple, lovely melody brought to mind its words, and she found herself gently singing a phrase from its chorus:

Calon lan, yn llawn daioni
Techach yw na lili dlos...

The bland piety and morality of the words made her look inwards at her own soul. Was she always *'yn llawn daioni'* in the way she'd like to be? Emphatically not, she thought: she had treated John harshly, horribly, punishing him for her own bleak misery, and for days she had been harbouring a sullen grudge against Simon, deliberately avoiding any contact with him - even eye-contact; and all for what? For doing his duty as he saw it, however painful it was, for the sake of all. She must make amends for that today, and sincerely beg his pardon, even if that was uncongenial to her own proud spirit.

As she threw her head back to dry her hair, she caught sight of a thick stick of driftwood, whitened, smoothed and polished by sea and stones to an elegant beauty, but heavy and sound. Her lips twitched with amusement, but she felt remorse too: she had found that on the beach and put it there, leaning on a rock, as a safeguard against some possible lustful attack by one of the hands. She had even remembered a quaint old English word from some book she'd read as a child, and christened her weapon 'Cudgel'. Ridiculous, she thought, for in all these weeks no-one had attempted the least offence; but sinful too, for why should she be so suspicious and mistrustful of poor destitute men - mostly her own countrymen - even neighbours - whose minds were doubtless, like hers, on working to survive in this wilderness at the end of the earth?

She thought too of John, her lover, as forbidden to her now as Abelard was to Heloise, and her thoughts were a blend of love and shame. She had seen him at first as an alien, as an English toff - one of the *crachach* - who (she'd been sure, with all the shallow certainty of adolescence) looked down on her. But nearness had changed him in her eyes to a kind, loyal friend with whom she could laugh and be free to be fully a woman. That she should be with him for the rest of his or her life was now more fixed and unchangeable in her soul than anything else. And yet.... Yet she felt ashamed of the headlong rush of her blood, of her sensual obsession with his hard, beautiful body, of her furtive midnight visits to his cabin - to his bed - naked but for the flimsiest of silk nightgowns.

That animal lust - which had taken even Raven by surprise - had been clean contrary to everything she'd been taught about decency, chastity and restraint. When her father had found out about her visits, his tormented rage had driven him into calling her a tart and a whore, and, looking back now, calmly, she felt that those ugly, shameful words had been justified. Even more strongly, she felt bitter remorse at her abandonment of the teachings of her Christian faith; she was without doubt, in the Saviour's own words 'a whited sepulchre, beauteous outward, but within full of all uncleanness'. She must never again let her body lead her into grieving her God. Only when she was truly pure would she have peace of mind.

The silence and calm of her reverie were suddenly shattered by a harsh shriek, as a marsh bird shot up from among the reeds, screaming its panicky alarm call. An ugly fear stabbed into Eleanor's heart, and she leapt to her feet and stared across the waving buff-coloured plain of tall, dead, whispering reed-heads. But except for that soft whispering there was a silence, a silence that seemed itself menacing; a long, long silence. Yet something, someone, had made that bird fly up in terror.

She called, as firmly as she could: 'Who's there? Who

is it?' and was horrified to see two men in blue jerseys rise to their feet from among the reeds and move towards her. She was dismayed, but not surprised, to recognize Billy John Ffynnongroes and his sly crony, Jimmy Protheroe. Anger became mixed with her shock and terror: 'What do you want? What are you doing here? Are you spying on me? Go away at once!'

Billy, who of course led the way, gave a sickening smile and spread his arms wide in protest: 'Come on darling, that ain't a nice way to welcome friends, is it? We're on'y paying a social call, like. Thought you might be lonely down here, didn't we, Jim?'

Even in her fear, Eleanor could see that Protheroe was not, like Billy, bold and ingratiating, but full of uneasy tension, as he muttered: 'That's right, miss. We don't mean no harm, like.'

As Billy came close, she snatched up her blanket-towel and threw it over her shoulders, clutching it close across her body to hide her breasts from his leering gaze. 'O no,' he said, 'don't cover them up, darling. They're lovely, they are, and I ain't seen nothing like them since we left Australia. And there's a better thing yet, ain't there, under them trousers you got on? Come on, give a couple of poor bloody sailors a bit of a treat, isn't it? They deserve it, don't they, working so hard all day...? Just a quick look - that's all we want.'

She felt a wave of revulsion at the gross request: '*Ach y fi!* You're rotten cowards, sneaking up on me and saying disgusting things. Go away, or I'll...'

'Or you'll *what,* darling?' His voice hardened. 'I'm not letting you run off, and you can holler as much as you like - there's no bugger to hear you. Come on, let's have a little cuddle, eh? You'll like it once we get started. You did with Raven, didn't you? You let that bloody English toff feel your little pussy. You didn't holler then, did you? So let's not mess about. Come on!'

Eleanor's obvious fear, revulsion and helpless defiance stirred Billy's thick, earthy lust to intolerable heights, and at once words turned to brutal action. Stepping close, he tore off her blanket and crushed her bare breasts against his coarse jumper and sought to kiss her, at the same time forcing his right leg between hers till his bony knee butted painfully against her groin.

Her only reply was not in words, but in the reaction of any desperate cornered animal: jerking her head to and fro to avoid his kiss, she suddenly brought it down and over to her left, and buried her sharp teeth in his bare wrist. He let go with a cry of pain and fury and stood back, glancing at the blood tricking from his arm.

'*Iesu Mawr!* You bloody little vixen! You're going to get it now, you can be fucking sure of that!' He drew his left arm across and gave her a heavy, back-handed blow on the face which made her stagger back, sobbing with pain. 'See?' he said, his face close, glaring. 'That's what you'll get if you try to muck me about - a bloody good hiding.'

Sheer fury had now replaced fear in Eleanor; she returned his glare and spat full in his face, hissing at him: 'Dirty swine! You won't...' But she got no further, for, hooking one leg behind hers, like a bar-room brawler, he pushed hard at her chest and sent her sprawling, half-stunned, back in the rough tufts of alien grass.

He began to unbuckle his belt, and said over his shoulder: 'Right... You ready, Jim? Come on, hold that snotty bitch down for me while I get my cock out, will you? You can have a go when I've finished. Give her another good clout if she struggles.'

But he spoke to the empty air, for Protheroe, whey-faced, teeth chattering with terror, was fifty yards off, scuttling like a rabbit back through the reeds.

'O, he's gone, has he, the yellow rat? Never mind, that won't help you, darling. You'll keep still and open up them nice long legs for me in a minute, or by Christ you'll be sorry.' His lust for her was now swallowed up by a reckless hatred of her, her lover, of everybody else on the island - or in the world, for that matter. Kneeling, his legs splayed across her loins, he spoke quietly, with a cruel, deadly urgency: 'I'm going to have you, you slut; I'm going to shag you good and proper, and you're not gonna struggle no more, nor you're not gonna tell a bloody soul afterwards. I got a knife here,' and he drew his heavy sailor's sheath-knife to show her its glittering blade. 'It's sharp, darling, it's sharp. You thrash about and annoy me any more, and you're gonna lose that pretty face of yours for life - see? Not even that lousy English skunk Raven will fancy you then, will he? So come on, let's get these old trousers off of you.'

With a sudden slash of his knife he cut her leather belt and, shuffling backwards, hauled her trousers to her knees, taking her drawers with them. He gave a crow of triumph: 'Ah! That's more like it! There's a pretty little bush, isn't it? Don't you make any more fuss now, or you'll get it good and proper, like I said. You just be a good girl, and I won't hurt you. You'll like it. You'll feel what a real man can do.'

Till now, Eleanor had kept a defiant silence; her

lower body trapped by his weight, she could only writhe to and fro with her torso, and push vainly at his shoulders, but at this final outrage to her body she let loose a long, loud 'No-o-o!' - a high scream of despair that echoed from the cliffs, and sent seabirds rocketing up from their roosts.

Her terror fed his towering lust, and he grinned savagely: 'Screech all you like, *cariad*, no-one will hear....' He broke off, appalled, for beneath the cries of the birds he could hear, from the far end of the reed-bed, another cry, a human cry, not of despair but of fury. He was under the curse of Cain - hated by all, and doomed always to fail. He leapt up, buckling his belt again, and said with an animal snarl: 'O, that'll be your fancy-man, won't it? Come to spoil our nice bit of fun, damn and blast him! Never mind, I'll soon fix him, and then we'll see who gets to shag you.'

John Raven burst out of the reeds, running at full tilt. Gasping for breath, he took in at once the dark-clad man standing grinning, the girl flat on her back in the rough grass, her near-naked flesh startlingly white; he heard her terrified cries 'John! John! Help me!' Without a word, and without slackening his speed, he rushed at Billy; his old boxing skills came back unbidden, and with fearful accuracy and strength he caught Billy with a right-hander to the jaw, his forward speed adding to the muscular force behind the blow, his hard knuckles thudding against bone. Billy, letting out a yell of surprise and pain, crashed to the ground alongside Eleanor, who nimbly rolled away from him and sprang to her feet, pulling her trousers back up again, for the instinct of modesty drove her, even in this horrible crisis.

John Raven then made his first - potentially disastrous - mistake: he behaved like a sportsman, a gentleman. He acted as if in a boxing-ring at his college, supervised by a stern referee under the Marquess of Queensberry's Rules. He stood back, fists poised, and let his opponent come round from the blow. He said: 'Had enough, have you? Want some more? Get up, you lousy bastard.' He should, of course, have waded in while Billy was still floored, and given him enough brutal kicks to head and body to ensure that, beaten to a pulp, he stayed down for a very long time. He forgot - perhaps didn't know - the first and only rule of unarmed combat: that there were no rules - it was either him or you.

Billy, on the other hand, was not only hardened by a lifetime of drunken brawls, he was also infinitely cunning. He got painfully to his knees, holding his jaw, and said: 'Christ, brassbounder, you got a damn good right there, you have, and no mistake. I don't want no more of…..' Then, in mid-sentence, he hurled himself forward and upward from his crouch, and with all his weight behind his spring, butted his head into Raven's unguarded abdomen, so that he, with a gasp and a yell of surprise, fell flat on his back, and in an instant Billy was kneeling over him, pinning him to the turf with one hand, while with the other hand he dealt Raven crunching blows to the head, his hard knuckles hammering Raven's head into the wet turf. Jammed between the thick tufts of grass, his head was a fixed target, for Raven could not ride the punches by moving it.

As Raven lay there, winded and only half-conscious, Billy drew out the knife with which he'd threatened Eleanor, and enjoyed a moment of sadistic triumph: 'I nearly carved up your bloody mate Grant once, up the River Plate - remember? I'd have fixed him proper if them dago cops hadn't turned up and beaten the shit out of me. Well, there ain't none of them here, are there, so never mind your fancy boxing, by God I'll put my mark on....'

He got no further with his cruel threat. He had forgotten that Eleanor was behind him, and that she was a strong young woman with a score to settle with him. Nor did he know anything about the formidable piece of timber called Cudgel. Naked to the waist, a bruised but fierce Amazon, Eleanor had snatched up the beautiful sea-carved weapon; she now drew it back over her head and, with a wordless savage scream, swung it vertically, two-handed, to land with a sickening dull crack on the back of Billy's bare head. Without a sound he crumpled sideways and Raven was able to scramble groggily to his feet. As he did so, the club once more landed viciously, this time on Billy's upper arm. While Raven stood, still dazed and winded, irresolute, two more heavy blows thudded on the seaman's inert body. Raven looked, almost in fear, at Eleanor, hideously transformed into a harpy by her hysterical, uncontrollable rage. Her hair was tangled, wild, still wet, plastered across her head and face, with brown blades of dead grass stuck in it from her fall; one eye was closed to a slit by a huge bruise, and blood trickled down her cheek from a cut made by a ring on Billy's finger; her teeth showed in a face drawn back, contorted by a berserk grin, and her breasts heaved, for her struggles had robbed her of breath. Her wild, animal exertions had sent her trousers sliding to the ground. She was a naked Fury in the grimmest classical mode, and her dark, pitiless eyes gleamed and blazed... murder!

CHAPTER NINE

'Raven, you fool! *For God's sake stop her!* She'll kill him!' Grant's voice was high, panicky, breathless. He and two of the hands, running flat out, were pounding through the reeds, fifty yards away. He had seen, from far off, the white club rising and falling, and now, moments later and close up, was astonished at what he saw - that the victim was now the savage attacker, that the previous attacker was prone on the rough turf, and that the usually strong and active Raven appeared to be standing by, helpless.

As for Raven, he was shaken and winded by the combat; he was only half-conscious from Billy's blows to his head, and was now transfixed by the present horror, and by his mental vision of the even more terrible danger that Eleanor had escaped. It had all happened so quickly - in minutes - and the fortunes of battle had changed so bewilderingly too. But Grant's voice brought him back to reality, to the present crisis.

Risking a severe blow from the club himself, he stepped across the fallen would-be rapist as Eleanor raised the heavy stick above her head for another blow, and, thrusting himself against her naked body, reached up to grasp her wrists and halt the swing. Silent, sobbing for breath, she struggled for a second or so to complete the blow, and Raven was amazed at the strength lent to her arms by her fear and vengeful rage. Then his firm grip, the stillness he imposed, and his urgent cry of: 'No, Nelli, no! Stop now, for God's sake!' brought her back to something like herself, to a stark realization of what she was - a naked savage about to batter a helpless fellow-human to death.

She let her cudgel go, to thud into the grass, and, as

Raven released her arms, sank to her knees, raised her hands to cover her battered face, and, indifferent to her nakedness, bowed forward and began to weep uncontrollably, her tears accompanied by high wails, by sobs that turned into screams. Her attacker lay inert, harmless for the present, but she was still feeling the horror of his threats, of his brutal callous strength, of the cruel knife-point, with which he had scratched her cheek, as a mere foretaste of the mutilation he intended. Raven knelt by her, his arm round her shaking body, and, as Grant and the two seamen ran up, tried to quiet and comfort her, like a mother with a terrified child. 'Ssh, ssh, Nelli. You're safe now. I'm here, and Simon's here with two chaps to help him. This utter swine can't hurt you now - not ever again. Don't cry any more, darling.'

The three other men stood respectfully back, silent and shocked, and full of a deep loathing for the shipmate who had so obscenely abused a young woman whom they admired so much. She, like her mother before her, had nursed Davey through a bout of typhus, seriously risking her own health. More bitterly still, they remembered how her mother had nursed Billy John himself through the same plague, and had died as a result. And yet he had tried to rape her daughter, to treat her worse than he would a whore. It was lucky for Billy John that Grant and Raven - men of some authority - were still there. The two ABs, the brothers Tom and Eirian Evans, from the Parrog, the little harbour in Newport, were big, hard men. They had known Nelli Roberts since she was a toddler, shopping with her mother in the town; had they been alone then with Billy he would not have got to his feet for a very long time - if ever.

Grant spoke to them coldly, callously: 'Get that thing on its feet again, boys. Has he come round yet? No? Very well, drag him over to the stream and stick his head in it. That should do it. When you've got him going, march him up to the hut. I don't think he'll give you any trouble, but if he does you'll know what to do, eh?'

'By Christ we will, sir,' said Eirian. 'Come on, you bastard, you! Get up!' But Billy lay, still stunned by Eleanor's first fearsome blow. They seized his upper arms and began to drag him to the stream, but stopped when he let out a high scream of agony.

'Hold on, lads,' said Grant, kneeling beside Billy. 'Yes, I thought so: she's broken his right arm for him, and serve him bloody right, too. I'll have to set it as best I can, I suppose, and get bosun to make me a splint - though why the hell I should bother with his useless carcass I don't know. He wouldn't do it for me. Anyway, that seems to have brought him round, so away you go now; we'll follow.'

Eleanor meanwhile had begun to shiver violently as the sweat of the fight dried in the cool breeze on her bare flesh. 'Come on, Nelli,' said Raven. 'Let's get your clothes back on. You'll freeze if we don't.' Gently he pulled her shirt over her still-shaking body, then, having drawn her trousers back on, took some twine from his pocket to keep them up, finally tugging on her thick jersey. 'There, now... is that better?'

She nodded dumbly, then threw herself against him, clasping him, shaking his body too with her sobs. At last she could speak: 'John, thank you, thank you... It was so horrible - what he said, and the things he did to me. If you hadn't come he would have...'

'Ssh, Nelli, ssh… Don't think about it any more. It's over now; we did come.'

Looking over his shoulder, she became aware of Grant standing near: 'Thank you too, Simon…And Tom and Eirian Parrog were here as well, weren't they?'

'They were, Eleanor,' said Simon, 'and like them, I know the rest of the crowd will be behind you to a man about this appalling attack. And now, my dear girl, I have to apologize sincerely to you for this disgusting affair. I never thought it would come to this so soon, and so violently… But I should have seen that you needed protecting while you were down here alone. In future you will be; you'll see to that, won't you, old son?'

'I will,' said Raven. 'By God I will. But I'm sure, Nelli, that you need have no more fears, no fear of Billy John or anybody else.'

Grant said, with an attempt at some cheerfulness: 'You'll be glad to know that you've fractured that swine's upper arm.' Then he caught sight of Billy's knife lying in the grass. He picked it up. 'As for this, he said, 'he won't be needing it any more.' And, holding the heavy knife by the point of its blade, he drew his arm back in a cricketer's throw and sent the knife flying in a high, spinning, glittering arc, to land far off in the boggy soil among the reeds, where it would rust and rot away to the end of Time. 'There, Nelli, 'he said, smiling. 'How about that for a throw? Now you see why, when I played cricket, they always put me to field on the boundary.'

She attempted a smile, and wiped the tears from her swollen face with the back of her hand. 'Now then, John,' said Grant, 'you'd better find some nice clean long grass, and bathe Nelli's bruise with cold water before it gets any bigger. Perhaps then she could do the same for you. You're looking pretty battered too. When you're ready to talk, Eleanor, I'm afraid you and John will have to tell me exactly what happened. The other committee members and I will have to pass judgment, so we will need to know all the facts. We won't ask you to speak about it in public, you'll be glad to know. As for that beast, I'll put him under guard; I don't think your Newport friends Tom and Eirian will let him do any more mischief. As for you, would you like to rest now, in your bed? I'll see you're not disturbed. I only wish I had some medicine or other to calm you and give you sleep.'

'No thank you,' said Eleanor stoutly. 'I'd rather do anything than sit or lie idle and brood over this. I'm not sure you understand, either of you, why I wept so bitterly just now. It was not just the horror of being beaten and nearly raped, - of becoming just a sink for that creature's lust - it was the terrible guilt I felt - still feel - at my own actions - at nearly murdering a fellow human being, however wicked. Worse still, I was feeling a kind of fierce, terrible joy in doing it. As you said to John when you first arrived, I *would* have killed him.'

Raven put his arm tenderly around her: 'Come, Nelli, let's go back, so that you can rest. Don't torment yourself by talking about the horrors you've suffered.'

'No, John. I must first tell you the thoughts that are already tormenting me. I call myself a Christian, a follower and worshipper of Jesus, who forgave even the Romans who were torturing him to death. In my madness, I came so close to being a murderess, and only you stopped me. Yet even that revolting wretch Billy never tried to kill me. Killing must after all be the ultimate crime - much worse than rape. A rapist is vile, but he only makes a woman do what she does most willingly - even eagerly - with a man she loves. I need to pray long and earnestly for forgiveness, and in the meantime,' she looked Grant in the eye with a trace of her old spirit, 'in the meantime, I thank you and John and the Thomas boys from the bottom of my heart for saving me from disgusting degradation. But instead of resting, once you've finished with your enquiry, your trial of Billy John, I'm going, as arranged, with my good friend Davey to his onion-patch in the woods to fetch back a decent load, and then he and I will peel and chop some of them for your supper. Life must go on, and a good meal is an important part of life.'

Her spirits revived a little more as they left the fateful beach and began to walk to the camp, Grant tactfully walking some way ahead. 'John,' she said, 'I had no time to pray for rescue, yet you came like an answer to a prayer, and well ahead of the others. How did that happen?'

'You have your good friends bosun and Davey to thank for that, darling,' he said. 'Billy and Jimmy were so eager to get down to your beach that they didn't hide their axes properly in the wood. Bosun luckily came across them, shoved into a bush, quickly found out who was missing from his wood-cutting party, and came and told me. I was down by the galley, and I at once glanced across and saw that you were not there washing-up with Isaac and Davey. I called to the doctor "Where's Miss Eleanor?" and he said, "Gone down to her beach, man, like every day". I told him that Billy and Jimmy were missing, and Davey - God bless him - piped up: "O yes, they said last night they was going to pay a call on her - keep her company, like". I didn't wait to hear any more - I just legged it down here as fast as I could. It was a few minutes, I suppose, before Simon heard, and roped in a couple of hands to come with him.'

'O, bless little Davey,' Eleanor said devoutly. 'But for him I might...' She was, of course, unaware of the terrible irony: that Davey had been first the unwitting cause of her ordeal, and then - equally unwittingly - the cause of her rescue. She did not know that, in the clouded innocence of his mind, he served both good and evil, God and Satan, equally well.

*

'Are we all here? Very well, then. I'm going to make short work of this, you two. We're not going to have some farce of a trial. You both know what you did, and so do we. Miss Roberts and Mr Raven have told us all we need to know.'

Grant was sitting magisterially at the end of the long table in the hut, flanked by the other four members of the cabinet; at the other end, Billy John and Protheroe stood under the guard of the two burly Thomases; Billy, dazed, and with his face bruised and twisted in pain, clutched at the table's edge for support. With the cabinet sat Eleanor, ashy-pale at being forced to re-live those ghastly minutes at Cilfach Dawel.

'Just one minute, though, Mr Grant,' said Kellock, always the thinker, and never the man to be reticent. 'You got them two standing there as if they'd both done the same thing; but they haven't, have they? Protheroe hooked it the minute John started the worst of his dirty work. We know that, cos Mr Raven told us that he saw Jimmy dive into the reeds out of his way. So we ought to deal with him separate-like.'

'Thass right, mister,' said Welly. 'We got to do it proper. We got to be fair, even to this kinda trash.'

'Yes, very well, I'll agree to that. Protheroe, wait outside. One of you lads, go and watch him. Now then for you, John: you almost make me wish I were a captain in the good old days - Nelson's days. Then I could have had you tied up to a grating and got the bosun to take the skin off your back with the cat-o-nine-tails. However, we're not allowed to do that nowadays, but it's a pity, because in all my days at sea I've never met such a specimen as you: always moaning, always a rebel, always against anyone who has to give you an order; sullen at best, recklessly violent at worst, as I know to my cost, and as you showed again today. Only this time it was much worse: you laid your filthy hands on a decent young woman.'

Billy demonstrated his recklessness again, saying with a leering grin: 'Decent? Her? You ask your mate Raven about that.'

White with rage, Raven leapt to his feet, but Kellock laid a hand on his arm: 'Steady, mister! Don't start nothing. We'll weigh him off good and proper, only we got to do it right, cos one day this will all have to be gone through in a court on shore somewhere.'

'We'll make him pay for what he's done,' said Grant, 'don't you worry about that, Mr Raven. In the meantime, John, you can shut your dirty mouth and listen. You seem to have forgotten something. We're not aboard ship now; we're on land, and you've committed three serious crimes on New Zealand soil: you violently attacked Miss Roberts, you attempted to rape her, and you assaulted, and threatened serious bodily harm, both to her and to a superior officer. That's mutiny, in any country in the world. So when we get to New Zealand, I shall be breaking the law myself if I don't hand you over to the police there, with an account of your crimes, and a list of witnesses to prove them. After that, it will be up to their lawyers and juries and judges to decide what happens to you. My guess is that it will be a very long time indeed before you see the outside of a prison cell again. And I can tell you that no-one on this island - except perhaps for your precious crony Protheroe - will feel the slightest sympathy for you. Do you understand me?'

Billy, his shoulders drooped, his head bowed, nodded in silence. The stuffing had gone out of him as he at last faced the bitter cost of his lust: the prospect - which he had not even considered - of long years in a cold stone cell, with a hard bed, and nothing but a bucket for a privy, a world away from his homeland. And he had heard of the hatred many convicts had for rapists, and the brutal treatment they meted out to them. He was already hated and despised by his shipmates; soon, even fellow-criminals would be his enemies.

'However,' Grant went on, 'it might - and I say *might* - make a difference to the length of your sentence if I were able to say to a court that you had shown regret for your crimes and behaved properly since. Whether you do that will be up to you to decide. Now then, for the present: well, if I were aboard ship I would put you somewhere down the hold, in irons. Here, I haven't got a hold, and I haven't got irons, so this is what we've decided: you will be on bread and water only for at least a month; you will sleep under guard in the galley, for you're not fit to mix with decent hands; I've fixed up your arm as best I can, and when you are able to work again you will work extra hours. Now I'm not going to threaten even you, but if you think for one moment that I can't punish you more than that while we're here, by God you'll find you're wrong. Any more mischief from you, and you'll wish you were in a cell - or dead! Anything to say?'

John shook his bowed head in silence. 'Very well, take him away, Thomas, and watch him! And tell your brother to bring that skunk Protheroe in.'

'One moment!' As Billy John and his guard left, everyone was startled to hear the firm, clear voice of Eleanor. She went on, her head erect, her tone bold: 'I was one of the injured parties, so I have a right to speak. Let Protheroe go free.' There was a gasp of surprise and protest from all of the cabinet, but before they could speak, Eleanor had risen to her feet, speaking with fiery emotion: 'Let him go free, I say! Warn him, forbid him to consort with John Ffynnongroes, but then let him go. As you have heard from Mr Raven and me, he ran away as soon as he saw what John intended. He did nothing to harm me.'

Grant interrupted: 'Yes, but….'

'Wait! I have not finished. Like many on this island, I am a Christian, and I strive - often failing very badly - to follow my Saviour's example, in this case, of forgiveness. Did He not, as I said before, forgive his torturers while dying in agony at their callous hands? "Father, forgive them, for they know not what they do" were his words. Is it not at least possible that, a year from now, Protheroe will be a better man if we now show him mercy? Let him be judged by his future conduct.'

'Yes, that's all very well, miss,' said Kellock with his usual pedantic, analytical tone, 'but never mind stories outa the Bible; we got to deal with what's happening *now, here.* I reckon there wasn't no morality nor goodness about what Jimmy done. He scarpered because he was scared, that's all - scared of the consequences.'

Despite her respect for him, Eleanor replied to Kellock with anger, her face flushed: 'And who am I, who are you, who are all of you, to sit here as models of holy virtue? We Christians are told by the scriptures to fear God himself. Which of you - Christians or not - can say that you never refrained from some dubious action because of your fear of the consequences - punishment, disgrace, dismissal, or humiliation - if your guilt was detected? Let him who is without sin cast the first stone.' She paused, and there was total silence. 'You see? We are none of us pure, holy, uncorrupted, so remember that when you are passing judgment.'

Impressed by her passion, if not by her biblical references, Grant nodded and said: 'Considering what you have been through, Miss Roberts, I think you show extraordinary generosity, and I'm minded - if my fellow members agree - to take a chance and follow your advice. Bring Protheroe in now. We may yet make a man of him, even if he has been a mere toady and crony to a vile bully, but he will have to mend his ways. I shall forbid him to exchange one word with John Ffynnongroes; it may be that that will not only improve him, but also make John himself less dangerous. I've always suspected that Protheroe was the brains behind their previous escapades. We shall see. Bring him in again.'

*

If Grant and Raven had hoped that the 'trial' and punishment of Billy would heal Eleanor's spirit and cheer her, they were gravely mistaken. The determination and stoicism she had shown during the hearing could not last, once the proceedings were over, and, even while busy with her domestic chores, she was unable to banish from her mind the nightmarish thoughts of the vicious assault on her body and mind. Billy's bitter jibe about her 'decency' had also awoken her shame about her previous heedless, wanton behaviour with Raven; deep within her soul, she felt that his jeering was justified. To be regarded with contempt by a creature so despicable as Billy was to accept guilt and deepest despair as no more than her deserts. So she sank into a sump of silence, misery and the anxious tension of unfocused fear. Grant, in desperation, told Raven to forget his previous command, and keep company with her as much as he or she liked, but even that had no effect. Even John, though as loving and sympathetic as a man could be, got from her only silence, tears, and sullen, monosyllabic answers to every question or remark. She avoided, too, all physical contact with him. There were no more grateful embraces like the one just after her rescue. Every day she seemed to sink lower into black despair, and would hardly speak even to the other people she liked most, Welly and Davey.

The catharsis, the abrupt final crisis, came one evening a week or so after the trial. Grant and Raven were chatting in the hut after work, while the hands sprawled outside in the rare warm sunshine of the lengthening day. The door to the store-room - now Eleanor's bedroom -

opened; Eleanor came out, dishevelled and white-faced. She spoke curtly to Raven: 'Come outside. I want to talk to you in private.'

She led the way through the scattered crowd, who fell silent as she passed, and down the path leading to the beach. Halfway down she suddenly stopped and turned to face him; her left eye and cheek were still disfigured by a dark bruise, and her hair straggled, dirty and unkempt, to her shoulders. She spoke with the dead coldness of a robot: 'Have you got your knife with you?'

'Yes, of course, but…'

'Give it to me.'

'My knife? Why on earth do you…'

She cut in savagely: 'Don't babble and argue. Give it to me. Is it sharp?'

'Yes, very sharp, but…'

She held her hand out in silence, and Raven reluctantly drew the knife from the sheath at his belt. 'Here you are… but why? My God, you're not going to…?'

'Don't be so damned ridiculous, man. Don't worry, you'll get it back. And me, for what that's worth. Stay here.'

She strode off, and Raven sat on a damp fallen tree, gnawed by anxiety and self-doubt: should he have refused her the loan of that dangerous weapon? What in the world did she intend to do? In her present dark, frantic mood there was no telling.

After some fifteen minutes of sick fear he saw her approaching; saw her with horror, for all her long dark hair - hair that had been so silkily beautiful in glossy waves that subtly gleamed in the light - all that hair had been crudely hacked off, down almost to the scalp, so that her head was crowned by rough, jagged stubble, with here and there an ugly tuft. 'There,' she said, with a ghastly smile of triumph, 'Saint Paul said: "If a woman have long hair, it is her glory". Like a fool, I always liked that passage when I read it, and felt stupidly vain, for I fancied I saw myself in his words, and used to admire myself in shop windows, but now I thought it was time I lost a bit of my glory.'

For a moment, Raven was too dumbfounded to speak. At last he said: 'Good God, Eleanor, darling, whatever made you do such a terrible harm to yourself? Why do you seem almost to hate your own body? Your hair was so lovely...'

He went to embrace her, but she shook him off and stepped sharply back: 'No, keep away, John! I don't want to be treated like a silly sick child! I don't want anyone - any man - to touch me.... Not after that filthy ruffian...'

'But I love you, Nelli, and you and I were once so ...so close, as lovers. I want to help you. So does everybody.'

'No-one can help me - no-one - all the while I'm on this horrible island with that creature.'

'But he's been stopped from hurting you. He'll be under guard and he'll be watched, day and night. He can't do you any more harm.'

Yes, but I shall have to keep seeing him, and he will see me. He's evil and he's cunning. Some day, somehow, he may find a way to attack me again. And don't forget, he hates you, John, more than ever now. *Ach y fi!* How I hate it that one of your names is the same as his. I can't bear to hear it now.'

'That's easy, Nelli; call me Jack; that's what I'm always called at home.'

Calmer now, less frantic, she gave him the ghost of a smile. 'Very well then, Jack it is. But, Jack, I am still more miserable and more afraid than I have ever been in my life. I'm desperate, or I wouldn't have done this to myself. I don't think you, or any man, can imagine what it is like to be the object of this hidden, poisonous lust. But perhaps now at least none of the crowd here will fancy me, as you men say. After all, there are many more male creatures on this island. Suppose one of the others...'

Raven shook his head vigorously: 'Now, Nelli, you are talking nonsense. The crowd are all on your side. Left to themselves, they'd have punished Billy much more than we did, believe me. I reckon the Thomas boys would have finished him off. Nelli, there is no chance of any further harm to you, and anyway, the steamer from New Zealand will be here soon. We've been here a month....'

'Yes, a month, and there's no sign of the wretched thing yet. Remember, we were told by the notice on the door on the first day that she would be late because she was in dock, and I remember Simon himself saying that once a ship was in a dockyard she might be a long time getting out again. And you have to remember too that no-one, no-one in the world, knows that we are here. It might be another month - two months - before she turns up. And in the meantime I'm being driven mad, while you - and I dare say all the rest of you men - think I'm just being a silly irrational woman.' She paused, her face stony, and then blurted out: 'What about Yorry Jones' idea? You remember - the idea he suggested at the general meeting? That we send a boat to Bluff Harbour to tell them we're here? Then they'd charter a rescue ship, I'm sure, especially if they knew there were so many of us here. After all, the supplies of biscuit and flour won't last for ever, with so many mouths to feed. Listen, Jack: you and I could go in that boat - and I suppose one or two others. You'd have to be there to navigate it, and if you go, then I must too. I'm not a bit loving at the moment, I know, for I hate the whole world, and especially myself; but you are a part of me now. I'm a repellent specimen at the moment, but as long as you want me, I will not let anybody or anything separate us - ever. And I know how to manage a boat under sail - I've spent hours sailing, at home in Newport. We could find others to come, I'm sure.'

'Now you really are being crazy, Nelli. Remember what Simon said at the time: it might well be throwing lives away to no purpose.'

'Yes, it might. But I wonder if you, and Simon too, for that matter, realize how dangerous it is in other ways if we just stay here, week after week? Never mind evil human actions, what about all the other dangers? Suppose someone gets badly injured while working in the wood with an axe or a saw? Suppose some disease were to break out - dysentery, cholera, pneumonia, for instance? Especially pneumonia, in a cold wet place like this island; I've seen some of the men coming back from the forest with their clothes soaking wet - they're so careless, sometimes. None of us has a shred of medical skill or knowledge, and we've no medicines, nor even bandages. You see? There are dangers either way, not counting the possible evil actions of that man - and maybe others. You say the crowd are with me, but you cannot see into all their souls. Only God can do that.'

'Yes, but Nelli, we are not going to be sailing at Newport on a fine sunny day in the summer; we're in fifty degrees of south latitude. Up to windward of this island, the nearest land is Cape Horn, thousands of miles off. The waves here can sweep all the way round the globe, with no land to stop them or break their force. Dammit, you've seen for yourself that, even in a brand-new three-thousand-ton barque, well handled, it's by no means safe. When it blows hard - as it often does around here - you can get seas forty feet high or more, with breaking crests. Every year, big, well-found ships disappear; so, for a small boat...'

She abruptly broke in on his warnings: 'How far is it to Bluff Harbour?'

'About three hundred miles, but...'

'How long would it take us to get there?'

He thought for a moment, calculating: 'Well, in ideal conditions - a decent beam wind and no breaking seas - say four days. Three, if you were very lucky, but...'

'Never mind all the "buts"; we'd have a sporting chance, wouldn't we?'

'A chance, yes, but a damned sight bigger chance of being drowned.'

'I know that, of course.' She was silent a moment, brooding, and then burst out, angrily: 'You don't see, do you? You're so blind to everything but winds and seas and ships and ropes and sails! You're as obtuse as most men when it comes to understanding women! You don't begin to see that, if I'm with you, I'd a hundred times rather face the dangers of the sea and the wind than live in this cursed place, where evil, vile hatred may fester in secret, in silence. The sea, the wind - they are just the mighty forces of Nature; they are not for us or against us. If it is God's will, I'll survive them; if not, so be it. I'm not afraid to meet my Maker. I'm prepared to risk sudden death at the hand of Nature to avoid the dull, endless, dark misery that I endure on this godforsaken island.' She added, with a sudden spurt of petulant, spiteful malice: 'Of course, if you're too frightened, I suppose I'll have to put up with it.'

Raven, stung into anger by her taunt, dropped his sympathetic tone: 'By God, that's a cruel, rotten thing to say to someone you claim to love! Don't start chucking insults at me, just because I don't instantly agree with you! I'll face whatever has to be faced as well as most men, but I'm a sailor - a professional. The sea has been my life for years. I know fifty times more about it than you do. You say I'll have to be there to navigate, but I won't be able to navigate properly, because I haven't got the instruments I need for that. I know that at sea you have to weigh things up sensibly - not make wild thoughtless gestures. For instance, you and I could never make that voyage on our own; we'd need to find at least two others mad enough to come with us. So your hare-brained scheme might chuck away three other lives, as well as yours. But if you think I wouldn't risk my life to help or save you, then by God, you're obtuse too - you don't begin to understand me. Christ, we wouldn't have your galley if the brassbounders and I hadn't taken a hell of a chance, going back to the wreck! But of course, if you think I'm just a coward, you'd better not have anything more to do with me, had you?'

His rage made her realize how clumsy, thoughtless and cruel her words had been. She softened, and put her hand out to hold his: 'I'm so sorry, *cariad*.... So sorry. ...I didn't really mean that - I was just frustrated, and you are right to be angry with me - that was a cruel thing to say. Please forgive me. But all the same, I mean all the rest of it, and I'm going to suggest my scheme to Simon to-morrow.'

'Very well, Nelli; talk to him. But I can tell you now what he'll say.'

She gave him a look of defiance, but of a defiance that was friendly now, and no longer bitter: 'Really, Jack? Well, we shall see, shan't we? You're a fine young sailor, as you say yourself, so modestly; but you're not Admiral of the Fleet yet, are you? Nor have you the divine power to read the minds of other men. We shall see, Jack, we shall see. Tomorrow.'

CHAPTER TEN

John Raven had been shocked, shaken to the core, by Eleanor's savage destruction of her hair and her looks; now she herself was to be not only shocked, but severely tested too, early the next day, before she had had a chance to speak to Grant.

She was busy, soon after dawn, in the galley. Bosun had ingeniously knocked up a rough table with sawn planks from one of the bigger, straighter trees, and Eleanor was bending over it, beheading and gutting some of the previous day's catch of hake for breakfast. She heard raised voices from outside the galley, and stopped work to listen. In her present state, every unusual noise was an alarm. She had been aware, since daylight, of the astonishment and pity in the looks she'd received from the doctor and Davey, when they saw the ruin of her hair. Tactfully, they had said nothing, but their very tact made her feel the pressure she was under – the pressure of being the centre of everyone's attention. So she was sure that the argument outside was to do with her.

She was right, for she heard Welly say, in the loudest and fiercest of whispers: 'No, shove off, you! You t'ink she want to talk to a low-down louse like you, after what you done? You mad, man – so *git!*'

She moved to look outside. Welly, his back to her, was waving the big frying-pan like a club. Backing warily away from him, white-faced and pleading, was - of all people – Jimmy Protheroe. 'Just for a minute, doctor, only a minute! I swear to God I won't say nothing nor do nothing wrong to her. I just want to...'

'You ain't saying nuttin', and you ain't doing nuttin'! You just gonna haul your dirty rotten arse outa here before I….'

But before he could finish his tirade, Eleanor cut in, nervously but firmly: 'Wait, Welly! Let him speak. He can do no harm to me here. Protheroe, say what you need to say, and then go. You can't expect me to want to talk with you, can you?'

'No miss, no. I don't expect nothing. I don't deserve nothing. But I just want to say what's on my mind. Then I'll go.'

'Very well. Say it, and have done. I've work to do here.'

'Right, miss, it's this.' He gulped nervously, brushing back the lank black hair from his face, his words coming in stuttering bursts; he was pale, fearful, aware of the menacing presence of the powerful Jamaican behind him. 'For any part I played in…in what happened down at the beach, I'm sorry, sorry from the bottom of my heart. I'd give anything to be back two days ago, and act different this time. I tried hard to persuade Billy not to... to do it – honest I did. Going down there to spy on you was a dirty thing to do, I know, and I can't get out of that, except to say sorry. But I didn't want Billy to... to harm you, like, and you know that I never laid a finger on you. I never even wanted you to know we was there, but you know Billy. He got me mixed up in what he done…I was always a bit afraid of him, like… But that's finished now… I've finished with him for good. I don't care if he gets hold of me one day and beats me up – I've finished with him. I've been a fool and a dirty rat – same as the doctor says – and I'm sorry, miss. I can't say more than that. I never realized that sooner or later, Billy would get me mixed up in something so bad as this. Well, I can't expect you to forgive me …not now, anyway…but p'raps one day…'

Listening to his halting words, Eleanor had been struggling with her own feelings towards this abject culprit. Her first feelings of anger and revulsion began to ebb as she heard his incoherent pleas. She realized how much he was suffering from shame and humiliation, and how much this public confession had cost this normally glib, self-assured, confident man. She was disturbed too by the unexpectedness of it; she had expected no more than sullen silence and avoidance from Protheroe, and here he was at her feet, so to speak, begging for mercy. She had preached to them all about Christian forbearance and mercy only yesterday; now she herself was being sorely tried. She'd always wanted to be *yn llawn daioni* – full of goodness – and follow her Saviour's example, but by heaven it was hard!

She mustered up a calm, neutral manner; it was the best she could do: 'Very well. You are right, I can't at this moment feel forgiving, but I appreciate your courage in coming forward and speaking as you did, and I will accept your apologies. But I know you are an intelligent man, and you must realize how shocked, terrified, disgusted and angry that attack made me feel. You will have to give me time, and, above all, for your own sake you will have to *change* – be a better man – and then perhaps, one day, I, and all your shipmates too, will forgive you. Remember as well, above all, that one day you will stand, as we all will, before the judgment seat of God, and answer to a much higher power than any on this island – a power who will know your innermost thoughts, and whose judgment on the guilty may be more terrible than we can imagine, even in our worst nightmares.'

'O yes, miss, I know all about that; I was always made to go to chapel when I was a boy. I'll try as hard as I can to prove to you and the others that I've done with all the grumbling and scheming and mischief and that. I'll go now. Thank you, Miss Roberts, for hearing me out, and for speaking up for me, back there when I was on trial, like. Not many would have done that, miss, not many. So I swear by Almighty God that if there's ever anything I can do to make up for what I done, I'll do it, whatever it is.'

'Very well – we shall see.' She felt inwardly divided: her Christian heart was full of a generous sympathy for a penitent at the lowest ebb of self-respect; her sceptical, reasoning head felt she was probably being hoodwinked and cheated by a man long noted for his cunning. All this penitence might just be play-acting. In the end, her heart won: 'You've spoken words today, Protheroe; now you will have to show by your deeds that you meant them. As Our Lord said of the false prophets: "By their fruits ye shall know them". Remember that always. Now you and I must do our day's work.'

He said quietly, 'Thank you, miss,' and, as he turned away, she saw him draw his jersey sleeve across his moist eyes as he went to face another day of contemptuous silence from his work-mates.

The doctor gave her a grave smile and said: 'You's a real Christian, Nelli, but you bin too easy on that skunk. I wouldn't trust him no further than I could throw him. You's a bit too good for this rough old world, I reckon... But now then: we got work to do. You got them fish ready for the skillet yet? The boys gonna be real hungry by now.'

*

The clouds raced across the sky, driven by a stiff northerly breeze, but between them were glimpses of a sun which was becoming stronger every day, so the committee abandoned the gloomy, windowless hut, and sat on the woodpiles in the clearing to hear Eleanor's plea. The official foc'sle representative, Jimmy Protheroe, was of course missing; no-one had told him of the meeting, and if they had, he would have had enough common sense to stay away.

The five remaining members had listened in a tactful and sympathetic silence to Eleanor's proposal about the boat expedition to Bluff Cove, which she had delivered, at first nervously and haltingly, but later with a growing confidence and conviction.

Grant's reply was also sympathetic, though firmly negative: 'Thank you, Eleanor, for being so clear and succinct. All of us will have a view on what you propose, and all will no doubt express their feelings later, but I must first say this: whatever democratic arrangements for command we may have evolved on this island, I – personally, as acting captain – am, under British law, responsible for the safety of my crew and passengers. Nothing we arrange to do here can change that, and when at some time in the future we arrive back on British soil, that is the test I shall have to face. I cannot abdicate that responsibility, nor even share it with others. So my position is quite different from that of the rest of the committee, and my view, I'm afraid, is the same as I expressed at our recent general meeting: I cannot agree to risking the lives of a boat's crew on a most dangerous voyage when, for all we know, a rescue steamer may be about to appear over the horizon. The look-out on duty might at any moment come running down from the hill to tell us she's anchored in Port Ross. We were told she would be delayed, but that doesn't mean she won't come. When she does, all our present trials will be over, and all of us will be safe. No-one will be drowned through a boat capsizing or foundering; no-one will be chilled, wet and starving, hopelessly lost in the Southern Ocean, somewhere between here and South America. Curly here will tell you that that is what probably happened to a boat's crew from the "General Grant" after she was wrecked here in the eighteen-sixties. No trace of them or their boat was ever found. Do we want to bring about another such tragedy? I think not. However, having said all that, I'll make way for the other members to speak.'

But before any of the four could utter a word, Eleanor was back on her feet, speaking with an urgent passion: 'I can understand your caution, Mr Grant, but you are still talking as if you were on the poop of the "Figaro" – and you're not. On this island we are just so many wretched survivors. You have all done your best to hold things together, to form our own civilization, but it hasn't worked, has it? I've been subjected to violence and disgusting humiliation, and it was only by mere chance, and only by minutes, that I escaped being raped. What if bosun had not happened to notice those abandoned axes? What if Davey had not known about those men's plans and told Mr Raven of them? I might now be disfigured, and carrying in my womb the seed of a man I loathe and despise. Only chance, or perhaps a higher power – which you, captain, I know, would not recognize – saved me. Being a man, you cannot fully realize how much I still suffer after an attack like that. Mr Raven too was brutally beaten, and only just escaped gross mutilation. He escaped only because I used extreme violence against his attacker. You yourself were afraid that I would kill him, and you were probably right – I was beside myself with fear and rage. Two savage attacks and a near-murder: not quite what you wanted in your little Utopian island republic, was it?'

Her recollected fear and the resultant anger had driven her to a sarcastic bitterness towards a man she liked and respected. She at once felt regret at that, and strove to be calmer, more reasonable: 'Nearly a month has gone by since we landed here; from what that notice said, there's probably another month to go, and as you yourself said, it might be even longer than that. You are a good man, and a good officer, but neither you nor your committee can guard me all day and all night for so long. I cannot expect it of you; I am not your only problem, nor am I for one moment suggesting that my life is a scrap more valuable than anyone else's. Simon, you cannot blame me for having this deadly fear and unease; you know that is not my normal outlook on life; you know that I am normally cheerful and confident. But I shall never be that, all the while we are on this island, and that man is one of our company.'

Grant made as if to speak, but Eleanor raised her hand to stop him: 'No, one more thing, then I'm finished. You haven't taken note of the other reason for this venture: the serious danger of an epidemic amongst us – cholera or pneumonia, for instance. If that happened, we should be totally helpless, and your precious steamer might find only a few physical wrecks, busy burying the corpses of the rest! Just listen, when we are all together, and you will hear some very ominous coughs and sneezes. As I said to Mr Raven, some of the men are very careless about getting wet while at work, and that is so dangerous in the dreadful cold, wet climate we have here. You must see we cannot be complacent about the future; you've all done very well so far, but remember what Burns said about the "best-laid schemes of mice and men" – that they "gang oft agley". I know a boat voyage will be dangerous, but Mr Raven says we could be at Bluff Harbour in a week, and in another week after that a steamer could be here in Port Ross.'

The men were silent for a moment, impressed by her eloquence and the passion behind it. Grant spoke with a rueful smile: 'You have spoken well and persuasively, Eleanor, but I am still far from convinced. Yes, you could indeed be at Bluff Harbour in a week or less, but you could also be at the bottom of the Southern Ocean in two days or less. But still, what do others think?'

Wellington Jones spoke first, his deep voice resonant with sympathy: 'I real sorry for Miss Eleanor. You all remember how she look when she came aboard in Chile – the most beautiful white girl I ever seen – and now look at her! That show you how she suffer from what that bastard did. The Lord knows I ain't no angel; I've screwed around plenty in my time – black gals, white gals, creole gals – but I never *made* em do it. No real man does that. Besides,' he added with a simple pride which brought a smile from his hearers, even from Eleanor, 'I never needed to – I was a good-lookin young buck in them days. If I was a few years younger, I'd go with her in that boat – only I ain't no sailor, and if I went, all you guys would starve. So I say this: I guess Mr Raven won't need no persuading to go, and if we can find two other volunteers, well, let em try. I reckon young Raven is one real good sailor. He'll get em through it if anyone can, I b'lieve.'

Raven blushed, and was for a moment disconcerted by praise from such an unexpected and unlikely quarter; only a short while back, he, with all his fellow-apprentices, had been the bane of Welly's life because of their cunning and ruthless pillaging of the officers' food-stocks. Then he said: 'Thank you for those kind words, doctor. Yes, of course I will go with her, since Eleanor so strongly wishes it. It's not safe or prudent, but if she wishes it, that is enough for me. I'm sure you all know that she and I feel we belong together, so I don't have to even think about it. But of course it is a different decision for others, where their…their personal, emotional feelings are not involved. I told Eleanor when she first broached the idea that it was a hare-brained scheme, and I still think so. She and I would not be surprised if no-one else was inclined to volunteer – though I know there isn't a man from the foc'sle who wouldn't cheerfully go if ordered to do so – with one or two obvious exceptions, of course.'

Grant nodded towards Kellock and said: 'Time for you to have your say, Kellock; I'm sure you have thoughts on the matter.'

'Yes, I got thoughts, but, like you p'raps, I ain't quite decided yet. Old Captin Bligh of the "Bounty", he got his boat a lot further than three hundred miles, but then he was a lot further north, where it ain't so stormy. Still, we got decent boats rigged with masts and sails, and if young Raven is careful I'd give em a sporting chance – but no more than that, mind. And then again, it might do us all good to know that summat was being done to get us off this place. I can feel the lads getting bored, listless, fed up with the same old chores every day, and not getting anywhere. It ain't like being aboard ship, cos there, with any luck, every day you're one day nearer the end of the voyage. And – sorry to put it brutal, like – but if the boat didn't get there, the rest of us wouldn't be no worse off, would we? Sooner or later that old steam-kettle is gonna turn up anyway. I'd go myself, only...'

'No, you would not go, Curly,' said Grant, 'because I cannot be without my Prime Minister and philosopher.' Once again, the company smiled, and Grant went on: 'Now bosun, the floor is yours.'

'Well, mister, it's chancy, but if you got two more volunteers – no more than that, mind, or you'd have to carry too much food and water – I'd say it's worth it. Twenty years ago I'd have volunteered myself...'

'You are not going either, my old friend,' said Grant affably. 'I cannot possibly do without you here. You're the only one who really knows how to make or do anything properly. And. incidentally, I'm going to rule out the brassbounders too. I've a special duty towards them because of their age, and anyway, they'd probably think it was just a great lark, and they'd all volunteer, the young idiots.'

'Mind you,' said the ever-practical bosun, 'no-one can go anywhere for a while. There's a hell of a lot wants doing to the quarter-boat to fit her up for this trip – a week's work at least.'

Eleanor spoke, more calm and determined than ever: 'Everyone's given his opinion, but we are left with all sorts of "ifs" and "buts" and "maybes". Why not settle it once and for all by having a meeting, explaining the plan, and asking for two more volunteers? If there aren't any, the matter's settled. We just stay here at the mercy of some steamer arriving, some time. If volunteers come forward, then I should say, by the rules of democracy, the expedition is on. We have three votes for, against two members undecided. To my thinking that is a majority in favour.'

Grant spoke like a man cornered: 'You would make a good barrister, Eleanor, if women were allowed at the Bar. I feel out-manoeuvred; here we are, discussing the practicalities of this voyage when I have not yet decided – and neither has Curly – on the basic principle – whether there will *be* an expedition. However,' and he stole a glance at Eleanor's ugly, ravaged hair, 'I can see how desperate you are now, so I will call a meeting for this evening, and if there are suitable volunteers, I'll reluctantly agree.' He added, the atheist in him scoffing affectionately: 'You will need an awful lot of luck, but I should say that you, Eleanor, are likely to be much more favoured by the higher powers aloft than most of us, so that might improve your chances on this desperate voyage.'

She smiled back, softened by his gentle, humorous kindness: 'I can't count on any such thing from above, Simon, for that would depend also on the sanctity and virtue of those with me in the boat. How sanctified and pure of heart is the average AB – or Mr Raven, for that matter?'

*

The evening meeting was held under louring skies and a blustering wind. The hands sat around on the woodpiles, puzzled and muttering.

'I reckon there's something big to be talked about,' said Yorry Splott. 'Must be something to do with what Billy done.'

'P'raps they wants us to vote on whether to string him up,' said his neighbour grimly. 'And I'd vote for that like a shot, the dirty rotten bastard.'

'Aye,' said Lewis. 'He've a-put the Old Man's daughter in a proper state, poor maid. She've a-gone and ruined her looks. Out of her mind, she must a bin, to do that.'

'O yes, I agree, it was a nasty thing for that lout to do to a woman,' said the prim Isaac Hughes, unsympathetically irritated, 'even if she wasn't quite so respectable as she might have been. But then, what's done is done, and I can't see what good there is in holding another dratted meeting. It's a nuisance to me, because I haven't half-finished clearing up after supper yet. It means I'll have to be working very late tonight.'

'Shut your miserable face, Isaac,' said Yorry's neighbour. 'She's the one who suffered, and she's worth ten of you, boy, any day.'

As for the two guilty men, Billy John sat under guard in the dark galley, while Jimmy Protheroe lurked, shunned by all, at the back of the clearing, on the outskirts of the crowd, his mind struggling to deal with daunting new thoughts and feelings.

The crowd sat in total silence – the silence of astonishment - while Grant explained the purpose of the meeting. This was not at all what they had been expecting, but, being seamen, they all soon understood that if two people were going, there would have to be two others, to keep the boat sailing day and night. Grant ended his introduction solemnly: 'Now, I'll be quite candid with you all: anyone who volunteers for this trip can be virtually certain to suffer long, cold, wet and horribly uncomfortable days and nights in a twenty-foot cockleshell of a boat in a cold, stormy latitude. Much more importantly, I don't rate the chances of this expedition at more than about fifty-fifty, though of course we shall do our best to fit the boat out properly. Mr Raven, as you know, is a skilful sailor and navigator, but he will have no sextant or log-tables to fix his position – only the boat compass, so he will not be able to navigate any better than Christopher Columbus could – and the Southern Ocean is a very big place to get lost in. So anyone taking part in this trip is taking a very big risk indeed. Again, I'll be frank with you: I'm not in favour of this enterprise, but the committee as a whole is, if two suitable volunteers come forward. Neither I nor they will put any pressure on any of you, nor will we think any the worse of those who don't volunteer. Men with wives and young families have every right to avoid the kind of risk that this boat voyage will entail. No apprentice will be allowed to volunteer, and any man who does volunteer must sign the log-book to witness that he goes of his own accord, not on my orders. Now then, let us see whether we shall have a crew or not. Stand and raise your hand if you are willing to join Miss Roberts and Mr Raven.'

At once, two hands shot up, and two of the crew rose to their feet. The crowd's astonishment at this whole business grew when they saw who it was that had shown such swift certainty – the tough, middle-aged Swede, Carl Johanssen, and the small scrawny peggy, Davey.

Grant too was startled: 'Johanssen! Good for you,

but you're a married man, aren't you? With children?'

'Ja, but the kids – they grown up now. Gone to Stockholm to verk in offices. They don't need old Poppa no more.'

'No – but your wife…?

'If my Gretta was here, she say, "Go help that poor gal". I sure she would. And I don't care about no small boat or rough weather or cold; I done plenty herring-fishing when I at home, and the Baltic plenty rough and cold sometimes. I go because I liked Miss Eleanor's mother, God rest her. She best, most wonderful woman I ever know. So I like Miss Eleanor too, and I sorry for her – real sorry. I don't boast, but I handy feller in a boat. If I go, we get to Bluff Harbour, damn sure t'ing.'

'Good for you, Carl,' said Grant, visibly moved. 'I can't think of a more suitable chap to go. But Davey…'

'Don't say no, mister,' said the boy, desperately. I'm like Carl – I'd do anything for Miss. Go round the world with her, I would. She nursed me when I had that horrible old fever. She might easily have caught it off of me. That's why I…I love her. And it was my fault that them two knew about her beach. That was real stupid and wicked of me. So I know I got to make up for that if I can. I don't care what happens to me, sir. So please let me go.'

Grant, with tears in his eyes at the boy's simple courage and sincerity, said gently: 'No, Davey, I can't let you go. You're too young, and you're not strong enough, or used to this kind of sailoring. But we all admire your pluck, and we know you'll be a real man one day.'

There was a low rumble of agreement and approval from all the hands. Davey switched his pleading gaze to Eleanor, who sat near Grant, but she replied with an affectionate smile and a gentle shake of her head.

Suddenly a sharp angry voice spoke up from the back of the gathering: 'What about me, mister? I stood and put my hand up straightaway, like them two, but you never saw me.' The men swung round, and gave a roar of incredulous rage when they saw who the third volunteer was – Jimmy Protheroe!

Even the quick-thinking Grant was for a moment dumbfounded. When he spoke it was with cold rage: *'You,* Protheroe? Is this some sort of cruel joke, eh? What in the name of God makes you think Miss Roberts would get into a boat with you – one of the causes of her trouble? Christ Almighty, I'm asking for real men, not low-down slimy bastards like you.' He paused, and there was a low, savage growl of agreement with his words from the crowd. Then he went on, with evident relief: 'Very well, then; if there are no other volunteers, that puts the kibosh on the whole idea, and we can...'

But Eleanor would not let him finish; she jumped up, her nerves overcome by indignation: 'No, I will not have my idea scotched like that! Haven't I got more right than anyone to have a voice in this affair? Mr Grant, is Protheroe incompetent as a sailor?'

'No, I wouldn't say that, but...'

'Or cowardly about doing his duty when it's dangerous – going aloft in a gale, and so on?'

'No, to be fair, even to him, I've never seen him hang back, but still...'

'Then for God's sake let the poor creature speak his mind. He spent a long time with me earlier this morning, saying how sorry he was for his actions, and swearing that he would do anything to make amends. What possible evil motive could he have in making this offer? What possible harm could he do to me, in a boat with Mr Raven and Carl present? None. A man can change. If he chooses to share a cold watery death with me – trying to help all of you, don't forget – why should we deny him this chance of…of redemption? Stop sitting there, high and mighty, in judgment, and try to imagine how you might feel in his place, and for God's sake let the poor man try to regain some respect – and self-respect. According to you, Mr Grant, it may well be the last thing he does in this life. Well, let it be a good one then.'

She sat down again, in a silence produced by an awed, incredulous respect for her passionate plea for one of her enemies. There was even a grudging respect for her former tormentor. Men turned to look at him as he spoke, and Lewis muttered to his neighbour: 'Well, fair play to un, Jimmy have got guts to do that, b'y.'

Protheroe said simply: 'Thank you, miss. I won't let you down, I promise, and no-one here will care tuppence if I go to feed the fishes. I've finished with all them stupid shenanigans I got up to with Billy John Ffynnongroes. Where did they ever get me? I swear to God I'll do my best, and if I do anything to harm you – why, let the others sling me over the side – they're big enough to do it. But look, Mr Grant: if Miss Roberts can't stand the idea of me being in the boat – well then, she's got a right to say no, and hope for a better man to come forward.'

'No,' said Eleanor, looking steadily and directly at him. 'I accept you as one of the crew – though the others will have to agree too. But remember this: you have spoken a lot of words today; from now on – for the rest of your life – you will have to prove their sincerity by your deeds. Words alone are nothing.'

Even the sceptical Kellock was awestruck: 'Spoken like a saint, miss. There's not one in a thousand would have spoken up for him like that.' Then, to re-establish his free-thinking credentials, he added: 'Not that I believe in saints of course. But if there was such things, you'd be one.'

Grant too was moved: 'I can see I was too hasty, Eleanor. As Curly says, you have shown incredible magnanimity, and I don't wish to over-rule you. However, I shall have to secure the agreement of Mr Raven and our friend Carl. You will – all four of you – have to work, and suffer perhaps, as a team, so you must be united, and on at least civil terms.' He turned to Johanssen: 'Carl, what do you say?'

'I not expect this, sir, but if Miss Eleanor say all right, then I don't say no. But, by yimminy, he best not do her no harm, or I'll…'

Grant broke in smoothly: 'I think I can promise you, Carl, that there'll be no trouble like that. As Miss Roberts says, now he will have to prove himself worthy. Now – Mr Raven?'

'Well, he's not the last man I'd have picked, but he's the next-to-last. Up to now, none of us knows much to his credit. Still, as Miss Roberts demands it, I'll take him on. But, as she says, he'll have to prove himself true to his words, and he'll have to change his ways a lot. There's no room in a twenty-foot boat for a grousing, grumbling sea-lawyer.'

Despite his words, though, he felt uneasy about agreeing. Perhaps all of them had been sucked in by this chap? After all he'd always been noted for being about as trustworthy as a rattlesnake. He looked long at Protheroe for a sign of cocky triumph or duplicity, but could see only a face of tense determination. The chap was young, strong, active, and a good deal brighter than your average AB; and, as Eleanor had said, he couldn't hope to get away with any dirty tricks with himself and Carl there in the boat. All the same, he was still Jimmy Protheroe, one of Nelli's former enemies, and it seemed mad to pick him when, if they'd waited, some more of the crowd might have volunteered. But then his professional soul told him that the whole trip was mad anyway – so why worry about a little extra madness?

Raven was not the only man with things on his mind as the meeting broke up. The bosun too had a problem, but his was linguistic, and less profound than Raven's. He muttered to Kellock as they walked away together: 'Listen, Curly. I thought I could understand *Saesneg* – English – well enough, but I got a bit lost back there at the committee meeting this morning, on times. What did Grant mean about Miss Eleanor "sucking a sink"? What the hell was he on about? We ain't got no sinks by here, mun., and if we had got one, you wouldn't suck it.'

'Ah no,' said Curly with a smile, 'it wasn't quite that. He was just saying she was *succinct.* He meant she didn't beat about the bush, like.'

'God damn, now you're doing it! What bush, mun? And who'd beat a bush, anyway? What for?'

'Well, Reuben, me ole mate, he just meant she didn't go on talking a long time. She just put it short and plain.'

'Well then, why didn't he *say* that? You bloody English don't realize the problem us Welsh boys have. You can't speak a bloody word of our language, but you expect us to understand all the daft things you say. "Suck sink" indeed!'

'Ah well, when you bin to a posh school like Grant did, I s'pose you want to show you've learned summat out of the dictionary - just to show your old man's had something for his money, like.'

'All right then; but what was she on about – the captain's girl? It was something about burning mice and men. How the hell did mice come into it, and who'd want to burn them, poor little dabs? And she said something about a gang. Who the hell were they?'

'She must have gone to a good school too, I reckon. She was quoting some poetry by a chap called Burns – a Scotch geezer he was – and he was saying that even if you reckon you've made a good plan, it can all go wrong. And there wasn't no gang, Reub; "gang" is just the old Scottish way of saying "go".'

Bosun shook his head, more dissatisfied than ever: 'There you are then – they're both talking rubbish! That's what sitting for hours over a lot of damn books does for you; you just talk daft. And anyway, whoever heard of a bloody mouse making a plan? It don't make sense. Poor little beggar ain't got the brain to do that, mun. Why don't these so-called educated folk talk plain, so that all of us poor buggers what didn't get no proper schooling can start to understand them?'

CHAPTER ELEVEN

The night that followed, like all the others since the abortive rape, was a long, dreary one for Billy John Ffynnongroes. His straw mattress, laid on a piece of sailcloth on the very rough wooden floor of the galley, was lumpy and comfortless. His upper right arm still throbbed a dull pain through his body. He could sleep only on his left side or his back. From the open end of the galley came draughts of cold night air, and his blanket was barely able to keep him warm enough for sleep; his request for another had been curtly refused – there were no more to spare, for the crew of the boat would need two each.

His mind too forbade sleep for most of the interminable hours between dusk and dawn, for it would not be still. It would not be dulled and clouded with the blessed calm fog of sleep, but instead ceaselessly, mercilessly, ground out its unending, silent diatribe of hatred, resentment, paranoia and thwarted lust. Round and round and round in his mind went the images of those he hated – Raven, Eleanor, Grant and Jimmy Protheroe. Nothing, no other thoughts in the world, could banish those loathed spectres.

You're as good as anyone on this island, said this inner voice, and better than most. You were cock of the starboard watch once – their leader; now not one of your shipmates will even speak to you – except your jailers when they have to, and they hate your guts. Why did they all make such a goddam fuss about a bit of sport with a girl? Christ, every sailor has a bit of fanny – a quick screw or two – whenever he goes ashore. That bloody Raven did, more than most, before that damn trollop came aboard and tickled his fancy. He's no angel with women.

As for her, why did she have to do all that screeching and hollering and thrashing about? You wouldn't have hurt her if she'd behaved tidy and friendly. Bronwen from Cwmfelin never made no fuss about it, once you got her up in the hay-loft after a drop of home-brewed. You only had to wait till her old man Dai had gone off to the mart with a few calves, or gone on Sunday afternoons to teach Sunday-school at Gideon Chapel. Too old by half for her, he was, and a bit of a runt too. Couldn't do it proper, Bron said; the old boy used to be finished before she'd hardly got started – and even that was only every other Saturday night. Never on a Sunday of course; mustn't break the Sabbath! So it was no surprise that Bronwen hadn't got any kids! P'raps she had by now, mind – yours!

She was the right sort of girl for you, and she was just as good a looker as that stuck-up tart, give or take a few moles, and a bit of a squint. You didn't even have to ask good old Bronwen for a poke or two. All for it, she was. But this bible-punching piece! Anyone would think she was the blinking Virgin Mary, the fuss she made! Good God, if she'd only just laid back and let you get on with it, you'd both have had some fun, and no harm done. All right, you pulled a knife on her; that was a bit of a mistake, perhaps. A couple of good back-handers across the chops would have done the job, and afterwards she might have finished up wanting another go – you could never tell with women. You could bet that bloody *Sais* had been in there a few times, and she didn't squawk about him.

But there, you was only a common old AB, and a *crwt* off a hill farm before that – not good enough to be allowed into her drawers. And then, by Christ, after Raven had interfered, she had to go and smash your arm with that damn great stick. Would that arm ever get right again? All right for her, but what'd life be like for an ordinary working-man with only one good arm? And Jesus – the pain when the bucko set it! Never done it before, probably, and wasn't too tender or careful how he did it, neither. You could have yelled this galley down with the agony of it, only you didn't want to give the bastard that satisfaction. And nothing to ease the pain – not even a few tots of rum.

Now you're stuck here – no fresh air, just the stink of food and wood-smoke; no exercise; not a damn thing to do, day or night. Funny, though: the times at sea in dirty weather, when you hardly got any sleep, being rousted out all night: 'Furl this! Set that! Lee braces – haul! Weather braces – haul! Up stays'ls! Down stays'ls!' Never a wink of sleep! You used to dream about being able to spend all day and all night snoring in your bunk. Now you got nothing to do *but* sleep, and you can't get a sodding wink. Your mind just thinks, thinks, thinks, all the time, up and down, round and round, like a rat in a cage!

What about that meeting last night? You heard every bleeding word. Heard that crawling rat Protheroe sucking up to them all, saying what a wicked naughty man he'd been, and how he'd be better in future. Cunning, slippery bastard! He'd got away with it now – even wormed his way into the boat's crew. You couldn't believe the way they all fell for that holy, goody-goody guff he'd spewed out. You'd like to get the chance to settle with him good and proper – see how he liked being smashed up. If only he'd stuck to his job, down at the beach that day! He could have held her down and stopped her row, and had his own go at her afterwards. Then we could have told her not to say nothing to anyone; she might have been more frightened of two of us. Anyway, she might have liked it in the end, with two proper men, not one half-baked, lah-di-dah brassbounder, still wet behind the ears.

But then, like everything else you've ever done or tried, it all went wrong. You've never had any luck but bad luck all your life, boy. Now, with a smashed arm set by a bodger, perhaps you'll never get a berth as an AB again. You might finish up as a poor old wreck in the workhouse, with all the bloody riff-raff of the parish. Christ, if only you could do like God did in the Bible, whenever He got shirty – bring down a curse on all of them – Grant, Raven, Jimmy, that stuck-up madam – all of them! Make them suffer like you've suffered, or worse, maybe. Drown the bloody lot, guilty or not, like what He did in old Noah's day, or give them some horrible plague, like the poor old Egyptians got. That'd serve em right! And there's another funny thing: you thinking of all that stuff from the Bible! Poor old Mam, she used to drag all us kids down to Gideon Chapel every Sunday. That was when she still had some go in her, before Dad knocked it all out of her with them two big fists of his.

Yes, you'd pay out all of them, but especially Raven, that lousy English bastard. Why should he be always lucky and you always unlucky – eh? He's younger than you, no better-looking, no cleverer, no better sailor, and yet he's always had everything – rich parents, good schooling, college – everything that you didn't get. What did you get? You got the most miserable, bad-tempered sod in the village for a father. Everyone called him Wil Cas – nasty Will – but only behind his back, cos he was big and hard. Christ, the hidings you had from him, with that thick black leather belt of his! He bullied Mam and all the family too, except for his darling Elvet, his eldest son. That swine couldn't do nothing wrong, cos he was the image of his dad. He put on such a bloody act as a good son who loved and respected his parent. But you knew him: he was only after the farm, and the way Dad drank, it wouldn't be long before he got it to himself.

Then you'd have been his unpaid slave, working like a dog, just for a bed and enough to eat; milking early and late, slogging in cow-shit and pig-shit all day, traipsing about on the hill after the sheep in all weathers, sweating buckets in the summer with the hay and the corn, freezing your arse off on winter mornings – and all for nothing! For bugger-all!

You'd have seen Elvet, all toffed-up in a suit and tie, off to Cardigan market in a shiny trap, with a smart cob in the shafts, then coming back drunk, with sovereigns jingling in his pockets. Well, fuck that for a life! That's why you cleared off one day, down to Newport, where there was always ketches and schooners and smacks unloading coal or lime. You had no trouble getting a berth as third hand on a schooner, but by God the work was hard there too! Hard beyond! A run-down, leaky old tub she was, pumps going half the time to keep her afloat, ploughing up and down the Bristol Channel mostly, or over to Ireland, nearly always with dirty cargoes that had to be shovelled in and shovelled out. On deck in all weathers, if you weren't down at the cabin stove, boiling up beef, frying sausages, or making plum duff for the skipper and mate – and hard bastards they were too, if you did anything wrong! You thought you was lucky when Mam's brother,

Uncle Gareth – good old boy, he was – helped you get a berth as an AB on the 'Figaro', because he went to school with Jake Roberts, the old capten. But there again, you had no luck; Jake never liked you. He didn't like hands who stood up for theirselves on times.

So what good did it do you, going deep sea? None. You're still back where you were – bottom of the heap. Shut up in a cold draughty jail; looked down on by your messmates who'd liked to have shagged that bird themselves, but hadn't got the guts to do it – like that rat Jimmy!

You know the ropes better than most of em; you'd make a better bosun any day than that old Reuben Mathias. And if you'd got to be bosun, then later you might have passed for your third mate's ticket, like old Jake Roberts did, so they said. Then you'd have been aft, sitting at the cabin table, eating decent grub, and up on deck in charge, shouting at all the hands, giving em a kick now and then. But they've all kept you down; a good AB, strong, handy aloft and clever, but still on two pound fifteen a month and workhouse grub. Is that fair?

No, it isn't fair, and by God, you'll show em one day – especially that Raven. Some time – if he didn't get drowned in a day or two – he'd have that fancy tart Nelli all to himself, to do what he liked with. Wouldn't have to worry about her Mam and Dadi no more. And *her!* She'd whip all her clobber off for him, double-quick. You wouldn't hear her screeching 'No, no, no, you horrible man!' to him. They'd get into a nice warm bed, and she'd open her mouth and kiss him long and deep with her tongue; then, after a bit of that, she'd open them nice long, smooth white legs and take hold of his tool and – No! No, boy! For God's sake stop thinking of that kind of thing, or you'll go mad, alone here in this cold stinking hole of a galley.

You just wait. You'll get your chance with someone else one day – some nice friendly bint – not a bible-punching snob like her. Meantime, boy, think about what you can *do – now* – to start to pay em out, especially Raven, even if it takes years to do it.

This boat trip they were on about: if you could only get out of here you could soon put paid to that. Go down the beach, get hold of a decent slab of rock and smash every goddam boat to splinters... No, stuff that for an idea! Like the bucko said, there's a good chance that the lot of em will drown like rats. Pity about old Carl – he's a good old boy – got nothing against him - but as for Raven and the tart and that rat Jimmy, well, the sooner the crabs are picking the meat off of their bones on the sea-bed the better. You'll just have to hope for a decent gale to give em all a nice cold swim till they can't swim no more, then a breaking sea over their heads, and down they go, with lungs choking, full of salt water; then the wind and sea will have done your job for you!

But let's suppose they do get there, and a steamer's chartered to come back here. Will she and Raven be on it, or will they be off home on their own, straight from Bluff Harbour? If they're not on it, then there's no chance of getting even – not for a long time. But one day, years off, you'll be out of jail and back in Wales, and you'll find them, somehow. You won't have forgotten what you owe them, by God! Suppose by then they're married and settled down? It's a fair bet they'll be living somewhere around Newport. That's where she comes from, and Newport people always seem to want to go back there. Then you'll find them, and find a chance to get even too! Then they'll wonder what's hit em!

If they do come back on the steamer, there might still be a chance to settle Raven's hash quicker, but most likely Grant will get them to lock you up below on the trip back to New Zealand. Still, you never know: you might be able to talk someone into letting you have a walk on deck at night. You might see Raven leaning on the guard-rail, having a cigar after his supper. He might disappear overboard when no-one else was about. It'd be a bloody job to do him in with this arm so groggy, but you might be lucky, especially if he's had a few tots! They couldn't prove nothing then – not *prove* it. And if they couldn't prove it they couldn't give you no more time inside, nor top you. Then, you never know, you might get a chance somehow, to give them the slip when the steamer gets to New Zealand. Like, say, pretending you're really ill, and getting sent to a hospital. You've heard of blokes bunking off like that. And then you could ship aboard a steamship, as a fireman, say, and get back home before the rest of them. Then you could disappear – get right away – and poor little Nelli would have to stay a bleeding spinster, crying her poor little eyes out for her darling brass-bounder.

But what *now?* Think, boy, think! Right: the first thing is to get free to move about without them two thugs from the Parrog watching you all the time. But how? How? There's only one way. It'll be the most horrible thing you've ever done, but you'll have to do it all the same: eat humble pie. Suck up to them, especially Grant, like Jimmy, the crafty sod. (But, fair play to him, he put on a damn good show, from what you could hear. Sounded like a chapel deacon!) Start tomorrow; get to see Grant and *crawl,* lower than a snake's belly. Say how sorry you are, what a wicked man you've been, say you'll be a real good, tidy boy from now on. Cringe, cry, beg – anything. And keep it up too, never mind how many insults you get back off that swine. Say you've been shamed by Jimmy's good example – that might go down well! Christ, it'll be horrible for a real man like you, but you got to do it. Get yourself free, then wait and wait and wait.

Don't think no more about it; try and get to see the bucko tomorrow morning, and show him what a wonderful, holy Christian character you are now. Show them that a marvellous miracle's happened, and you're now Saint William of Ffynnon-bloody-groes!

*

In the blowing, blustering drizzle next morning five figures in glistening black oilskins stood clustered around one of the big quarter-boats. Bosun Mathias and sailmaker Jac-y-Bont huddled together, muttering technicalities, bent over the boat's gunwales, peering closely at the details of her structure. Kellock stood back a little, in deference to the real professionals, while Raven and Eleanor stood silent at the bow, soberly taking in the boat's tiny size, compared with the three-thousand-ton barque that had brought them here to this chill, damp, windy island.

They turned round at the sound of hasty steps on the shingle as Grant approached, frowning. Bosun straightened up and said, with muted irritation: 'Ah, there you are, mister. We can start now. You did say "straight after breakfast".'

'I know. Sorry to keep you all. Eirian Evans stopped

me just as I was leaving. He says that damn swine Billy John wants to see me urgently, I told Evans he'd have to wait till I was finished here.'

'Can't think what he can want to say to you,' said Raven. 'He's barely uttered a word so far. Don't believe anything he says, anyway. I know him.'

'Never mind about him now. Let's start thinking about what needs doing to this boat to make her a bit more seaworthy for a long trip in what may be pretty rough seas.'

'Yes,' said bosun, 'there's a hell of a lot wants doing.'

'I think,' said Grant, 'that we'd all agree that the first thing she needs is some good waterproof decking over her bow half – back to a bit behind the mast. Otherwise she'll fill from the first big breaking sea.'

'Yes,' said Raven. 'And anyway, we'll need some sort of shelter from wind and rain and spray when we're off-watch and resting. But where the hell can we get suitable planking for a deck?'

Bosun snorted: 'Look behind you, mun. There's our wood – only a couple of yards off.' He nodded towards the other quarter-boat.

Eleanor was startled: 'What? Break that boat up for planking? Surely you might want…'

'It's the only way, miss. What shall we want with it when you're gone? We can leave just the whaler for fishing and maybe sealing.'

'Aye,' said Jac. 'And if we take some curved strakes from this boat's sides, they'll make a nice whaleback deck, what'll shed the water quickly. It'd be a bit leaky, though, so we'd…'

'Whoa there! Hang on a minute, you two,' said Grant. 'You're not in a Clyde shipyard, you know. You're saying "make that, fix this" and so on. All right, you have the saws to cut the strakes out to size, but where are you going to get all the fastenings you'll need – nails, screws, and so on?'

Jac and the bosun exchanged knowing and complacent grins: 'You don't know me and Jac properly yet,' said bosun, 'or you wouldn't ask that. D'you think I'd come away from the old hooker without my tool-bag? I got my auger and a screwdriver and a box of decent brass screws. Anyway, we can get screws from the other boat if we take out the thwarts. How about you, Jac?'

'I got my little bag too, mister – my palm and needle and shears and a good ball of twine. And we got the canvas and the cordage from the other boat as well.'

Grant shook his head with a grateful smile: 'Thank God for some old heads on old shoulders. Well done, gents!'

Eleanor whispered to Raven: 'I'm getting a bit lost here. I know the thwarts are the seats across the boat, but what are strakes?'

'They're just the overlapping planks of the boat's sides.'

'Thank you. I'll need you now and then at first as a nautical glossary.' She took his hand in a gentle squeeze, and – for the first time for many weeks – looked in his eyes and smiled. She was beginning to see the tiniest glint of light in a dark hell of fear and misery.

'Right,' said Grant. 'We'll have a cambered foredeck from the other boat's timbers. But it'll be as leaky as hell when a big lump of sea lands on it. Anyone below will get a wet arse and no fish, if you'll pardon the expression, Eleanor.'

'Aye, they would if we just put on a decking bare,' said bosun, 'but we've still got some of the heavy canvas them boys got from the wreck, so we'll stretch a cover of that over the wood. That'll make the deck a lot less slippery if someone has to go up there. And before we do that, we can caulk the deck the old-fashioned way - shred up bits of rope to make oakum, and hammer that down into the cracks. Pity we ain't got no tar nor pitch to set it properly.'

'Old Welly could help you there,' said the resourceful Kellock. 'Get him to render down some beef fat, and put that in with the oakum. That'd set good and hard in the cold. It'd stink a bit after a time, but them in this boat won't be short of fresh air – you can depend on that.'

The bosun was eager, carried away like a boy in his hobby: 'And I know: at the after end of the deck we can fix a plank on edge, sticking up as a breakwater to stop the water from sluicing back into the boat.'

'So far, so good,' said Grant. 'Now we've got two remaining problems: how to increase her speed in fair weather, and how to make her safe in a real blow. Let's take the second first, because it's more important.'

Jac piped up, infected by his old friend's enthusiasm: 'I can easy make some small stout sails from the heavy canvas – a little spitfire jib, and a trysail to set instead of the lugsail. Those'd keep her going well in heavy weather.'

'In all the books,' said Raven, 'they say that in really heavy weather you need a good drogue – a sea-anchor. But where are we going to find one of those?'

Jac turned to glare at him and tapped his own forehead: 'Out of here, boy, out of here. D'you think I couldn't knock you up one of those? Give me a bit of credit, mun, isn't it, after thirty-five years at sea! All I got to do is make a good, stout, square frame of wood, say about a foot-and-a-half across; cut out four long bits of canvas, tapering down; stitch them to the frame and stitch the sides of cloth together – see? Then you got a long, square, tapering bag with a small hole at the bottom. I'll stitch a small weight in one corner of the frame so that it floats upright, not flat. Then I'll put real strong diagonal bars across the frame; then, where the bars cross in the middle, you make fast a good length of the best rope from the old ship – about fifteen fathoms, say – lead that through the bow fairlead and make it well fast inboard – to the mast, maybe.'

'Aye,' put in the bosun, 'and you better be sure you parcel the warp with canvas where it comes in through the fairlead, or it'll chafe through and part, and then...'

'Jac was put out: 'Why you got to interrupt me all the time, Reuben? I'm doing this bit of it. Take your bloody turn, boy!'

Diplomatically, Eleanor asked: 'How can you call that an anchor if it's just floating, not holding on to the sea-bed?'

Equally smoothly, Grant explained: 'Well, you see, though it's not fastened to the sea-bed, we call it an anchor because, as it's submerged, it won't drift to leeward in the wind, as the boat will. And as it's like a giant tapering sausage, open at the tied end, it will act like a very powerful drag – like a kind of underwater kite. Then, as the boat is blown to leeward by the gale, the warp to the sea-anchor will tighten, and the anchor will act as a kind of brake. The boat won't drift nearly so fast, and – much more important – the drag of the sea-anchor will force the boat to come head-to-wind, so that nearly all the spray and solid water will land on the new deck and run off back into the sea. Your intrepid young Captain Cook here will, I hope, hoist one of Jac's new storm-sails, sheeted in really flat, to stop her yawing about. It's your only way of surviving a storm in a small boat – and in a big ship too, sometimes.'

'Mind,' said the bosun, 'you'll still ship a good bit of water, so you'll need a couple of buckets for bailing. You know what they say in Fishguard, miss: the best pump in the world is a frightened man with a bucket.'

'And then, when the storm's gone,' said Jac, not to be left out, 'you haul in on a light trip-line, which I'm going to rig to the top of the frame. Then the sea-anchor falls over flat, and you can get it in easy.'

'I've thought of another thing,' said the bosun, in his element now. 'This boat was designed to take fifteen or twenty people in it – that's over a ton weight. With only four, she'll need a good bit of ballast to keep her upright when you're carrying sail; else you'll have no grip on the water. It'd be like trying to sail a haystack to windward.'

'Yes, a good thought, bosun,' said Grant. 'Of course, at first you'll have a fair weight of food and water, but you'll also need some good big flattish rocks off the beach, well wedged in, so that they don't shift when she heels.'

'But surely,' said Eleanor, 'it would be dangerous to put more weight in the boat? I mean, if she should heel, and ship water over the lee gunwale, she'd sink like a stone.'

Grant was silent for a moment to give his words more weight; then he spoke quietly and soberly: 'Eleanor, if your young skipper lets her heel that far, you'll all be dead anyway. You would never right her if she capsized, and the cold of the water would kill you all in twenty minutes or less. You're not going fooling about in a dinghy on the Thames in July, you know.'

'No,' said Raven. 'I'll be as careful as hell, Simon, you know that, and I'll make sure the other helmsmen are too. But with luck we'll get some fine days with a decent breeze, and no breaking seas. Then we need to make this tub go faster and better to windward.'

Kellock broke his long (and very uncharacteristic) silence: 'Yes, I been thinking how you could get her to go better on the wind. You can't fit no deep keel on her, like a yacht would have, but you could fit lee-boards, like the Thames barges do – and the Dutch ones too. In the docks in London, where I worked as a nipper, I used to see a lot of them. You fix two flat, straight planks – one on each side of the boat – swinging from their top ends on some sort of bolt in the top strake. You lower the one on the lee side when you're tacking, and change round when you go about. You could have cords from the bottom of each board leading fore and aft, to raise and lower em and keep em in position. What d'you think, gents? Can do?'

'Good idea, yes,' said bosun, 'but he'll have to use them only in fair weather, mind. In a strong blow they'd make you more likely to capsize. But some of the wood that grows here is like iron; I dare say I could fix a decent peg of that through the top strakes, for your boards to swing on.'

'Don't see how,' said Raven. 'You've got no drill, have you?'

'You got a lot to learn, you have, mister,' said bosun severely. 'We got a poker in the hut; we can make a fire on the beach. When you got a red-hot poker, you got a drill, haven't you? The old shipwrights knew that, and they never went to no damn fancy college.'

Jac-y-Bont piped up again, unwilling to be left out: 'I been thinking too. That lugsail is a good sail off the wind, or in a beam wind, but if you have to get to windward in a light breeze you'll need a good foresail, to set on the fore-stay. I can soon knock one up out of this other boat's lug-sail. If I had time I could make you a real big one – long in the foot. That'd pull like a carthorse, that would.'

Grant lifted his hands to arrest the flow: 'Don't give him any fancy kites to fly, Jac, or he'll have the boat bot-tom-up on the first day – I know him.'

Jac answered sententiously: 'If he's a proper sailor who knows what sail to set and when, he won't do that. If he ain't, they're all bound for Davey Jones' locker any-way.'

There was once more a solemn silence as the dan-gers of the voyage slid into all their minds. It was left to Raven to dispel the sudden chill: 'Don't look so down, all of you. I'll be very careful; I'm not a daft young brass-bounder any more. And' – here he took Eleanor's hand and squeezed it affectionately – 'I've got the best reason in the world to be careful. We will get to Bluff Harbour, safe and sound. I promise all of you that.'

But the finality in his tone did not end the confer-ence, for the two old craftsmen had now got the bit be-tween their teeth, and had not exhausted their fertile minds. Jac said: 'As well as them storm-sails I was talking about, I can fit you a row of reef-points in the lugsail, so you can shorten sail, but still keep her going in stiff breezes.'

Grant protested: 'This is all very well, Jac, but all that will take a month, not a week.'

'Don't you believe it, mister. There's three or four of the boys know enough to help me with splicing rope and roping sails and fitting thimbles in the corners. That Jimmy Protheroe is a good hand at that, fair play to him. We'll get it done.'

Then the bosun: 'If we bring the decking back a bit beyond the mast there'll be room for storing food as well as sleeping. I'll fit some boards across to keep the palliasses up out of the bilge, but *Duw,* it ain't going to be comfortable. You'll be damn lucky if it stays dry in there. It won't be like a posh hotel, I'm telling you.'

'I'm sure you're right there, Reuben,' said Grant, and then smacked his hands together in a business-like gesture: 'Time to stop talking and get on with it. Both of you take all the hands you need for those jobs. I'm no chippy, but I fancy myself as a bit of a rigger, Jac.'

'All right then, mister: I'll get you to fit the shrouds from this other boat to double up these – we don't want her dismasted in a blow. And you can make a decent strop to go at the masthead to take the foresail halyard block. And I want to see some tidy splicing, mind. Three tucks, and no bits of yarn sticking out.'

'Aye, aye,' said Grant amused at the reversal of authority. 'Consider it done, ship-shape and Bristol fashion, Jac. And where we'd be without chaps like you two, I don't know.'

'I do then,' said bosun. 'We'd still be in Penarth dock, under the coal tips in the old hooker, cos no ship ever gets to sea without a few old hands to show the others the ropes.'

As Raven and Eleanor walked back to the hut, Raven was surprised to sense Eleanor's spirits rising. He said: 'You seem more cheerful now, *cariad.*'

'Yes, I am, thank God. It's so good to feel that things are going to be *done,* not just talked about. I feel as if I'm going to be let out of a horrible prison. Come to think about it' – and she shook her cropped, ragged head – 'I do look as if I've been in one.'

Raven felt his own spirits rise; she'd never referred to the dreadful massacre of her hair before, let alone joke about it. 'But he said seriously: 'You do know, don't you, how dangerous it's going to be – this trip? We've got little more than a fifty-fifty chance, if I'm to be totally honest with you.'

She took his hand and said simply and quietly: 'I trust you, Jack. You will get us there, no matter how hard it is. I know it.'

'I'll do my best,' he said, moved and sobered by her sincere faith in him. Then, being English, and a little embarrassed by deep emotion, he escaped to a lighter note. 'After dinner I'll go and give bosun a hand with dismantling the quarter-boat. But I'm not looking forward to that: I know what a grumpy old devil he can be when he's busy.'

'Yes, and I expect I can help Jac-y-Bont with cutting out the canvas for the sails.'

Raven laughed: 'Phew! That'll be a test of your courage all right; he's twice as cantankerous as bosun. These old chaps have got no time for us amateurs, but, as Simon says, they're worth their weight in gold.'

*

After his midday meal, Grant went to the little store-room for privacy, saying to Eirian Evans, 'Get that specimen over here, will you? I'll see him now.'

'Aye, aye, sir. D'you want me to stay, in case he…?

'What? With only one arm? No, Evans, thank you all the same. I could deal with that customer if he had both. What's this all about, do you know?'

'No, sir. He just says it's personal and important.'

Despite the strength of his loathing of John, Grant was shocked when the prisoner came into the store, an abject figure, his face pale and drawn tight by his constant pain, his shoulders bent and shrunken, his hair matted and his beard wild, his eyes cast down in apparent shame. Only once or twice did he raise them to meet Grant's gaze.

Coldly, his face set in a grim glare, Grant said: 'Well? What is it? Don't be long about it – I've got work to do.'

'No, sir, I won't keep you. Well, first of all I got to thank you for seeing me, after… after what happened. Well, it's like this, sir: I been thinking and thinking and thinking for hours on end in that galley - I got nothing else to do, like - and I see now how bad, low-down and disgusting I was that day. I know I've always been a bit of a scallywag on board, but I've never sunk that low before. So I want to say sorry to you and to Miss Roberts for what I done. I suppose there's no chance of me seeing her, to say sorry, face-to-face?'

'None whatever. Good God, you must know that, man! And you can't surely think that just saying sorry will put it all right again?'

'No, sir, I understand that…. Well, will you please tell her from me that I'm real sorry – sorry *o'r galon* - from my heart – as we say in Welsh – for the terrible things I said and the terrible way I treated her that day. I can't believe now, sir, that I did such things to a real nice, kind young lady like her. She and her mam was like saints to us chaps for'ard when we had that fever on board – and specially to me. I'm as disgusted at it as you are – as she is – sir. Please, you got to believe me, Mr Grant. I mean every word I've said.'

Grant replied with the same stony coldness in his voice: 'Very well, I'll tell her what you have said. How she reacts to your apology is up to her, not to me. As for your future, that too is out of my hands, as I told you at the hearing.'

'O, I know, sir, I know. You got to do your duty – hand me over to the cops; and I know I'll have to do a lot of time in jug. I can't complain – I deserve it.'

'You certainly do, and as I also said, there is no question of my keeping quiet, and so breaking the law myself.'

'No, sir, of course not. I done it, so I'll have to serve my time and not complain. But sir, you did say back then that if I acted tidy from now on you might be able to help me in court.'

'I did say that, yes, but until now I have seen no sign of any regret or remorse from you. Good God, at the hearing you had the insolence to fling an insult at the woman you'd so grossly abused.'

'That's so, sir, but you see, at first I was so laid out – in such pain – that I couldn't think about or feel things properly. I'm real ashamed that I said such a dirty thing. Now I've had time to see what a low-down, cruel, randy bastard I was, and by God, sir I'll try to make up for it. I'll give you my solemn oath, sir, that I'll make no more trouble for you. I can't do much yet, but when my arm's better,

I'll do any job you say, for as long as you say. And I haven't thanked you yet, sir, for setting my arm. You done your best for me, I'm sure. I can't complain neither about her breaking it, can I? It was only natural for her to lash out when she got the chance. I dare say my sister Beti would have done the same, if anyone had treated her like I did Miss Eleanor. So, if I keep my word, when I'm in the dock, you might speak up for me, sir?'

Grant was silent for a while, his cold composure a little disturbed. His first reaction had been to dismiss this worthless ruffian with contempt, but now he was less sure. John gave every appearance of humble remorse, and in view of his normally cocky nature, and the long history of mutual dislike between them, this penitence must have cost him a lot in self-esteem. Grant thought: You accepted the word of this fellow's crony Protheroe. Is it fair to totally, instantly, disbelieve and reject John? By Heaven, poor old King Duncan in 'Macbeth' was dead right: 'There's no art to find the mind's construction in the face'.

At last he said coldly: 'Very well, but all that is a long time ahead. What I say or do on your behalf will depend entirely on your conduct from now on. You have a hell of a lot to make up for. Of course, when the steamer does arrive, I shall have to tell her captain all the facts about you, and it is likely that he will then lock you up and put you under guard down below. That will be up to him. In the meantime, I will allow you out of the galley in the daytime, but you must stay in the clearing. I will ask the hands to vote on whether they will allow you to sleep in the hut, and that will be up to them. But I must tell you that you are not exactly popular with them. In fact, I may add that if I had not been there in charge, I'm certain you would have been lynched on the spot. So you see, law and order have their uses, however much you may dislike them. I will also promise you this: if you misbehave again, in any way, you will be a hell of a lot worse off than you are now. What you've had so far will seem like a picnic.'

'Yes, I understand, sir. That's fair enough. I don't deserve no better. I won't take up no more of your time, sir and I want to thank you for listening to me. I won't make no more trouble, sir, on my bible oath, and as soon as my arm's right I'll work at anything you say. One day, sir,' he added with desperate earnestness, 'you'll see how well I keep my word.'

The humble penitence and self-abasement on his lips and in his face were utterly convincing, profoundly sincere; but behind it all, as he turned to go, his vengeful mind ground out the bitter thought: Yes, by Christ, you *will* see, you jumped-up English bastard. You will see that you'll never get the better of Billy John from Ffynnon-groes, and some time – don't know when - one or two of you swine will pay dear for what you've done to him. You just wait!

*

'There you are then, mister,' said the bosun. That's the best we can do.'

Ten days later, the same group that had met to make plans for the voyage was back on the beach in spring sunshine and a good westerly breeze. Bosun and Jac-y-Bont, the old professionals, were divided between pride at their ingenuity and shame at the poor quality of their workmanship. With no proper tools – no tenon-saws, chisels, planes, sand-paper or spokeshaves – the new deck was a rough old job, but it would have to do.

But to other eyes, the lifeboat now looked yacht-like in the sun. A cambered fore-deck, nine or ten feet long, stretched back to abaft the mast; under it, planking from the cannibalized boat was wedged to form a small decking, to keep the bedding out of the bilge, and Kellock's lee-boards hung from each side amidships.

'We haven't put the ballast in yet,' said bosun. 'We've got it ready, but that'll make the boat a lot harder to shift, so we thought we'd wait till she was moved down to the water.'

'Yes,' said Grant. 'Good idea. We'll leave that job till last.'

Above the boat, the sails slatted idly in the wind. The new triangular foresail was now neatly roped on its leading edge, the luff, and its other edges were turned and stitched to prevent fraying. Small metal rings called thimbles were sewn into each corner: the head, the tack at the front lower corner, and the clew at the rear lower corner, so that the sail could be hoisted and trimmed by halyards and sheets. The sailmaker and his crew had been 'sailorizing', happy for a change from the boring landsmen's chores. Across the belly of the big lug mainsail was a neat row of reef-points – cords threaded through the sail and sewn in, and now hanging down on either side of the sail. In a strong blow the bottom of the sail could be rolled up and secured by them, and at either end of the row, stout rings called reef-cringles were sewn in to provide a strong anchorage for the new bottom corners of the reefed sail.

Grant whistled his admiration: 'You've done wonders, boys. You've turned her into a regular yacht. Now she'll make it, I reckon. Why can't all sailors be like you two, not like the object I've just been talking to?'

'We're still working on the storm-sails,' said Jac. 'We'll finish today. There again, they'll be a rough old job – they'd make a good sailor cry. But there you are, they'll have to do. As for that Billy John, there's a bad apple in every barrel.'

'You're right there, Jac. Now I'm going to talk to Mr Raven here like a Dutch uncle, since he's going to be captain for the first time in his life.' He took Raven down the beach, leaving Eleanor walking round the boat, admiring the changes, and discussing them in her native tongue with the two old men.

'Now then,' said Grant, 'No more chat and waffle. I'm going to give you orders, as your superior officer, and you had better listen carefully and remember them all. You are going to have your own, and three other peoples' lives in your hands – your hands alone - so this is serious business. I've got a lot of faith in you; if I hadn't, I wouldn't have allowed this enterprise to take place, but this is something you've never had to do before. As a captain, you are responsible for every damn thing that anybody in your boat does at any time – just as I'm now responsible for anything you do. Very well then, let's get down to brass tacks: In my judgement you're a good boat-handler, but I don't think you've ever made a long-distance passage over open water, have you? Well, I have done a little of that; years ago; my father kept a thirty-foot ketch down in Poole, and I've been down-Channel with him in that quite often – as far as Santander once. I don't want to start showing off, because you know only too well – and so do all the hands – what a balls-up I made of gybing my boat on the way here on that first day. But I can remind you of one obvious fact: on a long passage you are almost certain to encounter lots of different weather, some of it very unpleasant indeed. You can't avoid it and you can't shelter from it, so you have to learn to deal with it, however bad it is. You're committed to your voyage, and that's that. Obviously, the trips that Dad and I did were nothing like as dangerous as the one you're undertaking: he had a well-found, properly rigged boat, larger than yours, fully decked-in, except for a small cockpit – and that could fill without filling the boat itself. She had a solid lead keel to balance the power of her sails, she had gear for navigation, and there were ports down-wind where we could have found shelter in really bad weather; She also had lots of spare cordage and sails. Still, you've got plenty on your side too: you're a real seaman, you've got guts, and you know exactly what the seas in this part of the world can be like. But seeing them from "Figaro's" poop and seeing them from sea-level in an open boat are very different experiences.

'You've got to think all the time about safety, not speed. You're not doing a really long voyage as the crow flies, and you'll have plenty of food and water – we'll see to that. With any luck, you'll get some days and nights of decent sailing breezes, and then you should set all the sail you can, and use Curly's wonderful lee-boards if you're close-hauled, but only if the wind's moderate or light. You've no proper keel and those lee-boards will break in heavy weather. They'll also increase the danger of capsizing in a blow, by giving the wind more sideways leverage.

'Let's look on the bright side: with a decent west or south-west breeze, under full sail, you could make a hundred and twenty miles a day – though perhaps you'd better not have the foresail set after dark, because if it did pipe up, someone would have to go out on that fore-deck to douse it and bring it in. You'd better detail Protheroe to do that job, by the way. He's lighter and a lot more active than Carl. And make sure he has a lifeline on before he gets up on that deck. It'll be sensible in a decent breeze for all of you to sit up to windward to give her an extra knot or two, but for God's sake don't start racing with the lee gunwale nearly under water. Play safe all the time. If you're going to change sails, try to do it in daylight; if you're in any doubt about the wind strength at night, lower the lugsail and hoist the foresail in its place. If you've got a good following wind, or a beam wind, you'll be surprised to see the speed you'll make with just that, though you wouldn't do too much to windward.

'If there's a gale you'll get short breaking seas on top of the swells. Well, if you kept on sailing, two or three of those wave-crests could break over the gunwale and fill this boat, and that'd be the end of all of you – no second chance. Down sails then, and out with the sea-anchor – in plenty of time, not at the last moment. I've seen the effect of that once in my Dad's boat, and it's nothing short of miraculous. Up comes her head into the seas, and, since you're not trying to drive her anywhere, she just floats like a duck, passively. She'll rise to really big, steep seas, and they'll pass harmlessly under her. If you also hoist the spitfire jib on the mast, and sheet it in really tight, that will keep her from yawing about. If the storm goes on for any length of time, keep checking the canvas wrapping on the warp where it comes in through the fairlead; I'll tell Jac to give you plenty of spare canvas, and remember: that bit of canvas might be the only thing between you and death.'

'Yes,' said Raven, I see. I think it'd be a good idea for us to practise setting the sea-anchor on a fine day. None of us has done it before, I suppose, and we might need to set it in rough weather in the dark. And I think I'll stick to the ordinary ship routine of watches – Eleanor and I will be the port watch, and Carl and Protheroe the starboard, with Carl in charge, of course.'

'Right. Now, navigation: I'll give you pencil and paper out of the ship's old account-book.'

'Yes, but with the best will in the world, it's going to be all by guess and by God.'

'Exactly, and perhaps, even to my atheistic mind, it's a pity we haven't got the latter. He would have got you there safely, provided He was in a good mood. But there you are: in my creed you've only got yourself to depend on. Now then, you must take Eleanor's excellent sketch-map of the islands for the first stage, so that you don't pile up on Enderby Island. We'll start you at dawn to get you well clear of the whole archipelago in daylight. Use a whole double page to make a plot. Bluff Harbour is near enough due north, three hundred miles off. You'll have your boat compass – and make sure no idiot uses it with a knife or anything metal in his pocket. The magnetic variation is about seventeen degrees west. You and Carl must try to make a close estimate of the course made good, and the distance run every watch – and write it all down. Aim to be slightly east of New Zealand when you reach its latitude, for two reasons: one, that'll keep you clear of the Snares Rocks – well named, for they're a nasty unlit trap for ships, and two, because that way you won't finish up on a lee shore in a blow. It'll be a lot safer to aim to miss the land to the east, and tack your way back west. When you sight land, you'll know that you have to turn south to run down the coast to Bluff. There's probably no lights on the east coast, so heave-to at night.'

'Thank you for all that, Simon. But, hell, it's not going to be easy. No sextant, no log tables, so no fix. As you said, we're back four centuries.'

'Yes, you'll need a lot of skill and a modicum of luck, but I'm beginning to think you'll make it. There's one thing in your favour: a sea-anchor is quite useless if you're close to a lee shore, but your lee shore is Chile – hundreds and hundreds of miles off, so you don't have to worry about that. Did you ever read or see "The Tempest"? No? I thought not, you philistine. Well, old Bill Shakespeare knew his stuff about the sea all right. In a bad storm on a lee shore he makes his ship's bosun yell: "Blow, till thou burst thy wind, if room enough!" I sometimes reckon he must have been a sailor once to know that - that in a bad blow ships are much safer miles away from the land. Landlubbers always think a sailor loves to see the shore when he's out in a storm. Idiots! It's just the opposite!'

Eleanor had strolled across the join them, and said: 'How much longer is this lecture going on, Simon? I'm getting cold and bored with standing about. And, on the subject of being cold, wouldn't it be a good idea if we took some extra warm clothes? I mean, if we're just sitting in a boat we can't get much exercise, and if the wind should come from the south, it's going to be very cold. It's not too bad on the island now, and you've got some proper shelter; so some of you could spare us an extra jersey or two, surely?'

'What a very good idea! This is the advantage of

having a woman in the crew, John – they're so much more practical than we men are, and they think ahead. You wouldn't have thought of that until you were three days out in a freezing south-west gale.' Eleanor was standing close to Raven, and Simon put his hands on their shoulders in a kind of secular benediction: 'You're looking worried, John. Don't be; I feel that you will all make it, and when you do, once you've got them to charter a steamer to come and fetch us, there's no need to wait for us there. Cable old Powell, tell him what's happened to the ship, and tell him to cable you enough money for your fares home – and the two hands, of course - and then – off you go! Once they know about us, you've done your job, and all you need then is a passage home.'

Eleanor's answer was fervent and earnest, rather than happy: 'Thank God! Thank God that, once I am in that boat, whatever happens – good or bad - I know that I will never have to see that man again – ever. To me, almost any risk is worth taking for that, and I am so grateful that three other souls – one of them, I trust and believe, a redeemed soul – are willing to go with me, to make that possible. And, on the subject of redeemed souls, I feel strongly that from now on we should treat Jimmy Protheroe in exactly the same way as we'd treat Carl Johanssen; he has, in a way, offered his life as a supreme penance, and therefore, bygones must be bygones. In such an enterprise as this, which may end in death for all of us, there must be mutual respect and trust. But,' she added with a smile at Grant, 'whatever you poor gloomy atheists think, I believe in a Power that will get us safely to harbour, and to a life of safety and peace of mind.'

Grant replied to her fervour in a characteristic

blend of sympathy, kindness and dry, ironic humour: 'And I, from my gloomy, godless depths, hope that you are right in all you say, and that this Someone up there will send you blue skies, calm seas and good sailing breezes all the way to Bluff, and I hope also that this young man will remember enough of what he's been taught about navigation not to end up in Fiji or Samoa.'

'O, come on, Simon,' said Raven, keeping to Grant's lighter tone: 'Fair play, as our Welsh friends keep saying. I wasn't the best in Conway at navigation, but I wasn't the worst either.'

'There you are, Eleanor,' said Grant with the warmest of smiles, 'there's a small crumb of comfort for you. Make sure he looks at your sketch-map as soon as you start, so that he doesn't run the boat into Enderby Island on the first morning. Then, once you're clear of this archipelago, New Zealand's due north, near enough – even you can't miss it, John.'

All smiled brave smiles, as their banter skated over the dread reality that yawned ahead. None of them could forget the sight of the mountainous forty-foot waves marching in ranks with tumbling, white crests from the far-off Horn. Only a few weeks ago they had seen them from the relative safety of the deck of a fast, well-found three-thousand-ton Clyde-built steel barque. Even she, with all her weight and bulk, had been the plaything of those waves, tossed up and down like a toy. In a day or two, Eleanor and Raven might see them again from a half-open, twenty-foot wooden lifeboat with improvised sails and navigation equipment appropriate to the fifteenth century. There was no turning back now, so it was best either to make silly jokes about their plight, or to pray as they had never prayed before. Or, perhaps, both.

CHAPTER TWELVE

In the half-light of dawn the next day the landing beach, a place which, for countless centuries, had seen little of human life and activity, was astir with bustling humanity. The cloudless sky was pale, the stars fading into the light which was beginning to appear over the eastern shore of the harbour. Though the breeze was gentle, the air was chilly on that spring morning and the hands were glad to be busy; while some were loading the biscuit, bully-beef tins and the three breakers, or small barrels, of water into the boat's bilge, others were lugging the thick flat stones that were to be the boat's ballast down to the edge of the tide, while the remainder were clearing any big rocks or stones from the boat's path to the water. Though the whole crowd was there, except for Billy John and his jailer, there was quiet, for the men were all too aware of the solemnity of the occasion; a small part of their company was leaving; they had all been together for a long time, and all the men felt a strong affection for Eleanor. Carl Johanssen too had always been popular, and even John Raven, despite being an officer and English to boot, was liked and respected. As for Jimmy Protheroe, few of the crowd had yet entirely forgiven him, but most thought, well, fair play to him, he was risking his neck to make up for his crime. What more could he do than that?

The bosun and sailmaker were in charge. The two old men were tired from their long hours of work on the boat, and, while proud of their efforts, still half-ashamed of what they saw as the roughness of their workmanship. But it was the best they could have done in the circumstances. It would have to do.

Grant and Raven stood talking, a little apart from the bustle round the boat, for some last cautionary words. 'You've got an ideal day for your start, John – light south-westerly breeze and fine weather for the moment, but you'll be damn lucky if it stays like this all the way. Do for God's sake keep a weather eye open for storms. You've no barometer, so look out for a cloud-bow to the south, a backing wind and rain-showers – they're usually the first signs of a bad blow. And *play safe!* Be ready for dirty weather before it starts, if you can; don't worry too much about speed. As we've agreed, it would be best to steer to the east of the land, so point her north-by-east. And another thing: keep a good lookout for the rescue steamer. Personally, I'm not expecting her to appear for weeks, but you're going to be on a reciprocal course to her, so it's just possible you might sight her, and get a safe lift back here. But that's a very long shot indeed. So.... good luck, old son, till we meet again somewhere, some time. You've got a risky trip ahead, but I couldn't be sending a better skipper. You will all make it, I'm sure.' The emotion on both sides was powerful, and for a moment broke down the normal English reserve, as both men joined in a quick hug of farewell.

Wellington Jones was much less restrained. The long hours and days that he and Eleanor had shared in the galley had given him a strong fatherly love and sympathy for the troubled Welsh girl, and tears rolled plentifully down his grizzled cheeks as he embraced her: 'God bless you, honey. You bin the best cook's help I ever did see, and the prettiest too. You bin through bad times, I know, losing your mammy and daddy, and then having that terrible trouble with that goddam skunk Billy, but that's all behind you now, darling. You gonna to be with your man now, and you gonna be safe. That Jimmy Protheroe ain't going to do you no more wrong; I told him last night: "If I hears you made one wrong move with Miss Nelli, you gonna to get this big old kitchen knife straight through your ribs, boy." I guess he believed me, miss.'

Eleanor was deeply moved, and amused too, at the good old Jamaican's affectionate ferocity. She returned his hug and kissed his stubbly cheek: 'Goodbye, Welly. You're the kindest man I've ever known. I don't know how I would have endured these last weeks without you and the boring jobs you made me do. I never want to see another mackerel as long as I live! Isn't it strange, though? If we hadn't been cast away here on this island I would never have known you – not properly, anyway. I'd have been in the cabin or on the poop, and you'd have just been a man I glimpsed now and then, popping in and out of your galley on the main-deck. I'm so glad we became such good friends.'

She turned to where little Davey stood, his tears running unashamedly down his cheeks: 'And goodbye to you too, Davey *bach*. You'll have to do more washing-up when I'm gone, I'm afraid. And keep hunting for more vegetables to go with your onions. I'm sure there's a patch of potatoes out there somewhere, and they would be so good for the men. And don't be so down-hearted; this is not goodbye, for I'm sure we'll meet again in Newport one day.' The boy was too overcome to speak, but just gave her a brief hug and ran off up the path to the clearing, sobbing loudly.

All was ready now. While the boat's crew stood aside by the water's edge, the rest of the crowd, under the bosun's orders, stood evenly divided on either side of the boat, grasping the gunwales. In a high, strident voice the bosun yelled: 'Come on then, boys – lift and *larnch!* Lift and *larnch!* – Hi-*ho!* Hi-*ho!* Two-six… *heavy!* Two-six… *heavy!'* until the boat had rasped its way over the black shingle to the sea's edge. He was using the way labouring men of all countries and colours in the world had used for centuries to multiply their strength, until wonderful machines came along to help a few of them, and make the rest redundant. They halted their efforts at the water's edge while the ballast stones were loaded and securely wedged and lashed in place.

'There you are then, old son,' said Grant. 'All of you hop in before we push her out. You might as well start dry-shod; no doubt you'll get all the water you want later. How do I say: "Good luck to you all" in Welsh, Eleanor?'

Eleanor, though tense and white-faced, managed a cheerful reply: 'You say: *"Lwc dda i chi gyd,"* Simon – only I'll wager you can't say that.'

'True enough, Nelli, and I'm not even going to try. Consider it said then, and the very best of luck to all of you. I'll see you again soon.'

As the boat floated off, and became alive, Holy Parry from Solva raised his voice in the old hymn 'Guide me, O thou great Jehovah', and at once the whole crowd joined in with a real fervour. Being Welshmen of that time, they were mostly chapel members when at home, and had the skill to add silvery tenor and rich bass parts above and below the melody, producing a delicious harmony, which rose and echoed back from the slopes behind the beach. Eleanor – and Raven too – would remember those sounds till the end of their days, would remember sitting together in the stern-sheets as the boat at last floated free and began to move, and as Carl and Jim shipped the long ash oars and pulled lustily at them to make an offing. The sheer familiarity and sweetness of the music brought the tears to Eleanor's eyes, and even the men ashore brushed their cheeks furtively. As the boat drew slowly away from the beach, the music became fainter and fainter until it ended, and the boat's crew could just hear three cheers from the now far-off crowd.

Raven jolted himself back to his business as a skipper: 'Right: boat oars, boys, while I ship the rudder. Then it's up mainsail, up foresail.' As the men hauled down on the halyards, the two white sails crept up the mast and forestay, shaking and booming gently in the breeze. The mainsail, called technically a standing lugsail, was starkly simple: a peaked spar, called the yard, fastened to an iron ring called a traveller, which held it in to the mast, and, hanging from that yard, a four-sided sail, loose-footed at the bottom, having no boom. It was virtually a sail from the Stone Age, but for Jac's neat row of reef-points.

As the lug went up, first the peak of the sail, then the whole sail caught the breeze. The yard swung ponderously out to starboard. 'In, main sheet,' said Raven, and as Eleanor dutifully hauled in on the sheet-rope the canvas was transformed from a flapping bag of wind to a shapely white wing, and the smooth water began to chuckle under the bow. That murmur increased as the foresail too caught the wind and was sheeted in. The boat heeled slightly to starboard and Raven felt the tiller come alive in his hands.

As the shelter of the shore receded, the wind became stronger and steadier across the wide water of Port Ross. 'Check sheets,' Raven called. 'We're almost dead before the wind now.'

Eleanor was puzzled: 'Check? What do you mean – "check"?'

With a hasty irritation Raven said: 'It means pay it out a bit, loosen it. We're pressing her too much. I thought you'd know that. Well! Leave it at that. Now listen, all of you: no sheet is ever to be made fast to anything. You can save your hands by taking a turn with it round a thwart, but *never, ever,* make it fast – not if you want to stay alive. And with the wind on the quarter as it is now, give the sail plenty of sheet. Pay out the sheet until the sail flaps, then bring the sheet back in until the sail just goes to sleep, as they say. Then you know it's pulling at its best.'

As they all settled down to their places in the boat, Eleanor murmured sulkily to Raven: 'There was no need to get cross with me back then. I can't be expected to understand all your sailing-ship jargon straightaway, so I didn't know what "check" meant. Do you enjoy trying to make me look like an idiot in front of these men?'

'Sorry, Nelli. I didn't mean to shout. I won't do it again.'

She was too nettled to leave it at that: 'No! I'm one of your crew. You've every right to shout at me if I'm idle or stupid or careless – but not if I'm just bewildered by your weird terms for everything. You always forget that with you I'm using my second language all the time anyway.'

'I understand, Nell.' He put his hand on hers in a gesture of apology. The two sails, now full of wind, spread out wide to starboard, and all the time the boat gathered speed. To balance the force of the sails, the whole crew now sat on the port side.

Eleanor looked back along the creamy track of their wake, and could just make out the crowd as a tiny black blob on the beach, against the background of low, sloping grass, dense leafless brown forest above, and above that again the high, grey, rock-strewn fells, rising to the bald, lifeless summits of the island. Suddenly, her horror of Auckland Island fell away, and she said: 'Beautiful.... wild.... unspoilt ..... just like the world before Man came into it.'

'Wasn't Man there from the start?' said Raven. 'You know - Adam?'

'No. I'm afraid that's one bit of the Bible I don't believe. I don't see Man as part of paradise; Man seems to spoil everything' She was about to add, 'As I know to my cost,' but then thought: No, I won't spoil today by raking up past nightmares.

'Well,' Raven said, 'I can't say I felt that place was much of a paradise anyway.'

'No, it's not for humans, perhaps, but it is for the birds, the fish, the other creatures. They love it, I think. It's their home.' As if in confirmation, and dead on cue, there was a quiet splash and a sound of heavy panting astern, and they all turned to see the blunt head, spiky whiskers and genial calm face of a big bull seal, which had surfaced, perhaps out of curiosity. The seal looked at them and the boat with an expression of only the mildest interest, then noiselessly dived again. Touched, and amused too, Eleanor said: 'There you are – it's as if he was glad to see us going, but bidding us a kind farewell all the same.'

'The place lonely now,' said Carl, 'but all these islands seen plenty whalers and sealers years ago. All gone now.'

The thought of those bloody trades, of the whales

transfixed and tortured by sharp harpoons, and of the smooth skins of slaughtered seals adorning the bodies of rich American and European women cast a dark shadow in Eleanor's mind. She said: 'It's better now. They've all come back. The rocks are full of seals, and higher up on the cliffs there's hundreds of nests of albatrosses Look! There's an albatross now, right over our heads! He's on the same course as us, but look how graceful and fast he is. And just look at all those birds on the water over there, swimming and diving. They're like black and white pigeons.'

'Ja, cape pigeons – that what they call them,' said Carl.

'They must be finding plenty of little fish down there,' said Jimmy. 'Good going so far, mister.'

'Yes, ideal. Flat water and the wind abaft the beam – couldn't be better. That little hump of an island off the port bow is Ocean Island, and the big one to starboard is Ewing Island, so we've done three miles already. How many knots d'you think we're doing, Carl?'

'I reckon five, mister, maybe five and half.'

'Yes, I'd agree with that. So in an hour or so we'll have the North-East Cape of Enderby Island abeam, and then there's nothing between us and Bluff Harbour.'

'Ja,' said Carl. 'No land, but whole lot of sea and maybe lot of wind too, I t'ink. But she good sea-boat now.'

'We will get there,' said Eleanor fervently. 'I know we will. They've done marvels with this boat in only a week or so. But surely we should give this boat a name? You call her "she", so it should be a woman's name. I've been thinking: Dadi's ship was "Figaro", and that's the name of a man in an opera. Well, I've heard people singing arias from that opera in eisteddfod concerts, and I remember Figaro had a fiancée called Susannah. So why not call her "Susan" for short?'

'Right,' said Raven. '"Susan" it is. It's a bit late, but God bless "Susan" and all who sail in her, and by Jove, I reckon we need blessing more than most.'

With such a good fair wind on the quarter, Raven could steer as if he were steering a steam-launch. He headed for the gap between the two small islands, and once through that, he headed north-east for Pebble Point, the extreme south-east corner of the big, green, low-lying Enderby Island. As the land fell away to port, Port Ross widened and they entered Rose Island Sound. The sea's ripples turned into small wavelets, through which "Susan" ploughed her way, disdainfully flinging them aside, her bow rising and falling in a quick, happy rhythm. As, flying along, she struck the steep little waves, the overlapping planks of her bows gave out loud, deep crunches, as if she were ploughing through heaps of small shingle. Raven turned for a moment from his study of the course ahead to look at Eleanor, close beside him on the stern-sheet bench, and smiled. She had forgotten their tiff about "check", and he got back a smile of sheer, deep happiness that made his heart – his whole inside – turn over, it seemed. At last, at last, she was becoming her real self again – the Eleanor who had changed him from a boorish overgrown schoolboy and random, unfeeling lecher into a proper, young, passionate human being. She looked very different, of course: gone were the cool, native elegance, the smooth, perfect features and matchless long dark hair that had so electrified him in Chile. Instead, a ruddy, weather-beaten face grinned above a cocoon of thick, clumsy jersey and gleaming black oilskins, her face now framed by a stiff, jagged, ragged crown of short black hair, now beginning to turn into a brush, a mop, which the wind ruffled brusquely. She laid her hand on his with all the old, frank directness of a lover, and her eyes said: Nothing has changed. We are in a small, half-open boat with an old man from Sweden and a scapegrace from Wales – possibly reformed, possibly not – sailing perhaps to our deaths. But between you and me nothing has changed, nothing will change – not even in death itself.

Then a sudden stiffer gust heeled the boat more steeply to starboard, and Raven woke up to his present duty: 'Check sheets, boys! Let's bring her back up. Well – that'll do. Sorry about that.' Eleanor took her hand away, and they exchanged rueful smiles like conspirators.

The boat snored along, and soon they were back in smoother water, as they drew into the shelter of Enderby Island to windward. Raven steered her close in to Pebble Point, calling out: 'Look out for skerries, Carl. There's none marked on the chart, but look out anyway.'

'Ja, mister. I vatch good. I don't see nothing yet.'

As they reached the point, the whole low green eastern shore-line of the island opened out, and soon Raven called again: 'In both sheets. I'm bringing her up into the wind a bit more. Well, that'll do. Pass me the compass, Nelli. Yes, I thought so. We're on our proper course now – north-by-east. Next stop, Bluff Harbour.'

There was a brief cheer from the two seamen, and Raven called: 'Jim, pass me that canvas parcel from under the foredeck. That's the log-book. Eleanor, will you write the log for us – in English, please! There's a pencil in there too. Enter this: "October 2nd, 1896, 8.45 am: North-East

Cape of Enderby Island abeam to port, one mile. Course, north-by-east, estimated speed six knots, weather fair, moderate south-westerly breeze. All plain sail."'

'All plain sail'; those bald, drab words! How well Eleanor remembered her father writing exactly that phrase, seated in his roomy chair at his desk in 'Figaro's' beautifully-pannelled chartroom – so long ago, it seemed, though it was actually only two months or so. She was stirred, not only by the memory of him, but also by her sadness at the death of his huge, beautiful barque, her sails spreading eighty feet wide and a hundred-and-eighty feet high, and on her counter the curt, proud, resonant words: 'Figaro, Cardiff'.

'All plain sail': how little justice that did, even to this perilously small craft! Though the main-sheet, which was her charge, was mainly held by its turn round the thwart, she could still feel its pull – like that of a willing horse – a pull that was taking them away from the wild, savage beauty of the lonely Auckland Islands, and towards ..... what? Only God knew that, and, mercifully, He kept that knowledge to Himself.

From where she sat, between Jack and Jimmy Protheroe, she could look up at the rare Southern Ocean sun gleaming on the stout, varnished, red-gold pitch-pine mast, and on the taut, curved, carved shapes of the leaning sails. She could hear too the regular drum-beat as the boat's bow crunched the steep little waves at her forefoot. She caught Jack's eye, and could see that he too was exulting in the boat's speed and beauty, though, being English and professional, his response to her look of joy was more practical than poetic: 'Going well, eh? The old boys have done a first-rate job on her. She's going like a yacht in a regatta! Welcome, one and all, to the Southern Ocean – all of it. We've got to do three hundred miles; we've done seven miles now, so that leaves only two hundred-and-ninety-three. We're doing six knots at the moment, so at this rate it'll take us ....um... about...'

'Forty-eight hours and a bit – say forty-nine,' said Jimmy promptly. 'Two days and one hour to go.'

'Good heavens,' said Eleanor, smiling. 'I'm very impressed. Your mathematics are dazzling, Jim!'

'Yes, well, I used to win prizes at school for my tables. I ain't quite so stupid as I look. Old Aggy Davies Crymych School used to say I'd be a bank manager one day. Never managed that, though, cos my dad took me out of school when I was twelve – said I could be doing something more useful in his forge.'

'O yes,' said Eleanor, 'I remember my father talking about Huw Protheroe Crymych Forge. Dadi thought a lot of him. I remember he made a splendid iron gate for us once, when I was little. Blacksmithing must have been an interesting job.'

'I s'pose, for some, but not for me, miss. My dad kept me at it all hours, and I got more kicks than ha'pence, as they say: blowing up the fire with the bellows, standing there holding things with the tongs while he hammered away at them; holding the twitch to keep the big old farm horses still while he shod them; sometimes I had to try to hold their damn great feet up and keep em still while he trimmed the hoof. I got cursed every time something went wrong, Hot beyond, it was, in the forge in summer. That's why I cleared out and fell into bad ways, as you might say – always trying to show I was cleverer than the rest. Always getting into trouble wherever I went...'

'All that's behind you now, Jim,' she said gently. 'You must think about the future now. So now your dad has to do without you?'

'No, miss – he's gone, I'm afraid. A year back, it was. He got a kick in the head from one of those racing ponies – always the worst to shoe, they were - so full of oats, and so quick to move. My mam sold up and went as housekeeper to a gent at Plas Bronafon, over Cilgerran way. Happy there, she is. The old chap – a nice old boy - lets me stay there in a spare servant's room when I'm home on leave.'

'When you two have quite finished gassing,' said Raven with mock severity, 'could you please give a thought to sailing this boat? Nelli, give your mainsail a bit more sheet, and Jim: look at the foresail luff – the way it's sagging! Jim, for God's sake get up off your backside and give the halyard a swig-up. What a crew, eh, Carl?'

'They get bedder, I t'ink, pretty soon. Don't you start hazing everybody already, skipper. We got plenty far to go.'

They fell silent, each with his or her own thoughts. Looking back along the boat's small wake, they watched the low green Enderby Island, and the smooth, sculptured misty summits of the main island behind shrink into a low blur on the southern horizon. Goodbye then to its cool, drizzling, windy safety, the sheltering goblin forest of twisted trees, the warmth of the galley fire, the bunks in the long wooden hut, and the sound of many voices calling, gossiping, laughing. Ahead, there was nothing but the limitless, shifting, restless plain of the sea; no land for thousands of miles to port or starboard, 'Susan's' bow rising and falling abruptly, pointed to the South Island of

New Zealand, which they must find soon, or starve, or die of thirst.

Raven, showing his growing qualities as a leader, sensed their underlying fears – which he himself of course shared – and was once again practical and positive: 'Right then; it's now nearly eleven by my watch. In half-an-hour we'll all have a bite of some bully and biscuit, and a drop to drink – not too much, for we don't know how long it's got to last. Then Eleanor and I will take the afternoon watch, and you two can get your heads down if you want to in the for'ard cabin – if you can call it a cabin.'

'A caboosh, I'd call it,' said Jim. 'A little rough old sort of den.'

'Very well, then, a caboosh, if you like. I'm thinking it may be hard to get to sleep later, if it gets rough, so take your chance now – I should. Then you two – the starboard watch I'm going to call you – take over at four. In the mean time, while we're all awake, I want you both to take a trick at the tiller, to get used to sailing her on a compass course. Have you ever sailed a small boat, Jim? No, I thought probably not, so you really need to practise. Take your knife off and put it for'ard somewhere. No-one is to come near this compass with any metal about him – understood? Come on, have a go now. Remember, let her run, as much as you can. Be as easy on the tiller as possible. Every time there's an extra puff of wind she'll try to bring her head up into it, so you need to meet that swing; bring the tiller up towards you as she heels. It's just like sailing a big ship – and you've done plenty of that – only it all happens a lot faster. But a chap who can do sums as quickly as you can should soon learn. If you look at the water up to windward you can often see the puff coming.'

As Protheroe got up to take the helm, Eleanor shifted into his place to make room for Jack. (Shall we call him "Jack" now, as Eleanor so much prefers that name?) She found it so strange that she had for hours been sitting shoulder to shoulder, touching, a man who, only a couple of weeks ago, had come with that other man to *Cilfach Dawel* to spy on her nakedness. Since he had publicly repented, her Christian faith had obliged her to forgive, as Jesus had in his torment; she was still firm in that resolve, but sometimes a pragmatic human doubt – and some resentment – crept into her mind, when she saw his handsome, mobile face and saw his determined, cheerful obedience and willingness. Was all that pleasant surface simply a façade behind which evil still lurked? Was it true redemption or just a cleverly-acted pretence, the cunning of a serpent? Stolidly, her faith replied: You must trust him and believe in his repentance until you have proof that it is false and treacherous. As Hamlet had said to the old counsellor: 'Give every man his deserts, and who shall scape whipping?'

At noon they broached the first of their tins of bully and biscuit, and tapped the first breaker of water, and found how hungry and dry they had been. 'Easy on that water, mind,' said Raven. 'Sip it, don't gulp it. And let's keep all the tins and their lids when they're empty. Then if – when – it rains we may be able to catch some fresh water in that bit of canvas, and run it into a tin.'

As they all munched and sipped, an unspoken union began to grow, as if the meal were a kind of sacramental ritual. Now, said that feeling, we are one. We represent three nations, we speak – or can speak - three different languages, but now we are one – the crew of the

'Susan'. We shall live or die together.

After the meal the two seamen crawled into the cramped caboosh under the fore-deck and stretched out, fully clad, on the palliasses in there. Up in the bow, the boat's motion was – or seemed – more jerky and abrupt, but they were seasoned sailors and used to comfortless berths and short, snatched sleeps, and they were not awake long.

'Now they're gone,' said Eleanor coolly, 'I think I'll use the lavatory bucket. They did just now, and very discreet they were too. But, like everything else, these things are so much more difficult for us women, so you will please be a gentleman, and avert your gaze for a few moments?'

Concentrating, as bidden, on the sails and the steering, Raven felt a growing joy at Eleanor's recovery from her silent misery and self-hatred. At last, the old cheerful, candid Nelli had been reborn. And yet he sensed that, underneath that cheerful surface, she had still not fully recovered from the nightmare of Billy John's brutal, brutish sexual attack. Raven could feel that physically, sexually, she was still wounded, disabled. She had once or twice looked lovingly at him and touched his hand, but only briefly, as a quick gesture. He could feel the reluctance, the fear behind those quick fleshly contacts; it would clearly be a very long time – if ever – before she became again the sensual, passionate girl who had shared his bunk in the night watches so impossibly long ago.

He sensed that much the same thoughts were in her head too; it was time to be his cheerful workaday self again. What was the use in brooding over past nightmares? When she was once more back beside him he said:

'Come on, Nelli: you have a practice on the tiller too. You've done a lot of small-boat sailing in Newport, haven't you? She's going like a train, so you won't need much rudder. But keep your eye on the weather quarter, and be ready for the stiffer gusts. Now we're drawing clear of the shelter of the land, you can start to feel the swells, can't you? But never mind, they're long and smooth – we don't need to worry about them.'

Sure enough, Eleanor could feel a growing difference in the boat's motion: as well as tramping, chopping through the waves that overtook her from the port quarter, she was now slowly lifting and falling as great smooth ridges of water, their tops perhaps twenty feet apart, slowly marched from the west across their path. With her hand on the tiller, she could feel the boat like a living thing. It was like holding the reins of a lively, willing horse that needed guiding, but not urging. She was absorbed by the delight in that feeling, and proud of her skill in this age-old craft. She remembered reading in a newspaper before she left Wales about some German man who had invented a machine called a glider, in which he was actually able to fly like a bird. That must be very like sailing a boat – balancing your craft on the wind, carving a path through the air. But flying was, so far, just a new dangerous oddity; she felt glad that under the boat was the solid reassurance of water.

More and more, as Jack had said, she felt the boat rising and falling several feet in a steady rhythm; felt the boat's speed slackening as she sank into a trough and the lower parts of the sails lost the wind, then surging ahead as she rose, and both sails filled again. The wind was still from the south-west, but these long, smooth hills of water marched, one behind the other, from the west, from the Horn, for there was nothing to hinder their endless progress round the earth.

She was reminded of the big globe in her Haverfordwest class-room, and recalled the whimsical thought she'd had as a child: how odd that, when He made the world, God had put nearly all the dry land in the northern hemisphere! You would think He'd have spread it more evenly. That would have made things better and safer for deep-sea sailors like her father. But her teacher, the gaunt and spinsterish Miss Gwyther, had been shocked and furious when Eleanor made that suggestion to her. It was not, she said, for anyone, especially a foolish child, to question God's designs and purposes. The world was as it was, and that was that. There was divine reason, purpose and perfection behind all He had devised, and arguments about such things amounted practically to blasphemy. She had gone bright red with indignation, and the wattles of her scrawny neck had wobbled as she shook her head. She had never approved much of this pretty, outspoken Welsh-speaking girl from the wilds of North Pembrokeshire. When she heard her giggling and gossiping in Welsh with another girl from Cardigan, she was always filled with impotent anger and the suspicion (usually correct) that she was the butt of their laughter.

Eleanor smiled to herself at the recollection, and Raven said: 'You're looking happy, Nelli. What's made you smile?'

'O, nothing – just something silly from my schooldays. Never mind, it stops me brooding about the past – and the present too.'

'Brooding?'

'Well, not exactly brooding, but wondering what lies ahead. I've told you I trust you, but I can't for the life of me see how you can navigate this boat. I mean, aboard the ship my father had drawers full of charts; he had a sextant and a chronometer, log-tables, parallel rulers, dividers – all sorts of clever devices. You have nothing but a little compass. I just can't see how you will manage. Perhaps – and this is a feeling that is growing in my mind – I have been foolish, reckless and – worst of all – selfish, to let my fear and disgust at what happened at the cove persuade the rest of you to take such a risk with your lives.'

'No, no, be easy about that, Nelli. We all came as volunteers, and we came because we saw how fear and horror were destroying you. One of us came, so he says, out of repentance, the other two out of affection – no – out of love. I know that Carl loves you as a father might, and as for me, you know how I love you. What sort of a lover would I be if I wasn't prepared to take a bit of a chance to rescue you from that suffering? And I'm confident we shall get to Bluff Harbour. It is not so far – only three hundred miles, and if the weather stays like this we shall cover over a hundred miles a day. But you've seen the weather in these latitudes; we shall be very lucky indeed if it does stay like this. Even now the breeze is strengthening; when we change watches at four I think we'll take a reef in the mainsail, to be on the safe side. As for the navigation: yes, it's going to be hit-and-miss, I'm afraid. As you say, we've got none of the right kit here, but that doesn't mean we're helpless. We'll just have to navigate as Columbus and Drake and all those old chaps did. I'm aiming the boat a bit to the east of New Zealand; Carl and I will make an estimate of the distance covered and the course made good every watch, you can write that down in the log, and I'll make a rough plot of it on a blank page at the back. We know the distance we have to cover to the north, so when we calculate that we've run that distance, plus a bit more, we shall know that the South Island is due west – on our left, as you might say. So then we just steer west until we come to it.'

'But....'

'Yes, I know what you're thinking. Then we shall have to take damn good care that we don't run into it in the dark – or in a fog – and get wrecked. We'll have to heave-to at night. Then, when we sight the land, we turn to port again and follow the coast till we sight the harbour. There's bound to be some lights and buoys there. Luckily, with the wind generally from the west, we'll be in sheltered water, off a windward shore, so we won't get blown onto rocks. But as for now, I don't like the look of that cloud-bow to the south, behind us. The wind is freshening, isn't it? I can see you're having to use more rudder all the time to keep her on course. Very well: we'll be all right till four, I reckon, but then I'm going to reef the mainsail and douse the foresail for the night, as Simon advised. Can't be too careful.'

Sure enough, the first interruption to the peace of their voyage happened just before four o'clock: what with the mild wind from astern, their thick clothes, and the regular rhythm of the waves passing under them, both were beginning to feel warm and drowsy. After all, they had started the voyage at first light, and, because of tension and anxiety, neither had slept well the night before. Suddenly, they were jolted out of their languor by the hiss of a breaking wave that, steeper and larger than the rest, slapped against 'Susan's' quarter, throwing spray into the boat, lifting her stern sharply, and forcing her to slew round to port, at the same time heeling her over till the starboard gunwale was almost submerged.

Startled out of his torpor, Raven yelled: 'Helm up, Nelli, for God's sake, or she'll broach-to! Up – up – more, more…! Well, that'll do.' At the same time he eased the sheet so that it juddered round the thwart, the big sail flapped and rattled in the wind and the boat came back onto her northerly course, and back too to a safe angle of heel.

'My God, Nelli, we were damn careless then. That could have been the end of the trip. And d'you know why? We've been on watch a lot too long – over eight hours. That mustn't happen again. It's my fault – I should have foreseen this. We must have proper watches and rest times from now on, and no-one must ever be on the tiller for more than an hour at a time. Ah – good men,' he called, as he saw Carl and Jim crawling backwards out of the caboosh, their backsides lifting the thick canvas curtain that hung from the end of the fore-deck to provide some shelter from the wind. That fore-peak 'door' had been Jac-y-Bont's last refinement to the boat's fitting-out.

'I thought you wouldn't need rousting out after that schemozzle. Apologies, gents; that was my fault. We've been steering too long – over eight hours. That's much too long. She nearly broached-to.' Broaching-to was the end for many a sailing-ship. If a vessel running before the wind was caught by a steep wave and swung round broadside-on to the wind and waves, she was at the mercy of the next wave – stationary, and therefore unable to steer, heeled over, and likely to be overwhelmed.

'We're going too fast – that's the trouble. If we get some canvas off her and steer properly she'll have time to rise to the waves. Jim, put the life-line on and get up on the fore-deck, will you, to gather in the foresail. Nelli, stand by to pay out the halyard so that he can pull the sail down. Let the tack go, Jim, and bring the whole caboodle - sheets and all - back into the boat. When he's safely back in, Carl, you and I will reef the mainsail. We'll have to luff up and spill the wind to do that, Nelli, so when you've let go the halyard, come back and take the tiller. Let her come up to take the seas on her bow, but keep some way on her, and for God's sake don't put her about on the other tack. We'll be as quick as we can. Damn good job we're doing this in daylight, I reckon. Right, Jim, up you go, and take care, mind. Just hang on if she heels. Remember the old saying: - "One hand for the ship, the other for yourself".'

Sliding, heaving, flat on his stomach on the wet, canvas-covered fore-deck, Protheroe struggled to the bow, hauled the sail down as Eleanor slacked away the halyard, then cast off the tack and called: 'Right, miss. All gone for'ard. Pull the whole lot back.' Having done that, Eleanor watched in silence as he pushed himself back, the fore-deck tilting sharply this way and that as the boat rolled in the following sea. She found herself feeling as anxious for him as if he had been a brother, not her former enemy. That, she felt, was a good sign of their new unity.

After that, reefing the main was another ticklish job, as Raven had hinted; the boat had to be brought up, almost into the wind's eye, so that the sail could be hauled right in, and yet Eleanor had to keep her under way. As the boat swung round to port, the wind's strength became much greater, and the slack sail thundered, shaking the whole boat. This, she thought, is very different from a leisurely summer jaunt off Cerrig-y-Drwy.

But at last it was done, and Raven took the tiller again and bore away to bring her back on her down-wind course. As he did so, he called to Carl: 'We're going to get that wind you were talking about. Look at the compass; the wind's backed several points while we were doing that. It's nearly south now – nearly dead astern. Not a good sign, eh? Let her go like this till the end of your watch at six o'clock, but call me if you're worried about anything. Then we may have to get the main off her, and run with the foresail only.'

'Ja, that's good idea, mister. The foresail's a good lifting sail, not pressing. Now you and miss get some sleep. It's the first dog-watch now, so you only got two hours. You been working long time – too much maybe.' The two hands watched in silence as Raven and Eleanor disappeared, crawling into the caboosh. Protheroe, perhaps less redeemed than Nelli had hoped, looked at Carl with the beginning of a sly, prurient grin, but the big Swede shook his head angrily, and said: 'Stow that, you! You mind your own bloddy business, boy, and pay out a bit more on that mainsheet.'

In the cold, damp fug of their little hutch Eleanor and Raven lay close together, huddled for warmth. The release from the buffeting of the eternal wind was blissful, yet Eleanor seemed irritable, perhaps from exhaustion: 'Do you mean to say we've only got two hours in this dog-kennel? Those two had four. Where's the sense in these short dog-watches? Just one of your stupid sea-going customs, I suppose? You've always done it, so you keep on doing it?'

'Not at all – it's very sensible. It means you split the day and night up into seven bits, not six. That means you get a different pattern on succeeding days; otherwise, some poor devils would get the middle watch – midnight till four – every night. That's what they call the graveyard watch, because it's so awful. Fancy you – a captain's daughter – not realizing that! Now for God's sake let's get some sleep – though you could give me just a little kiss before we drop off.'

Unfortunately, his tone had been a trifle too didactic and smug for her strongly independent nature, and she replied curtly: 'I could, but I don't choose to kiss bossy know-alls.'

Raven smiled as he settled to sleep. He thought back to his mother and father, snapping at each other about pettifogging trifles over their breakfast boiled eggs and toast. This was what it would be like when he and Nelli were married – not always totally amorous and harmonious! Silly books said, 'They married and were happy ever after', but real life was not like that. Nothing could be perfect all the time! He whispered: 'As you wish, Miss Roberts, ma'am, as you wish.'

CHAPTER THIRTEEN

When a cold, reluctant dawn broke over the Southern Ocean, it revealed the little boat still dashing through ever-growing seas, the stout foresail, now hoisted on the mainsail halyards, taut with wind, the spray from the wave-tops rattling now and then on the oilskins of the two figures in the stern – Raven at the tiller, Eleanor sitting beside him, except when, clutching for hand-holds to steady her in the boat's crazy, jolting motion, she used the bucket to bale out the boat's bilges, for now solid lumps of water were coming inboard as each overtaking wave-crest rapped against 'Susan's' port quarter.

Raven sweated despite the cold wind, for he was now fighting the waves, constantly hauling and thrusting the tiller this way and that, as each big wave towered over the stern, bore them along, the boat surfing at a giddying speed on its crest, then slid under them, leaving them slowed down in its trough, waiting for the next menacing grey, white-topped wall of water.

He was silent, but his seaman's mind was racked by internal debate: this was terrific progress. Already, he reckoned, they had reeled off over a hundred – maybe a hundred and twenty – of the three hundred miles they had to cover. But still, it wouldn't do, this headlong, reckless career. With his hand on the tiller, he could feel that, with every wave, the boat was getting harder and harder to manage. The steep seas were, as they approached, throwing the stern up so high that the rudder was only half in the water, making the speeding boat less and less under his control. He was having moments of sheer sick panic when, for a few heart-stopping seconds, the rudder-blade lost its power and grip, and the boat started to slew round to port. It was no good. It seemed a damn shame to waste this strong following wind, but this would *not* do. It was all becoming too dangerous; he must take Simon's advice – safety before speed. Though Nelli was close beside him, he was forced by the wind's roar and the wash of the sea to yell in her ear: 'It's no good, Nelli. We'll have to put out the sea-anchor. Go for'ard and roust the boys out.'

The two men came aft cautiously, hanging on, dragged from the heavy sleep of exhaustion, for they too had had four hours of constant struggle and anxiety. Raven's orders were brief, and in any case the men knew what they would be: 'Out sea-anchor, boys! We're going to broach-to in a minute if we go on like this. Carl, make the warp well fast to the mast first. Jim, I'm sorry, but you'll have to get up on the foredeck. Don't forget your life-line, for God's sake. And be sure to get the parcelled bit of the anchor-warp into the bow fairlead first, *before* you put the drogue in the water, because once that warp gets the full tension on it you won't be able to shift it. Pay the warp out under control, so that we don't give it a sudden jerk. And bring the tripping-line back into the boat, for when we need to get the anchor in again.'

Protheroe nodded and said nothing, but Raven could see the dead-white pallor of his cheeks, could see the fear in his eyes, could see him gulp, and could see and hear that his teeth were chattering, and not just from cold. He remembered, with a flash of guilt, the first grim maxim of his officer's training: 'Never order a man to do something you'd be afraid to do yourself.'

'I tell you what,' he said. 'You take the tiller, Jim,

while I go up there. It's my idea, so it's up to me to do it, isn't it?'

Protheroe was too wrought-up to be respectful: 'Don't talk so bloody daft, mun! Who's going to navigate this tub if your life-line parted, and you went into the drink? If I go in, it won't matter so much, will it? I'm only a no-good skate.'

It was not the time to argue. 'Right. Good man! Well, when I see a chance, I'm going to luff up into the wind and seas. That'll be the bad bit for you, so for God's sake just hang on when she heels. Then, when I give you a shout, drop the drogue in. When you start to feel the strain coming on the warp, slowly pay out the whole lot – all fifteen fathoms of it. That should pull her head round. Understood?' Protheroe nodded stoically, and Raven reached out and grasped his hand: 'Good man. Off you go, and hang on, for God's sake on that foredeck! But wait till I say the word. Carl, get the spitfire jib out. Then, as soon as the drogue's pulled her head round, douse the foresail, hoist the spitfire jib in its place, and sheet it in really tight. We'll have that up for a riding-sail, to stop her yawing about on the warp.'

What with the boat's mad speed as she surfed down the front slopes of the giant combers and her vicious motion as she rocked from side to side, and what with the hoarse, loud blustering of the gale in his ears, Raven was finding it desperately hard to think calmly and sensibly. He needed to crane his head round over his right shoulder to try to pick out an approaching wave less high-crested with foam than the rest. The waves were coming at him at a good twenty-five knots, but they were now so big – there was now a distance of quite sixty yards of dark grey sea between their crests – that the speeding boat would have time enough to round up into the wind before the next great comber arrived. His mouth was dry and felt sour; that, he knew, was the sick, coppery taste of fear. It seemed scarcely credible that a few fathoms of rope with a canvas bag on its end could save them from the brutal seas, but it was that or nothing.

Icy, stinging spray dashed painfully into his face as he peered to windward; for the wind now had a savage force, it was only when the boat was on the crest of a wave that he could see any distance. But – yes! There it was - a gap in the white tops of the overtaking seas. Now or never! Jim was crouching just behind the foredeck, a life-line round his waist, Carl behind him again, ready to pay out the long warp. One end was now made fast to the mast, and the Swede had, like the true seaman he was, got the bight – the middle section of the rope – neatly coiled at his feet.

Raven yelled: 'Up you go, Jim! I'm bringing her up into the wind. Don't forget: make sure the parcelled bit of the rope is in the fairlead before you drop the sea-anchor. Right?' Both men nodded. 'Here we go, then! And *hang on,* Jim, for God's sake!'

He thrust the tiller away from him, and the speeding boat, lurching drunkenly to starboard, began to swing round to port to face the great wind-roughened wall of water that approached. 'Let go, Jim, as soon as you can!' he screamed into the wind. 'Nelli, get the bucket and bale like hell. We'll ship a good bit at first.'

Sure enough, as the boat came beam-on to the wave, solid gouts of water came in over the port gunwale. Only now, when they were facing the wind and not flying before it, did they realize its fearsome strength. It was hard to look to windward with the deadly force of the gale in his face; it was even harder to think straight, as the wind roared and the foresail thundered madly while Carl struggled to douse it and get it into the boat. There were some horrible moments as the boat lay helpless, beam-on to the wind; though the helm was hard down. There was no sail behind the mast now, and the bow stubbornly refused to point up into the wind. Instead, the boat drifted, helpless, wallowing, sideways before the gale, Eleanor frantically baling with the bucket, sobbing for breath, as the ocean strove furiously to overwhelm and drown them.

Then Raven saw Protheroe fling the drogue over the port bow, saw it sink into the boiling sea, saw him clinging to the boat with one hand and paying the warp out with the other; Carl was uncoiling the warp slowly, only a little at a time, so that no deadly coil or kink in the rope could entangle Protheroe and drag him overside. Raven thought: My God, I should have warned them about that. But never mind, good old Carl didn't need to be told! The boat meanwhile was now moving at perhaps three knots to leeward, a helpless log.

Then they heard his cry: 'Warp's paid out! She's got her anchor.'

Then… Then… It was like a miracle, a blessed miracle! Raven saw the rope that had at first led out abeam to port, gradually tighten as the boat drifted and the anchor began to grip the water. Being wholly below the surface, the drogue felt no leeward thrust from the wind, and its shape made it act as a strong brake, as Simon had said it would. He saw the rope draw slowly round, till it pointed dead into the wind's eye, and drew the bow powerfully round to face the seas. And at once their plight was transformed! Any spray now rattled harmlessly onto the new foredeck, and streamed back into the sea. At first 'Susan' yawed this way and that as the gusts took her, but once Carl was able to hoist the small, strong spitfire jib behind the mast, and sheet it in tightly, the yawing stopped and the little craft faithfully, obediently, faced up into the wind and stayed there, the small sail acting like a weather-vane.

And now, in that little lifeboat, in that wild south-westerly gale in the open Southern Ocean – perhaps the most dangerous area of sea on the face of the globe – there was at last peace – of a kind. No longer trying to defy the waves, hurtling through them on her own compass course, fighting the sea, the boat and her crew had yielded to the elements. The wind and the waves were as bad as ever, but now that she had surrendered, they passed harmlessly over and under her and were gone. Each huge, steep ridge of water, crowned with hissing foam, roared up out of the south-west, impossibly high above her bow; the stout warp, held by Jac-y-Bont's home-made drogue, seemed to tow her up its slope until, with a rattle of flying spray, it passed under her keel.

The boat no longer threw its crew about; she pitched into the ruffles of sea on the surface of the huge combers, but hardly rolled at all. Still, it was as well that they were all hardened sailors, for the boat rose and fell perhaps thirty feet at a time, as if it were being lifted and lowered by a giant crane. All of them felt hollow and queasy in their stomachs, for it was now mid-morning, and they had not eaten since last night's supper.

'Are you feeling all right, Nelli?' asked Raven.

'I'm not sure.... my head feels as if it's spinning round inside. But I've never been sea-sick in my life, and I'm not proposing to start now. When I first joined the ship in Chile, when we were at anchor for weeks and weeks, rolling in that swell – then I felt pretty poorly sometimes.'

'I know; but this is a bit extreme for all of us, eh, Carl? I think we ought to have a bite to eat; then we may feel better. We must all be starving, and anyway there's nothing for us to do now, apart from baling and keeping a lookout.'

'A lookout for what, mister?' said Protheroe, who had come aft to join them after his perilous spell on the foredeck. A little of the old, unredeemed Jimmy Protheroe, sea-lawyer, was beginning to show itself in arguments with anyone in authority.

'I don't know... a ship, maybe, running for the Horn… or a steamer. We don't show up much in this sea, so a windjammer might run us down – she'd be doing fourteen knots or so under tops'ls and fore-course in this blow.'

'All right, mister: say we see a damn great barque or a steamer headed straight for us. Then what do we do? Wave our hankies at it? We got no flares nor rockets nor nothing, and we can't move without getting in the sea-anchor, can we?'

'I'll tell you what we'll do, clever dick,' said Raven, too happy with the new peace and safety to be annoyed. 'We're making stern-way, so if we put the rudder hard over, we can make her veer across, one way or the other. That might help. But for now, stow your damn sealawyering, sit here and get some bully and biscuit down you. You must be pretty wet after being on that foredeck.'

'To the bloody skin, mister.'

'Yes, I thought so. You did well up there, man; you should be proud of that. It was damn chancy for you, sprawled out up there with not much to hang on to. When you've eaten you'd better crawl back into the caboosh and try to get warm and dry again. Wrap up in blankets, and stay as long as you like. We'll start the routine watches this evening at six. Meanwhile, there's nothing for anyone to do now but try to keep warm.'

'Ja,' said Carl. 'But this a lod bedder now – not fighting sea – she too strong for us. Now ve joost rest on the vaves – like sea-bird. This storm pass, like everything pass. Then ve make sail again.'

Long hours indeed passed as the sullen day dragged by and a thousand waves, marching inexorably round the globe, lifted them high into the roar of the wind, slid under them, and left them in the relative calm of a huge deep valley. A first, as each black-grey wall towered over them, rushing at them, all the crew were convinced that their end was nigh, but as wave after wave passed under them, their faith in Jac-y-Bont's little canvas bag, and its fifteen fathoms of good rope grew and grew.

Several times, great wandering albatrosses came by, hovering in the wind with steady wings, or hurtling headlong before it. One particular bird made itself their companion. As if intrigued by the presence of such a tiny craft in that huge watery desert, it hovered and circled persistently round them, its huge black-tipped wings almost half the length of their boat. Sometimes it settled on the water alongside, as if to show them how to survive a

Southern Ocean gale, taking effortlessly to the air to skim over the worst wave-crests, to land again sociably close as the wave passed. How I wish, thought Eleanor with a rueful smile, that we could do that! How wonderful it must be to live in mastery of all three elements – land, water and air! She had been silently praying for the safety of the boat and her crew, and she saw the magnificent bird as a sign of hope – a messenger to tell her that her prayers had been heard. This grey, savage, trackless ocean was its home; it could fly over it, get its food from it, or rest on its rugged surface, and do so for months on end. Surely, her thoughts said, we too can survive on this hellish sea for a few days, if God is merciful to us, and (her practical mind added) as long as the warp doesn't part. Then she chided herself: why could she not be more spiritual, more a child of God, and trust in His mercy alone, and not even think about bits of rope? It must be Jack's earthy, pragmatic influence! But never mind: his love for her had made him undertake this horribly dangerous voyage without a second thought when he saw the depth of her suffering and fear, and thank God they had him here, with his courage, common-sense and steady leadership. She could tell from his face that he often felt a fear as great as hers; but he had the gift of true courage, the kind that was needed to master that fear and defy it, and show others how to defy it too. He would never be a priest, a scholar or a philosopher, but one day he would be a wonderful sea-captain.

'Carl,' said Raven, 'you might as well turn in again and get warm. There's nothing for us to do out here now but wait and bale. But before you go, have a good look over the side for a moment and tell me this: how fast you think she's drifting to leeward?'

'I say.... knot and half – maybe two.'

'Yes, I agree. A hell of a lot less than we would have made without the drogue. But still, that means that in twenty-four hours she'll go nearly fifty miles to the north-east. By the time this gale blows itself out, we'll be a hell of a long way to leeward of our proper course. Never mind; can't be helped. She's a lot safer and more comfortable now, and there's nothing else we could have done. All right, old son; off you go and get your head down for a while.'

'Wouldn't it be wonderful,' said Eleanor when the Swede had gone, 'if we had a little cabin aft? The wind's so cold, coming from the Antarctic, and we've been too busy to notice that it's started raining.'

'Very well then, let's make ourselves as comfortable as we can. Let's drag the mainsail back into the stern-sheets. We'll double it over; you lie on one half and pull the other half over, to keep the wind and rain off you. I'll keep a lookout, and tell you when to jump up and start baling again, and in two hours we'll change places.'

*

It was a big, seemingly interminable storm. All day, all night, and all the next day the wind howled over them, the little craft climbed the steep walls of water and slid down into vast troughs. Lumps of spray from the wave-crests slopped in over the gunwales, and the lookout was kept busy baling. 'Susan' had now drifted out of any shipping-lane, and the horizon – when one could see it from the top of a wave – was always bare, but for the endless ranks of great seas. For two days and nights the crew shuffled themselves around between the caboosh and the stern, those off-duty snatching the short, heavy sleep of exhaustion, all of them huddled together at times to eat and drink – though none had a normal appetite. Their hectic fear had been replaced by anxiety, cold boredom and weariness.

When the bleak dangers and grinding monotony of their days and nights were at their worst, it was Raven's determined cheerfulness that kept them hopeful: 'Yes, it's bad here,' he said at dinner-time of the second day, 'but luckily we've got plenty of water under us – thousands of fathoms, I think.'

'Thousands of fathoms,' said Eleanor acidly. 'And that is supposed to be *good* news?'

'Yes – you ask Carl. Where the sea's shallower, the waves are much steeper – that's what makes Cape Horn seas so bad.'

'That's right,' said Protheroe cheerfully, 'and you look at it this way, miss: if you're - say, five foot nine tall, then six foot of water is enough to drown you anyway. So it don't matter how much more than that there is under you, does it?'

'Aye,' said Raven, 'and best of all, there's no land to leeward for thousands of miles – not till you get to South America.'

'You sailors, said Eleanor, 'are so full of comfort to us landlubbers. Those thoughts have cheered me up immensely: thousands of fathoms under us, and thousands of miles to the nearest land to leeward. Soon you will be telling me that fresh air and sea-bathing are good for me and my complexion.' It did Raven's heart good to see both the seamen grin at her ironies; that showed there was nothing wrong with their morale, nor Nelli's either, for that matter.

It was not until the third morning of the storm that Raven, struggling backwards out of the cold fug of the caboosh, felt a difference in the air and in the sea: 'Looking better, Carl,' he said, rubbing the sleep from his eyes. 'The seas have gone down a lot. Let's have a look at the compass.... Yes, I thought so. The wind's veered right round into the north-west, and there's no more breaking seas. And look,' he pointed to a low arch of blue sky. 'You can see the sky clearing, up to windward. I think we've seen the worst of it now, and we're all still alive.'

'Alive,' said Eleanor, 'yes, alive, but very tired and stiff and very damp and very bruised all over, and, most of all, very, very cold. Otherwise – we're fine.'

'Yes,' said Raven guardedly, 'fine, but...'

'Heavens! I might have known there'd be a "but"! But *what?'*

'Well, the storm's taken us a long way to eastward of our course, and now the wind's gone round to the north-west, so if we're steering for Bluff Harbour it's a dead header – right on the nose. New Zealand's dead to windward now, so we shall need Curly's lee-boards when we do make sail – which we can't for a while; it's still blowing too hard.'

'Ve get there,' said Carl stolidly. 'Ve get there. Take long time, beating up into vind, but she good boat, and ve get there vun day.'

*

The long savage storm that they had weathered had struck Auckland Island too. 'Figaro's' crew, though sheltered from the worst of it in their wooded valley, had heard its wild roar through the trees, had felt it battering and shaking both hut and galley. Staggering in its gusts, they had toiled in the driving rain, under Jac-y-Bont's direction, to secure the galley roof by passing lengths of rope over it, and tying their ends to big rocks, hanging clear of the ground.

On that third day the wind still blustered in the woods, and gloomy clouds still raced across the lowering sky. Grant and bosun sat after breakfast in the galley. 'Weather's clearing up, mister,' said bosun. 'No need to look so worried. We saved the galley roof all right. Thank God them boys got all that halyard rope from the wreck, though – else we'd have been in trouble.'

Grant shook his head soberly: 'The storm's been bad here. This roof nearly went, and it's still too bad for work outside. But what about the boat and her crew? Just think what it must have been like for them! I wonder if she's still afloat and the right way up.'

'I been thinking the very same. But look at it this way, we done our best for them. We couldn't have done no more.'

'I know. But it was I who let them go, bosun. I shouldn't have done that - I can see that now. Shall we ever see any of them alive again? I wonder.'

'Aw, don't blame yourself, mun. You acted for the best – we all thought so. What's done is done – no good looking back. Nobody I know of blames you for it. That poor dab was in such a state; she couldn't have stood being on the same island as that rat Billy much longer. And anyway, why don't we look on the bright side for a change? I bet you they're all fit and well and that young Raven is looking to make sail again soon. And I bet you too that they've been grateful to Jac for his sea-anchor these last two days.'

'You may be right; but there's something else bothering me – Billy John.'

'What about the young bastard? He's safe enough with them two big Parrog boys looking after him, isn't he? They're off down to the stream with him now. They wouldn't want him doing his daily business in the galley.'

'I know, but I still feel uneasy about keeping him more or less locked up. He did as much as any man could to apologize when he came to see me. I just feel he should get something from me in return. That's the other thing troubling me.'

'Good God, mister, he owes you a hell of a lot already. If you hadn't been here I think some of the lads would have half-killed him – p'raps finished him off altogether. As for being locked up, he'll have to get used to that. He'll get years in clink when you hand him over to the law, and they hear what the swine did. It wasn't just rape, remember: he threatened to cut her up, and he actually tried to do that to Raven. They'll put him in for bloody years – I hope.'

'Yes, but here and now it's different for him: in prison he'll be put to work, and he'll be allowed to talk to the other convicts at times. Here he's just left to brood like a caged animal, day after day. Don't forget, we've no idea how many more days or weeks we're going to be stuck here, even if the boat does get through. He may get worse than he was before. Mind you, Eirian says that since Billy spoke to me, he's changed his ways – he's polite and cheerful and obedient – never grumbles.'

'Well, all I can say, mister, is that it'll be a damn long time before I and the other lads will trust him or be friends with him. Remember, you offered them the chance to have him back in the hut to sleep, and not one of them said yes. All right, he said he was sorry, but that's only words, mun. He behaved worse than the worst kind of animal to a decent helpless girl. The lads have all got wives or sweethearts – some of them have got daughters. They're not going to forgive him in a hurry. *Iesu Mawr,* mister, I didn't think you, of all people, would go soft on him.'

'I'm not going soft, Reuben. When we get to Bluff Harbour I'll hand him over to be weighed off, but I don't want to make him any more vicious than he has been. Our precious sea-lawyer Protheroe says he's reformed, and we've believed him. I can't see John could do much harm here. He can't escape, because we're all trapped here anyway. I'll just give him a bit more scope – let him work with the others and so on. His arm is a bit better now; he could do light jobs, I reckon.'

'Well, mister, if you put him to work in the wood with an axe, all I can say is – for Christ's sake don't turn your back on him!' Mathias tilted his cap back, sighed, and shook his head sadly: 'But, like you say, God knows how much longer we're going to be here. Like you said before, once they get that rescue ship into a dry-dock, nobody knows how many things they'll need to put right, or how long they'll be about it, especially if she's an old boat. In the meantime, a lot of the bully has gone, though there's still plenty of biscuit and flour. It's good that little

Davey has found that big patch of spuds, but the lads need meat too, if they're to work hard and stay healthy. We've got to start some serious seal-hunting, as well as fishing. There's lots of good meat on a seal. I've tasted it; years ago, up in Canada; it wasn't too bad – a bit fishy, that's all. As for that varmint Billy, I reckon it's Raven he really hates, whatever he may say. The capten's girl loves Raven – you can see that – and she hates Billy. It's the old story – jealousy, and that's a bloody dangerous state of mind, especially in a wild place like this.'

So preoccupied were the two men that they had not noticed that Isaac Hughes steward was – very quietly, so as not to miss a word of their conference - washing dishes just outside the galley. Naturally, in ten minutes the whole crew knew the gist of what had been discussed, and were generally much in disagreement with Grant's decision about Billy.

Curly Kellock was of course the most judicious in his verdict: 'Well, I s'pose even that bloody skate deserves some sort of second chance.'

Yorry Splott was much more hostile: 'That dirty bastard? *Ach y fi!* I'm never going to work with him.'

Wellington Jones was even more decisive: 'I ain't having that low-down skunk working in my galley – not ever! I don't want to be strung up for murder – and that's what'd happen. I got enough to worry about without that. Jesus, you guys should see the way the stock of bully has gone down. Two more weeks, and it'll all be gone, and still no steamer. Bosun's right; he was saying to me yesterday that we got to start hunting them seals straightaway, and Davey and some of you others could do a bit of climbing and get some birds' eggs off the cliffs – must be plenty up there, with all the damn squawking we hear all the time. It'd do some of you hoodlums and scrimshankers good to get up off your arses now and then. And remember: we saw them tracks in the grass the day we got here. There might still be other animals – pigs, sheep, cattle, I don't know what. You could look for them too, if you want to eat.'

Even the ever-cheerful Lewis was dismayed: 'Aye, we'll have to feed ourselves now, boys. Still no bliddy steamer… been here well over a month now.'

'That ship will come one day, man,' said the doctor. 'That young Raven will get to Bluff Harbour – then they'll charter some sort of steamer, once they know we're here. We'll wake up one morning and hear her whistle blowing from Port Ross.'

'Get to Bluff?' said Lewis. I hopes to God they all do, but with a storm like we've just had? For all we know, they may all be dead now, poor dabs.'

'You put a lot of the bully into that boat, didn't you?' said Isaac peevishly.

'Course we did,'' said Lewis. 'We couldn't tell how long the trip would take em, and what else would they live on, eh?'

'So all the rest of us are suffering because of the four of them in that damned boat – and all because of that girl of the old capten's, and the fuss she made about Billy John's shenanigans.'

'Sometimes, Isaac,' said Welly, quietly and coldly, 'I'd like to screw that whining head right off of your neck, so help me.'

Lewis said fervently: 'Aye, and I'll give you a hand with that any time, doctor.'

'All right, but we'll see how you people in the crowd like it when the bully's run out because a load of it went off in that boat on that stupid trip.'

Welly's fury boiled over: 'You bugger off out of my galley right now, before I do you a mischief, you miserable old grizzler. Them in the boat – even that Jimmy – are the bravest people I know. You ain't fit to lick their boots, man. One day you'll be glad of what they done.... Now – *git!'*

*

At dawn on the fourth morning after the storm began, Raven was at last able to say; 'Right! Come on, folks! Roust yourselves out! We've got no more than a decent moderate breeze now. We're going to make sail. Just the lug-sail to start with, Carl. I'm going to put her on the wind, close-hauled on the port tack. Jim, heave in on the tripping-line, and get the sea-anchor inboard and stowed. Carl, get the riding sail down, bend on the lugsail and hoist it. Jim, when the sea-anchor's in, lower the starboard lee-board. We'll see if she can sail like one of Curly's blessed barges. Nelli, start getting some breakfast ready. I think we've all got our appetites back, now the seas have gone down – just swells and a good sailing breeze. Stewardess: I'll have coffee, two rashers of bacon- smoked back rashers, mind - two fried eggs and some grilled kidneys, please. And toast, of course. And, obviously, marmalade.'

'Damn,' said Jim from for'ard, 'ain't we gonna have some sausages? *A beth am ychydig o fadarch wedi ffrio?'*

'What's he saying?' said Raven, suspicious – as the English usually are – that anything said in their presence in an unknown tongue is mocking or derogatory.

'Calm down, 'said Eleanor. 'He's only asking for a few fried mushrooms. What's the harm in that?'

'Why can't he ask in English, so that Carl and I can understand?'

'O, and why should he? We Welsh are a linguistic majority in this boat, and anyway, I'm the one who will be cooking this wonderful breakfast. So why should Jim and I always have to talk in your clumsy Saxon tongue?'

The old imp of subversive mischief was growing all the time in Jim Protheroe: 'D'you know, miss, I reckon you ought to teach him the language of Heaven, as we call it. Then, if he's mate on another Welsh ship, he can curse the hands in their own tongue.'

'"The language of Heaven",' said Raven sardonically. 'Don't say that even God has to understand your weird lingo?'

'Undoubtedly He does,' Eleanor replied tartly. 'After all, it was in existence long before English was. But as for teaching it to Mister Raven, Jim, that would be a long hard job, I fear.'

'No, miss,' said Jim, eager now to disconcert both of them. 'Not when you're wedded to him, eh? I've read that the Dutch planters out in the East Indies used to find a nice, good-looking native girl, and be friendly to her – I mean *very, very* friendly - and then, when they was tucked up comfy in bed together, she'd have lots of time to teach him – teach him the local language, I mean. In Dutch they used to call girls like that "pillow dictionaries". Now that was a good idea, wasn't it?'

Half-annoyed, half-amused, Eleanor blushed deeply and said to Raven: 'Mister Mate, this is beginning to seem like impudence and insubordination from one who claims to be a redeemed character. Can you not discipline this fellow?'

'Yes, I could land him one he wouldn't forget in a hurry. Mates are allowed to do that, you know. But I don't want to damage him, because if this wind drops much more I may need him to row us to Bluff Harbour. Now let's for God's sake get the anchor in and the sails up, without all this damn silly gossip, and then have breakfast, and no more stupid chat.'

'Aye aye, sir,' said Eleanor, and when, ten minutes later, the sail was up and the boat under way, she added: 'And I don't think I'll bother about anything too fancy this morning.' She handed each of them a big dry biscuit, hard as a paving-stone, on which she'd laid a hacked-off slice of bully beef. 'Breakfast is served, gentlemen. Will you say grace, Jim?'

'Of course, madam,' said Jim, and intoned with a parson-like piety: 'Give us this day our daily workhouse tooth-breakers, and may the Lord make us duly thankful, even for this horrible scran.'

All their spirits rose now that the anchor was in; the boat had slewed round to starboard off the wind, the sail flapping as it climbed the mast, then filling into its beautiful curves, 'Susan' heeling gently to starboard. She had begun at last to forge ahead, so that the rudder took charge, and she became a living, moving thing again, the water beginning to chuckle once more under her bow.

'I'll tell you what,' said Raven, grinning. 'These leeboards are going to make things a lot better when we're working to windward like this. I can get her sailing several points closer than before – she'll go up into the wind like a yacht. Good old Curly and his barges!'

'But you're not able to steer a course for New Zealand yet, I suppose?' said Eleanor. 'I suppose also that it's hard for you to know where we are, after just drifting for so long – over three days?'

'Indeed, but at least, thanks to the compass, I've a fair idea of the direction of our drift – just about due north-east, and, as for how far we went, Carl and I reckon about a hundred or maybe a hundred and twenty miles – so it was a good job there was no land in that direction. So we're still south and east of Bluff Harbour, and north-by-west, which is the best she'll point, is not a bad course. Mind you, we're a long, long way to leeward of the course we wanted, so later on I'll put her about on the starboard tack, to make a bit of ground to the west. What you need to pray for now, Eleanor, since you're the holiest of a damned unholy crew, is a good steady wind – no more storms and no flat calms either.'

They sailed on over a sea totally transformed; the huge, fierce-crested, steep, dark-grey waves had subsided to become smooth, harmless, light-blue lumps of swell, over which a pleasant breeze blew. The sun shone down from a clear blue sky, the boat leaned gently to starboard, ploughing a steady course over the ever-shifting swells, flinging aside the little choppy wavelets that the breeze had raised, leaving a small creamy wake behind her. An hour later, Raven called to the men lolling for'ard, 'Carl, Jim, up with the foresail. We'll have all plain sail again. The breeze is dropping off all the time, so we need to wake this boat up a bit. When you've done that, stow the sea-anchor and its warp away. But, Carl, as you're doing that, check the parcelling on the warp where it went through the fairlead. That warp had a hell of a strain on it for a long time, so the canvas may be a bit chafed, and after all, we may need to put the damn thing out again. Then you can get your heads down till twelve, if you want to.'

Eleanor looked at him reproachfully when they'd gone: 'You should not call that little wood-and canvas contraption which preserved our lives through that terrible storm a "damn thing", Jack. I was just reflecting on the great debt we owe to those two old men, Reuben Mathias bosun and Jac-y-Bont sails, one from the slopes of the Preselis, the other from a cottage in Pengelli woods – so many thousands of miles from here. And, from what you've just said, we owe a lot to Curly from the London docks as well. Thank God for such wonderful men, with so many years of sea experience between them. We'd all be dead now, but for their foresight and skill – and energy too, for they worked from dawn to dusk for a whole week to give us that deck and that sea-anchor and that spitfire jib and these lee-boards. Those "damn things", plus God's mercy, saved us from a miserable cold, wet death.'

'I know, I know. I shouldn't have said that. As my mother always used to say, "Heaven helps those who help themselves".'

*

That night, both Raven and Nelli were exhausted by the time their long first watch ended at midnight, for now that she was sailing properly, the boat demanded all their attention, to make sure that she was sailing as close to the wind as possible, at the best speed possible. It was good to be making free progress again at last, even if there was much weary beating to windward to be done. But her sharp, jerky motion through the short seas which had got up was a constant stress on their stiff, aching limbs and joints. Every second, the jolting boat threw them this way or that, and for two hours now they had been dying for the moment when they could lie down and rest. Raven had found himself glancing constantly at his moonlit watch to monitor the slow, dragging hours till midnight, when he could roust out Carl and Jim for the middle (or 'graveyard') watch.

When the time came to change watches, he and Eleanor, though cold, stiff and exhausted, were happy at the thought of rest, warmth, shelter and sleep. However, even in the caboosh it was chilly and incredibly noisy, for the bow constantly smacked hard into the little waves, and the boat's overlapping planks made it sound as if they were hammering into hard shingle, for only a quarter of an inch of larch wood divided them from the fathomless Southern Ocean.

The lovers lay close together for warmth, fully dressed but for boots and oilskin coats, the latter laid on top of their blankets for added warmth. They would have four hours of undisturbed rest in a bed of sorts together, and they were young – twenty-one and twenty – and yet they lay still and slept soundly, deeply, with no amorous or sensual touches or caresses. It was, they both knew, neither the time nor the place for those.

They brushed their cold lips together briefly, Eleanor whispered: '*Nos da, cariad* - goodnight, darling,' and was almost instantly unconscious. Raven laid his arm across her muffled body and murmured back,

'Goodnight, Nelli' and snuggled closer for warmth and comfort. But, as the captain of their little craft, he was not so soon asleep, for he had practical concerns on his mind. Were those two chaps at the helm getting the best out of the boat to windward? Was the wind still steady from the north-west? When should he put her about onto the starboard tack? Might they soon need to ration the food and water?

Then gentler thoughts took over his mind, as he heard and felt the give-and-take of Nelli's breath. With a wry smile he thought back to the heady, reckless, guilty, sensual moments he'd spent with her aboard the barque – snatched moments of delicious pleasure, haunted, tainted by the fear of discovery – discovery by one who was not only his lover's father, but also his omnipotent captain, the stocky, choleric Welshman who styled himself 'Master under God', and who looked quite capable of felling an ox.

What would he not have given in those days for four hours' unchallenged sleep – or hectic, glorious lack of sleep – with the most beautiful girl he had ever met, who – best of all – had seemed to return his own over-mastering passion? Now, in that cramped, damp, draughty hutch, slamming and sawing through the waves, they were alone and free. Ah, but back then, aboard the 'Figaro', despite the guilt and fear, it had been naked flesh to flesh in a warm cabin – no thick rough trousers, jerseys, or jackets that swaddled their bodies and kept them apart, deadening the senses. But one day, one day, no matter how long it took, Nelli would be her old confident self again, the horror of Billy John's attack would be a thing of the past, and they would be together again properly: no fear, no haste, no guilt, and, by God, no clothes either! And they would be lovers until they were old and grey – that was as certain as anything in the universe.

But alas, that four hours' rest was not to be. Half-way through the watch, Raven and Eleanor were woken from their heavy sleep by an eager shout from Jimmy at the tiller: 'Skipper! Come aft quick! I think I saw a light just now – off the starboard bow.'

Raven scrambled hastily out of the caboosh, dragging on his oilskin coat, for the night was chilly under the clear moon and stars. He clattered aft to where the two seamen sat. 'A light? Where away now, then?'

'Broad on the starboard bow. Can't tell how far off.'

'I can't see a damn thing out there. Have you seen it Carl?'

'No, I see nutting.'

'That's because you're getting on a bit, mate,' said Jim, with the scorn of youth. 'It's only faint, and it keeps coming and – Look! There it is! Now d'you believe me?'

'Yes, I saw it too then. Well spotted, Jim. It keeps disappearing because we only see it when we're on top of a swell, and so is she. There! There it is again! It can't be very high above the water, or it would show more often. What course are you on?'

'Same as you said – on the wind, full and by. North-by-west it was when I last saw the compass.'

'Right: bear away off the wind until you're pointing straight at that light. Let's have a bit more main-sheet out, Carl.'

'Vy you do that, mister? If she under vay ve don't catch her, I t'ink.'

'No, probably not, but you never know. It's worth a try, and it'll show us which way she's heading. I can't take a proper bearing of her, can I, in this dark? Let me take the tiller now, Jim. I'll try to keep this boat on the course we're heading now.'

'Bit of a puzzle, ain't it, mister?' said Jim. 'I mean, it's a white light, so it's got to be either the masthead light of a steamer coming straight at us, or the stern light of a ship going away from us. But then, if it was a masthead light of a steamer under way, it'd get closer pretty quick, and if it was a stern light we'd surely have seen her passing us.'

'Yes, and if it was a masthead light it'd be well up above the water, so it wouldn't keep blanking out.'

Jim scratched his head thoughtfully: 'So that only leaves...?'

'A riding-light – you know, like an anchor-light.'

'What, mister! Out here, bloody miles from anywhere? Anchored? Don't talk so blinking... *There!* Did you see that?'

'Yes! Just a glimpse of a green starboard navigation light. So she's under way, heading across our bows, left to right. But this gets odder and odder: If she's a sailing-ship under way, what's that bright white light? If she's a steamer, and that's her masthead light, how come it's so bright?'

Eleanor appeared, hauling on her coat, and yawning: 'What is it? Is something wrong?'

'No, nothing wrong. There's a ship ahead, but there's something odd about her. She seems to be heading across our bows, but her bearing isn't changing, and she's got a bright white light only just above her green starboard light. I can't understand it; even in this light breeze you'd expect her to move a bit. But she doesn't.'

'Dawn come soon,' said Carl. 'Then ve see vat's

vat, eh?'

With a maddening slowness, the morning hours dragged by. Though 'Susan' was doing no more than three or four knots, the lights grew steadily brighter and at last they were visible every time their little boat rose on a swell. 'Right,' said Raven. 'That shows us one thing: she's not moving, or hardly at all. And I'm beginning to think I know why: she's been damaged somehow in the storm, and can't move. Jim, you've got the best pair of eyes in this boat; before long you may be able to see at least her topmasts – unless of course she's a steamer.'

But it was another hour before Protheroe cried: 'Yes! There it is! I can see a topmast. See? Just to the left of the light?'

'Yes, I see it now,' said Raven. 'Well done, Jim. Odd, though, to see only one mast.'

'Ah! There! Another mast! Just to the left again – you see it?'

'Yes – but then that's odd again. It's a shorter mast with no yards on it, so it must be her mizen, so – unless she's a brigantine, where's....'

'Heavens! You donkeys!' said Eleanor scornfully. 'I'm only a passenger and a landlubber, but I can answer the question you were going to ask: you're looking at her mainmast and mizen; you can't see a foremast, because that's what's damaged, and that's why she's not moving.'

'H'm,' said Raven, a little irritated by the blow to his professional dignity. 'You may well be right, I suppose,' he said, a trifle pompously. In his heart he knew she was, and was kicking himself. 'In due course we shall see, shan't we?'

'Aha,' said Jim half an hour later as, now in full

daylight, all the vessel's spars were visible. 'Now you can see what's what. You was dead right miss,' he added with deliberate tactlessness. There was still something of the rebel left in him, and he enjoyed seeing an officer being taken down a peg. 'Look, mister: her foremast's broke off at the cross-trees. You can see the topmast and t'gallant mast sloping down over her bulwark.'

'Yes, I see, said Raven, tight-lipped. 'You were quite right, Eleanor. Well done. Good thinking.'

Eleanor said nothing, but allowed herself a quiet, private smile of complacency.

At last, as the boat closed in on the enigmatic craft ahead, the whole ship was visible, and an odd sight she was too: short – less than half of 'Figaro's' length, high-sided, her bows tubby and rounded, her yards antiquely short, her bowsprit, by contrast, extravagantly long, and angled upwards like a prodigious old broomstick.

'Good God!' said Raven, 'she looks like something left over from Nelson's day!'

'Nelson's day?' said Protheroe. 'Older than that, mun. More like Noah's day.'

'You boys not seen vun of these before?' said Carl, with the air of a man who has seen everything that floats, whom nothing surprises. 'She Yankee valer. You not see many of them now. My Uncle Sven, he make trip on valer from Nantucket ven he young – long time back. Only vun trip – he say never again, by yimminy.'

'Not a place for catching whales here, surely?' said Raven.

'No, but she down to her marks – she got her full cargo now, I t'ink. She on her vay round the Horn, back to Massachusetts.'

'Not for a while she ain't,' said Jim. 'Not with all that top-hamper hanging over her side. She's a bit of a wreck.'

'Yes,' said Raven. 'And with all that damage aloft, I reckon she dare not set the sails she's still got on the main and mizzen. Half the upper stays must be gone. She's got a hell of a lot to do before she makes sail again.'

'That would explain the bright light you first saw,' said Eleanor. 'It was there to enable them to work on the fallen mast and spars during the night. Are you going to speak to her, or get back onto our proper course again?'

'Speak to her, of course,' said Raven. 'She'll be able to give us an accurate position, even if she is dismasted. I'd dearly like to know what our longitude is.'

It was full daylight now, the welcome sun beginning to rise from the eastern horizon, and they were now only a few cables' lengths from the stricken whaler. The sharp-eyed Jim was first to notice the next oddities: 'That's rum too, mister: there's only three fellers working on that fallen hamper, and all of em's black. There's only one other chap on deck – by the wheel there, aft. He's white – a bit fat too. How many hands usually on a whaler, Carl?'

'Mebbe… thirty, forty or so. They have big crews. So much verk to do – catch the vales, tow them back, cut them up, boil up blubber, put oil into damn big casks, then stow the casks all avay below. Too much bloddy verk, my uncle say, all for few dollars.'

'I don't like the look of this, Jack,' said Eleanor. 'I think something terrible must have happened to this ship. Why are there only three men working when she's so badly damaged? Where is all her crew? Perhaps she's had some awful disease amongst them. God knows we suffered enough aboard the "Figaro" from that. We shall have to be very careful about going aboard her, Jack. We must make sure she's not a plague-ship.'

Now they could all see the three black sailors crawling, struggling amidst the fearful raffle of stays, halyards, braces, canvas and splintered timbers. The morning sun gleamed back from the bright blades of their axes as they cut through the nightmare tangle. They worked with the headlong energy of desperation, but they were a pitifully puny band for such a task.

'Let go the sheets,' called Raven, and the boat's sails fluttered in the gentle breeze as she lost way. 'Ship ahoy, there! What ship?'

From the man aft – now seen as tall, portly, wearing a seemly long black coat and a broad-brimmed black hat – came a solemn, powerful, deep voice: 'The whaler "Pawtucket", New Bedford, Massachusetts. What boat?'

'Party from the Welsh barque "Figaro", Cardiff, wrecked six weeks ago on Auckland Island. We're bound for Bluff Harbour to seek rescue for the rest of her crew,' Raven replied. 'Our food is running low on the island, and we have no medicines. Where is your crew? Have you had some plague aboard?'

'None, sir, none,' intoned the mellow voice, in the manner of a preacher more than that of a sailor. 'No plague but the plague of wretched human vice and wickedness. That was plague enough, the Lord knows.'

Totally nonplussed by the strange reply, Raven showed his true English quality of polite, puzzled reticence. 'Oh… Yes… I see... Er…I'm sorry. Well, sir, may we come aboard? We should be most grateful if you could provide us with our position. We have been blown far out of our course by the storm.'

'Indeed you may come aboard, sir. It seems we are both in need of succour. But, as for your position, there we shall fail you, I fear, for we are lost too, and as our blessed Saviour once said: "If the blind lead the blind, both shall fall into the ditch." However, we shall give you all the help we can with food and water.' He turned and delivered his fruity yet stentorian voice to one of the men working for'ard: 'Noah, come aft and help me lower the boarding-ladder.'

'There you are, mister. I was right, you was wrong,' said Protheroe with all his old confident cheek. 'The old boy hollered out "Noah"! I told you this packet was older than Nelson's. So I reckon them chaps working for'ard must be Noah and his two lads, Shem and Japheth. Some of them blokes in the Old Testament lived for hundreds of years, remember, so why not them?' He grinned at Eleanor: 'See, miss, I know all about old Noah and his sons. I've been a bit of a rascal in my time, but I went regular to bible classes when I was a nipper.'

CHAPTER FOURTEEN

From the waist of the ship a boarding-ladder – roped at the sides, but with narrow wooden rungs – came tumbling down. The other two black seamen had come back aft from their hopeless struggles with the fallen mast, and one of them threw down a heaving-line for Jimmy to seize, and, hauling in on that, he and Carl ranged the boat close alongside the whaler's black hull and brought the bottom of the ladder into the stern of the boat.

As the tubby old ship rolled in the swell, 'Susan' rose and fell several feet with every roll. Raven said: 'You go first, Eleanor; and would you .... ?'

She stood grasping the ladder and said shortly: 'Before you say another word, no, I would *not* like any help. I can manage perfectly well, thank you.'

As she took her first nimble step onto the ladder and left the boat – perhaps for ever – her mind flashed back to the moment when, over a year ago, at Caleta Buena on the Chile coast, she had made the opposite transfer from the liner 'Magellan', which had brought her and her mother from Liverpool, to 'Figaro's' boat – perhaps the very same boat that she was now leaving. Events had moved a full circle, but then her mother and father, both fit and well and happy, had been fondly, and slightly anxiously, watching her; and now they had gone forever. There were even whole days now when she did not think of them. Time moved on relentlessly, and yet, perhaps, mercifully.

At the top of the ladder a white hand on one side and a black hand on the other held her, to steady her as she put one leg over the high wooden bulwark, straddled it, then swung the other leg over to make an undignified landing on the whaler's deck.

'You next, mister?' said Jim politely, holding the ladder for Raven.

'No, Jim. Carl, you go up next, then me. You and I, Jim, will need to unstep the mast. I'm going to ask them if they will hoist the boat inboard for us, in case we should need it again, so you'll have to stay here to hook on the falls.'

Once the boat's forestay and mast shrouds had been cast off, and the mast and yard laid flat on the thwarts, Raven followed Carl up the ladder and swung expertly over the bulwark to the deck, where he found himself face-to-face with the whaler's crew – one portly white man, one middle-aged black seaman and two young ones.

'Welcome aboard, sir,' said the apparent commander, his mellow voice booming from under his broad-brimmed black hat. 'Allow me to introduce…'

But Raven, always first and foremost the sailor, raised a hand: 'Just a moment, sir, by your leave: may we first hoist the boat, and do introductions later? She could get damaged by banging against your ship's side if we leave her.'

'Ah yes, you do right to interrupt me, sir. We must attend to seamen's matters first. Noah, will you see to that?'

'I will, Mr Tucker, only, begging your pardon, you gonna have to help us. That's a doggone heavy old boat, I guess, and we only got six men to hoist it.'

'*And* an able-bodied woman,' said Eleanor, with a touch of indignation, 'who is not afraid of hard work, or of getting her hands rough and dirty if need be.'

'I real sorry for that, miss;' said Noah with a broad grin. 'I guess I shouldn't have left you out. I sure won't do that again – I'd be too scared!'

Eleanor forgave him with a silent smile, and Noah, tall and lanky, with the same sort of tight, grizzled curls as Wellington Jones', turned to his young assistants: 'Come on then, you young varmints, look lively! You heard what the man jus' said. We'll use this pair of davits here. Lower them falls nice and gentle. You don't want the lower blocks to lay out that pore feller down there, does you?'

The davits were the small pair of arched cranes used for lowering and hoisting boats, and the falls – the tackles for lifting boats - hung from them. These were lowered carefully to Jim, so that he could hook them on to eye-bolts in the boat, before clambering aboard himself and hauling up the ladder behind him. Then, in that chilly morning air, all eight of them were able to warm themselves by some lusty hauling. The quarter-boat, as Noah had said, was heavy, and even with all of them tailing on to the falls, they were obliged to lift one end at a time, snatching a quick turn on a cleat, and then grasping the other fall. Heaving flat out, they were a good twenty minutes getting 'Susan' up, and they would have been longer than that but for Jimmy, their shantyman, who led them in a song to help them to time their heaves together:

As I was a-walking down Paradise Street,
To me way hay, blow the man down,
A pretty young damsel I happened to meet,
Gimme some time to blow the man down!

By the time the upper and lower blocks of the falls came together, and the boat was fully hoisted, the verses – despite the feminine presence in the party – had become remarkably pornographic, and the shantyman himself was too breathless to continue. They all cheered as Raven finally called: 'Well! High enough! Make fast at that!' For the small boat's crew, it had been a blessed relief to feel a steady deck under their feet, and to be able to move freely, to walk, and to fling all their weight on the falls. As well as that, their concerted efforts and their achievement of a difficult job had already, it seemed, formed all eight of them into a new, united crew, though five different races of humanity had hauled and strained on those ropes.

The transition from boat to ship had especially cheered Eleanor, for she saw it as another stage in her escape from darkness and terror. She flopped, panting, red-faced, against the shoulder-high wooden bulwark, and turned her dark, cropped head to give Raven one of her old smiles: 'Phew! That was a struggle! Jimmy Protheroe's shanty was useful, even if the words were quite disgusting. Anyway, I need a watch below after all that, *capten bach.*'

'Not the slightest chance of that, Ordinary Seawoman Roberts! No idling! We've got to unload the biscuit and bully and water-breakers from the boat, not to mention the small matter of a dismasting to attend to.'

'Aye, sir,' said the portly commander, 'but before that I think introductions are now called for. My name is Nathaniel Tucker. I was the late captain's steward and ship's purser. These excellent fellows from the foc'sle, my sole companions for some weeks now, are Noah Brown, whom I have created bosun, with his young comrades George Miller and Amos Bacon.'

The ABs had been furtively wiping their sweaty,

grimy hands on their trousers, preliminary to the handshakes all round. They ducked their heads with an old-fashioned courtesy as they shook Eleanor's hand; despite her rough male attire, her boyish, cropped hair, and her hearty and muscular efforts at the ropes, they saw in her a lady to be respected.

Raven did the honours for his small band, and then said to the stately Tucker: 'So you, sir, are not the captain or mate of this ship?'

'Indeed not, sir. I am a mere landlubber – the ship's purser a mere pen-pusher. Noah has been our sailing master. I have little knowledge of ropes and spars, and none of navigation. You, as a former second mate of a large barque, have those skills, I take it?'

'I have, though as yet I have no official rank as mate, on paper. However, my late captain, Eleanor's father, was a stern and conscientious schoolmaster, and taught me and the other apprentices how to find a latitude at noon, and how to get a running fix by taking morning and evening sun-sights. He also got us up on deck at night to point out to us some useful stars for navigation.'

'Well then, Mr Raven, I am convinced that you would make a far better captain than I, if you should feel inclined to throw in your lot with us. We are certainly in need of help, since not one of us has the slightest skill in navigation. Our intention has been to make for New Zealand, but whether we are near that destination I know not. We have been sailing by guess and by God, as you sailors say.'

'Your guesses have been good ones, Mr Tucker, or perhaps God has been kind to you. My guess – for we have no means of navigating either, apart from a small boat-compass, – is that we are now about a hundred miles south-east of Bluff Harbour, on the South Island, which was our destination too. Tell me: have you a sextant on board – and log-tables – and a chronometer – and, of course, the chart for this area?'

'Indeed, we have all of those. And fortunately, since it was always my duty to wind up the chronometer every morning, I have continued to do so, merely out of habit. Will that be of help to you?'

'Help? It is essential to obtaining our longitude. I think that by evening, if the sun continues to shine, I shall know pretty exactly where we are.'

There were smiles of relief from all the other seven, the whaler's men sensing that, in this young man, all sorts of good possibilities were dawning. Raven went on: 'But before I go any further, and give any orders, one thing must be clear: I was the official skipper of that boat, by order of my captain, back at the island. Am I now to be the official skipper of this ship? Someone must be master. If it is to be me, I must have the consent of all of you from the whaler, and that consent must be written in your log-book and signed by all of you, on behalf of your ship's owners. When we get back to the world of law and officialdom, I do not wish to be seen as the head of some pirate gang who has taken the ship by force, and enslaved all of you.'

This time, the relief of the whaler's crew showed itself in outright laughter, even the solemn Tucker joining in. 'My dear young man,' he said, 'I have never seen a person less like a pirate, in appearance or manner, than yourself. On the contrary, we see you as a saviour from Heaven.' The black sailors nodded vigorously in agreement.

Eleanor spoke up, smiling broadly: 'No, Mr Tucker, there I must disagree with you. I know him well enough to know that there is little that is heavenly about him. But still, you will not regret having him as your master. Without him we should not be standing here now. We should all be countless fathoms down on the bed of the sea.'

'Very well,' said Raven. 'Thank you, sir, for your kind words, and thank you, Miss Roberts, for your slightly mixed comments on my skill and moral fibre. I'll do my best, though obviously my sea experience is limited; my captain, Simon Grant, would fill the position much better, but he is marooned on Auckland Island, many miles away, so you'll have to make do with me. But let's be clear about one thing.' Here he cast a glance at the two grinning young hands, who struck him as showing the same signs of foolish adolescent immaturity and mischief as those of the traditional windjammer apprentice – including himself, not so long ago. 'If you all agree to make me your captain, you will have to do what I say, when I say it, whether you like it or not. If I'm going to be in charge, I'm not having any shenanigans – an order will be an order.'

Tucker nodded: 'That is perfectly reasonable, sir. I think I can promise you that you will have no mutineers here.'

'Very good. I've no wish to be like Captain Bligh of the "Bounty", dealing out fifty lashes, but I must be in charge. And now, before we do anything else, perhaps you would find me the sextant and log-tables? This would be a good time to take a morning sun-sight.'

'Excellent,' said Tucker, beaming. 'And after that

may I suggest that we have a late breakfast? I caught some rather fine cod-like fish yesterday, and I have developed some skill as a bread-baker. We took in fresh supplies of flour and yeast in Hawaii, so I can offer you loaves and fishes – a suitably biblical dish for a celebration, I think. It will not take me long to fry the fish. Perhaps you would like to take your seats in the officers' mess-room, while I cook, and these lads go back to their heavy task of clearing the wreckage for'ard.'

'No,' said Raven, opening his account as captain. 'I don't want you chaps doing any more chopping at ropes and spars and slinging stuff overboard until Carl and I – and you too, Noah – have had a good look at the damage, and decided what to do about it. In this calm sea the fallen mast doesn't present any danger, and if you chaps go on hacking away with axes we may destroy or lose something that could be very useful later. If we're to get to Bluff, we've got to get this ship jury-rigged; - you know - repair enough of the damage aloft and get some more canvas on her, with whatever sort of lash-up we can manage, so that we can sail her again. The main and mizen masts have got to be properly stayed, and we need some more sail for'ard to balance her.'

'That be long job, mister,' said Carl gloomily.

'It will, but we have to get her fit to face storms again; you know how quickly the weather can change in these parts. Let's just hope we get some calm days to do the job. Give me a few minutes to do a sun-sight, and then we'll go for'ard and have a closer look. Will you come with us, Noah?'

Raven's heart sank as, ten minutes later, having now successfully got one position-line on the chart, he stood by the fringe of the chaos for'ard. As Jimmy Protheroe had spotted, most of the foremast had been felled by the gale, and now lay, slanting downwards, over the starboard bulwark, held there by a nightmare, twisted raffle of shrouds and running rigging. Like most masts of that time, it had been made in three jointed pieces – lower mast, topmast and topgallant (usually shortened to t'gallant) mast. The storm had parted some of her upper portside stays, and though the stout lower mast still stood intact, the topmast had broken off just above its lower joint. Looking up, Raven could see the colour of fresh wood in the jagged splinters that stuck up from the breaking-point.

'What happened, Noah?'

'Well, mister, we'd had her hove-to under a couple of storm stays'ls in the worst of the blow, and this old tub, she rode the seas like a cork. Didn't hardly get the decks wet. But - let's see – not yesterday morning but the day before, the weather got a bit finer, and Mr Tucker he say to me: "Noah, the weather's better. Can't you make sail again now? We need to get to land." Well, sir, I thought it still a bit too rough for that, but like a blamed fool I says: "All right, Mr Tucker sir, we try her with the fore-tops'l and the headsails." But I was an old fool, sir. I been at sea long, long time, an I should a knowed better. In my heart – in here, sir – I knew it was wrong, but anyway I send the boys aloft, they cast off the gaskets and I sheet the sails in. But very soon after I done it, the storm he say: "I ain't done with punishing you sinners yet," and he gave the most almightiest blast, and down came the whole damn shebang. Thank God I'd at least had the sense to get them boys back down on deck. But there, I got to confess to you, mister, that it was all my fault. That Mr Tucker, he good man and no fool, but he don' know B from a bull's foot when it comes to sailing, so I can't blame him. God knows I'm real sorry, sir, to have brought all this trouble on you.'

Raven put a hand on Noah's muscular shoulder: 'Noah, it's done with, man. Who doesn't make mistakes? It was a terrible mistake on our old captain's part that put us ashore on Auckland Island, and he'd been a first-rate skipper for years. As for me, well, once, off the River Plate, I was too busy hazing a cabin-boy for throwing up in the scuppers to notice a *pampero* coming up astern, and you know what vicious storms they can be. Don't let it get you down, man; you know what they say: A man who never made a mistake never made anything. Besides, if your ship hadn't been dismasted we would probably never have sighted you, so maybe you've done us all a good turn.'

'You's kind, sir, an I know we gonna git along fine, but now you know you got a dad-blamed old fool in your crew.'

'Enough, Noah – it's over. Let's get down to business. First of all, we've got to get the mainmast properly stayed, or that too will go when we make sail. The triatic stay, you know, the stay between the two mastheads, has obviously gone, and so has the main t'gallant forestay, so the first job will be to rig new ones. Have you got spare cordage down below?'

'Mister, we got ever' damn thing under the sun below there. These old hookers, they make long, long voyages – two years and more sometimes, so they carry plenty of spares. I guess the old stays, they worn out and rotted a bit by the sun and the wet. We been out near enough two years now, so we need new stuff up there.'

'Yes, you're right. But I didn't know there were ships about still using rope stays held tight by dead-eyes and lanyards. It was all steel wire and bottle-screws on our barque, but then she was brand-new.'

'You know when this old tub was launched? Eighteen-hundred-and-sixty-one, they say, and there's other whalers out there in the Pacific older than that. These old Quakers that run the whaling, back in Nantucket and New Bedford, they're mighty careful with their ships – and with their money too. They spend more of that money on their ships than they do on their crews - that's certain-sure. I expect they know the bible real good, but they've forgot that bit about the labourer being worthy of his hire.'

There was a cheerful cry from Eleanor aft: 'Jack! Noah! Breakfast! Come on, all of you.' Raven lost his preoccupation with rigging repairs, and allowed his nostrils to take in the Elysian delight of the mingled smells of frying fish and fresh coffee.

For the four who had been shaken, wind-swept, wetted and horribly cramped for days in a twenty-foot boat, it was indeed an earthly paradise to be sitting comfortably in shelter down below, on proper chairs, round a proper table, with plates and knives and forks before them, on a good solid ship, which did no more than roll gently in the swells. For the black sailors too it was like a blessing, a miracle, to be sitting in that previously sacred place, the officers' mess-room, not in the crowded, comfortless foc'sle.

On their plates were neat, hefty fillets of fish, which had been dusted with flour and fried, and on each side-plate was a thick slice of real fresh bread, a thing which 'Figaro's' people had not seen or tasted since they left Australia, weeks ago. Like most cooks, Tucker was a perfectionist: 'Be wary of bones, good people, in your fish. Alas, I have not yet acquired a real cook's skill. And as for the butter, it is only tinned stuff, and not of the freshest.'

The new commander, tortured by ravenous hunger, went to seize his knife and fork to begin, but was halted by a sharp jab in the ribs from the elbow of Nelli, who sat beside him. She had seen Tucker clasp his hands together and raise his eyes to the deckhead above; he was obviously a pious man, and wished to say a grace with which to solemnize this first meal together. The whaler's men, who knew what to expect, had already bowed their heads above their tempting plates and closed their eyes, fervently making their own silent, more earthly, prayer - that the grace would not be so long that their fish became cold.

Tucker's mellifluous voice boomed out, loud in that confined space: 'Lord God, Thou knowest how thy servants here have suffered in the tempest which Thou sent to try us, and Thou knowest too how we four were lost on Thy mighty ocean. With this prayer, and with this simple repast we celebrate the arrival, by Thy grace, of friends from afar, poor lost souls like ourselves, who have nevertheless, I believe, the power and skill to help us and guide us to a safe haven. We offer Thee thanks for this our food, for our survival in the tempest, and for this blessed succour which came when our hopes had well-nigh died. Through our Lord and Saviour Jesus Christ – Amen.'

They all murmured a heartfelt 'Amen', and – hungry though they were – still bent motionless over their plates for a few seconds, for they were all genuinely moved by his old-fashioned eloquence and solemnity.

Glancing sideways, Raven saw a tear or two trickling from Eleanor's eyes. He gave her knee a gentle squeeze, as if to say: 'I understand', and she turned to smile gratefully at him.

Tucker's voice boomed again: 'Thank you, good folks; and now let us fall to and sample our victuals.' This time there was no reply but the light clatter of knives and forks on plates, and the cheerful rattle of cups in saucers as the delicious bread, fish and coffee went down to grateful stomachs.

After a while, when their first fierce hunger had been satisfied, Tucker said to Raven: 'I am astonished, sir, at your setting out over such a perilous sea in so small a boat. I have heard sailors say that a New Zealand rescue steamer calls at those southern islands regularly to search for castaways, since the islands are on a direct line between the main Australian ports and Cape Horn. Would it not have been more prudent to wait for that?'

'It would indeed, and perhaps, as you imply, our voyage in an open boat was foolhardy. But it was forced upon us by the utterly cruel and disgusting behaviour of one of our seamen towards Eleanor here. She was desperate to leave the island, and I and these two good men volunteered to help her. In this company, and on this happy occasion, I will not describe what kind of attack she suffered, for I have no wish to bring back evil memories to her. As you can still see, she was bruised and wounded in the attack, and so was I in effecting her rescue. In a sense, she rescued herself, for I made a poor fist of my fight with her attacker, and she, in turn, had to rescue me. Perhaps it was a rough form of justice, but while I was on the ground, being savagely beaten, Eleanor recovered sufficiently to get to her feet and hit the attacker so hard with a heavy piece of driftwood that she broke his arm.'

'Indeed?' said Tucker, enigmatically.

'Yes, sir,' said Eleanor, bowing her head, shamefaced: 'I have always tried to be a Christian, and follow our Saviour's example of forgiveness. I never intended to inflict such a severe injury on my attacker, but you must understand that I was demented with fear and rage at his brutality. Indeed, I am deeply ashamed to say that, but for Mr Raven and our commander Mr Grant, I might well have gone on to kill the wretch who tried to .... who attacked me.'

'Indeed?' said Tucker again, solemnly.

Carl was indignant at what he felt was Tucker's disapproval; he spoke up stoutly: 'She did good t'ing, sir. That man, he a bloddy rotten dirty bastard!' Having always to speak in a foreign tongue, which he had learned mainly in foc'sles, Carl frequently misjudged the vocabulary appropriate to the occasion.

'No, no, Mr Johanssen,' said Tucker. 'I think you misunderstand me: I was not about to criticize Eleanor for her action. It is good scripture. Did not God declare to Moses in the book of Exodus that justice demanded "Eye for eye, tooth for tooth, hand for hand, foot for foot"? Indeed, I have often felt that, in dealing with utter scoundrels, the Old Testament offers better practical advice than the New. Perhaps I am an erring sinner in thinking that, but I cannot help it.'

'And now, what about your disaster, Mr Tucker?' said Raven. 'What on earth became of your officers and the rest of your crew, if it was not an outbreak of disease?'

'Ah, sir, that is a story I must tell you at another

time, for it is a longish tale, and you no doubt wish to start your labours for'ard. In addition, it is a story of such shameful cruelty and depravity that I cannot in conscience narrate it in the presence of a pure and refined young woman. So, if you have all had sufficient nourishment for now, I will clear away and wash the dishes. Would you, madam, care to help me?'

'Gladly, sir. I think I should be more hindrance than help among that fearful tangle for'ard.'

While Raven led his five-strong party to their daunting task, Eleanor and Tucker busied themselves in the small, neat pantry just for'ard of the mess-room. After a long and active silence, Tucker cleared his throat and said hesitantly, with some embarrassment: 'Tell me, Eleanor, am I right in thinking that you and Mr Raven have a - shall we say - personal attachment, beyond that of fellow-survivors?'

Eleanor, taken by surprise, blushed, but replied firmly: 'Yes, sir, you are quite right. We are indeed ...'

He cut in: 'You are not, I take it, lawfully married?'

'O no. We met about a year ago when my mother and I joined my father's ship. Since then there has been no opportunity for any ceremony; indeed, my parents did not approve of our attachment, for reasons which I will not go into now. We fell in love almost at once; we have been through some terrible times together, for my mother died of the typhus and my father perished in the wreck. Indeed, Jack was the last person on earth to exchange words with him. All the rest of us escaped, but with only some food supplies and the clothes we stood up in; then I suffered this appalling attack you have heard about. I can see that you are a good, God-fearing man, but I have to confess to you that, in all these troubles, my faith in God was sorely shaken, but my faith in Jack – never! We have exchanged no rings, but we will be married one day – we are certain of that. Utterly certain.'

'My dear, if your souls are united, what do trinkets matter? I scarcely know either of you, but I too am certain that you will have a long and happy life together. However, (his tone became decisive and firmly moral) we must observe and maintain Christian standards, for a marriage ceremony is one of the most important sacraments of our lives. As your union has not so far been sanctified, that means that you will require a cabin each. Fortunately, we have several small spare cabins, as, in these whalers, the expert harpooners rank as mates. I will show you your quarters at dinner-time.' He paused, then turned with some relief to mundane matters: 'I think we will cook them some pork for dinner.'

Eleanor's heart sank as she visualized the briny, slimy, woody lumps of salt pork that used to come out of the casks aboard 'Figaro'. She said, without enthusiasm: 'Shall I take out some pieces to chop up and put in soak?'

'No indeed, Eleanor. There will be no need for that. I am referring to fresh pork. We bartered ourselves some pigs in one of the islands of Samoa, and Noah – who is an excellent butcher – slaughtered the last of them a few days ago. I think I can find us a front shoulder joint, and between us I expect we can devise some gravy sauce, and to accompany that we will bake some yams – some sweet potatoes. We obtained also several sacks of those from the islanders, and they – as our sailors say – are mighty good eating.'

Eleanor gaped and beamed: 'Fresh meat and fresh

vegetables too! Sir, this will not be dinner. For us, this will be manna in the wilderness!'

Meanwhile Raven, in a more workaday mood, was taking stock up for'ard. In full daylight, the whaler seemed, to his eyes, the most extraordinary craft he had ever clapped eyes on. Though not much less in beam than 'Figaro', she was, he judged, only about a third of the barque's length. Everything about her was antique – rope rigging, the shrouds set up with dead-eyes and lanyards, all the decks and bulwarks of wood, and, for'ard of everything, pointing up to the skies ahead, that prodigious bowsprit that they had all noticed earlier – a good thirty feet long, he guessed. Strangest of all, right amidships between the foremast and the mainmast, was a massive square brick structure like the base of a tower, about eighteen feet wide by ten feet long. Set in its top, which was about four feet high, were two huge metal cauldrons; underneath those was the wide grate of a furnace, and under that again a metal tray, about six inches deep, that covered the whole area of the bottom of the structure.

Along the ship's sides were old-fashioned wooden davits – two pairs to port, three to starboard – but only one of her boats remained. Overall, the most striking feature was the scrupulous cleanliness of everything; the ship was like a man-of-war – every piece of wood scrubbed white or gleaming with varnish, everything metal burnished till it shone.

He noticed Noah looking at him with amusement. 'You not seen an old whaler before, mister?'

'No, never. Well, only at sea, in the distance. Good God, she's a funny old hooker, nearly as wide as she is long, but she's as smart as a British battleship – all spit and polish.'

'Ah yes. Well, it must be a good six weeks since we tried out our last whale – you know, cut off the blubber and boiled it down to get the oil. Lordy, mister, when we doing that the decks be like a pigsty for dirt – running with blood and oil so you kin hardly stand. But when all that done, the Old Man he make us scrub, scrub, scrub, morning till night. If'n you don't do that, the ship stink to high heaven.'

'I suppose the blubber gets boiled in that brick furnace arrangement amidships?'

'Yessir, that's the try-works. That be sending up a cloud like a pillar of black smoke for two days, maybe, when we trying out; it be just like that cloud of fire and smoke that God send to Moses and the Israelites to guide em through the wilderness.'

'And that big trough underneath?'

'Ah, we fill that with seawater before we light the fire, else the furnace scorch the wood underneath – maybe set the ship on fire.'

'You must need a hell of a lot of wood or coal to fuel a furnace that size?'

'No, only some wood at the start. When the blubber melt, it leave lots of dried-out chips in the oil. We skim them out and use them for the fire. They do burn real good.'

'H'm ... All very clever. And the oil's very valuable, I expect? A cargo of it worth a lot?'

'Thousands of dollars, sir, back in New Bedford. But foremast hands don't get much of that money for their pains. I tell you mister: this is the most dangerous, dirty and most cruellest trade I ever did see. I nearly wept at first to see how them poor critters suffered, stuck with harpoons, hunted till they plumb exhausted, then pierced in their vitals with the lances. I tell you, I never go whaling again. We lost three men, too, when a big old sperm whale, he just come up fast right under a boat and crunch it to splinters – jus like a dog with a stick. I'll dig ditches or sweep streets before I do this job again.'

'I think I'd be with you there, Noah. But now then, let's get down to business: we've got to first stay the masts, then fix up some kind of jury-rig to get us to Bluff – she won't sail as she is. Of course, one way or another, we've got to get rid of all the hamper lying over the side, but I think we need first to decide what sort of jury-rig we want to finish up with before we start discarding anything else. I mean, if we use the anchor-windlass and rig up some leading-blocks we can haul things back up on deck.'

Jimmy Protheroe and Carl had been looking sagely at the wreckage overboard, and came over to join them. Jimmy said: 'We don't reckon we can do much about the topmast, mister – not with only six of us, not even if Miss Eleanor and the old chap was to come and help with the pulley-hauly. It's too big and heavy, and broken anyway.'

'Ja,' said Carl, 'but if we get the t'gallant mast free of it, that mast be useful, and that much lighter to pull up.'

'Yes, you're both right,' said Raven, 'and that's given me an idea for our jury-rig: we cut the topmast free and let it go. As Jim says, it's too big for us to handle. But I agree we could get the t'gallant mast up – it's much shorter and lighter. Then somehow – I haven't yet quite worked out how – we sway the t'gallant mast up and fix it to the lower mast, and use that to set three headsails out to the bowsprit – God knows that's long enough – and that will give us a much more balanced sail-plan, in case we have to go to windward. Now then, this is what we do: two of us – Noah and I – go aloft and get rid of the stump of the topmast and rig a new main-topmast forestay to make the mainmast safer, you two lads scramble down among the wreckage, unbend the sails and take off the two yards, while two – Carl and Jim – stay on deck to haul up everything they've freed. And of course, we save all the rope we can. The hands going over the side will have to wear life-lines; it'll be a pretty difficult climb for you, I'm afraid, boys, and I don't want anyone going for a swim – though I expect you'll get pretty wet anyway.'

'Don't you fret about that, mister,' said Noah with a wide grin. 'You going to send George and Amos down: they can swim like fishes and clamber like monkeys. Only trouble with them is, they ain't got the brains of one monkey between em.'

Far from being upset at the insult, the two young blacks showed their teeth in wide smiles, and burst into high-pitched laughter, almost as if they had been praised. 'Don' you listen to that poor old guy, mister,' said George Brown. 'He just jealous cos he too blamed old to get down there and back. He damn near ready for that ole rocking-chair on the front stoop.'

'Thass right,' said Amos. 'Don't you pay him no mind. We go down there with our knives; we cut all the buntlines and clewlines and rovings loose, so the sails are free, then you guys haul on the sheet-ropes, and up they come. Believe me, sir, we smart enough for that.'

(The rovings were the short lashings holding each sail to its yard, while the buntlines and clewlines were light ropes used to gather the sail in ready for furling.)

'Yes,' said his friend, 'and when we done that we cut the yards free from the mast, so you can haul them up too.'

'Carl,' said Raven, 'some of the stuff to come up will be heavy, so you might need to get a good length of decent rope and take some turns round that old anchor-windlass's drum. If you need to, get Eleanor to help you by heaving back on the rope to keep the turns tight on the drum. Right, everybody? Thank God we've got another calm day, so let's get on with it – no more gassing! Noah, show me where all the tools are kept; you and I are going to need a saw and a maul – you know a big hammer.'

All set to work, and Raven was glad and proud to hear young George and Amos chattering, laughing and singing in their high voices as they struggled perilously among the wreckage overside – proud because he sensed that, by visualizing a solution to their problems, he had given them a purpose and an aim, and therefore a hope for the future, to replace their despairing, aimless hacking at ropes and spars. Halfway through the morning he glanced down from his jobs aloft to see Eleanor vigorously hauling at the rope on the windlass, helping Carl and Jim.

By that time, the old stump of the topmast was gone; he and Noah had cut through the lashings and knocked out the fid – the heavy bolt that held the jointed mast together. The stays to the mainmast had also been replaced. They climbed back down the ratlines and joined the deck working-party. They had made good progress too: for all their nonsense and chatter, the two young whaler hands had done well: fathom upon fathom of rope rigging had been loosed, hauled aboard, and neatly coiled down. Carl was in the act of showing Eleanor how to lay down the coils neatly and clockwise, or right-handed. The lads in the wreckage had now freed the tops'l yard. It was a massively heavy piece of wood, some twenty-five feet long, and would need careful handling, for the old ship still rolled to and fro and pitched into the shifting swells.

'Jim,' said Raven, 'get a good-sized block and nip up and shackle it to the top of the lower mast, then come back down, take the end of this thick rope here, reeve it through the block and bring the end back down again; I'll chuck the other end down to the lads, so that they can make it fast to one end of the yard. We'll sway the mast up like that, and then stow it on the deck. Carl, Jim, stand by to steady it as it comes up. Eleanor and I will work the windlass; Nelli, will you nip down aft to the pantry and ask Mr Tucker to come up? We'll need him to take your place backing up on the rope from the windlass.'

'All right, I will,' she replied, 'but I just hope it won't cause him to spoil our dinner, because that is going to be a treat.'

'Why? What are we having?'

'Not telling. It's wait-and-see dinner, as my *mamgu* – my granny – used to say.'

She hurried off aft, her cheeky gaiety leaving Raven stirred with wonder and joy at the capacity of the human soul to heal itself after horrible wounding. Even her hair had recovered somewhat; it no longer looked ugly, savagely hacked, but simply boyishly cropped, to match her male attire.

The anchor-windlass was a strange old contrivance, immensely powerful but laboriously slow. It consisted of a horizontal steel barrel, revolving between massive wooden pillars, and driven by a system of cogs geared to a kind of see-saw with a cross-wise handle at each end. As you pumped the ends of the see-saw up and down, you made the drum revolve slowly; three turns of rope were taken round it, two people pumped while a third hauled back on the end of the rope, to keep the turns tight on the drum, so that the turns would grip and not slip. As Jim had said of the ship, the contraption might have come out of the ark.

But it worked; groaning under the strain, the rope raised one end of the mast and hauled it upwards till its other end slid over the bulwark. Leaving his place at the pump-handle, Raven carefully, cautiously, slacked off the rope, allowing the turns to render round the drum, lowering the mast so that the three black seamen could lay it tidily on deck. A cheer went up from all of them as it came to rest, and young Amos said cheerfully, 'Hey, that was easy, man! No trouble!'

Noah chided him with mock-severity: 'That because someone with a head on his shoulders told you what to do, you young lunkhead. 'And if'n it's so blamed easy, just you git down there agin with this rope and make it fast to the t'gallant yard. We'll get that up next. I know you two aim to sit about on your butts chawing t'backer, but it ain't time for that yet, not by no means. So away you go now.'

Soon the smaller, lighter, t'gallant yard was swayed up and lowered to the deck, where it lay beside the heaps and folds of the rescued sails. 'Now sir,' said Tucker cheerfully, almost - for him - playfully, 'you have had a long and hard morning's work and it is near two of the clock. Do you wish to continue, while your dinner becomes ruined in the oven, or do we now lay aft for a meal of roast fresh pork, baked sweet potatoes and gravy sauce? The choice is yours.'

Raven smiled broadly: 'I've no wish to become the most hated man in the southern hemisphere, so dinner it is, lads, and we'll have an hours' stand-easy afterwards too. We've earned it, eh? Mind you, after that we've got the biggest job so far – getting the t'gallant mast free from the broken topmast, and hoisting that inboard. That's going to be our new jury topmast. So get your strength up, all of you.'

As they all piled aft with loud cheers, their nostrils were assailed by the heavenly odours of fresh meat cooking; for the boat's crew especially a meal like that was, as Prospero said on his island, 'such stuff as dreams are made on'.

An hour later they all lolled, replete, on their chairs in the mess-room, their stomachs well stocked with Tucker's excellent cooking. Jimmy Protheroe's appreciation showed itself in a resounding belch, and he said: 'Pardon all, I'm sure, but it was your good grub done that, Mr Tucker. You ought to be a chef in one of them big hotels. Even my old mam, God bless her, can't cook like that.'

There was a contented rumble of agreement, but Tucker had not exhausted his store of delights: 'We still have some fresh young coconuts, which might form a suitable dessert, and after that, gentlemen, if anyone wishes, we have plenty of tobacco – both leaf and plug – as well as clay pipes. These ships, you see, were well stocked for very long voyages.'

'Ja,' said Carl. 'A pipe of tobacco – that be good. I miss that on the island for long time.'

'Me too, sir,' said Protheroe, and Raven, who had picked up the smoking habit in the half-deck among his fellow-apprentices, also showed his pleasure: 'Excellent! I've been dying for a puff for ages.'

'Do you smoke too, Mr Tucker?' said Eleanor, with some distaste. 'If not, shall we retire and wash the dishes? I have no wish to stay here if this place is going to stink of tobacco-smoke. I did not mind smelling the good cigars that my father smoked, but sailors' clay pipes full of cheap shag tobacco – faugh!'

Tucker was apologetic: 'Well, ma'am, I'm afraid that I am minded to join these gentlemen in a pipe. The pleasures of the flesh, alas ...... But I will not have you washing all the plates on your own. I will show you to your cabin where, if you wish, you may enjoy a siesta after your meal in slightly purer air.'

'Thank you, sir, that would be much more to my taste, for smoking' – and here she shot a severe glance at Raven – 'is not a habit I much admire.' She stalked out, leaving Raven red-faced and well aware of the suppressed mirth of the hands around him at his discomfiture, but nevertheless defiantly stuffing a new clay pipe with the blessed nicotinous weed.

'Now sir,' he said when Tucker returned to the mess-room, 'you have not yet explained why this is a ghost-ship, virtually without a crew. You didn't wish to explain in front of Eleanor, but now you are free to talk. We three have all been at sea for years, so we are not squeamish, and will not be easily shocked. We all have much to do when we muster again this afternoon, but for the present, we have all earned an hour's rest, while you tell us your tale, so fire away.'

'Very well. You shall have the tale, as you call it, but I fear it will be neither pleasant nor edifying. If you wish, we can repair to the captain's saloon, where the chairs are softer and easier. Who is to gainsay us, since you, despite your youth, are now our captain?'

CHAPTER FIFTEEN

Settling himself comfortably into his chair, Tucker took several deep draws at his pipe, and began: 'I must, I think, begin by telling you that, except for the captain, mates and expert harpooners, the crews of whaling ships are abominably badly paid. They are promised a "lay" – a share of the profits of the voyage – but it is a very small share – perhaps one two-hundredth, which even after a successful two- or three-year voyage, does not amount to much. And for this pittance they will have many times faced the deadly danger of attacking a sperm whale over fifty feet long and weighing perhaps sixty tons, with teeth and jaws capable of catching and devouring huge deep-sea squids. And you need to remember that they have to mount their attack on the monster from a boat no bigger than yours, but much more lightly built. Furthermore, the godly Quaker owners will have denied them much of even that miserable pittance by charging them high prices for clothes, boots, tobacco and so forth, which they have bought from the ship's stores. As the ship's purser, I was in charge of this robbery, and felt great shame to be so.

'As an inevitable consequence, this ship, like most whalers, had many undesirable characters aboard. I do not, I must emphasize, include these gentlemen here in that description. They had their own reasons for joining.'

The black sailors grinned and nodded, and Noah said: 'Thass right, mister. You folks got to remember that it's only thirty or so years since they stopped the slavery. I kin remember real well the days when my momma and pappy belonged to a Mr Wilson, over on a cotton plantation in Missouri. He was a good enough master; he let them live together in one of the plantation huts – else I wouldn't be here now, would I? But still they was things that he owned, and he could have done pretty much what he liked with them. Of course, I had to pick the cotton and tote the bales as soon as I old enough. These here young bucks, they lucky. They always bin free.'

Amos spoke up: 'Yeah, we free. My folks come up north to get away from all that. But it still damn hard for black boy to git decent job. That why I signed on this old hooker. I just had to, or go on the bum. Same with George here. I guessed when the skipper signed me on that it would be a hard ship, but I didn't know how hard.'

'So you see, Mr Raven,' said Tucker, 'it is a last resort for most of the hands. Consequently, our ship was full of the dregs and scourings of every territory in the Pacific and elsewhere – Russians, Americans, Britons, Maoris, Australians, Portuguese, Kanakas – the black people of the islands. In short, they were a lawless riff-raff, kept at their heavy, dull and often very dangerous work by the most brutal discipline from the mates and harpooners, who had themselves often come from similar disreputable backgrounds. Several of the hands were stranded beachcombers, others were runaway escaped convicts, fugitive scoundrels, deserters from other whalers, and so on.

'Now, to get fresh supplies of food, water and firewood, during their very long voyages, these whalers must perforce put in to the Pacific islands at times, and it is to our shame that, for the black islanders, sometimes their first experience of the white man is their meeting with this scum – a harsh word to use for my fellow-humans, but I can find no other. They are godless rascals, often bearers of the deadly diseases of our so-called civilization – especially those of the venereal kind - and craving, after so long at sea, for women on whom to satisfy their lusts. Not surprisingly, their brutal crudity and arrogance has often caused bloody conflict between them and the Kanakas.

'Fortunately, most of the larger islands have long been under the benign influence of Christian missionaries, who, years ago, showed the most remarkable courage in coming to live amongst these islanders, some of whom lived lives stained by tribal wars and cruelty, and even the ultimate abomination of cannibalism. The missionaries' influence, and indeed, their mere presence, have made quarrels between whalers and Kanakas much less frequent, but there are still small, remote atolls where the light of true religion has not yet dawned, and the old evils may survive. The island of my story was one of those.

'However, enough of this preamble; I must turn to my story of the "Pawtucket" and her crew. Well then, a month ago we were sailing, with a full crew and nearly full holds, among the islands of the Samoa group, searching for one or two more sperm whales with which to complete our cargo of whale-oil, spermaceti, baleen, and even some ambergris.'

Jimmy Protheroe looked puzzled, and interrupted: 'Hold on a minute, mister, if you don't mind. What are all them things you mentioned? I know about whale-oil for lamps, but that's all.'

Noah put in helpfully: 'Well, feller, the spermaceti, that's the real good, kinda waxy oil that comes from the whale's head; that go to make real fine candles; the baleen is the bendy whalebone. That goes to make stuff like ribs for umbrellas…'

'Yes,' said Tucker, smiling, 'and also to provide our

fine ladies with bustles and corsets, with which they strive to improve or disguise the shapes given to them by their Creator. As for the ambergris, that is a strange ugly deposit sometimes found in the whale's bowels, which, when refined, can be used to make the most heavenly perfumes for those same fine ladies to improve the natural odour of their bodies. This substance, being so rare, is quite literally worth its weight in gold. We have a little of that, I believe, locked securely in the captain's cabin. But do, gentlemen, please allow me to try once more to begin my story.

'Now then, to obtain water and firewood we made for a small island in that group of islands, and anchored one morning in its lagoon, having steered through the narrow gap in its surrounding reef. What the island's name was I have no notion, for our Captain did not bother to confide much in his subordinates. But it was, in my eyes that morning, a place of stunning beauty, with a white-sanded beach, on which a warm sun shone. The beach was fringed by coconut palms and, behind them was a thickly-wooded hill, rising to a low peak – an earthly paradise, in short. Here and there we saw clearings where crops were growing, and here and there smoke drifted up from cooking-fires in the clusters of thatched huts – another Eden, it seemed.

'We were met on the beach by a score of natives, men and women, all grass-skirted, weaponless, smiling and friendly. Though the older folk of both sexes tended towards fatness, even obesity, the young men were fine specimens – tall, broad-shouldered, athletic in build. But as for the young women – the *wahines,* as the sailors called them…' Here Tucker's face and voice became transformed, as if by ecstatic recollection. 'As for them, they were comely beyond words or imagination to men long at sea – lithe, shapely, bare-breasted, clad in only wisps of grass which, we later found, they happily discarded when they wished to dance. Their skins were not black, but of a…' he paused, to summon up the right words, 'of a sort of splendid, glossy, bronzed, mahogany colour, ravishing to behold. They were graceful, and… ah… yes, so where was I? I have lost my thread I fear.'

Raven politely stifled his amusement: 'You had just landed on the beach and met the islanders – most notably the female islanders.'

'Ah, yes! You must pardon an old fellow's weaknesses. Well, the meeting was most friendly, and we communicated well enough by sign-language, and besides, we had Kwato, a seaman from Fiji, who was able to gather some notion of what they were saying in their island dialect. I think that they must have had little or no experience of whalers, for they much admired our clothes and our boat, and looked out with wonder at our ship, which, I guess, seemed to them of immense size.

'However, despite their wonder and awe, the Kanakas were most friendly. They showed us an inlet where a cataract of crystal-clear water tumbled down rocks into a pool, where we could conveniently fill our water-butts, and they took us to a nearby part of the forest where many trees had been felled by a storm, and were now a ready source of excellent dry firewood.

'While some of our whale-boats' crews were busy filling casks with the island's wonderful pure water, and other crews busy chopping and sawing wood for the galley fire, the kindly islanders were not idle. They all disappeared up a path leading to their village, and returned, staggering under the weight of big rush baskets crammed with the most excellent fruits and vegetables - bananas, papayas, pineapples, yams, breadfruit, and a tasty root vegetable called taro. To us, who had been for months condemned to a dull and dismal diet of stale water, dry biscuit, as hard as roof-tiles, dried peas and beans, and lumps of salt beef and pork more like wood in texture, this was a blessed cornucopia, and the natives seemed like dusky and very cheerful angels of mercy.

'They made us understand that they were willing to barter fruit and vegetables, live pigs and turtle-meat in exchange for our goods. They especially prized metal goods – pans, knives, axes and so on, they having no metal goods on the island, apart from a few hoes and spades obtained from occasional trading schooners.

'For a week or more life with them proceeded in total harmony, and every day canoes full of happy islanders came alongside; the natives clambered aboard by the main chains, and wandered about the decks, gaping at our masts, rigging and furled sails, and even enjoying crunching our hard ship's biscuits with their splendid strong white teeth. The only jar to the harmony was their custom of helping themselves to any portable ship's stores they could lay hands on. They assumed – perhaps not unnaturally - that, because we were welcome to a share of anything of theirs, we would be equally liberal towards them of our possessions. I have read that your great Captain Cook had the like problem in Tahiti. But of course, we could not allow them to cut off great lengths of rope from the running rigging, or loot the mess-room of its crockery and cutlery.

'Every night we were bidden to feast with them at their village, and every night our men stuffed themselves with great masses of roast pork, baked yams and taro, washed down at first with delicious coconut milk, and later, as the evening wore on, with draughts of a potent liquor called kava, which they make by pounding the roots of the kava plant to a powder, and then mixing it with water to make a grey, intoxicating brew. It was not much to my taste; we drank it out of cups formed from coconut shells, and one draught was enough to make me very relaxed and unsteady. But our hardened topers quaffed it as if it were lemonade, so that later they could scarce row themselves back to the ship.

'But what made me most uneasy was the behaviour of the *wahines*.. Flushed with kava, they would shed every scrap of clothing and dance naked in the firelight, weaving in and out among the seated sailors, writhing their bodies with the greatest sensuality, and swaying their ripe, perfectly-formed buttocks before our sailors' hungry eyes.'

Tucker here took out his handkerchief and wiped his moist face: 'I do beg your pardon, gentlemen, but, despite my strivings to maintain a decent purity of mind and body, my greatest weakness is a partiality to the female form in a state of nature. Even the recollection and narration of these scenes has produced in me a regrettable ….er ….excitement.'

Raven replied gracefully: 'Don't apologize, sir. Your descriptions were vivid enough to produce the same effects on us – eh, Jim?'

'O *Iesu mawr,* mister, you're right there!'

'Yes, yes,' said Tucker, recovering his composure.

'The shapely female form is indeed one of the very finest of God's works upon earth; indeed, my proclivity for it has been the source of many of my woes. But that is another story. Allow me to return to my narrative. I soon came to realize that the spontaneous liberality that the Kanakas displayed over their gifts and their hospitality extended also to the sexual act Their Mosaic laws evidently did not forbid either what we would call stealing or random, promiscuous fornication. These beautiful girls bestowed their utmost favours as freely as you and I might shake hands. To the riff-raff of our foc'sle, long starved of the company and touch of woman, and to the officers too, our stay at the island was an unending orgiastic paradise. I was shocked to hear them boasting of their repeated conquests – such that they could scarce stand unsupported, what with their strenuous couplings and their many cups of kava. The ship's normally busy daily routine was replaced by apathetic sloth and anarchy, even among the officers. But what concerned me even more was the callous brutality in their bragging. Instead of seeing their pleasure as a source of joy, happiness, innocent delight and affection to both partners – as God, I am sure, willed it to be – they spoke of and treated women as objects, as mere machines for sating their lusts.'

'So you wasn't tempted yourself, mister?' said Protheroe slily.

Tucker coloured: 'No, not precisely tempted; I think "obliged" would be a more accurate word. On the third night the tribal chief, a man of great good nature and of great obesity too, to denote his high rank in their society, presented me with his eldest daughter, a young woman of the most extraordinary beauty, and by signs suggested that I should take her off into the forest and pleasure her and myself in that dark seclusion. Being a man of middle age, and one who seeks always to live the chaste and devout life, I began to decline politely, but Kwato gripped me by the arm and said, urgently: "Mister, you say no, you make chief angry. He think you don't like his daughter. You make him b'lieve you think she not good enough for you. You maybe make big trouble for all of us." What could I do, gentlemen? My acceptance of his gift became a... a... political necessity, you might say. I was obliged, for the safety of all our company, to smile, bow, take the lady's hand and allow her to lead me into the darkness of the clustering trees. I saw it as my duty.'

'Yeah, and then what happened?' said Protheroe, grinning lasciviously.

'And then, young man,' said Tucker severely, 'I did my duty - twice, in fact. And for the rest of our stay, the same duty was every night expected – nay, demanded – of me, and despite my age I did not fall short of my obligations, as it were. Yes, you smile, Mr Raven, and I cannot blame you. No doubt it seems to you amusing that a dull, stodgy old pen-pusher like me should enjoy such favours from one so young and beautiful.

'But our island idyll, I began to feel, was becoming tense and dangerous. The men of the tribe were strong and warlike, used to carrying out bloody raids in their war-canoes on the people of other islands. At first they tolerated – even encouraged - the crew's copulations with their womenfolk – their sisters, daughters, nieces, perhaps even wives – but they must after a few days have felt anger at the whalers' violent and brutal lust, and at the disgusting and degrading practices which they forced upon those delightful girls – practices which I do not propose to describe to you now.

'The bloody storm broke upon us on the last night of our stay. On the first day, I must explain, the hospitable Kanakas had shown us the sights of their island, including a sacred grove near the inlet where their canoes were beached. It was a dark, somewhat sinister place, so thickly shaded by huge trees that the sun never shone in there, and in the midst of the grove were some primitive stone fire-places, and Kwato told us later that these were where, on special ceremonial occasions in the past, the bodies of their slaughtered captives from other tribes had been roasted for consumption by the men of the tribe, never by the women. Whether that revolting custom was still observed he could not say, but the place sent a cold shudder through me, as it showed another, cruel and savage, side to the islanders' cheerful and generous natures. But the main point of this visit for my narrative, is that we were told that this so-called sacred place was utterly forbidden- or *taboo*, as they called it – to any female person of any age or at any time – and that the punishment for breaches of this law was cruel indeed.

'Some French classical scholar once said: "Those whom the Gods would destroy, they first send mad". The conduct of our crew on this last night perfectly proved the truth of his observation. Some of them, knowing that this was their last chance of venereal pleasures for perhaps months, were more than usually depraved. They did not trouble to be discreet with their couplings – I cannot call it love-making – but instead threw the island girls to the ground in full view of all at the feast, sometimes subjecting the most attractive of them to repeated ravishings, lining up to take their turn, like dogs with a bitch in season. I could sense that the mood of the Kanakas – not surprisingly - was changing from one of genial hospitality to one of cold disgust and smouldering, sullen fury. My companions here shared my disgust and anger.'

'That's so, mister,' said Noah. 'Me and the boys, we didn't want to see them nice brown gals treated like animals by them matelots. We black people, as I said before, saw enough of that when we was slaves, when we was treated as *things,* not human beings made in the likeness of the Lord. Them sailors was worse than the slave-owners in the way they treated them gals. If ever there was savages on that island, it was our crew from the "Pawtucket", and by the Lord Jesus they got their reward. But I'm real sorry to cut in on you like that, Mr Tucker.'

'Not at all, my friend. My sentiments are exactly the same.'

'Mind you,' said Noah, 'We ain't pretending to be no hypocrites, like them whited sepulchres in the Bible. Them gals was too much of a temptation for us three as well. We all took gals off somewhere quiet on other nights and had us some fun with them. By hookey, them gals knew how to love a man real good, real good! But that was happy fun; we never hurt nobody, nor bullied em, we only took what them gals wanted to give, and we parted friends. I knows that ain't behaving like the Bible says, but we only poor sailors, what never sees a woman for months and months; most of the time, we don't git nothing but hard graft, plenty of knocks from the mates, and risking our lives fighting them terrible sperm whales.'

'If only all the hands had behaved as these fellows did,' Tucker continued, 'we should now have a complete and happy crew. But liquor and lust had brought Satan into the minds of the rest of the crew, and that in turn brought Satan into this new Eden. One of the crew – Briggs, a ruffian from Australia, I believe – persuaded several of the others that it would be a great jest after the feast to drag their hapless females down to the sacred grove for their nightly orgy. Hopelessly drunk on the kava he had swigged down, he yelled to the others: "Who gives a damn for these black bastards and their mumbo-jumbo? Let's show em, lads!". His suggestion met with roars of drunken approval from most of the hands. Their reckless, wicked folly made my blood run cold. I went at once to Captain Olsen and begged him to put a stop to this criminal madness, but he himself was too far gone in his cups to care. He merely slurred out: "Shut yer mouth, yer canting old Quaker! Let the boys have their fun while they can, for Christ's sake. What do I care about a bunch of Kanakas and their goddam *taboos*? Go on, sling your hook!"

'From that moment I knew, and so did my friends here, what would happen when the islanders suffered this final callous insult to their women and their religion. Our men were besotted with liquor, unarmed and greatly outnumbered – totally helpless to defend themselves. I had done my best to avert the coming slaughter, but in vain, and we four saw no reason why we should die for the folly of others, so without a word we slipped away unnoticed from the feast and hastened down to the beach. My instinct was to launch one of the whale-boats and row to the ship at once, but Noah, who is made of sterner stuff than I, said, "No, mister! If we take a boat now there won't be room for all of them to get off, if they should make it down to the beach. We got to wait and see what happens. There's going to be mighty trouble up there, I believe, but we can't leave them to die".

'So, mastering our fears, we waited, shivering, in the bright moonlight. To mar the beauty of the scene, we heard for some time the ugly, drunken racket from the feast, but then, suddenly, we heard the shrill screaming of the women as, I suppose, they were being dragged towards the gloomy, dreaded grove. Then, above the screams, we heard the clamour of enraged men shouting and, almost at once, yells of agony and terror. It was like hearing the terrible sounds rising from the mouth of Hell. We knew then that it would be folly to wait any longer. With a desperate effort, we shoved one of the boats into the water, but as it floated, and we were all about to scramble aboard, Amos cried: "Wait! One of them's coming!", and sure enough, a figure came out of the trees and came lurching and staggering towards us. We recognized him as O'Reilly, an Irishman from Cork. As he came closer, panting and whimpering with pain, we saw that he had one hand to his side, and that blood was streaming through his fingers. We seized him, and began to struggle to get him into the boat, but as we did so, his body went suddenly limp, he fell from our hands into the shallows and gasped out his last words: "Finished! The lot of us! They had spears, clubs..." Then, lying there in the little waves, he crossed himself as the Papists do, and murmured: "Christ Jesus and Mary... forgive me my..." But before he could finish his last prayer, a small wave broke over his head; he choked, and lay still for ever. The moon was so bright that we could see a thin, wandering stream of his blood staining the water on the fringe of what had been a paradise island. I too pray that he will be forgiven, for he was a wild man, but not, at heart, a bad one.'

Tucker paused, clearly troubled deeply by the memory of that night's horrors, and the whole group was silent in that safe, comfortable cabin.

'You have certainly been through hell,' said Raven, 'but how in the world did you escape from it – with only four of you? Seems to me you were in a death-trap in that lagoon.'

'Only by the help of One who is not of this world. Nothing but a miracle – indeed, several miracles - could have saved us. Our troubles were by no means over, for I knew that the natives, for revenge, would wish to capture the ship, loot it, and then set it afire, first murdering us, of course. Even as we pulled out to the ship I saw dark figures running from the path to the water's edge. One paused to give a final spear-thrust to O'Reilly's corpse; he must have seen us rowing towards the ship, and I heard him yell to the others. In a trice they were all racing along the beach to where the canoes were kept. I knew it would not be long before they attacked the ship itself, and I had seen how swift their canoes were. We reached the ship and scrambled aboard, abandoning the boat. I then became aware of our first blessing – a brisk, steady offshore breeze.

'These three men here showed unbelievable speed and skill; in no time they had slipped the anchor-cable; then George and Amos shot up the foremast ratlines, went out on the tops'l yard and loosed the gaskets, so that the sail dropped and unfolded, while Noah, down on deck, hauled like a madman to sheet in the sail, and in a matter of minutes that sail was set, spread to the wind, and drawing, and the "Pawtucket" was under way. I, poor lubber that I am, went to the wheel, with Noah shouting directions at me how to steer. And – this is the greatest miracle – the moon was so bright that Noah, up for'ard, could see the small gap in the reef through which we must go or perish. The ocean swells broke continuously on the coral reef, so that, from the lagoon, the reef appeared in the moonlight as a bright white strip. But that strip of foam was, of course, interrupted by the small gap where no waves broke. I had to steer for that blessed piece of darkness. Naturally, our progress was slow with only one sail set, so the boys came quickly down and loosed the big foresail. Gentlemen, I have never in my life seen sails fill and draw, and a ship gather speed, with such keen pleasure, and neither have I seen such feats of skill as these men performed that night. Noah was, at one and the same time, sheeting in sails, directing these lads, and conning the ship through that perilously narrow gap. It was another blessed benediction when, peering over the bulwark, I saw the ends of the reef sliding past to port and starboard. At least we had overcome one of our problems by escaping from out of that perilous trap.

'But our troubles were far from over; indeed the worst was yet to come. By the time we reached the gap, three canoes were shooting like arrows towards us. Despite their liberal draughts of kava, the Kanakas were able to paddle like demons. These good fellows abandoned sail-setting and began to prepare to defend the ship, for we knew that we faced the prospect of our own slaughter as well as the destruction of the ship. There would be no possibility of negotiations. Yet remember: I am a Quaker and resolutely pacifist in outlook. I was determined that there should be no more bloodshed if it could be avoided. But at all costs the islanders must be prevented from boarding us. Once they were on deck in numbers, with their spears and clubs at close quarters, we were dead men, skewered or brained. Noah told me that I was the most important man on board – the helmsman; on no account must I allow myself to be distracted from steering a straight course out to sea, with the sails full and drawing. He ran below and fetched up two rifles and some ammunition from the captain's store, while the boys armed themselves with what we call cutting-spades – fearful, razor-sharp blades on long wooden shafts, used for cutting the blubber from the whales.

'Despite warning rifle-shots over their heads, the leading canoe's stout paddlers came on steadily, too full of rage, I expect, to be deterred. The leading canoe came alongside under the main chains, where the shrouds, fastened well below the bulwarks, provide, as you will all know well, a handy ladder for an active boarder. We knew that these young, athletic men would find it only too easy to leap up, grasp the bottoms of the shrouds, and haul themselves aboard. In that strong moonlight, I saw Amos standing tense, leaning over the bulwark with his dreadful weapon poised. Then I saw him put all his strength into a murderous thrust at the first would-be boarder, and, over the warlike yelling of the Kanakas, I heard a cry of agony and terror as the man, terribly wounded in the shoulder, fell back, not into the canoe but into the sea. The attackers knew, as did we, that a body thrashing in the water and bleeding copiously, would attract sharks within minutes.

'I had been puzzled for a while to see Amos left alone at the ship's side, but now I saw why: Noah had been preparing his master-stroke, for now I saw him and George staggering under the weight of a massive anvil; Amos laid down his weapon and somehow they lifted that huge lump of steel, balanced it for a moment on the top of the bulwark, then dropped it, so that it smashed clean through the canoe's bottom, grievously wounding two of the islanders on its way.

'Bedlam and panic broke out alongside, while all the time, out of the shelter of the land, the breeze stiffened and the ship gathered way. Life is sometimes cheap in those parts of the world, but now a score or more of men were in the water, three of them now bleeding, and all of them screaming in terror of the sharks. The two following canoes had perforce to stop to pick up their floundering comrades; once they had done that, they now had both the canoes so dangerously overloaded that they, all three score of them, faced the hideous fate of being torn to pieces and devoured alive. I have no doubt they were brave men, but that horror they could not face. They took up their paddles again and turned back to the calm water of the lagoon. In a sense, the dreadful reputation of the shark was our saviour that night.'

'Yeah, and that good old anvil, mister,' said Noah.

'Yes, indeed, and the anvil. Very well: once they saw that, for the moment, the attack was over, our good fellows here shot up and down the shrouds and out along the yards, loosing all the sails – courses, tops'ls, t'gallants, spanker – so that with every minute our speed increased and the two canoes were left farther and farther astern. Two more canoes came out, but they must have seen that their hopes of boarding us were slim. This good old tub was now plunging along at, I suppose, six knots or so in a choppy sea, and able to manoeuvre this way and that, so that boarding would have been impossible. Besides, they knew now that we had firearms, and they probably assumed that, if we had to, we would use them lethally. They overtook us, for their canoes are as swift as racing-boats, but they did no more than yell curses and throw a few harmless spears before turning back to the lagoon.

'Thanks to Almighty God and these three splendid fellows, we escaped the fate suffered by many whalers in the past among these islands. With no missionary to soften the islanders' savage customs, it may well be that many of our shipmates' bodies ended up on the cooking-stones of that dismal grove, and provided feasts for later days.

'We four escaped unscathed, and my only regret about our escape is that, to save our lives, we were forced to injure – perhaps to kill – some of the Kanakas. Their revenge had been cruel, savage and bloody, but on the other hand, all the trouble had been started by our men; the natives had shown, until that last night, nothing but friendship, generosity and tolerance. But after this, I fear for the safety of any other whaling crew that puts in there, for the islanders now have little reason to welcome the white man.'

'A narrow shave,' said Raven solemnly, 'but by God you did well, all of you, to get out of that situation. No wonder then that you seem so... so united, such friends.'

'Well, mister,' said Noah, grinning, 'as for what me and the boys did, it's surprising what you kin do if you scared out of your wits. But this Mr Tucker now, he steered damn well for a purser,' He was tactfully easing the tension that had come from remembering the horrors of the island. 'But once we out to sea and all sail set, alow and aloft, I take the wheel off him and send him down to the galley. He cook a blamed sight better than he steer.'

'Yes, Noah,' said Tucker with a rueful smile, ' you and your friends steered, but none of us knew well in which direction to steer. We were hapless wanderers on God's largest ocean, and He alone knows how long we might have wandered thus, had it not been for His final blessing upon us – the miracle of chancing, in all that vast space, and in that moment in time, to meet a body of souls, one of whom could tell us, by his science and skill, exactly where we were. If that was not a miracle, my friends, then I, as they say, am a Dutchman.'

CHAPTER SIXTEEN

'So that is how they died, poor, stupid, heedless wretches,' said Eleanor quietly, 'all cruelly massacred for the filthy animal lusts of some of them. What a senseless, wicked waste of lives, and what an utter shame it is that a tribe of islanders, who had been at first nothing but friendly and generous in their strange fashion, should now have murders and perhaps tortures on their consciences, and will now hate us "civilized" people for the rest of their lives!'

Raven and Eleanor were alone in what had been the second mate's cabin, talking quietly after supper that night, after a long and exhausting day working on the foremast rigging. They sat together on the only possible sitting-place – the bunk - holding hands, her fluffy cropped head on his shoulder. They looked like an image of the first stages of a chaste, shy, callow courtship. She had insisted on hearing the grim story that Tucker had told. Raven had been reluctant to re-tell those dark horrors. He had appreciated that they might recall to her that terrible morning at the cove, but had finally given her the general outline, omitting the worst of the details.

While doing so, he had been wryly, sadly aware of the distance and reserve that now lay between them – of how their relationship had been marred by tragedy and violence. Unbidden, the memory returned of that time, only months ago, when they had last shared a bunk in his cabin – his second mate's cabin – aboard the 'Figaro'. Then, in the first headlong rush of youthful passion, in a great ship with the ocean roaring past, only half-an-inch of steel plate away from them, they had lain naked, caressing in a delicious foreplay that had never reached its consummation; her religion and her fear of pregnancy and of her parents had forbidden that. And now? No heat, no deep kisses, no touching of flesh; nothing but a trust, a loyalty, a friendship which no disasters could end. Life, with its bitter blows, had matured them all too quickly, but their mutual love, much sobered and inhibited, still remained, as permanent as a rock. They were still one.

And now the sickening, ugly story of lust and slaughter was out there, between them - they both felt that. She said, after a long silence: 'They were cruel and violent, those islanders…. And yet, who am I to judge them? Had you and Simon not stopped me, I might now have the murder of John Ffynnongroes on my conscience. They had, I suppose, stone-headed clubs; I had my thick cudgel. Like them, I was beside myself with rage; I would have battered my enemy's skull in if I had not been stopped. Morally, what is the difference between us? None. Since that horrible day, I have often had this thought: isn't it strange, ironic, that the urge of sexual desire, which God meant for Man's pleasure and continuance upon earth, should so often develop into a source of bitter hatred and violence? I can even understand now why some women – and men too – decide to avoid all involvement in sexual matters by joining holy orders, and spending their days in cloisters.' She raised her head to smile sadly at him: 'There! Your Nelli Roberts as a nun! You would never have expected such a thought from a determined Nonconformist like me, would you?'

Raven tightened his clasp of her hand: 'I can see, Nelli, that Tucker's story has upset and shocked and depressed you. But think: that was only one episode among all the millions of other events happening all over the world on that night. It isn't typical of how men behave with women, or of how women generally behave either. I mean, in a quite innocent way those *wahines* caused the trouble by the way they showed their bodies and gave themselves so freely to anyone. That doesn't excuse what the whalers did, of course, but then, neither does it mean that true, decent love between a man and a woman can't exist. Just think of your own mother and father – how much they loved and needed each other. Sometimes people laugh at the idea of a person dying of a broken heart, but I'm certain that, in a strange way, your father did exactly that. He was never himself again after your mother died. Everything of value had gone out of his life, destroyed by sorrow and, I suppose, some guilt.'

'I know. I know you are right to be positive and optimistic about human nature. I can see, for instance, that these four men on the "Pawtucket" are alive because they showed decency, wisdom, courage and a lot of skill and determination. I've got to be like them, and look ahead to a better time; but, Jack, it is hard to escape from the darkness of the mind. When you've been through horrors, they haunt you. When it was just the four of us in that cockleshell of a boat it was pain and hardship for my body, but better for my mind, my soul. We were so intent on simply surviving and, as far as I was concerned, being very doubtful that we would, that there was no time for these horrible, gloomy phantoms. It was all steering, sail-trimming, baling and watch-keeping in a strong, cold wind, often with driving rain as well, followed by four hours of the dead sleep of exhaustion. Now that we are on a proper ship, and for the moment safe from the sea and the wind, this hideous story of lust, folly and murder has brought all those phantoms back. Jack, I can't help it; I'm sorry to be such a drooping, despairing lump of a thing.'

'Nelli, you know you need never say "sorry" to me. But, once again, think: we are all still alive – all eight of us. Think of how you and the chaps from the whaler were saved, by the most amazing good fortune – as Simon would say – or by the grace of God, as we might say. It was by pure luck or grace that Simon and I were able to rescue you in time, and pure luck or the same grace that Tucker and his men had a bright moonlight night and a fair offshore wind. If they hadn't had both of those, they'd have been caught like rats in a trap. And, for that matter, if they hadn't lost their foremast we should never have sighted them.'

'Yes, God was good, to them and to me, and I know that despair is a sin ...But it is hard, Jack, to be hopeful and cheerful. I try, but it is hard. Just as you think you are free from the horrors of the past, back they come into the sea of your mind like a silent black octopus, rising up from the depths to drag you down again. Even if you can control your conscious mind, you can do nothing about the subconscious mind that composes your dreams.'

'You have bad dreams, Nelli? I didn't know.'

'No – how could you know? I had them when we were on the island, but I didn't tell you about them then. Now you're our commander; you have to deal with all our present, real, actual dangers and problems – and you've done so very well. I didn't want to burden you with still more.'

'I see. But for the moment we have a respite from danger, and we're alone together at last. So tell me about them, if you think it will help.'

'It's not one dream, but a whole series; each is different from the last in detail, but the same themes run through all of them. In my dreams it's always twilight, and I'm always walking alone and feeling cold, and I'm always searching for my mother and father, who are, I know, somewhere ahead of me, but I can never see them. Sometimes I am in a thick, very dark wood; I'm dressed in this sailor's gear, wearing heavy sea-boots, and stumbling over the roots of trees. Sometimes I am totally naked and barefoot, walking on a shingle beach, yet the stones don't hurt my feet. A freezing wind is blowing, and I am chilled to the bone.

'Always, always, I am being stalked, hunted, pursued by a man – Billy John Ffynnongroes, of course. I can never see him or hear him, but I just *know* he is there, behind me, and close in the shadows. I try to run to escape from him, but my feet are clogged by mud in the wood, or by shifting shingle on the beach. All the strength goes from my legs. I struggle frantically to run. I exhaust myself, yet I hardly move forward. I know the hunter is getting nearer and nearer, and as he does so I feel colder and colder. Then, just as I know that this phantom is about to seize me and rape me, I wake with a start. I find myself scared, sweating, panting and clutching myself in my groin – you know – to guard that part of my body that he lusts after. It's all so horrible.... When will I ever be free of this terrible fear and loathing?'

'You will be one day – soon, I hope, Nelli. I'm sure that time will make it fade away. It won't haunt you for ever.' He put an arm round her shoulder to draw her close for comfort and reassurance. She did not resist him, but neither did she relax and flow into his embrace as she had always done before, in that bright dawn of their love. He would have kissed her if she had turned her head towards him, but instead she stared blankly ahead.

Then, with an abrupt change of mood, she stood up, shook her head, and gave him a fleeting, shallow smile. 'Come on!' she said. 'Enough of this brooding! We're tired, and there's still a lot left to do on deck tomorrow, I dare say. My poor back is killing me, after all that bending over and hauling at the windlass. Tell me now what you've found out about our position today, Mister Great Navigator, and then we'll both try to get some sleep.'

'Well, I've been working with the log tables on my evening sun-sight, and now I've got a fix. I'll tell them all in the morning.'

'You can tell me now, Jack.'

'Well, our guesses were not that far out. I make us just over a hundred-and-fifty miles east-south-east of Bluff Cove.'

'Can you be sure about that?'

'Yes, quite sure. In this calm weather I was able to get a good clear horizon, and I took a meridian sight at noon as well, and that confirms the other two.'

'Marvellous! How clever you are, you sailors! And what a blessing it will be to all of us to *know* where we are, with no more guessing!'

'"Clever"?' said Raven. 'I don't know about that. "Competent" is all I'd claim for myself. I couldn't begin to compare with your Dad. He was a wizard – no other word for him. But I found it so good today just to have a sextant in my hands again. I'd almost forgotten what it felt like. Tomorrow, would you like to help me? I need someone to note down the exact chronometer time at the split second when I get the sun down onto the horizon. Old Tucker helped me today, but I'd much rather it was you. And I found the patent log in a locker today; when we eventually get under way we'll stream that astern, and I could do with someone to read the dial on that and note the distances run every day in the log-book. Would you like to do that?'

Her response was delighted, delightful and overwhelming. Her mercurial temperament was still able to surprise even Raven. She reached out, drew him to his feet and enveloped him in a long, firm hug of joy, tucking her chin over his shoulder. For a few moments they stood, swaying gently on their feet as the old ship rolled to the swells. She whispered close in his ear: 'Jack, Jack, you know I would. I'll do that, I'll do anything I can to help – anything. Clean out the lavatory – what do you call it? – the heads - every day if you like. Make a sailor out of me, not a useless lump of a passenger. I'll be your new brass-bounder! You can work my fingers to the bone, day and night. That would be so much better than this ghastly brooding over the past! I'll never be a heroine of the sea like Grace Darling, rowing a boat through a storm to rescue people, but I'll do my little best.'

Then she drew back slightly, turned her face to his, relaxed her body into his, head to toe, took his arms and drew them round her, and kissed him long and lovingly on the lips. It was not a languorous, open-mouthed kiss of urgent sexual desire, the prelude to the full contact of flesh, but a frank statement of a love, a commitment beyond mere sensuality, a declaration of deep loyalty, gratitude and admiration. Raven felt not only the joy of seeing the clouds lift from her soul, even if only for a short time, but also the inevitable surging, stiff, uncontrollable, physical return of his old passion for her.

At last she drew back, smiling close in his embrace, but wiping off a tear or two with the back of her hand. Raven smiled back, his eyes moist too. 'Phew!' he said softly. 'A brassbounder? You? I don't think so. I have never felt like this about a brassbounder, I'm glad to say. Kiss me like that again, *cariad*' The beautiful Welsh word of endearment now came naturally to his lips.

She shook her head and stood back slightly: 'No, *capten bach*. I'm going to disobey that order. On deck, with ropes and such, I'll always obey you to the letter, but not down below. I've already got you too excited.'

'How do you....'

'Don't ask such a silly question! When you hold me tight and our bodies are pressed together, I don't need to ask and you don't need to tell me. I'm going to take off this thick, clumsy sailor's gear and go to bed, but not till you've said *"Nos da"* and gone safely back to your cabin, my lad. Mr Tucker was very firm about that. He asked me very pointedly if we were married, and now knows that we are not, so he very properly gave us each a cabin. He does not want any hanky-panky – any improper actions - happening on a ship owned by good Quakers.'

'I see. As they say in the Navy: "No fornication under the white ensign"?'

'Exactly. And as I say, not under the stars and stripes either, so off you go, my boy. One very little kiss, and off you go.'

Off he went; but it was not such a very little kiss that she had given him. After he had gone, and she heard his cabin door shut, she sat for a while on her bunk. That close, pressing contact with his hard body had stirred her deeply, physically, and somewhere, at the back of her mind, some wild earthy part of her whispered: 'Go on, do what you said – take all your clothes off, but then go to Jack's bunk, not yours! Who's to stop you now?' But instantly some other much cooler, wiser and more powerful voice said: 'No! That is madness! You are not ready for that yet, and you know it. Leave the poor man in peace.'

She sighed, pulled off her thick navy-blue socks and began to haul her coarse woollen jersey over her head.

*

'And now, lady and gentlemen, all we have to do this morning is to get our new topmast up there, and rigged firmly enough to carry two decent headsails in a strong breeze. Otherwise, we'll never get this old girl to go to windward. I don't suppose she was any great shakes at that at the best of times, Noah?'

'No sir-ree! You kin take your bible oath on that. Six points off the wind was the best she could point, and even then she make a hell of a lot of leeway. She sure ain't no clipper.'

It was 'all hands on deck'; after another good breakfast; all eight survivors stood on the foredeck in the light breeze. On the deck lay the massive length of wood that had been her t'gallant mast. Somehow, this puny team – only six of them trained sailors – had to get this half-ton or so of pitch-pine up to a vertical position, then up thirty-five feet off the deck, still vertical, and then securely locked at its lower end to the top of the lower mast, and then strongly supported by stays fore and aft, and by shrouds at its sides, so that it could bear the strain of two big headsails in a near-gale.

It was a very tall order indeed, but Raven was not a man to quail or despair before an almost impossible task. He had been at sea now for nearly four years, and though his public school and his nautical college had not produced a philosopher or a sensitive poet or a great scholar, they had made him simply a good leader of men – determined, pragmatic, adaptable; harsh if need be, but energetic, optimistic, and skilled at carrying his crew with him, inspiring them to face work and danger. So he was now in his element, and he had found in Noah an excellent bosun to be his right-hand man.

'Right then, everybody: we've got a big job to do here, but we'll manage it if we do it a bit at a time. Now we're going to be lifting a very heavy lump of wood a long way off the deck, and that's got to be done damn carefully. I don't want anyone getting hurt or any more damage done to the rigging, so everyone has got to *think* – has got to *think* hard about every move he makes. Sorry, Eleanor: he or she makes. Now then, Noah, have you got a really good heavy tackle on board?' (Like all sailors, he pronounced the word as 'tay-kle'.)

'Tackle?' said Noah. 'Lordy, mister, we got a tackle could lift the whole of Creation! We rig it to the maintop, and we use it to haul the monstrous great thick strips of blubber off of the poor critters we kill. You want it rigged to the foretop, I guess? Okay.' He turned to the other black hands and said genially: 'Come on then, you no-good loafing bums! We go and drag it for'ard. Shift your asses!'

When it appeared, it was indeed a tackle of immense size, with two three-fold blocks and a tremendous length of good hemp fall. 'Crikey!' said Raven. 'You weren't joking, man. That's one hell of a big tackle, and just what we need. I reckon you'll need to use one of the halyards just to get the top block up there, it's so heavy. I reckon that if we take the fall of that tackle to the windlass, we can lift any damned thing.'

Twenty minutes later, the huge tackle was in place, and the lower block hooked to the top of the t'gallant mast as it lay on deck. 'Well done, boys,' said Raven. 'Now then, Noah, while the mast is handy down on deck. I want you and the lads to get three good lengths of thickish rope and secure one end of each to the head of the mast. They're going to be our temporary stays to keep the mast vertical as we hoist it up into position above the lower mast, so they've got to be plenty long enough to reach from the top right down to the deck, with enough left over to put round a cleat.'

That done, the whole crew set to work; Tucker and young George manned the pump-handles of the windlass, while Eleanor, happy and determined in her role as an ordinary seaman, put three turns of the fall round the windlass drum and stood by to back up the rope as it came off the turning drum. The other five stood by to guide the butt of the mast past obstacles as it was dragged along the deck.

'Ready, everyone?' called Raven. 'Right then, up she goes.' He raised his right arm, pointing a finger to the sky and moving it round in a clockwise circle: 'Heave away there - handsomely.' In sailors' international parlance that meant 'slowly'.

As the fall tightened, the whole tackle began to groan with the strain, and all the parts of the rope became bar-taut. The three-fold tackle was an immensely powerful device, but a very slow one. It took minutes of winching before the top of the mast, with its round block called the truck, began to stir and lift off the deck, being hauled for'ard, inboard, and up towards the fore-top. The men on the deck sweated and panted as they heaved the butt of the mast this way and that. Eleanor, gathering in the rope as it wound off the drum, and hauling back on it to stop the turns from slipping, bit her lower lip in concentration. She was only an ordinary seaman, but she could see how crucial her part in the operation was: if she allowed those turns to slip back, the huge spar would crash down onto whoever was under it. That was *not* going to happen!

Inch by inch the masthead rose to the diagonal, and Raven was able to send Amos to lend his weight on the windlass handles. Fathom by fathom, a mountain of rope began to rise behind Eleanor. At last the new jury topmast was vertical, parallel with, and side-by-side with the lower mast, and Raven called: 'Avast hoisting! Amos, make the fall well fast to the bitts – *well* fast, mind, or the whole bloody issue will land on our heads. Noah, up you go and lash the jury masthead to the crosstrees, just so that it's safe while we discuss the next step.' The crosstrees at the fore-top was a solid wooden platform built onto the mast where the joints of the mast met. It was several feet wide – wide enough for a lookout to stand on – and the shrouds normally fastened to its sides went up, slanting in, to support the mast above, and provided a ladder by which to climb up it.

When Noah was back down on deck Raven smiled, smacked his hands together and said: 'All right so far. Well done, everybody! We'll have a few moments' stand-easy while you catch your breath, and then we'll start on the hard part.' The young blacks groaned in unison, but they grinned as well; what else could you expect from an officer but shouts and bloody hard work? Raven said: 'All right, if you want me to be a real Yankee bucko I'll get myself a rope's end to take some skin off your backs.' But he was grinning too. He went on: 'Gather round and listen, so that you'll all know what I'm trying to do. Ask any questions you like, and tell me if you've got any suggestions of your own. This bit is going to be tricky, so we've all got to *know* what we're supposed to be doing. We're lucky that the swell's not too bad today, but she's still rolling a bit.

'This is what we're going to do now: we'll move the bottom block of this big old tackle to the bottom of our jury topmast, so that when we heave away, the topmast will rise up off the deck, vertical, and parallel with the lower mast. What we've got to do is *keep* it parallel as it goes up, and that won't be easy. What I've thought of is this: we fix two fairly tight rope collars round the two masts, one about eight feet above the other, so that as our new topmast goes up they'll help to keep it vertical, and held in close to the lower mast. Carl, will you cut off two short lengths of rope and make the collars? When the bottom of the new mast is about six feet below the crosstrees we stop hoisting and lash the two masts together as tightly as we can. All right so far? Anyone got other suggestions?'

'Ja, mister,' said Carl. 'It going to be hard work hoisting the topmast, cos the two masts will rub together all time – no? So while I fix the collars, we get plenty slush from the galley and grease both them masts down bloddy thick. That make em slide more easy' He added with a rare grin: 'These boys here – they like that job, I think.'

There was a concerted groan from Amos and George. Slush was the rancid grease left over from the cooking of the salt pork and beef, and slushing down – painting anything thickly with the disgusting stuff - was the job most hated by foc'sle hands.

'I'd do it most willingly, sir,' said Protheroe with an insincere smirk. 'Only I can't, because I'm a vegetarian. I can't be touching something that comes from meat.'

'Now that is a pity,' said Tucker, joining in the joke with ponderous humour, 'because I shall be cooking a leg of fresh pork tonight for the rest of us. However, I'm sure I can find you some dried peas instead.'

'All right, all right,' said Raven impatiently. 'No time for arsing about. Thank you Carl. An excellent idea. Amos and George, you don't mind, do you, boys?' Both of them rolled their eyes to heaven in despair, but Raven knew they'd do it. He thanked his lucky stars that three such good hands from the whaler had survived. If only all foc'sle crowds could be like them – smart, active and bright! 'Go on then, lads. Away you go to the galley for the slush-tub. And while they're off doing that we've got other things to discuss. Now, if we just relied on the collars, we'd have no proper control of the mast when it got high, so that's why we've got those three long ropes fast to the new mast-head, which we'll use as temporary stays to keep the thing vertical. Jim, you take one rope right for'ard, and take a turn with it round the anchor-bitts. Noah, you and Amos go port side, aft of the mast, and I will do the same starboard side. I see there's some really man-sized cleats on the bulwarks, so we'll take our turns round those and – everybody – for God's sake see that those turns don't get jammed. Mr Tucker, will you and George work the windlass, please, and Eleanor, will you back up the fall again?'

Fifteen minutes later the unfortunate Amos and George had finished their horrible task. The two masts were plastered with the filthy, evil-smelling grease, and so were the two sailors. 'Good!' said Raven genially. 'Well done, lads. Now, we've got to be pretty damn careful, or, as I said, somebody may get injured and we might lose this t'gallant mast – and we haven't got another one. So, as the mast starts to come up off the deck, all of us on the ropes have got to be clever. We've got to keep the ropes tight enough to keep the mast going up vertical, but not so tight as to stop the thing going up at all. We've *got* to keep three turns on the cleats, in case she rolls heavily. It's all got to work if we're to sail this old tub; so anyone who makes a balls-up of this will get my boot up his backside.'

Eleanor said with a cool smile: 'Or *her* backside, I presume? That would be only fair.'

But Raven was too preoccupied and tense to be amused: 'Let's get on with it, shall we? All to your positions! When I signal, hoist away on the windlass, only handsomely, mind.'

George muttered under his breath as he went for'ard, rubbing the grease off his hands and onto his trousers: 'Ain't no other way but slow with this goddam old heap of junk.'

'Ready all? Hoist away!'

The immensely powerful windlass and tackle brought the heel of the new jury topmast effortlessly up off the deck; it began to rise up the lower mast, as fathom after fathom of good hemp went through Eleanor's hands

Raven kept a sharp eye on the angle of the mast, snapping out orders to keep it vertical. The whole lift took an age, but at last he shouted: 'Well! High enough! Make fast at that, all of you. We'll do the final lashing, and put the fid in after dinner. Jolly well done, all. You've earned your dinners.'

Eleanor was happy to see his relaxed, smiling face. She realized that this was the largest and most important operation that he had ever been in charge of. She murmured as she joined him: 'Well done, Jack – or *da iawn wir!* as we'd say at home. And is my backside to be spared after all, *capten?*

Raven blushed: 'Sorry about that, Nelli. I didn't think when I shouted that.' Then it was her turn to blush as he whispered close in her ear: 'As for your backside, that is something that I cannot allow myself to even think about at the moment, Ordinary Seawoman Roberts.'

When the bell went at the end of the first dog-watch – at six o'clock – the new jury mast was finished, standing tall, proud and firmly stayed in the evening sunshine.

'There you are then, mister,' said Jimmy. 'That's that, and a hell of a job it was, too.'

'You're talking as if we'd finished, man. This is just the start – the first stage. We've still got to fit proper shrouds to that mast, as well as a proper forestay and a new triatic stay. Then we've got to get the blocks and halyards into position, get the staysails up on deck and try setting them. When all that's done, you can get ready for actually sailing her – steering, sail-trimming, lookout, clearing up this mess on deck. You're not in a bloody deck-chair on a cruise-liner, you know.'

'No, I've noticed that, mister - often.'

'Well, you know what they say in the Navy: "It serves yer right, you shouldn't a joined". That's enough for today, everyone. Back again in the morning. I can smell pork roasting in the galley. Too bad you don't like it, Jim.'

*

That evening, after a delicious supper, Raven and Eleanor met once more to talk in her cramped, dingy cabin. This time, there was no more discussion of ugly nightmares. Eleanor clearly had something else on her mind, some thing more practical. 'Jack,' she said, 'I've been thinking about what you said about our position – a hundred and fifty miles east-south-east of Bluff Cove, wasn't it?'

'Yes, and with this light air from the north, we should be able to get there in a few days, with a tack or two. Why?'

'Well, I haven't got a chart in front of me, but it would surely take us about the same time to go back to the island, less perhaps, with a northerly wind behind us?'

'Yes, but what on earth...?'

'No, wait! Suppose the "Figaro's" crew is still on the island? It must be well over a week since we left, and you know the food supplies were getting a bit short then.'

'Maybe, but surely by now the New Zealand steamer....'

'Jack, we don't know *anything* about her. She might have called there to pick them up, but then again she might not. We cannot know, one way or the other. You remember what the old hands said about dockyards and repairs. They may have weeks yet to wait. We have to keep on remembering one obvious fact: we know that there are castaways on Auckland Island, but nobody else in the world does. Probably that steamer calls there time after time, year after year, and finds nobody on the island, so they wouldn't feel the need for any hurry. And what worries me even more is that there are no medical supplies on the island. They might all die if an epidemic struck.'

'I suppose so, but ...'

'No, Jack! No "buts". You've done a wonderful job on the rigging, but you haven't been thinking straight about our strategy when we get started again. Neither have I. Listen, then: what the men on Auckland Island need is rescue from that awful place; what this ship needs is a crew. One officer and five seamen – you can't call that a crew. You've all done well so far, but we're a feeble band to man a ship of this size, especially if we get stormy weather again, which is more than likely. With so few people it would surely be a desperately hard job to furl one of the big sails in a strong breeze, wouldn't it? Don't you see? The two things fit together! If we go down there and pick them up, they will have escaped from the island, and we will have a full crew. Everybody benefits'

Raven, a little nettled (if we're to be honest) at this unexpected challenge to his authority, was doggedly resistant: 'I suppose so, but we might traipse all the way down there and find they've all gone. That'd mean a whole week wasted.'

His stubbornness angered her too: 'A week! What does a week matter? We're not a tea-clipper, racing the "Cutty Sark", are we, for Heaven's sake? If the poor chaps have been taken off, we about-turn and head back to Bluff Cove.'

'H'm: You say I'm not thinking straight, Nelli, but I think you've forgotten something very important. Remember how happy and relieved you were when you first got into the boat, to think that you need never see *him* again? You know who I mean. Well, obviously, he'd be among the crew we collected – the man of your nightmares, Nelli. You'd be back in his company again. I can't bear the idea of your suffering all that fear again, *cariad*.'

'Jack, I know you mean well, but you misjudge me, you underrate me. Just think: on the one hand there is the rescue of two dozen men, all but one of them totally innocent, on the other, my probably foolish and unnecessary fears. Which is the more important? I can't put my peace of mind before – possibly – the lives of all those men! Surely that wretch could be shut up securely somewhere in this ship?'

'Yes, I suppose so. Well, I can't decide now. I'll think about it – sleep on it – and anyway I ought to consult Tucker and the other whaler hands in the morning before doing what you suggest. Look, I'm dog-tired, Nelli, so I'll ...'

He rose to go, but as he did so, there was a polite tap at the door. He opened it and saw Jimmy Protheroe, who looked quickly from one to the other and said, with a hint of his old prurient slyness: 'Sorry to call on you so late, sir, miss. Is it a bad time? I mean, I don't want to interrupt nothing.'

'No,' said Eleanor, firmly but irritably, 'it is not a bad time if you have something important to say. But we are both very tired, and so are you, I suppose, so let's hear it, and try to keep it short. Is this something just between you and Mr Raven?'

'O no, miss, not by no means. I reckon it's something to interest both of you, and me and Carl too.'

'All right, then, Jim, spit it out,' said Raven, 'only it's late and I'm very weary.'

'Right then, it's like this: on that first day, when we came aboard, old man Tucker more or less invited you to take charge of this ship, and have all the powers of a *cap-ten* - right? And you agreed, and said they'd have to enter their agreement in the log-book, and all sign to it – and they did – right?'

'Yes,' said Raven wearily, 'right. But I wish I could see where all this rigmarole is getting us. You're getting as bad as Curly Kellock. Is this going to be one of your old tricks?'

'It certainly ain't, and I wish you wouldn't keep jumping to conclusions. I'm talking about law now, proper international maritime law. That ain't no trick of mine, is it? Hear me out, and you'll both be glad you did, I can promise you. Now then: when we first came across that bunch on the whaler, what would you, as a professional trained officer, say was their chance of getting that ship to port safely, in the state it was in then, and seeing that there was only four of em?'

'Almost none, I'd say. They were hundreds of miles from where they wanted to be; they were very badly damaged aloft, and didn't seem to have any idea of how to repair the damage. And on top of that, none of them had the least notion of how to navigate.'

'Exactly, sir,' said Protheroe, with growing self-importance. 'Couldn't put it better myself. So if we bring this ship safely to harbour, do you know what maritime law says? I've read all this up at home, so I know, and I've been thinking about it while we was working. It says, sir and madam, that the ship's insurers will then owe us four the total value of the ship itself, plus – what's much more important – the total value of its cargo. That's the law of salvage. I don't think the money would be divided equally between us; I think you, sir, being the *capten,* would get the lion's share, as they say, but there would be a tidy sum each for Carl and me too. Not for you, miss, I'm afraid, as you wouldn't count as crew.'

Eleanor said loftily: 'No, I would not. And in any case, Mr Raven and I are not interested in scheming and money-grubbing. We came aboard to save these poor souls from a miserable death, not to make a profit.'

'Of course you did, miss, and so did I. But just think: this ship has been at sea in the Pacific for two years or more.'

'Well,' said Raven, 'what's that to us?'

Protheroe took on the air of a patient schoolmaster with two very dull pupils: 'It means, of course, that her hold is full of barrels of oil, barrels of spermaceti, and a great deal of baleen – you know, the whalebone. I've read about these Yankee whalers – it's all in Melville's book "Moby Dick" – wonderful book. Have you read it?'

'Yes,' said Eleanor.

'No,' said Raven. 'Too busy learning how to navigate, and you can thank your lucky stars for that.'

'Yes, true enough, sir. We're all grateful for that. But you'll know then, miss, that these old Quakers what run the whaling business, back in Nantucket and New Bedford, are some of the richest men in America. This ship's hold is like a damn great gold-mine. All that stuff down there is worth thousands and thousands of dollars, and all its value – every red cent – is ours, because, if it hadn't been for us, the ship and its cargo would never have got safely into a harbour. And that, sir and miss, is the law. No-one can deny us our reward – so long as we do get the old hooker back to port safely.'

Raven, quite taken aback by this whole new situation, which raised issues beyond his limited experience of life, and which demanded immediate decisions on his part, said: 'What do you think, Eleanor?'

She, suddenly struck by this vision of a very large windfall, which might have the power to change their lives for the better, came down rapidly from her lofty moral perch. She smiled at Jim and said: 'Well, at last now I see the value of having a sea-lawyer in the crew. You're obviously well versed in these matters, Jim, and I suppose it would be simply foolish for us to forfeit our rights, for which we have certainly suffered and laboured. Remember, Jack, that one day we are going to need a house to live in.'

'Exactly, miss; you've got it! I mean, we've done a lot of work on this old hooker, and Mr Raven himself says there's a lot more to do, and if it should blow up rough again, it won't be no picnic, being so under-manned. Nor it won't be very safe, neither. And didn't Our Lord himself say: "The labourer is worthy of his hire"?'

'Yes,' said Eleanor, her face relaxing into a broad smile, 'and didn't Shakespeare himself say, "The devil can cite scripture for his own ends"?'

Protheroe put on a face of shock and injured virtue: 'Devil, miss? Where does he come into it? This is the law. There's no trickery nor immorality in what I'm suggesting.'

'Of course not,' she said. And since you're in such a moral humour, I've just thought of another suggestion to make to both of you. Mr Raven and I have been discussing the idea of going back to the island, not to Bluff. If we do that, we can have a proper crew, provided, of course, that the steamer hasn't taken them all away by the time we get there. My suggestion is this: whatever sum we get from the insurers, the first charge on it must be to pay the wages of all the men on the island for the whole of their stay there. After all, we shall all have quite a lot of money; they will have none, and neither will their wives and families.'

Protheroe's face fell: 'Ah well, miss, that's all very well, but ...'

Raven broke in, certain of his feelings and judgment on this issue at least: 'No, "buts" on that question, man! Good God, most of the poor beggars on the island are only paid two pounds fifteen a month! We'll have thousands of dollars between us, you say. What sort of a shipmate are you, eh? Don't worry: if I'm paid a lot more than you and Carl I'll contribute more, in proportion.'

'O well, if you put it like that....'

'We do,' said Eleanor firmly.

'Yes, all right then I'll agree to that, and I dare say good old Carl will too.'

'I'm quite certain he will,' said Raven. 'You're not married, are you? Well, Carl is, so he knows what it's like to have a wife at home in Sweden struggling to run a farm so small that every year he must spend months away at sea to earn enough money to keep a roof over their heads. You ask him, if you don't believe me.'

'Yes, yes, all right,' said Protheroe, rather ashamed

now of his protest, and his shame making him irritable: 'You don't have to get into the pulpit and preach at me about it, mister. But when you're standing at the garden gate of your nice tidy house that you've been able to buy in Newport, don't forget that if it hadn't been for me, you wouldn't have had the gate nor the house. *Chwarae teg,* (fair play) now, that's true, isn't it?'

'Chwarae teg,' said Eleanor, pacifically, 'it's true. And it's been wonderfully refreshing to see this law-abiding and generous side of your nature, Mr Protheroe. Surely, you will have your reward for it in the Great Hereafter, for do not the English have a very true old maxim: "Give the devil his due"?'

CHAPTER SEVENTEEN

The morning conference with Tucker and Noah was cordial and, considering the importance of its agenda, surprisingly brief.

'Another excellent meal, Mr Tucker,' said Raven, leaning back in his chair. 'Fried pork steaks for breakfast – a gourmet's paradise! Now then: I have asked you and Noah to stay while the hands get on with rigging staysails. With luck we shall soon be able to get your good old "Pawtucket" under way again.'

'And make for Bluff Cove, I take it?'

'That is just the point we wanted to discuss with you. As you know, with the exception of the grievous loss of Eleanor's father, the whole crew of the "Figaro" reached the island camp in safety. So there are now twenty-five of them living in a hut in a forest clearing. But this very good fortune has itself raised a problem, as Eleanor has pointed out to me. The New Zealand government has been generous and enlightened in its provision of food and shelter, but with such a large number of survivors, the food-stocks must be now running low, and the castaways will soon depend entirely on what they can get from hunting, fishing and collecting sea-birds' eggs. Even more serious is the fact that there are no medical supplies of any sort on the island. As you can imagine, Auckland Island is a cold, gloomy, wet and windy place. We fear that, as time goes by, an epidemic of some sort – pneumonia, influenza, dysentery – anything – is bound to strike.'

'Of course,' said Eleanor, 'it may be that the government steamer has already called and taken them off, but we have no way of knowing that, and we were warned by a notice that the rescue steamer might be a long time coming, as she was to be docked for repairs. That is why we are so anxious.'

'Yes, I understand perfectly the causes of your anxiety for your friends,' said Tucker, 'and I think I am beginning to see the drift of this conference. You are going to suggest that we head southwards to Auckland Island, not north-west to Bluff?'

'Yes,' said Raven, 'and if they are there, our calling there will be of huge advantage to all of us on the "Pawtucket", as well as to them. They will have been rescued, and we shall then have a full – if not over-full – complement of skilled seamen.'

'I see. And I assume it would be hazardous for us to undertake any long voyage, undermanned as we are?'

Raven shook his head emphatically: 'Quite out of the question. When you set off in a ship propelled by sails, it's vital to know that you can get those sails furled quickly in dirty weather. That we know we can't do. Though your ship's much smaller than our four-masted barque was, your principal sails – the tops'ls and courses – you know, the lowest sails on each mast – are pretty large. It's easy enough to set them, but with only six of us able to lay out along the yards....'

Out of the corner of his eye he saw Eleanor open her mouth to speak, and he turned to her, took her hand and smiled, shaking his head: 'No Nelli! I know what you're going to say, and it does you credit, but the answer is a definite "no"! I'm not letting you go up there. In any case, someone has got to steer, and someone else has got to man the ropes on deck. If the weather's decent I'll set the t'gallants, and if we have to furl those there'll be plenty for you and Nathaniel to do on deck, my girl.'

She smiled and returned his warm clasp of her hand: 'I was only thinking of what Mr Gilbert says in the "Mikado":

To lay aloft in a howling gale
May tickle a landsman's taste.'

'Ah yes' said Tucker. 'He and Mr Sullivan have been popular with us too. But,' he added with a roguish smile, 'remember how that song goes on:

But the happiest time that a sailor sees
Is when he's down at an inland town,
With his Nancy on his knees, yo-ho!
And his arm about her waist.'

Eleanor blushed deliciously, and Raven too smiled, but said with tolerant frustration, 'When you two have quite finished with your silly quotations, perhaps we can turn to our problems here and now. I thought Simon Grant was bad enough, quoting all the time. Now, let's suppose all our castaways are still on the island: we take them off, we maybe make some improvements in our rigging – we have a bosun and a sailmaker down there who are practically geniuses in such matters – and then – what?'

'I think,' said Tucker, 'that with so many more mouths to feed, we had better put in at Bluff Cove and stock up with biscuit, beef and pork in barrels, and would you like me to buy a real pig or two? We have a sty ready for them amidships. And perhaps some hens in lay? And I don't see why the officers aft shouldn't have some good bully-beef. And all of us need some fresh vegetables and lime-juice. We do not need an outbreak of scurvy.'

'That sounds all very fine,' said Eleanor, 'but remember, we haven't got any money for such things.'

Tucker spoke with pride and dignity: 'I am still the "Pawtucket's" purser. Nothing that has happened has changed that. As purser I can sign any bill for provisions in foreign ports. The bill will be cabled to our precious Owners, and it is up to them to cable the money back. It will give me great pleasure to present those Quaker moneybags with a steep bill or two, and, more importantly, when we arrive at New Bedford, Noah and I will back your claim for salvage to the hilt, shall we not, Noah?'

'We sure will, mister. When you folks first found us we was pretty near despair – didn't know what to do nor where to start. I sure don't know how you done it, sir, but you put some heart back into us; you showed us that we had it in us to save ourselves, once we had a leader. You done wonders, mister Jack.'

Raven was silent, embarrassed. Eleanor, bursting with pride at the old seaman's praise of her man, patted Raven's hand, and said, with the most affectionate satire: 'Yes, Noah. And he does them by shouting at people and swearing at them now and then. He's very good at that.'

Noah gave a huge, white-toothed grin and shook his head: 'No, missy, there was a sight more to it than that. Not many could have done what he done.'

'Amen to that,' said Tucker heartily, 'and I assure you I will do my best to see that you get your pound of flesh from those hypocrites and their insurers, for I believe that the latter are a mutual insurance company owned by the ship-owners themselves. They will bluster and prevaricate, but by Heaven I will see them wriggling on the hook in the end.'

Eleanor was puzzled: 'I don't quite understand your hostility to these men, Mr Tucker, if they are Quakers like yourself.'

Tucker shook his head with a melancholy grimace: 'Ah, that is a long story, Eleanor, with little enough credit on either side. Yes, I have long been a follower of our founder George Fox; indeed, I might say an enthusiast for the practices of the Friends – though not of course an enthusiast in the pejorative eighteenth century sense of a fanatic. Their abjuring of priests and ritual and liturgies, their dedication to the Christ within each one of them - all that is dear to me still. But what I cannot stomach is that men who profess a universal benevolence to all mankind should show such callous parsimony to the men in their employ. For when a whaler's cargo is sold for thousands of dollars, they pocket a good third of the profit, another third is ploughed back into the ship and its fittings and provisions, and the last third only is split most inequitably between the men who have suffered perhaps three years of cruel dangers, vile food and merciless discipline – if that is the word for it. The captains do well enough, the mates and harpooners passably, but I have known forecastle hands to end up being paid nothing, because they have been obliged to buy from the ship's stores tobacco, boots and clothing at exorbitant prices fixed by those sanctimonious humbugs.'

He paused in his long tirade. Eleanor said shrewdly: 'Yet you serve in their employ. That seems curious, does it not?'

'No doubt it does, and therein lies my share of the shame in this history. In our Society we become personally very close to one another. We do not sit in pews, gabble a few prayers, bawl some hymns, listen to a minister's tedious drivel, and then go thankfully home to our Sunday dinners. We gather as equal friends, and then wait in silence until the Spirit moves one of us to speak. My sin was to sacrifice not only my membership of the Friends, but also my marriage, to a most irregular liaison with a young and beautiful novice to our Society. I, in my misguided zeal, took it upon myself to instruct her in our beliefs, sometimes privately. I have mentioned to you my perhaps excessive fondness for the opposite sex. The eventual outcome was inevitable: she was overcome by my eloquence and piety, and I by her spell-binding bodily beauty. As I said, it is a sorry tale on both sides. The Quaker ship-owners offered me the position of purser on one of their ships, mainly to hide me and the scandal that I had caused to our Society. I took it to avoid the obloquy and disdain of the righteous folk of New Bedford. Now, among the mostly godless and disreputable crew of a whaler, I appear relatively virtuous, though in truth I am no more than one of those whited sepulchres we read of in Matthew. I imagine that, like me, most of a whaler's crew are escaping from something.'

His broad, tanned, kindly face was drawn with his sorrow, and one tear trickled down his cheek. 'As for me, in my folly I threw away a life of domestic calm with a loving and worthy wife, and an honest occupation as a counting-house clerk for a short spell of delicious licence, followed by years of this wretched wandering over the face of the globe. God alone knows whether I shall ever be forgiven and taken back by those I have shocked and hurt.'

He ended. Noah, Raven and Eleanor were silent in sympathy, torn between pity for his plight, and embarrassment at this baring of his soul. Only Tucker could break the silence and return to the here and now. He shook his head, as if to clear it of these spectres of the past, and forced a smile: 'Come, that is enough of my rambling self-pity and confessions. We have much to discuss and perform here, today.'

'Yes,' said Raven. 'For instance, you said just now "when we get back to New Bedford". Are you suggesting that – assuming we do get our former companions aboard – we ourselves take "Pawtucket" all the way back to her home port?'

'Most emphatically yes, sir, for that is the only way to be sure of getting your salvage claim paid in full. If you were simply to take her to New Zealand, and leave it to me and to others to get her back home, your claim would be seriously damaged. The lawyers in the Maritime Court in Boston would argue about it until they had filled their own pockets with the spoils – as happened in Dickens' "Bleak House", Eleanor, did it not?'

'No!' said Raven. 'No more literature, for God's sake! I can't stand it! So then, we stock up a bit at Bluff, and then eastward-ho for the Horn. With strong breezes in the Roaring Forties we'll soon be there!'

Noah gave one of his wide grins: 'Not so soon as you maybe think, mister. This is a good old, well-built hooker, and seaworthy as a cork, but eight knots is about all you'll get out of her. She built for wandering over oceans looking for whales, not "cracking on". When you hunting for sperm whales, you might as well be in one place as another, cos you never know where or when you'll sight em. We'll git back one day, that's all.'

'Okay,' said Raven, 'eight knots it is, then. It may be a nice change not to be cracking on at fourteen or fifteen knots, with the ship like a half-tide rock and the decks full half the time, just to please the Owners with a smart passage, to help them compete with the damn steam-kettles. Let's hope the forties will roar to get us round the Horn, and that then we'll get a decent south-east trade-wind to push us up to the Line. Right then, Noah: we finish rigging today, and get under way at first light tomorrow, eh? I'm beginning to think that things are looking a bit rosier for us now. What do you think, Mr Tucker?'

'I think, young man, that – though I hope I am not superstitious – it is much better not to say such things, for that is tempting Providence.'

*

When dawn broke the following morning, it did seem as if Tucker's caution had been wise, for, though the new sails were nearly ready to set, the breeze had dropped to the lightest of airs from the north, and Carl, reeving sheet-ropes on deck, was very glum: 'Not enough vind to shift this old tub, mister. She yust vallow, I t'ink.'

'Never mind, Carl,' said Raven cheerfully. 'Every mile we can make is…'

'Deck, there!' came a cry from Jimmy Protheroe, working aloft in the foremast cross-trees. 'Sail, dead ahead!' His sharp eyes had caught sight of something on the eastern horizon. Raven and Noah went quickly up the ratlines to join him, Raven carrying a telescope.

'Where away now, Jim?'

'Look! Just off the starboard bow now, going left to right. Must be heading south, maybe south-west. You can just see two little triangles – the tops of her gaff tops'ls, I expect.'

'Schooner, then,' said Noah. 'Sealer, probably, heading for the Auckland Islands too, to look for seals. I hear them poor critters got wiped out twenty years ago, but maybe some back there now.'

'There certainly are,' said Raven. 'We saw scores of them on our way up Ross Harbour, and on Enderby Island too…scores. That schooner will be there long before us. Perhaps she'll take off "Figaro's" crowd?'

Noah shook his head gloomily: 'She might, mister, but then, if she is a sealer, she might not. A sealing crew can be a rough, hard bunch – worse than whalers, even. They won't want to waste time and lose money by doing good deeds. They don't give a rat's ass about nobody. They might even be going there to rifle the Government store – they often do that, I've heard. But if that's so, I reckon they'll be unlucky this time. The most they'd do is to report your crowd back at Bluff, but I doubt even that.'

Soon the whole spread of the schooner's sails was visible over the horizon to the three in the cross-trees. Suddenly Noah's eyes widened in fear: 'O Jesus, mister! She's not keeping on her course – look! I be damned if she ain't hauled her wind and started heading straight for us.'

'Why would she do that?' asked Raven.

'Don't know, mister, but I don't like it. Sometimes the sealer's skipper is the worst scoundrel of the blamed lot.'

'What the hell's up with you, Noah? Why have you got the wind up? They've sighted us; they'll think it odd we're just hulling here – not moving. They'll likely have seen we've no foretopmast, no tops'l, no t'gallant. They'd be curious, wouldn't they? They may be coming to offer help.'

'Yeah, mister, and maybe not the kind of help we want - maybe just to help themselves. Give your glass to Jim, mister, while we shin down on deck and talk to ole man Tucker. He's a wise ole buzzard in his way, even if he do talk like a preacher-man.'

They gained the deck to find Tucker scanning the newcomer anxiously. Eleanor came up from the galley to join them. 'Hello,' she said in amused surprise. 'What's suddenly the matter with all of you?'

Raven jabbed a finger: 'That! That's what's the matter.' He called up to Protheroe: 'Get the glass on her. See if you can read her name.'

'That ain't easy, with her coming straight at us and ducking into the swells. Hold on…I can just see the letters on her bow now. The name starts with a "B", then an "O", I think…then "N" or "M" – I ain't sure.'

Noah spoke in a thin, shaky voice: 'O, Christ save us, Mr Tucker! It's her - the "Bonito", Cap'n Charlie Lopez!'

Now Tucker went a sickly pale: 'As you say, Noah, Christ save us!'

'I'm not clear,' said Raven, 'why you two should be so alarmed about a sealing-schooner.'

'The Pacific is an immense space, Jack,' said Tucker, 'but the world of the whalers and sealers who roam across it is a small one. You could almost say that we all know each other, at least by hearsay. Whalers constantly meet haphazard in mid-ocean and indulge in what we call a "gam" – an exchange of gossip. In good weather they will both heave-to and visit each other by boat. That is how we all know about the "Bonito" and her infamous skipper, Charlie Lopez – a wild, wicked and ruthless man who has collected a crew to match his own vicious ways. I've heard he's half-African, half-Portuguese from the Cape Verde Islands, but an American now, of course. His schooner works out of San Francisco, but he is known from the Sea of Japan to Pago Pago as trouble for all who cross him.'

'I don't understand,' said Eleanor. 'What harm can he do to other ships and men?'

Noah turned to her: 'They say, miss, that if he finds another schooner where he wants to hunt, out come all his hunters with their rifles, and it ain't seals they're shooting at.'

'But the other sealers must have rifles too?'

'Not so many as he's got, and all his hunters are murderous – and blamed good shots too.'

'His reputation is enough to win any battle,' said Tucker.

'You got to sheer off or git shot – that's about the size of it,' said Noah.

'I still don't see that we'll have any problem with him,' said Raven. 'We're not a sealer on his hunting-ground. What quarrel would he have with us?'

Noah said wearily: 'I kin see you don't understand Charlie Lopez yet. You tell him Mr Tucker, and quick too, cos we ain't got time to blather on.'

'Very well then: in a nutshell, the Pacific is a perfect place for men like Lopez – no law and order, no witnesses; it is a place even worse than the western states of America a generation ago. Now just think: you yourselves could see us that first day as a helpless, damaged, under-manned hulk. You have done some repairs, but to a sailor like Lopez this ship is still obviously damaged, and obviously under-manned, with only eight souls aboard.'

Noah could contain his frustration no longer: 'Jesus, man! Surely even a young limey like you can see why we so scared! You think Lopez won't see we damaged and got no proper crew? You think he don't know we maybe got thousands of dollars-worth of cargo under hatches? You was pleased when you realized you could git yourselves a fortune by salvaging this ship: you think Lopez won't think the damn same?'

'But we've taken charge of her now. You all agreed to that. And one way or another I'll get her to port and we'll get another crew.'

Tucker began to share Noah's impatience: 'You do not know Charlie Lopez, Raven, or you would know that such a scoundrel is not going to let a few helpless people keep such a treasure from his grasp.'

'Jesus, cain't you see yet?' said Noah. 'His plan will be to turn up at Bluff or somewhere else with this ship. He'll say he found her adrift, damaged and with no crew. He'll say he repaired her, put a few of his hands aboard her and brought her into harbour, and kin he have his forty thousand bucks, please?'

Eleanor flushed with indignation: 'But he couldn't get away with that, because we'd tell them that it was all lies and that...'

She tailed off as she saw Noah slowly shake his grizzled head. He said: 'Mr Tucker, you tell her, please.'

Tucker took her hand gently: 'My dear, if Lopez has his way, you and I, and every man jack of us would have been shot through the head and thrown to the fishes the moment he and his ruffians got aboard. Then who will be there to contradict him? The ocean is a huge and lonely place, and hides ugly secrets well.'

She went as white as a sheet: 'Then indeed, God preserve us! O, what can we do to save ourselves?'

Now that he understood the danger, Raven was fired up to a warlike determination: 'By God, we'll do *something!* We've got rifles and shotguns too – I've seen them. This hooker's got high thick bulwarks, and the brick tryworks too. She's like a fortress. I'm a decent shot; I'll let some bloody daylight into some of them! There's the cutting spades too – you fought off the kanakas with them!'

'Them kanakas didn't have no guns, you fool,' said Noah, 'and they was in canoes – that's how we beat em.'

Tucker raised both hands to placate the exasperated Noah. 'The fact is, Mr Raven, that if it comes to open warfare we are doomed. You are a brave man, but your courage would not save us. We are outnumbered three, perhaps four, to one, and our foes are desperadoes, armed to the teeth. Lopez could lay his schooner alongside close enough for twenty or more of his men to leap into the chains while others sniped at us from aloft. Then what chance would we have?'

'They soon be alongside, Mr Tucker,' said Noah, the sweat of fear on his face. 'What in Christ's name we gonna do?'

For a man of peace, who had spent his life among ledgers and invoices and receipts, Tucker showed a remarkable calm strength: 'We have to defeat them by craft, Noah. As a Quaker, I abhor bloodshed, and in any case violence will not save us. It must be by guile.'

*

Charlie Lopez, captain of the Frisco sealer 'Bonito', steadied his telescope against the main rigging and took a long, careful look at the tubby, stricken whaler ahead, rolling in the smooth swells with not a sail set. He said to his mate, 'Hey, Slim, take a look at that hooker, will you? I done right to alter course, I reckon. Git your glass on her and tell me what you see.'

Slim Connolly, once a hapless, beaten cabin-boy from County Mayo, now a harsh tyrant, mercilessly imposing order on a crew of fellow-outcasts, focused his glass and something like a grin cracked his long, leathery, mahogany-coloured face: 'Yep, I see sump'n mighty interesting, cap. I see a Yankee whaler – "Pawtucket" – out of New Bedford, likely. Right down to her marks with cargo. Not a damn sail set. Lost half of her foremast. Got some lash-up of a jury-rig topmast, but no yards on it. In a bad way, I'd say.'

'Yeah, but that ain't all. Look on deck. Ain't hardly anybody there working. That's damn queer, ain't it, this time of day, if she's disabled?'

'I kin see six...no, seven...no, eight, all told. There's a big fat oldish guy in a big black hat amidships, talking to a tall white guy with a cap on – a mate, maybe- and two other white guys, one a big fair-haired feller, a Swede, maybe. Then there's two others, one a slip of a boy, I reckon, with a big fuzz of hair like a kanaka, only he's white. And then there's three blacks, one old one talking with the fat guy and two young uns dragging sails about, I guess. If that's all they got aboard, they sure are in a fix.'

'Yeah, Slim, and ain't that a crying shame? A deep-laden whaler at the end of her voyage, with sperm oil and spermaceti and baleen, and God knows what under hatches – worth thousands of bucks – and no crew. I smell silver dollars, boy!'

'I'm with you there, cap. Them poor guys are just begging for some real sailors to come along and help em.'

'Yeah, and by jeez, to help ourselves too. Down top-s'ls, mister mate, we're going alongside for a good ole gam. We'll go aboard, and we'll just happen to take our six-shooters. You got one handy, Slim?'

'Sure have. I need it with the sort of bastards you've signed on for a crew.'

'Okay. Tell them bastards to git the gig ready for lowering. I'm real looking forward to a nice chat with them poor Yanks. And we'll keep it real friendly to start with. If we get em worried they'll get shooters out too, and that'd make it messy. Someone could git hurt, an it might be you or me.'

*

'Guile?' said Raven. 'That's all very well, but *how?'*

'By using our wits,' said Tucker. 'We have no chance by open warfare, as I've explained.'

'If we could keep them off till dark we could make sail, and escape that way.'

'Quite impracticable, I'm afraid. With what is at stake, they will keep a very good lookout, and their schooner is four times faster than this tub. No, God forgive us, we must be civil, unsuspicious and friendly, but lie our heads off about everything, especially about our intended destination at Auckland Island, but also about why there's so few of us, why half of us are not whalers, and why one is a woman.'

'As to that,' said Eleanor, 'I'm dressed in sailor's

gear and trousers, and my hair is short and wild. At a distance I'll pass for a lad. I know: I'll go below soon, before they get too close, and you can tell them I'm the cook's boy – the peggy.'

'She's nearly here,' said Raven. 'I can see the hands swinging out a boat. My God, Tucker, we've got to *think* – think of something that will keep them off this deck.'

Suddenly Eleanor was seized, struck, by a blinding revelation. She grabbed his arm: 'No! Wait, Jack! We don't think, we *remember* – remember what happened aboard "Figaro"! That creature Billy John went ashore, caused trouble, got thrown into jail, came back aboard infected with typhus from the jail, and spread it among the crew. Suppose that had happened to the "Pawtucket"?'

'My God, Nelli,' said Raven, 'you're a genius! You see, Mr Tucker, that story kills two birds with one stone: it gives us a damn good reason for warning them off, and also explains why there are so few of us on deck!'

'Yes, yes!' said Tucker, with great relief. 'It was in inspiration, Eleanor. Let me think now of some suitable lies to embroider the story. Yes, I have it: ten of the crew – no, eleven, I think, ten sounds too much like a round number – eleven of our company have died, fourteen more have been badly affected, but are mostly recuperating; but there are five others who are still dangerously infectious. The good Lord has spared the eight of us – a purser, a mate, a cook's boy and five seamen, but (since we don't want them to offer any sort of assistance) we expect enough men will be ready very soon to take the deck, so that we can make sail and head for Bluff Cove. By-the-bye, Eleanor, you had better go below now, before they get too close. And blessings on your head, my dear!'

Raven gritted his teeth: 'Now we've got to be damn

careful in everything we say – got to be consistent in our lies.'

'Indeed, yes. As Scott says:

What a tangled web we weave
When first we practise to deceive.'

'No quotations now, man, for God's sake! Look, down comes her mainsail… now the foresail and the headsails. Stand by to lie, everybody.'

'Yes, I'll still be the purser, but you're the second mate – Mr Crowe from…er...'

'Somerset! I can do the accent. We had a milkman from there once. We've got to play-act, and it's got to work. Remember, boys – nice and polite and smiling, not suspicious at all. But Amos, nip below and help Eleanor to get all the guns you can lay hands on ready and loaded – just in case. My revolver's down there, in my cabin. Give that to Eleanor.'

With shouts and the squealing of blocks, the schooner's sails came down with a run. Now the long, low, rakish black sealer came to a halt no more than twenty yards off 'Pawtucket's' starboard beam, and lay still, rolling and pitching lethargically in the slow swells, a black menace on that fine spring morning, the sea a perfect blue, the sun beaming warmly on the predator and on its prey, the helpless, beamy, sluggish, wall-sided whaler. The ships lay parallel, but facing in opposite directions. The schooner's starboard bulwark was now lined with bearded, savage-looking men, their clothes stained with blood and grease, the marks of their grisly trade. They were the outcasts and misfits of many communities of the Pacific and Atlantic seaboards - kanakas, Scandinavians, Portuguese from the

Cape Verdes, Spanish from the Canaries, and the dregs of the slums of California. They were united in only two things – a scent of prey and a lust for the resulting dollars.

Lopez picked up a tin speaking-trumpet, set his face in a genial smile, and hailed: 'Ship ahoy! What ship?'

Tucker boomed back, needing no trumpet: ' "Pawtucket", whaler, New Bedford. What ship?'

'"Bonito", sealer, out of Frisco. You folks look to be in a real fix. Tell you what, we'll lower our gig, and me and my mate Slim Connolly will come across for a bit of a gam. Ain't seen nobody since we left the Sea of Japan. And maybe we can help? Sure don't like to pass by when folks are in trouble.'

Back came Tucker's equally unctuous and lying reply: 'You are kindness itself, sir – good Samaritans. God be praised that there are such folk as you at sea in these wicked times! However, much as we would like to spend time with you and entertain you, alas, a gam is quite out of the question. We are a stricken ship, sir, a plague-ship. As you are to leeward of us, I beg you, for your own sakes, to come no closer. God forbid we should infect you and your crew with such a painful and indeed deadly disease as typhus – jail-fever.'

Doubt and disappointment were audible in Lopez' tone: 'Jeez! Typhus! D'you mean you're the only folk alive on board?'

Tucker was becoming smoother, more confident in his ability to lie convincingly: 'O no, God be praised, we are the only ones fit to be on deck at the moment, but we have men below in their bunks whom we expect to be fit soon – our captain, Captain Olsen, being one of them. We have buried only eleven of our company so far, but we still have five in acute danger, and highly infectious. In the next day or so, they will go one way or another - towards recovery, or sinking from their present agonies into the final coma.'

'You ain't captain then, sir?'

'No sir, only a mere purser – a pen-pusher, and now perforce a cook. By God's grace I, and our second mate here, Mr Crowe, and, as you see, five seamen and the cook's boy, have escaped the plague.'

'Hey, typhus – that's a real bad plague. How come you got that aboard?'

'Drunken folly, sir. One of our crew beat a barman and smashed up the bar in Pago Pago. He was arrested and spent five nights in a most unsavoury jail there. You know what those places are like – ridden with disease. He came back aboard, at first showing no symptoms, but in a week he and most of the foc'sle hands were down with it. Our captain, a good soul indeed, caught it by going down into the foc'sle to dose the sufferers, and so, for the moment, there are few indeed of us to man the deck. But soon, we trust, we shall have a dozen survivors fit enough to join us at work.'

'Too bad, too bad. So where're you headed, once you git started?'

'O, Bluff Harbour, of course. It is the only place close enough to consider. As you see, the plague was not our only disaster. That last storm – perhaps you suffered from it too? – damaged us badly, but Mr Crowe here and his five men have done wonders, as you see, to fix up a jury-rig.'

'You done real good, Mr Crowe. You've done a damn good job on that foremast, with such a small crew. I could do with a mate like you!'

Raven plunged into his role of a crude Somerset whaler's mate: 'Ar, but twas a roight bloody job, sir. That ole storm were a real bastard of a blow. Foremast snapped off like a bleeding carrot, and the whole damn issue was hanging down overside. Chroist, you never sin such a fuckin mess in all your life, sir. Had to kick a few black arses – and whoite ones too – to git it sorted out, and some of it back up aloft. Aye, a long hard job with only these few goddam sojers to work with.'

'You sound like a limey, Mr Crowe.'

'Thass right, cap'n. Somerset and proud of it! Born in Bridgwater, bin at sea all me life, though. Fetched up years ago in Boston – but that's a long story, with a few jails in it. But, like Mr Tucker here said, you don't wanner bother about us, like. With a few more hands on deck I can git this poxy ole tub to Bluff. B'lieve me, cap'n you don't wanner come near us, less you want to be pitching half yer crowd into the drink, like we done. And anyways, sir, if you was to come over for a gam, you'd likely be the first to get it. How it is we ain't got it, Gawd knows. And, by Chroist, twas summat crool to see the pain them poor buggers had fore they snuffed it. Couldn't eat, couldn't drink, and they had such headaches, they wanted to pull their whole bloody heads off, some of em.'

Listening in a tense silence at the foot of the companionway, Eleanor was amazed at the skill with which Tucker and Jack were playing their parts: Tucker lending credit to his lies by exaggerating his usual pious, sanctimonious manner, Jack by totally transforming himself, his smooth, musical, English-public-school voice hideously coarsened into an ugly, grating, foul-mouthed rasp. It was lucky too, that because of his long razor-less spell, his wild shaggy hair and rampant whiskers made him look the part of a tough whaler's mate, not a college-trained, young, middle-class officer from a first-rate British ship.

She would have been amused, but for the terror of their situation. What if this gang of ruffians did not believe them? What if they did, but decided, with the lure of all those dollars under their noses, to chance their lives anyway? They did not look like men who valued their lives much. Most terrifying of all, what might be her own fate, once they realized at close quarters that she was a young woman? What if they did not shoot her at once, but instead passed her round as some sort of human plaything, so that she suffered days or weeks of hideous degradation before her inevitable death at their hands?

Raven and Tucker too were made uneasy by a long silence from the schooner. They could see Lopez and Connolly deep in conversation, with much gesticulation, head-shaking and keen looks towards the whaler. One thing was painfully clear: they had not given up yet; they were still too tempted by the plunder in front of them.

Then Lopez' voice came across the water again, still carefully polite and friendly: 'A real shame, that. Still, I guess you'll soon be under way again, back to Bluff?'

Raven paused for an instant before replying. It was clear that every one of Lopez' apparently innocent and casual questions was a part of his strategy, so every answer needed the same Machiavellian skill and duplicity. It was so important to appear relaxed, straightforward and trusting, but even more vital to lie convincingly about everything, especially their future plans. It was also important to make him believe that the whaler was unable to move yet – to believe that they were much more helpless than they really were. 'Waal, as to that, sir, it'll have to be Bluff, of course – nowhere else for bloody miles. But as to when, well, thass another matter. We got her rigged now, passable-like, but that ain't our only problem. When we was running before that gale, a big following sea hit the rudder such a fuckin slam that it smashed the steering-gear on deck to buggery. It damn near chucked the poor sod at the wheel overboard. An I ain't sure yet whether the bloody pintle ain't buggered too, so that the rudder won't turn. So one way or another, we don' know whether we're on our arse or our elbow, as they say. But, any road, you keep clear of us, sir. Don't you catch the plague off of us. We'll git there one day. But much obliged, all the same.'

Raven was thinking as he uttered the coarse lies: With any luck, if we do get away somehow, he'll never dream that we'd be headed south, so he'll chase us the wrong way.

'Hell,' Lopez called again. 'I kin see you're made of the right stuff for a mate.' Then he abruptly changed his tack: 'I guess, Mr Tucker, that when you do git back to Massachusetts you'll have a decent cargo to unload? I see your old hooker's down to her marks. Worth a load a bucks, eh?'

Tucker had been expecting that one, and lied with a deceitful, confident smoothness that made his Quaker soul ashamed: 'Alas, sir, it would if there were a good market in New Bedford for rocks and gravel, for there is more ballast under our hatches than anything else. Tell me, captain, have you had a prosperous voyage this year?'

'*Prosperous?* By Christ above, sir, we have *not*.

We've scoured every goddam island and skerry from the Aleutians to New Zealand and got nearly nothin for our trouble. We're headed south now, for them miserable, cold, windy islands down there – that's how desperate we are.' One of the protagonists had at last spoken the truth!

'And we, sir, have suffered alike, and for the same reason: the whole ocean, I fear, has been hunted and fished out by our forefathers. True, we have some tiers of barrels down below, but they are full of poor stuff – oil from bowheads and the like – worth little. We have sighted but one pod of sperm whales – only one, in all our wanderings. We launched the boats, of course, but one of the males in the pod was a rogue whale, and we gained nothing but two smashed boats and one dead harpooner. Poor fellow, he fell from the boat almost into the monster's jaws, and that was the last we saw of him. In the end, Captain Olsen was so sick of this disastrous voyage that we put in at Hawaii and took in enough ballast to get us safely home. What our precious Owners will make of it all, I dread to think, with no good quality oil and a big bill for ballast, not to mention the lost hands'

Tucker was desperately hoping that by now he had thrown enough cold water on their hopes to make them set sail and leave. Instead, he was disturbed to see Connolly the mate prodding Lopez' arm and pointing at 'Figaro's' quarter-boat, where it hung from the davits amidships. By heavens, Tucker thought, I had forgotten about her!

Lopez' voice came back, harsher and more suspicious: 'That boat you got there, mister: that don't look like no whale-boat to me – big, heavy, half decked-in. How come you got that aboard? And what happened to the guys that were in her?'

'Alas, poor souls,' said Tucker with convincing sincerity. 'All perished, I'm sure. We came across that boat floating bottom-up after the storm. She had the name "Figaro" and the word "Cardiff" on her transom. Cardiff is a port in Wales, is it not? As you see, she had been fitted with some rough decking, but all to no avail, I fear. The ocean has swallowed not only them but also, I presume, all the other members of "Figaro's" crew. The ship itself foundered in that last storm, I expect, but no-one will ever know for sure. Ours is a cruel vocation, Mr Lopez. We recovered the boat from the sea in case we too might need a substantial lifeboat one day, for, as you can see, all but one of our own boats were destroyed by the storm.' Tucker had discovered in himself a masterly talent for improvisation, skilfully mixing truth with invention, a talent that might yet fit him perfectly for a career in politics.

There was a long silence from the schooner. Then Lopez called out: 'Yeah, I see. Reckon we'll hull here alongside for a spell, just to see you get rigged and repaired okay. Even if we can't come aboard, we'll be right happy to lend you gear and tools and stuff if you need it.' His voice regained all its virtuous bonhomie: 'We'll do anything we can to help, you know that.'

'That is wonderfully good of you, sir, but we would not want to delay your hunting.' He picked up on Jack's last lie: 'It will be some days, you see, before we shall be able to sail and steer properly. And now, in the meantime, sir, if you will excuse us, I and my mate must go below to see how our patients are faring this morning. God send that we have not another body to commit to the deep. Our foc'sle is still more like a hospital, and tending these people is an exhausting task, believe me.'

'Hey, you're a damn brave bunch, and the best of luck to you. But,' Lopez added, his voice throbbing with nobility, 'we just can't abandon our fellow-sailors in distress. Tell you what: we'll stay, till tomorrow at least.'

He put the trumpet down, and the colloquy was over – a tense, blackly-comic interchange between a vicious predator and a vulnerable prey – an interchange where truth and honesty had had no place on either side, and hypocrisy and lies had reigned supreme.

Then, on each gently-rolling deck, reality took over.

'What d'you reckon, Slim?' asked Lopez.

'Ain't it plain to you yet? They're all goddam liars! We can't check up on a damn thing they've said. They know well enough what we're after, so all they can do is stall - try and put us off. Jeez, I'd do the same if I was them. We can't see what his cargo is, but I never yet heard of a Yankee whaler taking in ballast. We can see his masts and rigging, but we got no bloody idea whether his rudder and steering-gear are damaged or not. And most of all, Charlie, we don't know whether anyone aboard that ship has – or has had – the typhus. They all look healthy enough to me. I bet my last bottom dollar, cap, that you've been fed a load of bullshit. They're trying to make suckers out of us.'

'No, trust me, you're wrong there, Slim, specially about the typhus. How else can you explain that there's only eight guys aboard, and out of them one's a fat ole purser and another only some bit of a cook's boy? Them whalers always have crews of thirty or thirty-five. So where's the rest of them? Why ain't they all up on deck, like our crowd, watching and listening to what's going on? Listen: if there's even a chance they got typhus on board, you won't see me or anyone else from this packet setting foot on that ole hooker. I saw men dying of that jail fever in Chile once, and I'm telling you, it wasn't pretty – a God-awful long, slow death, with pain all the way. No, what we'll do is just stay here, close and quiet. We got em just where we want em. If they've got the wind up, and if what they said about the steering-gear ain't true, they may try to give us the slip in the dark. Then we'll *know* they've just been codding us all along. We'll keep a damn good look-out, and if they set sail we catch em and board em and feed em all to the fishes. Then we'll see what he's really got under hatches.'

'Okay, you're captain. But I lay you're wasting time, and maybe missing the chance of makin us all rich.'

On the whaler too the talk was more realistic than the absurd charade of mutual good will that had preceded it.

'Do you think, Mr Raven,' said Tucker, 'that we have finally convinced them?'

'No, I'm afraid not. If we had, they would now be hoisting sail. As it is…'

'As it is, I believe that they are undecided – divided in their opinions. I have been watching that precious pair of rascals carefully, and, by his gestures and manner, I fancy that the mate is much more in favour of an immediate direct attack than his captain. So I suppose that all we can do is to continue as if they were not there?'

'No, that would be no good. If at some time we pretend to have cured this mythical steering problem, and set sail, we shall then have to do what we said we would –

head for Bluff Cove. Well, I just can't imagine them letting us get there. With this lash-up of a rig that trip will take days. And then, don't forget that you told them we had hands down below who would soon be fit for work on deck. When Lopez sees that that is not happening, our main story – or lie – will lose all credibility; after all, he has only our word for it that there is any illness on board. And in the meantime, we cannot set sail yet because we have to appear to be mending our steering-gear. Noah, you'd better come and help me play-acting at that, while the others get all the halyards and sheets rove, so that, if and when we get a chance, we can get moving at the drop of a hat.'

'Okay, mister, I'll do my best, but I tell you, we better pretend real good. Them bastards'll be watching us like hawks, day and night. If'n they didn't, we could slip away, soon as it got dark. There's a nice northerly breeze getting up today; we might be able to git outa sight by morning. Then they'd likely chase us the wrong way. But there – what's the use of hoping? They'll keep their eyes peeled…'

Jimmy Protheroe, working at the sheets nearby, gave a cold, mirthless laugh: 'Yes, unless, just sculling about here with nothing to do, the silly buggers went and got pissed.'

Raven looked up sharply, but before he could speak, Tucker said: 'I take it, young man, that that low expression you just used meant "got drunk"? I fear there is little chance of that. They have been long at sea, and all their liquor will have gone, whereas we…'

Raven cut in abruptly: '*What?* Whereas we *what?*'

Tucker said, with a heavy sigh: 'Whereas we, sir,

have liquor enough below to swim in. Captain Olsen replenished his supplies very amply at the chandler's in Hawaii. He made me enter them in the ledger as cordage and salt beef, to fool the Owners. Alas, he was…'

'Never mind about that, man! What exactly have you got locked away in the lazarette?'

Tucker replied casually, not noticing Raven's sudden urgency: 'Oh, two kegs of rum, two of brandy, even a case of bottles of Scottish whisky – a potent brew, I believe.'

Eleanor's voice suddenly cut in: 'Rum, brandy, whisky? What on earth are you all talking….'

Raven was pre-occupied and harsh: 'I told you to keep below, Nelli, out of sight, not to come traipsing up on deck.'

She replied sullenly: 'I know you did, captain sir, but I got bored. Anyway, they're not watching us at the moment; they've all gone below for breakfast, I expect.'

But Raven was no longer listening to her. He clenched one fist and smashed it into the palm of his other hand: '*Got it!* That's it! That's how we get away – rum, brandy, whisky! Thank God you said that, Jim – about them getting pissed!'

Tucker was exasperated: 'I do wish, young man, that you would tell us why you are gibbering about liquor like a half-wit. I don't for the life of me see…'

'No, you don't see, do you – any of you? You're all too bloody thick! Then listen to me: this evening we give them every last drop of our booze, liquor – whatever you like to call it. Every damned drop! I'm relying on you, Mr Tucker, to give them some plausible reason for the offer. You're about the best liar I've ever come across, so you'll be able to think of something convincing. Have we got a speaking-trumpet like Lopez had? Good, because I want you to make sure that that whole bloody crowd of savages knows about our generous gift. Once they do, it'll be more than even Lopez and his mate can do to stop them swigging it down, I reckon. They won't have had a drop for a long time. We lower your whaleboat; Amos and I will ferry the stuff across in that, while you give them one of your humbug speeches about their goodness and our heartfelt gratitude, et cetera, et cetera. We make a great performance of keeping our possibly infected bodies away from all contact with them, our wonderful newfound friends and would-be saviours. They haul up the kegs out of the boat with ropes. We come back, hoist the boat, but keep it ready. Then we sit back and see what happens. We can pray, if you like, that the whole bunch of them will get drunk, pissed, pie-eyed, pickled, slewed – whatever you like to call it – until they're lying about like logs, and *then*, and *then*, lady and gentlemen, we make our very quiet exit, after a further small expedition that I have in mind.'

He dropped his excited rhetoric and said soberly, bleakly: 'And if that doesn't work, if they all keep sober, if that just makes them see we've been lying through our teeth all along – then, shipmates, it's goodnight to the lot of us. And if that happens, if the worst comes to the worst, Eleanor, you will have your revolver, and you may want to keep the last bullet for yourself.'

CHAPTER EIGHTEEN

All that day, any observer – and there were several very keen observers aboard the sealer – could see a constant flurry of earnest activity aboard the 'Pawtucket'. Tucker, Eleanor and Protheroe tramped to and fro between the galley and store-room aft and the foc'sle for'ard, laden with mess-tins, buckets, mops and bundles of blankets, assiduously tending their phantom patients. Raven and Noah, 'mending' the steering-gear, were hard for the observers to see, as they were within the wheelhouse shelter, but they did their best to add plausibility to the deadly farce by going to and fro carrying rope-coils, marlin-spikes, hammers and large spanners, and every now and then hammering loudly and calling urgently to one another.. Only the three seamen, Carl, Amos and George, working at the sails, sheets and halyards, were in the realm of reality: they were actually doing what they appeared to be doing.

Aboard the sealer, Lopez and his mate Connolly were keenly watching the charade, while at the same time bawling at the hands cleaning and painting on deck. They saw no point in giving their crowd a day off while they themselves scrutinized their prey.

Between his forays to the foc'sle, and secure from prying eyes, Tucker was also busily employed in a real, if unusual, task. Eleanor, hurrying below during the late morning, was amazed to find him in the mess-room, kneeling over the tubs of rum and brandy, which he had brought out of the lazarette, the officers' food-store, and stood on their ends. He was gently prising out the spiles – the tapering wooden pegs which sealed the barrels. Beside the barrels on the deck stood a large green bottle.

'Nathaniel,' she said, 'what in the world are you doing with those tubs?'

'Ah, Eleanor, I am seeking to make a slight additional improvement to your young man's excellent scheme. I have taken this bottle from our few medical supplies. It contains laudanum, which is, as you know, a powerful tincture of opium, and is normally our standard remedy for toothaches and so forth. I think it may well prolong the slumbers of our foes yonder. The longer and more profound their sleep, the better for us.'

'Yes, but you will have to be very careful to hide the fact that the spiles have been removed and replaced. And won't they taste this drug in their liquor?'

'I think not. These are liquors with a strong flavour, I am told; and I doubt that those ruffians over there will be delicate or discriminating drinkers. Besides, I shall add only a little of the drug to each barrel. And as for the whisky, those bottles are sealed, and I dare not tamper with them. Our situation is so perilous that the least mistake could be fatal.'

As the fine spring evening began to darken over the sea, and the day-long bustle aboard the whaler came to an end, the second mate, Mr Crowe, and Tucker came to the starboard bulwark amidships, Tucker wielding the tin speaking-trumpet to add yet more volume to his powerful voice. They looked across at their predator; many of its crew, tired from their day of forced labour, were lolling about, smoking or chewing tobacco on the hatches, lazily contemplating their victim, for they all understood Lopez' game well enough, and were confidently looking forward to profiting handsomely from it themselves.

Tucker's voice boomed out across the water, pregnant with gratitude and goodwill: 'Captain ahoy! Captain Lopez! Ah, there you are! Sir, we have what we hope may be good news for you, but no more than your just reward, since you have offered to be such good Samaritans to us. Mr Crowe and I, in between tending our sick and attempting to mend our steering-gear, have been considering our future and its possible problems. Our captain and most of the other sufferers are recovering fast, which of course is good news. But on the other hand, I have been reading our Medical Guide, and something in it has made me anxious: it insists, as a matter of vital importance, that patients recuperating from typhus must on no account drink any form of alcohol.'

At the back of his mind he worried a little about this glib flow of lies. Did the Guide say that? Had Lopez got a copy of the Guide, so that he could check up on that? Would he? No matter - in for a penny, in for a pound!

'Our problem is that our captain and all our harpooners are much addicted to alcohol, and know that we are well supplied with it, for our commander purchased lavish amounts of it in Hawaii. If, once recovered, they begin imbibing this strong drink, the foc'sle hands will demand their share too, and this may well lead to mutiny and disorder, as well as to serious relapses into illness. I, of course, as a mere purser, would have no authority to prevent that disaster. So we are forced to take desperate measures, no matter what the subsequent cost to ourselves from the captain's wrath. As a Quaker, I have no taste myself for strong liquors, and I brought all our stock up on deck with a view to jettisoning it over the side. But Mr Crowe here, who is a good fellow and certainly does not share my distaste for strong drink, has suggested to me that, instead of doing that, we should, in sincere gratitude, offer it to you and your men.'

Lopez had no chance to reply, much less to decline, for a huge cheer came up from all his crowd – hunters and seamen alike, and, as more men tumbled up from below, there was uncontrolled hubbub as they heard the wonderful and incredible news. Eleanor, listening from below, was impressed by Jack's cunning in having the offer made very loudly and publicly to the whole crew, so giving Lopez no chance to refuse without starting a mutiny.

Albert Crowe, crude and coarse as ever, now took the trumpet: 'Waal, twas the least we could do, wadn't it? These ole Quakers – fornicating ole killjoys, they are. Oi wouldn't let him ditch all that lovely booze, Oi wouldn't. Your boys ain't ill, are they? And Oi dessay they like a tipple now and then, so why waste good liquor? Oi told him: Give it to them good ole boys on the "Bonito" or Oi'll drink the whole fuckin lot meself – and then where will yer be?'

A huge roar of laughter came from the schooner's deck; so many men were at the bulwark that the whole ship was listing over towards the whaler. Crowe lifted a hand to still the racket: 'Moind you, Oi've kep a few bottles for meself.' This raised another burst of guffaws. 'Still, that leaves you a good old drop to drink our healths with. There's two firkins of rum and two of brandy – that's a good few gallons. Then there's two cases of a dozen bottles of Scotch whisky. Have you tried that stuff? That's better than rye, and bloody good stuff to keep the cold out, that is. So that's a decent drink all round for yer, ain't it?'

Among their bawling throng, Lopez and Connolly were conferring, not cheering. Connolly said urgently: 'What are they up to now? This sounds to me like another goddam trick. I don't believe nothing of what them bastards say. You be careful, cap'n. Remember what I said about all their other yarns. We got no way of knowing what's true and what ain't.'

Lopez grinned, unconcerned: 'Sounds like the boys ain't gonna give us much choice, don't it? Anyway, what trick? I know that old buzzard. He's just trying to bribe us – to win time, to buy us off. But it won't do him no good, will it? We'll soon know if he's lying. He says he's got hands who'll soon be ready to work on deck. Well, we'll be able to see if that happens, shan't we? He can't fool us about that. His ship's helpless, especially if her pintle's bent or broke. (The pintle was one of the massive metal fixtures on the ship's stern on which the rudder hinged.) Anyway, if he did try to give us the slip in the night, we know where he's got to go, and we'd soon catch up with that old tub. And if that happened – if they've been lying all along – then by Christ above they'll be sorry, all of them. Shooting will be too good for them. Listen, Slim: I ain't gonna give him no chance to slip away – I ain't that kinda fool. We'll let the boys have a few drinks, but there's got to be two on deck all the time who are sober enough to keep a good lookout. They can have a drink later. You see to that, Slim.'

He picked up his speaking-trumpet and called: 'Hey, Mr Tucker sir, you're a real good guy! We're mighty obliged to you, but Jeez, your skipper will be plenty mad with you when he finds out what you've done. We finished all our booze long ago, and this sealing is a tedious, cold, dirty old job. I'll send a couple of lads over in a boat for it.'

Tucker raised a hand. 'No, no, sir, I must stop you there! Remember, the plague is still virulent with us – that would be much too dangerous. We will send a boat to you, and we have first washed each keg and bottle in sea-water to kill off any possible infection. God forbid that we should infect our would-be saviours!'

Crowe said, more practically: 'He's right, cap'n. You don't want to get close to us. We'll put slings on the barrels and cases, and bring em across in our boat. You just lower some ropes down into the boat when we git alongside, and haul em up.'

He and Tucker exchanged significant looks as another cheer came from the crowded deck. A rough, hurly-burly scramble for suitable lengths of rope began without any order from Lopez or Connolly. Still showing a face of innocent geniality, Raven muttered: 'Looks promising. That crowd are half out of control already.'

The whaler's boat was swiftly lowered and loaded, and with vigorous strokes of the oars, approached the schooner, Crowe and Amos rowing, George standing in the stern-sheets wielding the boat-steerer's long oar. (When the whale-boat was at its normal deadly business of fighting huge sperm whales it needed often to twist and turn far more rapidly than it could with a rudder.) The boat slid alongside the schooner's low midship rail, and in no time, to vociferous cheers, the tubs and cases were on her deck.

'Thass it, boys! Now fill yer bloody boots!' cried the affable Crowe. 'You ain't going nowhere t'morrer, are yer? No more are we, and Oi'm right shagged-out, what with the steering gear and them poor buggers for'ard, so, like Oi say, we've kep a few bottles for ourselves. Damn shame we can't have a gam and few drinks all together, sociable-like, but there you are – it ain't to be.'

He had been deliberately addressing the crew, but now he looked over to where Lopez stood: 'Can't thank you enough, sir, givin up yer time like this.' He added, ambiguously: 'Ain't many sealer skippers around like you, sir. So our very best to you and your boys. Can't stop though; got to git back to being nursemaids to the poor sods with the plague. Mr Tucker do reckon there's another one – maybe two – will have to go over-side t'morrer, poor bastards.' He shook his head sadly.

Lopez waved farewell, calling: 'Real sorry for that, Mr Crowe. It's been right handsome of you two gents to think of us. See yer t'morrer!' Raven was pleased to note that his waving hand already held a whisky-bottle.

Ten minutes later the boat had been hoisted and Raven, Tucker and Noah stood by the davits: 'Well,' said Raven, 'what do you think? And for God's sake don't let anybody grin or look pleased. We're still a plague-ship, don't forget.'

Noah looked suitably gloomy, but said: 'Looks good to me, mister. Them guys won't have had their supper yet, and if their cook gets a skinful, perhaps they won't get nothing at all to eat tonight. All that booze on an empty stomach, never mind that jollop that Mr Tucker added – that sure should put em out for a while. Listen to that racket,' he added, as the sound of angry voices came across the water. 'I do b'lieve the cap'n and the hunters aft are gittin mad with the foc'sle crowd about who gits what to drink.'

'So much the better,' said Tucker shrewdly. 'That will make them drink all the faster, so as to stop the others getting it. But sirs, inwardly I feel the deepest shame. I have already seen naked kanakas sliced by cutting-spades, and a score more sent, possibly, to the sharks. Now I am using vile alcoholic potions to drug and delude simple men.'

'Needs must,' said Noah, 'when the debbil drives, they say. And besides, them guys out there ain't so simple.'

'Come on,' said Raven. 'We've got to give all our mythical patients their suppers and tidy their bunks, don't forget. That Connolly is damned clever, so don't let him catch you staring at the "Bonito". We ignore the sealer and look busy.'

Twilight fell after an hour of this pointless busyness between galley and foc'sle. Then it was their own supper-time, though no-one had much of an appetite. Eleanor was white and silent; Raven, totally preoccupied, scarcely noticed the food on his plate. Through the open door they heard from the schooner the sounds of a happy carousal – shouts, toasts, obscene songs from both for'ard hands and the hunters and officers aft.

Raven at last pushed a half-eaten meal away. 'Now then, listen, all of you. I've been thinking hard. We've got to do more than this, or we may get caught, no matter how drunk they get. This ship is so slow – especially under a jury-rig – that it's very possible that at dawn our mast-heads would still be in sight, if there was just one of them sober enough to go aloft with a telescope. That would sober all of them up quickly enough, and the "Bonito" is so fast she'd catch us in no time. And that, you all know, would be the finish, for all of us. So it follows that that schooner has got to be more disabled than we are, and I think I know how to manage that. It'll be a desperate business, but we've no choice. This is what we do, and we do it in complete silence. Once we start, there will be no orders from me. You have all got to *know* what to do, so listen carefully now.'

There was a dead silence for a moment. None of them had the least idea of what he was planning, but they all realized at once that it was sure to be horribly dangerous and all too liable to failure.

He began again, tense and laconic: 'We wait until all's quiet aboard the sealer, and that may take hours. Then I and one seaman go across again in the whale-boat. We get up on her deck. We shall have to hope that no-one is keeping a proper watch, or that, if anyone is, we can lay him out cold before he can shout. Once on deck, we get out our knives and cut off and throw overboard all her running rigging – halyards, sheets, topping-lifts – everything, especially the ropes controlling her big sails – foresail and mainsail, and both tops'ls.'

He paused and turned to Jimmy Protheroe, who sat near, white and sweating: 'Jim, I want you to come with me. You've got good eye-sight, and besides,' he added, in an attempt to ease the tension by a little banter, 'you're the craftiest bugger I've ever met. That's a request, mind, not an order. You'll come?'

Silently, mopping his moist face, Protheroe nodded.

'Good. Now then: once Jim and I have left, Mr Tucker, you'll take the wheel, please; Noah and George go to the foremast, Carl and Amos to the mainmast. *Listen*: as soon as you see or hear us coming back, hoist every staysail and, with this northerly wind on the port beam, sheet them in to reach on the port tack. Then all of you run aft and set the spanker. One other thing: Amos, as soon as the sails are set, nip round and douse every light on the ship. And mind, for God's sake don't forget the stern-light! *Do not wait for us to get aboard!* This ship will be slow to gather way, so Jim and I will be able to scramble aboard at the main chains. We shan't stop to hoist the boat, of course. Clear so far?'

They all nodded, their faces set in grim lines of a determination that was not very far from despair.

'Right. Now, Mr Tucker, when she starts to answer the helm, steer straight ahead to clear the schooner's stern, and for God's sake don't hit her! Eleanor, will you help Carl and Amos at the mainmast, and then all of you come aft to set the two mizzen staysails. Remember, there'll be no orders from start to finish, until we get clear.'

He paused, swallowed, and, with a glance at Jim, said: 'If, on the other hand, you hear shouts, fighting and gunshots it'll mean Jim and I are dead ducks, so you just go ahead, steer north by north-west for Bluff, and hope for the best. You may well get a good start, so you might make it. All clear, then – all agreed? Any questions?'

There was a brief tense silence; then they were startled by a loud, emphatic 'Yes!' from Eleanor. She went on: 'But it's an objection, really, not a question. I don't agree with your plans. You have forgotten something very important – the boat-steerer. You will need a third person in the boat.'

Raven flushed red with anger and embarrassment at an attack from such a quarter: 'I've forgotten nothing!

Jim and I can row and steer – we're not landlubbers. There's no-one to spare for a boat-steerer.'

Eleanor jumped to her feet, even angrier: 'There is! There's me! Are you suggesting I'm a landlubber? After all the time I was at the helm in the lifeboat in that storm? If you are, you make me sick with your superior, patronizing attitude!'

Tucker rose, his hands raised, palms down, to allay the lovers' mutual rage. 'Please! Raven, Eleanor! This is no time for…'

Noah cut in with the voice of calm reason: 'You jus cool down now, mister, and listen. There's maybe somethin in what she say. You know she ain't no fool at sea now.'

'Yes, I know that, man. But we haven't got time to fall out about piffling details.'

'Indeed no,' said Tucker fervently. 'We have enemies enough only yards away.'

But Eleanor fought on: 'It's not a detail, Nathaniel; it's important, yet he won't listen. Very well, I will keep calm and I'll be very brief, but I *will* have my say. I'll just tell you what I think. I agree that our captain has devised an excellent way of crippling our enemy. But I insist that the plan will work much better with a boat-steerer, and I know – and he knows, really – that I'm able to do that job.'

Gradually, as she went on, the anger went out of her voice as she turned to pleading and informality: 'Just think, Jack: when you're coming alongside that schooner it'll be vital not to bump the oars or the boat against her side. You yourself say everything's got to be noiseless. That will be much easier with me at the steering-oar. You will be able to ship your oars yards away. And by the way, you ought to wrap some cloth round the oars where they fit in the rowlocks, so as to muffle the sound they make, and, talking of sounds, why don't you and Jim take off your great clumping seaboots, and do your job barefoot? And when the boat is alongside and you and Jim are at your dirty work on deck, I can hold on to the chains and keep the boat away from hitting the side. Then, when you've finished, you won't have to waste time casting off a painter. I'll be your painter.' She ended with half a smile.

'But Eleanor, it's going to be so damned dangerous. That's why I've got to go myself, and that's why I haven't ordered anyone to come with me – though I know every man here has the guts to do it. But you, Nelli – I don't want you anywhere near that hell-ship out there.'

'But Jack, don't you see? You said yourself that if this trick didn't work we'd all probably be dead. So what does it matter where I am? In fact, if everything goes wrong tonight, I would think it better for me to be in the boat alongside their schooner. In the dark they'd never see I was a woman, so they'd just shoot me then and there. I'd infinitely prefer that to being captured alive. Remember, Jack, what I went through on the island. Just think what would happen to me if I were captured alive.'

'I know all that, Nelli, but still…'

'Jack… captain… I am telling you this: when that boat is lowered, I am dropping down into her stern, and if that is mutiny you'd better put me in irons here and now.'

'Don't look to me as if you got much choice, skipper,' said Protheroe, with a touch of his native impertinence, 'cos you ain't go no irons handy, have you?'

*

Then, once it was fully dark, the torturing hours of waiting began, with all the whaler's puny crew listening, listening, to the seemingly endless, ugly riot of sound from the schooner – cries, yells, the smashing of glass, bawdy singing, and now and then the sound of a vicious, mindless quarrel between near-speechless drunkards.

Nine ....ten ... eleven ..... twelve o'clock passed, and only then, and only gradually, did the vile noise subside. On the whaler's deck the men urgently readied the boat for lowering and, for the hundredth time, checked that the halyards and sheets were ready too.

Raven, Eleanor and Jim stood amidships, side by side, shivering as the air grew colder and the danger nearer. 'Not long now, I reckon, Jim,' Raven muttered. 'Got your knife, Jim? Really sharp? Good. You take the foremast, I'll do the mainmast. We'll both be working right over their heads, but that can't be helped. And you've got one of the big belaying-pins tucked in your belt? Good. So have I. Remember, don't use it unless you have to, but there might be a semi-sober watchman or two on deck.'

'Don't you worry. The bastards won't be watching nothing when I've done with them.'

'Right. Now remember: we don't want to hang about, but it's a lot more important to be thorough than to be quick. If it's possible, get rid of everything – halyards, sheets, sheet-blocks – the bloody lot. They've got no steam on that hooker, so that will fix them good and proper for quite a few hours. Another thing: be as *quiet* as you can; don't let coils of rope or blocks land on deck with a thump. When you've cut a halyard, try to feed it quietly over the side – the port side. And try to catch the last bit of it as it drops from aloft.'

'Softly, softly catchee monkey, eh?'

'Exactly. And for God's sake don't fall over anything in the dark either, or we're both for the chop. And one more thing: we're doing this job barefoot – no clumping about in boots. So if you stub your toe on a ringbolt, don't yell!'

'See that? I think we may be lucky, mister. See them two coves amidships, sitting on the for'ard hatch? Well, half-an-hour back I seen a chap come up from the foc'sle, and I could see in the light from the scuttle that he had a bottle in each hand, and he went back down empty-handed, so them watchmen are getting their share. I bet you that wasn't what Charlie Lopez ordered.'

'Good! So much the better for us if they're sozzled. Wait ... Look at that! Hasn't one of them just laid himself down on the hatch?'

'Yeah. And look! There goes the other one! Must have rolled into the scuppers.'

'Right, Jim. Here we go. Time to lower away.'

No sound now came from the schooner but the lap of small waves against her side and the gentle frapping of the halyards against the masts. Silently, the whaler's crew mustered around the davits where the whale-boat hung. The falls were released from the cleats and the boat descended in silence to the water – in silence because Noah had remembered to oil the blocks with a feather and melted grease.

Tucker went to the wheel, where, thanks to the shelter of the wheelhouse, he would be invisible. Raven held up his hand for total stillness. Not a sound now came from the sealer, nor did anyone move on her deck. Raven,

Protheroe and Eleanor stood ready at the rail. Noah came to grip Raven's hand in both of his. Not a word was spoken.

The three took it in turn to nimbly mount the bulwark, then slide down a rope into the boat. Jim used his muffled oar to shove the boat off, and with infinite care both men began to row, while Eleanor, standing in the stern-sheets, leant on the long steering-oar to point the boat's bows at the schooner's main chains.

A few near-silent strokes were enough. Eleanor, facing forward, could see that they could now glide alongside, so she raised a hand to say 'Easy-all'. With meticulous care the oars were boated, and all three reached out to grasp the schooner's lower rigging and hold the boat off a foot from her side. Eleanor, her teeth chattering with the night's chill and the deadlier chill of fear, held the boat steady as the two young men stood, grasped the lanyards at the foot of the shrouds, and silently, athletically, disappeared from her view.

Raven and Jim exchanged nods and went about their destructive business, Prothero having to use extravagant care in stepping over the inert bodies of the so-called lookouts. Up from the open companionways to foc'sle and mess-room came the sounds of sottish snoring, mumbling and clumsy movements as men turned in their sleep.

Raven took out his knife, honed razor-sharp on the whaler's grindstone, and began his ugly work. Despite his fear and urgency, he felt a twinge of professional guilt at this vandal-like wrecking of the beautiful pattern of the schooner's running rigging. It was like slashing the muscles and tendons of a graceful speedy animal. Gingerly he freed the mainsail halyard from its pin, took the coil to the ship's side, fed the end of it over the bulwark and, every nerve jumping at any sound, paid it all out into the sea. Then, slipping quickly to the halyard's other end at the lowered gaff, he hacked it free from the spar and its blocks. Then followed the most ticklish part; he had to let go of the severed end and, going to the ship's side, pull down on the rope he'd led over the side. This was tricky, because the cut end would go up the mast to the cross-trees, unreeve through its block – he hoped with all his soul that the block wouldn't squeal too much – and then drop down out of his control. All he could do was to stand directly underneath, so that the heavy hemp rope fell on him, not on the deck.

Despite his care, some lengths of rope did rap on the deck and he listened, his heart in his mouth, for steps or shouts from below. But still the only sound was that of snoring; his mouth twitched in a grin; the strong spirits and Tucker's opium were doing their work well!

Then, in the midst of his satisfaction, his heart seemed to stop dead. From up for'ard, where Jim was at work, he heard the sound of coughing and of clumsy foot-steps on the ladder up from the foc'sle. Great God! One of them coming up on deck! This could be the finish for all of them! Time to *do* something – and fast! Darting for'ard, he found Protheroe crouching for cover behind the fore-mast; he had his heavy hardwood belaying-pin in his hand. Raven sank beside him in the darkness and laid a hand on his arm to say 'Wait!' Because one seaman had come on deck it didn't necessarily mean he had heard them, but he must be kept as quiet as possible, in case he awoke one of the 'watchmen'. Sure enough, as the man came stumbling over the high coaming, he made for the ship's side and vomited his liquor long and painfully into the sea.

Raven let go of Jim's arm and breathed 'Yes!' into his ear. Instantly, catlike, Protheroe was on his feet and in two seconds, while his left hand grasped the man's collar, the right brought his wooden club down with a crunching blow on the back of the seaman's skull. He made no cry, but his legs buckled and Protheroe lowered him gently into a heap in the scuppers.

Jim came scuttling back to the foot of the foremast; Raven whispered in his ear: 'Well done. That should do it. Done the foresail halyards? Good. Now see to the tops'l halyards and all the blocks on the gaff. I'll go and do the same; then we'll skedaddle. Keep an eye on him. If he starts to come round, give him another.'

Then both returned to their work, stripping the schooner of its vital muscles, slashing at the strops which fastened the blocks to the gaffs, the spars which spread the tops of the sails, then turning their attention to the tops'l halyards, stripping the masts of every scrap of rope. Raven came back for'ard and together, ears cocked for sounds from below, they worked hastily but carefully to strip the headsails – the jibs that went out to the bowsprit – of their halyards. But, with the flying jib still to do, they started at the sounds from aft of deep, drunken coughs and loud retching.

Raven whispered urgently 'Time!' and seconds later Eleanor, looking up from the boat, was glad beyond all words to see the pale ovals of their faces over the starboard bulwark. The lightly-built boat dipped and rocked as first Jim, then Raven, dropped into it. Even now, despite their haste and ugly fear, they kept to the solemn maritime convention that the captain must always be the last into the boat. Such is habit!

With not a word spoken, Eleanor shoved off the stern, the oars were shipped, two powerful strokes from Raven swung the bow round, and the rowers bent their backs to send the boat shooting towards the whaler. As they did so, they heard the quiet, rumpling thunder of sails flapping. Eleanor could see, against the starry sky, one staysail after another climbing its stay, shaking for a moment and then stiffening into its firm curved shape as the sheets were hauled taut. Behind her, all was still quiet on the sealer, and nothing moved on her deck.

By the time the whale-boat was alongside, the stout old ship had started to move, sluggishly, but with a quiet murmur, through the water. A wooden-stepped boarding-ladder rattled as it unrolled down to them. 'You first, Nelli,' whispered Raven. Up she went, and Carl's huge hands were there to grasp her and steady her over the bulwark. In her state of cold terror, her words of thanks came out in the wrong language for that occasion: *'O, dioch yn fawr i ti, Carl!'* But Carl needed no translation – her eyes said everything. Raven and Protheroe received no such gallant attention, but simply clambered up, sprawled splay-legged over the bulwark and landed anyhow on the deck.

As Raven leapt to his feet, Noah, busy unfastening the boarding-ladder, whispered, 'You done real good, mister.'

'No time for talking, man! Three more stays'ls to set. Get that done, and then get every man jack down aft to set the spanker tops'l – and at the bloody double too! I'll take the wheel now. Nelli, go round and make sure every light is doused.'

True to his orders, Tucker had the slow-moving ship pointing exactly where she had before – roughly east, with the north wind on her port beam. Without a word Raven motioned him away and grasped the spokes. He saw and felt at once that they were still very far from safe. The two ships had lain for many hours parallel, beam-on to the wind, but pointing in opposite directions, only some thirty or forty yards apart, the schooner, unfortunately, down-wind. The moderate breeze was moving the 'Pawtucket' ahead, but the old girl was no clipper, able to sprint ahead in the lightest breeze; instead, under the pressure of the wind on her sails, she was making a dangerous amount of leeway, drifting sideways towards her perilously-close enemy. For every yard forward she sagged a good foot sideways, but if he were to steer her closer to the wind she'd stop altogether. Hold your nerve, man, he said inwardly. Outwardly, he croaked quietly in almost his Albert Crowe manner at the men working at the mizenmast: 'For Christ's sake pull your fingers out, you bloody sojers, or we'll be into her! *Come on!*'

He could just make out the aftermost point of the schooner – the end of her long main boom, which projected some feet over her counter. The 'Pawtucket's' aftermost part – her spanker boom – must clear that. It was going to be a close-run thing; the gap between them was shrinking, shrinking. If only this old hooker would *move*! If the spars fouled, or – much worse – if the hulls collided, that must wake up the drunkest of drunks. They would tumble up on deck, see the whaler moving, and then know they'd been hoodwinked all along. Lopez would be further enraged by the brutal destruction of his rigging.

But they'd no doubt got spare blocks and cordage down below. In a few hours they could re-rig after a fashion, and that schooner was so fast! If the whaler's crew were to survive, it was vital that the sealers should all sleep till well after dawn.

Closing one eye, he took a rough bearing of the sealer's boom-end. If that bearing didn't shift, or shifted to the left, it was inevitable that they'd hit her. The gap had now narrowed to half. My God, he thought, she's less than a cricket-pitch away!

And then, suddenly, he felt a strong gust of wind ruffle his hair, felt, with unutterable joy, the wheel come alive in his hands as the good old girl surged forward and tried to luff up into the blustering squall. Thank God – some good luck for a change! He let her come up a few points; he heard the growing chuckle of her wash, he saw the big, gaff-rigged spanker sail at last hoisted, sheeted in and pulling well, and, turning his head to starboard, saw the schooner's counter horribly close, but drawing rapidly astern.

'Noah!' he called quietly. 'Come back here. We're going clear, but we're not safe yet by a damn long chalk. Tell everybody: dead silence, and no lights of any sort anywhere – not even a match. Aloft now and set the main t'gallant, and tell em to be bloody quick about it.'

Fifteen minutes later the schooner's stern-light was a distant twinkle in the wake, but Raven's manner was still urgent, unrelaxed. This was still no time for triumph. He called to Amos nearby: 'Get Noah and Mr Tucker here, pronto!'

When they assembled, Raven began: 'So far, so good, but we're heading east – the wrong way, of course.

I'm going to bear away and put her before the wind, so free up the sheets for that, and square off the t'gallant yard.' A few quiet orders from Noah sent the hands scuttling to set the sails for the new course. Then Raven went on: 'We'll go south for a mile or so, then gybe her round to head north-west by west, the course for Bluff....'

Tucker was open-mouthed with astonishment and displeasure: 'But you young fool, that's...'

'Wait, wait! Hear me out. I know what you're going to say: that's what Lopez is expecting, so he might still be able to overhaul us. But no, of course we're not really going to Bluff. But think: just suppose that, at dawn, one of those sots wakes up, sees that we've gone, and catches sight of the morning sun on our t'gallant sail? We can't be sure to be clear out of sight by then, can we? So then, I reckon, Lopez will think that that part of our story was true, and when he's re-rigged, he'll chase us that way. But obviously, by the time he's re-rigged, we will be well out of sight, so – once we're quite sure of that - we up helm again and run down south to Auckland Island. I've taken care not to mention Auckland to them, so surely he'll never dream that we'd go that way. There's no ship repair yards down there, are there? Just a few bare, cold, uninhabited islands and then nothing but sea till you get to Antarctica and the ice. No, I reckon he will head for Bluff, and if he doesn't find us on the way there, he'll try further north – Otago Harbour, say. So, I trust, he will not come within miles of us and then, I fervently hope, we will never see that shipload of murderous bastards again. How richly that ship deserves to be sent to the bottom by one of these new torpedo things that the Navy uses, but alas we didn't have one for them.'

Tucker shook his head, and at last his broad cheeks were split in a beaming smile. 'And to think,' he said, 'that up to now I have always considered sailors, with all their faults, to at least be plain honest souls! But you, sir, have proved yourself a worthy modern successor to the great Niccolo Machiavelli himself, and I – to my soul's peril – have been your assistant in the deepest, most mendacious, chicanery.'

'Indeed, sir, you are right to be wary of him.' They all turned to see Eleanor behind them, and there was a smile in her voice. 'He is a double-dyed villain through and through. How else could such a man have inveigled and wormed his way into my innocent and girlish affections? I know him well, gentlemen. Never trust him!'

Raven replied with a pretended sternness: 'I am trying to steer this damn ship properly. How can I concentrate if you are bothering me with silly chit-chat? Noah, let's attend to business: I think we've gone down-wind enough, so I'm going to bring her round to starboard to steer west. Tell the lads to stand by to sheet in on the starboard tack.'

'Okay, mister. But by the Lord Jesus, sir, if you talking about steering, you ran us mighty close to that schooner's main boom just now. We was all a-sweating to see how close!'

'Close?' said Raven. 'There was nothing to worry about. I should say I missed it by a good eighteen inches... well, no, perhaps ....fifteen.'

CHAPTER NINETEEN

A sunny dawn, and the slim black schooner 'Bonito' rolling sharply in the bright daylight, broadside-on to the steep little waves kicked up by the northerly breeze, and pitching to the long, slow swell from the west. The lop of the sea dislodged a heavy wooden block, and it slid down the slope of the deck, hitting the cheek of AB Schultz, one of the appointed lookouts, as he lay in a drink-sodden sleep amidships.

The blow knocked him into a bleary, woozy consciousness and the awareness of a skull-splitting headache. A block? Why was that sculling about loose? He became aware of a strange, total silence on the ship. There was wind, but no sound of taut halyards frapping against the mast. Was he dreaming? Then came a quiet rumble and a sharp clink as an empty bottle rolled up against a ringbolt. Into his thick, dense brain there came the sound of low groans.

He opened his eyes, wincing at the stab of the bright sun. The upturned sole of a boot was close to his bleary eyes; he followed the line of the serge-clad leg and body. One of his shipmates was flat on his face in the scupper, groaning as the motion jolted his head.

Schultz sat up abruptly, and at once a deadly nausea drove him to retch long and convulsively onto the deck. That bloody whisky! Why did I have to drink the lot?

Struggling to his knees, he saw that the fallen man was Tommy Kanaka, and saw too that the curly bush of his head was matted with dried blood; saw also, not far off, the inert carcass of Dutchy Lindstrom, his fellow supposed lookout. Staggering at last to his feet, unsteady in the ship's sharp rolling motion, he became aware of more oddities: the mainmast staysails were in a chaotic heap on the main hatch; further for'ard, two inner jibs were the same. Still stupid with pain and drunkenness, he turned his eyes to the masts: something about them was wrong – but what? Then, with a wrench of fear and horror, he saw the fearful signs of destruction: no taut halyards going down to the fife-rails at the foot of the masts! And at the end of the booms, no sheets, no blocks! Holy God, some a them bastards from the whaler - they must have come aboard and cut off and slung overboard every inch of running rigging while we was out cold! Jesus Christ, Lopez will kill us for this – we wasn't supposed to drink nothing!

In his terror he stumbled over to the prone body of the other 'lookout' and stirred him roughly with his boot, yelling: 'Dutchy! Dutchy! Wake up! Look what some bastards have done! We gonna git killed for this!'

The strident voice awoke the drunken skipper and mate, sprawled on sofas below in the mess-room. Lopez growled: 'Slim, git up there and tell them idiots to quit shouting. My head's bad enough without that racket. I bin drunk and hung-over often enough before, but never like this. What was in that goddam liquor? Shut them noisy bastards up and then roust out the rest of the crowd. You was right; that was just a trick, that booze. And it was spiked too. Now, by Christ, I'll make em suffer!'

Connolly blundered up on deck and Lopez heard him exclaim in horror: 'Holy God! What the hell has happened here?' Then he yelled back down the companionway: 'Make em suffer, will you, you bloody stupid mutt? Well, will you just come up here and see for yourself. You ain't seen nothing yet – you don't know the half of it.'

Lopez, pale and sick, at once took in the utter ruin of his ship's rigging. He saw Schultz swaying, clutching a shroud, his face a mask of misery and terror; saw Tommy Kanaka stretched out; saw Lindstrom struggling to his feet. In a terrible whisper Lopez said: 'You pair of miserable useless bastards! What happened?'

Schultz gibbered: 'They… they… There was six of em…got aboard in the dark. We never seen em coming. They… they laid us out before we could shout…. Look at Dutchy Lindstrom – he's only just coming round. We couldn't help it, cap'n.'

Without a word Lopez chopped him to the deck with a heavy back-hand blow, then drew back and kicked him savagely in the ribs: 'Liar! Bloody goddam liar! Six of em got aboard and you didn't see em nor hear em? And what about these bottles? Who swigged all that whisky down? Who gave you those? I'm gonna string you both up and take the skin off of yer backs till you tell me.'

'Never mind him,' said Connolly. 'Just take a look out there on the starboard beam, will yer, where the whaler was. Where is she now? I don't know, nor you don't know neither. Did you think they'd hang around to see how we felt this morning? You may be that stupid, but I can see they ain't. I'll get aloft with a glass, but she'll be miles off by now – outa sight, most likely. Wouldn't it be better to start getting rigged again, stead of beating the shit outa these useless skunks?'

'How long's it gonna take us to get re-rigged, Slim?'

'No idea. You tell me – you're the clever one, you say. Don't ask me for no more advice; just do what you think. I'm off this hooker as soon as we touch land. I kept telling you, but what was the use? Too goddam stupid to run a bumboat, you are, Lopez.'

'Less of your bloody lip, paddy, or you'll be gitting a hiding too!'

'What? From you? Bullshit! I been a boxer in my time, and I can fight real dirty too. I've laid out plenty of bigger and better men than you, dago. I'm off aloft, but I'll see sod-all, that's for sure.'

Frustrated, Lopez turned on the two terrified seamen: 'You miserable skunks, douse yer heads under the pump, and then git all hands on deck. I'll deal with you two real good later. If you hadn a bin pissed as arseholes no-one could a got aboard without you knowing. I guess Tommy Kanaka just came up on deck to take a puke while they was busy, so they laid him out. He's the only one to get hurt so far, but I promise you there'll be two more soon. Now... *git!*

He pounded his fists on the bulwark in impotent fury. Cleared off, have they? I'll get em yet! I know where they're headed, and we can do three times their speed, once we get rigged. I'll make em suffer, I will, before they go into the drink. And I'll git my salvage in the end, too. They'll find, by Christ, that they can't fool Charlie Lopez.

Then, as men emerged from the foc'sle scuttle, groaning and clutching their heads, he yelled: 'You and you! Down to the bosun's store and help him bring up all the spare cordage and blocks – pronto!' He ground his teeth and muttered savagely: 'I'll git under way somehow by noon. They won't have gotten far in that old tub – not to Bluff anyways. And when I git aboard you – look out, you goddam Yankees! I'm gonna feed the fishes on what's left of you!'

*

When dawn broke over the whaler, Raven was still at the wheel. The old 'Pawtucket', as if glad to be moving and free at last, was plunging sedately along, leaning, every sail taut and drawing, reeling off the miles from the crippled schooner with ponderous slaps and deep, dull booms as her bluff bows butted the short seas, sending light showers of spray over the weather bulwark as she pounded her way westward.

Noah came up from his cabin, yawning, stretching, rubbing his tight grizzled curls. 'By damn, mister, that the best sleep I've had for many a weary night.'

'Morning, bosun! Good for you! Get all the hands up now, will you? Before the watch on deck goes below I want to set the main tops'l. What do you think? Easy enough to set it, but can we furl it? There's no sign of a gale at present, and I need more speed.'

'Mister, we'll go set it, and in this wind we'll furl it too if'n we need to.'

They both staggered and took an involuntary step as the whaler, with a deep boom, dropped her bow into a trough and almost stopped. 'You feel that?' said Raven. 'That's been growing for the last two hours – a swell from the west, running clean across the north wind. We both know what that means – some damned dirty weather ahead.'

'Yeah, for sure we in for another bad westerly blow – t'morrer, maybe. But don't you mind, mister, she'll stand it. The only reason she got damaged before was my blame stupidity in setting too much canvas, like I told you that first day you come aboard. You too good a sailor to do that. If'n it gits too bad, you just heave her to with a couple of storm stays'ls, an she ride anything like a cork. Make a lotta leeway o course.'

'I believe you. So it makes sense to push her as far to the west as we can while we've got this decent north wind. Then she might fetch Auckland Island on the one tack, even in a blow. But we've got to be careful; that top-s'l's a big, deep old sail, isn't it?'

Noah shook his head, smiling, his eyes moist: 'You dead right there. An I tell you what, Mr Raven, sir: scuse me talking like this, but you's a real man, with an old head on them young shoulders. Ain't many your age with the guts and brains to do what you done last night with them devils. You the skipper for me, Jack. Be damned if I've seen your like.'

Raven gave an embarrassed grin: 'Good of you to say that, Noah, but I couldn't have done it without the rest of you. And after all, we were caught like rats in a trap - we had to do something pretty desperate.'

'Maybe, maybe, but by the good Lord, you was a blame good King Rat! But you want that tops'l set, so I'll stop blathering and boot them guys aloft to let go the gaskets. And when that sail's set, I'm back here to take over that wheel. How come you didn't roust me out to give yourself a spell? You bin there at it since two o'clock.'

'Yes, s'pose I have. I remember some time having to get George to fetch a bucket, so I could have a leak. I've been nursing her along to get the best speed out of her. But there's something important to do before you set that top-s'l.' He raised his voice: 'Jim, it's full daylight now. Nip up to the main t'gallant crosstrees with the telescope and have a real good look astern – and I hope to God you see nothing of that bloody schooner. They may all be awake by now, and looking for us. But if we can't see their mastheads, they can't see ours.'

Eleanor appeared on deck, rubbing her eyes and shivering in the cool brisk wind. 'Jack, you poor thing!' she said in a motherly tone. 'Have you been at that wheel all night? You must be exhausted!'

'Yes, I do feel a bit tired, now it's daylight and everyone's turning-to. I've been concentrating too much on learning to steer this good old hooker to feel tired till now. I haven't done a trick at the wheel since I was a brassbounder. Jim's aloft with a glass to make sure we're not being followed. Then we're going to set that big main tops'l. I want you on deck at the foot of the mast to help, letting go the clewlines and buntlines, and then hauling in the sheets.'

'Aye aye, *capten bach, syr!'* she said with a playful grin.

'Did you sleep well, Nelli?'

'Not at first, because of all the excitement and anxiety. But once I knew you were at the helm and could feel the ship well under way, I slept better than I have ever done. All that dreadful fear and tension had exhausted me too. Once that was gone, it was as if I'd drunk a pint of Mr Tucker's laudanum. Now I feel ashamed to have been so torpid and idle, all that time. Listen, my lad: once that sail's set, Noah will take the wheel and you'll have some breakfast, and then get into your bunk and stay there snoring – all day if you like!'

'Aye aye, ma'am, just as you say. Except that I'll need to be back up on deck at noon. There will be things to do by then. Anyway, you look lively now, Roberts, and stand by to slack off the main tops'l buntlines!'

'Sir!' Able Seawoman Roberts stamped her feet to attention and gave a mocking salute. 'I will, *capten,* when somebody shows me which ropes they are. I'm not very "able" yet, you know.'

A thin cry came down from Protheroe: 'Deck, there! Nothing, mister! Nothing, nowhere astern! We've lost the buggers!'

The brief shout gave them both a flood of joy and blessed relief. 'Thank God, Jack!' said Eleanor fervently, 'but thank you too!' She stepped close behind him, linked her arms around his waist, drew him close, binding their bodies together, and breathed in his ear: 'My hero! – as helpless heroines in silly books always say! But I'm not really mocking now, Jack, I mean it. You took a horrible risk, and now we owe our lives to you.'

'Jim came too, don't forget.'

'I know, and all credit to him. But you devised the plan, thought it out and decided to do it. You knew – so did we all – that if it failed, that would have been the end of us, and what my end might have been like – that doesn't bear thinking of. Taking on that fearful responsibility – the decision to *do* something, to attack that schooner, and not just dither and hope for the best – that's what showed you to be a real *capten* and a real hero. I'm so proud of you, Jack!'

This frank, odd, back-to-front public embrace, this flow of loving praise, brought back all Raven's awkward, comical, English embarrassment: 'Thanks, Nelli. Good of you to say so. I've had Noah here, saying much the same. Didn't hug me though, I'm very glad to say. But come on, we've got important things to do now, Nelli. I've got to steer, and they need you at the mainmast, so….'

'All right, all right, I'm going. You're almost as bad as a horrible mate we had once called Albert Crowe!' And as she went she drew back her hand and gave him a hefty, affectionate whack on the behind.

He called after her: 'Ow! That hurt! Striking a superior officer! That's serious! Fifty lashes for you, sailor!'

By now, while Noah waited on deck, Carl, Jim, Amos and George had swarmed up the shrouds and were edging out sideways along the foot-ropes of the topsail yard. One by one, the rope gaskets holding in the folds of the sail were loosed, so that the sail became a huge, rumpling, booming bag of wind. Raven steered the ship downwind to ease the wind pressure on the sail. Noah, Nelli and Tucker let go the clewlines and buntlines, and the big sail descended, its ponderous flaps shaking the whole mast, so that the men coming down from the yard had to hang on tight.

Noah yelled: 'Sheets!' and all three put all their weight into hauling on the sheet-tackles, which drew down and fastened the sail's bottom corners. That was a heavy job that was completed only when the men from aloft added their strength. At last the sail was set; it filled, was quiet, and took up its beautiful curved shape. Now it was time to get the ship back on her westerly course and trim the angle of the sail to the wind. Raven shouted: 'Braces! Bring her to reach on the starboard tack!'

Noah called: 'All hands! Lee braces – haul! Put your goddam backs into it!' This was a massive heave for so few, and it needed Jimmy's high, rhythmic chant to coordinate their efforts: 'Two-six – *hup!* Two-six – *heavy!* Two-six – *hi!* Two-six – *break her!'* Slowly, while Noah slacked off the weather brace, the powerful tackles swung the yard and its sail round to lie diagonally across the ship. Raven eased her gently round to due west; as the ship came broadside-on to the brisk wind, she sedately gathered speed. With a loud *boom* she stuck her bluff bow into a steep, short sea, throwing up a burst of solid spray, which the breeze drove back over the bulwark to drench the party on deck, but, instead of curses, Raven heard child-like, happy squeals and shrieks of surprise and shock. He grinned and thought: That sounds good. We're going to be all right now.

Noah came aft, also grinning: 'That's more like sailing, eh? That's give em all a wet arse and no fish, Jack. You git below now, sir, and git your head down. You've had a long trick at that ole wheel – too damn long – so away you go now. I keep her going due west, eh?'

'Aye aye; due west. But I want a shake at noon, mind. I'm going to alter course then.'

*

Gloomy twilight, and a ship rolling sluggishly in a light wind. John Raven lay on a greasy, bloodstained deck, writhing, struggling, to free himself from the strong hands holding him down, but unable to rise an inch from the planks. Wrenching his head sideways, he could see Jimmy Protheroe lying prone nearby, the back of his head bloody, his bleeding face full of harsh reproach. He was saying in a low, droning voice: 'It's all up, Raven, you fool. All up with the lot of us...all up... all up... you shouldn't a done it, you bloody pup... now we're all finished.'

In the dim, dirty-brown light Raven saw Lopez' face

above him, very close. He could smell the brandy and tobacco on his breath. Lopez' voice was low, grating: 'He's goddam right there, Mr lying bastard Raven – or Crowe – or whatever you call yerself now. It's all up with the fucking lot of you. Thought you'd give us the slip, did you? Cut my rigging up, would you? Well, I got a knife too.' Raven felt a sharp agony as the cold steel point of the knife pricked his neck. Terror made all his muscles fail; he could only shout 'No! No! No!'

From the dimness behind Lopez he heard the gruff Welsh voice of his old captain, Jacob Roberts – Eleanor's father – booming: 'You bloody stupid *Sais*, Raven! I should never have made you up to third mate. What sort of an officer have *you* turned out to be?'

Lopez gave a low, thick chuckle: 'Don't you worry, cap. He's gonna feed the fishes, but not till I've done with him, and that'll take a while.'

Then Lopez grasped his shoulders and shook him hard, harder, and all at once John was not on deck, but in a dark, stuffy cabin. The face above him was not Lopez' face but Eleanor's, white and tense. It was Eleanor's hands grasping, shaking his shoulders. Then it was Eleanor's voice speaking, full of a frantic anxiety, which burst out in her native tongue: '*O Iesu Mawr, beth sy'n bod? Beth sy'n bod, cariad?* (What's the matter, darling?) Jack, Jack, are you ill?'

Raven jolted awake, but the nightmare's horror had not gone. Whimpering, sweating, he gasped hoarsely: 'O Nelli, Nelli, thank Christ it's you! Thank God! I've been having a most horrible dream. My plan had all gone wrong. Jim and I were on the schooner, captured. Lopez was pushing me down onto the deck. He had a knife…he was going to…it was all so *real!'*

'Jack, Jack, *don't!* Don't even try to remember any more of it. It was only a horrible dream – a nightmare. Forget it! Put it all behind you.'

Raven attempted a smile: 'What a captain! What a hero! Lying here blubbing like a baby! Pathetic, isn't it?'

'No, Jack, it's the most natural thing in the world, after the agony of mind you must have gone through last night. No-one can control his or her subconscious mind. You know that I've suffered in the same way.' She too gave a little smile: 'Maybe even Nelson had dreams like that.'

'My God, I was so frightened last night, Nelli, aboard that schooner – more than I've ever been. My mouth was all dry, with a horrible, sick, coppery taste in it. No, I'll never be a hero, I'm afraid.'

'Jack, you donkey, that's what *makes* you a hero – having that fear, but being able to conquer it, to hide it from your crew, to turn it into action. If I were your old English queen, I'd give you the Victoria Cross on the spot. As it is, you will have to be content with this.' Gently pushing him back onto his pillow, she covered his mouth with hers in a kiss which began as one of motherly comfort, but grew into a long, glued kiss in which pity and gratitude flowed slowly into sheer, deep, headlong desire. At last she felt her own cold husk of grief, terror and physical revulsion crack, split open, to allow much of her old reckless passion for him to burst into vivid life again. Murmuring wordlessly, she moved to spread her whole upper body over his, and, the long kiss over, they lay breathless at first, cheek to cheek, unspeaking, drinking in, savouring, the intense pleasure of the reunion of their bodies.

Raven's head was whirling, impotent, though he sensed that Nature had made one part of his body only too painfully potent. In minutes he had been passively dragged from extreme, sweating terror into, first, simple relief, and then into fierce, strident pleasure, feeling the delicious sensation of her earnest lips and tongue, feeling too her breasts pressed against his body. He brought his arms from beneath his blankets to enfold her, hold her quite still. Then he breathed hoarsely: 'I know what I would like us to do now, Nelli.'

'*Cariad*, you can tell that my body feels and wants the same, but we mustn't, must we? It's not the time or place. It's noon; you have got captainish things to do, and I'm going to try hard to be a good girl till we're married. Besides,' she sat up on the edge of his bunk, a little withdrawn from him, 'what happened to me on the island was so gross, so disgusting, so horrible, that I still haven't quite got over it. I still don't feel I can happily open the most intimate parts of my body to a man's hands – not even to yours, my darling, though a part of me longs to feel your gentle hands on my body – anywhere on my body. I'm so sorry, Jack. I know it's irrational and stupid, but I can't help it. At present we're much alike, Jack. Your dreams are haunted by terror of what might so easily have happened to you on that schooner, mine by horrible fear of what so nearly happened to me in the cove. After all, it was only by chance that you realized so soon that I might be in trouble. And as for my fate if I'd been captured alive by that rabble manning the sealer, well, I can't bear to think of it. So I'm not ready to…'

He took her hand and said simply: 'Nell, *cariad,* you and I are going to be together till we die. You're not stupid to obey deep feelings like those. They will pass in time, and we have all the time in the world. There'll come a time when we can make love how we like, as often as we like; when your body will be mine, and mine yours to touch and explore. Nightmares won't last forever. And now, my love, you'd better let me get up on deck.'

Minutes later, up on deck, he took his captain's look round at the sky and the sea to windward and the set of the sails. He felt a flood of affection for the stout old 'Pawtucket' as she butted, shouldered, tumbled and thumped her way through the steep beam seas. He went aft, to where Noah stood at the wheel.

'She's going well, bosun, but it's time to get off this westerly course. This is the way we said we'd go, so this is the course "Bonito" will steer when she's rigged. I've been thinking things out: we started out at two o'clock last night. Let's guess that it was about eight o'clock before they were up and doing. We were very under-canvassed, doing five knots at the most, so by then we were only thirty miles away from them. I reckon it would take them three or four hours to get fully re-rigged, but once her sails were set, she'd go twice our speed at least. I've been trying to think myself into Lopez' head: he will rule out our going east, I'm sure, with a crew of our size, and thousands of miles to the nearest Chilean port – say Talcahuano. He will think we will indeed head for Bluff and hope to beat him to it. But he may think, especially when the wind changes to west or south-west, that we'd head further north, up the east coast – to Otago, say. He will never, I hope and believe, think that we'd head south, so that's where we must go – and go *now*. So I'll take the wheel. Away you go now and muster the hands to square the yards as I bring her round to port. Then send Carl aft to take the wheel while you and I get below for some dinner. I've just realized that I'm bloody starving. How about you?'

'Bloody starving is right, mister. Guess we didn't eat so good last night, with them murdering bastards so close on the beam.'

Once off the wind, the whaler's speed was reduced; as she sedately made her way south by west, the following seas made her roll, the masts moving in wide arcs across the sky, the yard-arms sometimes dipping close to the water. To compound the motion, the huge, growing westerly swells alternately raised and dropped her fifteen or so feet. Down in the mess-room Tucker and Eleanor had been forced to fit the fiddles – the small upright slats of wood that formed a low wall round the table's edge to stop cutlery and plates from clattering to the deck. Only strong stomachs like this crew's could fancy the steaming savoury plates of cracker-hash today.

'Sorry about this motion, everybody,' said Raven. 'But don't worry, there's worse to come. I can feel this good north wind easing all the time and the swell from the west growing. Noah and I are sure we're in for a westerly gale soon; the barometer's dropping too.'

'So it will be a long time before we see Auckland Island?' asked Eleanor gloomily.

'No, cheer up, Nelli. If a gale comes from due west we should be able to head straight for Enderby Island, as we've come a good way west already. Under shortened sail we can stay on this course, even in a gale. - for a while, anyway. The only problem is this: with the fine weather we've had so far I've been able to get good sun-sights, so I know where we are now, but if we get days of cloud and wind it'll be all dead reckoning from now on, so we'll have to heave-to every evening. We may come across some ice-floes or small bergs; and besides, I don't want to find Enderby Island by hitting it in the dark. But this old barque won't mind a gale of wind, will she, Noah?'

'No sir-*ree!* She ain't no clipper, nor she ain't no yacht, but you handle her right and the debbil himself couldn't sink her.'

*

As a cloudy dawn broke over Ross Harbour, AB Tydfil Jones, high up at the lookout post on the slopes of Mount Hooker, Auckland Island, sprang to his feet and, gasping for breath, started to drag bunches of small dry branches from under a rocky overhang. That done, he shoved a malodorous fat-soaked bundle of rags under them and pulled a match-box from his pocket. Overhead, the last of the gale blustered among the rocks, but here, in this little dip, there was blessed calm and shelter. He muttered to himself as the match spluttered into life and was held to the rags: 'Now come on, you bugger! Catch light! Catch light, for God's sake, can't you?'

It could. Little dark-red flames and black smoke, reeking of rancid beef fat, arose. The tinder-dry twigs caught, then the crisply-crackling flames took hold of the small branches. As the smoke rose, the blustering wind caught it and streamed it eastward over Ross Harbour. 'Good boy, good boy,' the seaman muttered excitedly, as, reaching into the shallow cave, he hauled out thicker lengths of cord-wood to build the small blaze into a majestic bonfire. Good old Reuben bosun, he thought. We all cursed him when he made us drag all this dry wood right up here to the top of the cliff, but he was dead right. I've got a good old blaze going in ten minutes. *Da iawn!* Well done, old Reub! And look out there! A blinking ship at last! Now I'll pile on some of the greener stuff and some of these damn great old sods of grass. Now it's daylight it's smoke we wants. Someone aboard that hooker will surely see that lot! Let's have another look at her afore I goes down: she's a long way off still – wish I had a telescope by here. But I can see she's a small barque. She's headed straight for us, but she's coming real slow cos she's only using stays'ls. Can't see no proper square-sails set. Bloody odd, that, with the wind abeam. Never mind – off I goes!

After throwing on some more branches he set off, trotting and stumbling down the rough track, stony here, boggy there, that the lookouts had made during the long weeks of their stay. The path wound across a plain between rocky outcrops and huge wild tufts of coarse grass, till it plunged down a steep slope into clusters of massive, dripping tree-ferns among the rocks, and then into a gloomy belt of thick, twisted rata trees, where a cleared path led down to the camp.

The camp was silent as he ran out from the forest. A smudge of smoke rose up from the banked-up galley fire. He burst noisily, unceremoniously, panting, into the hut and ran down the row of bunks, yelling: '*Bois! Bois!* Wake up, you lazy buggers! There's a ship in the offing. Come on!'

He did the same, more politely, in the store where, in Eleanor's absence, Grant and bosun now slept: 'Mister Grant, sir! *Capten!* There's a ship coming in! Honest, a ship! Not far off, neither!'

Both officers had had years of experience of sudden, urgent awakenings, and both sat up, dazed but struggling for alertness: 'A ship? What ship?' said Grant. 'D'you mean the rescue steamer? And don't yell, man – we're not deaf. Calm down, for God's sake!'

The breathless Jones gulped with the effort at restraint. His chest heaving from his long run down, he said: 'No, not a steamer, sir – a smallish barque, I'd say. But she's still a good way off, and it ain't good light yet. She's off to the left of Enderby Island, heading due south for the gap between it and that little Rose Island.'

'Good for her. She's got a clear channel a mile wide there. The other side of Rose Island the channel's got a nasty little skerry of rocks slap in the middle. Her skipper must know this place. We'll go down to the cove; she should appear round the point soon. You've lit the fire, of course?'

'O aye sir, and a good smoky one too. But you don't need to hurry too much; she's coming real slow cos she's a tubby old thing, and only got her fore-and-aft sails set. Of course, she was end-on to me, so I can't tell you much more about her.'

'No, but well done indeed, Jones. Come on, bosun, let's get our duds on and get down there.'

In the bunkhouse too there was hectic chaos as the men, laughing and joking in their relief, huddled on their clothes. Curly Kellock, grinning, bawled out the old Navy wake-up cry: 'Carm on! Turn out, turn out! Hands off cocks, and on wiv yer socks!'

Ten minutes later, on that dull, chill, windy Auckland morning, the shore of the cove was lined with an eager, untidy mob, all gazing earnestly at the gap between Rose Island and the much bigger Enderby Island. It struck Grant that the last time they had gathered there it had been to say goodbye to the four in the quarter-boat. Where were they now, after two deadly storms? Alive? Dead? They'd been gone so long, and their boat was so small and frail. When, if ever, would he see them again?

The everlasting wind had raised small choppy waves in the strait's grey water. The men were silent now, their souls fixed on rescue and release from this dreary, wet, windy underworld. 'Yes!' Grant cried. 'Look, you can see her masts above the corner of Rose Island!' A cheer went up. 'But Jones was right: she's taking it damn slowly. You can see now, she's only got umpteen stays'ls and the spanker set. Odd, that, Reuben. If I were her skipper, I'd have at least the tops'ls set, to push her through the tide out there.'

'Ah, but I can see why now,' said bosun. 'Now she's getting closer you can see there's something wrong with her foremast. She ain't got no proper topmast nor t'gallant mast – only a little stump thing. A lame duck, she is. But fair play, her skipper knows his business. Now he's clear of the island he's luffed up a bit, heading straight for where we're standing. He knows his way round this place, no mistake. A Yankee whaler, I'd say. mister. She looks as if she's got a full cargo, so she's likely come in here to do some repairs, and take on fresh water, ready for the trip back to Nantucket. Well, God knows we got plenty of water for him here.'

'Aye, but from what I've heard about whalers, he may have been hoping to help himself to grub from the Government store, as well as water. So if he's seen all of us here, and our smoke, he'll know he's in for a disappointment there.'

There was a dead silence on the beach now. Grant was suddenly struck to the heart by a spasm of emotion – a spasm in which grief and guilt were evenly mixed. So here it was at last – a ship, but only an old whaler. Had it been the rescue steamer he'd been longing for, it might have been carrying the crew of the quarter-boat, safe and sound despite the horrific storms they'd gone through. As it was - she was just a whaler. All they could hope for from her was a trip to Bluff Harbour. That was something. But Raven and his party had been gone for a good three weeks now. They had not got to Bluff Harbour to alert the steamer - that was certain. That meant that he had sent three young people and a splendid older seaman to their deaths. He'd allowed himself to be persuaded, against his better judgment, by Eleanor, because of his love and pity for her, and now, for ever, the guilt was his. A whole family wiped out; mother by typhus, father by shipwreck and despair, and now a beautiful daughter, barely twenty – all gone. He'd been the captain, the 'master under God', as Eleanor's father used to say, and he had failed in his duty of total responsibility. And now they were all gone.

As she came into calmer water and less breeze in the lee of Mount Hooker's two-thousand-foot bulk, the old barque came upright and slowed till there was only a ripple under her bluff bows. The men on the beach, quiet with longing for their release, murmured a comment now and then: 'She's a whaler all right, said Holy Parry. 'Funny-looking old thing – big white davits port and starboard, but only one boat on em.'

'Aye,' said Lewis. 'And another damn funny, thing:

there's not many on deck yet. On'y half-a-dozen, if that. Drat, you'd think all her crowd would a been turned out by now, to get the hook down and the sails off of her.'

Slowly she glided on till she was precisely in the middle of the cove. Then they heard faintly the rumpling of her sails as their sheets were slackened, the bow-wave disappearing as she luffed up into the wind, losing way. There was a total, rapt silence on the beach at the sight of her. For endless dull weeks the men had seen nothing but the island, with its grim twisted forests, high rocky slopes, its racing clouds, rough water, the seals and the sea-birds, and, of course, each other. Now at last a vessel had appeared, with new people on her, from the outside world – a vessel which, though ancient, slow and lamed by storms, might yet change their lives.

As the ship came to a halt they heard clearly a cry from aft: 'Let go!' They saw a man on the foc'sle raise a heavy hammer, heard a sharp clink as he knocked out the pin holding the chain, and then the sound most stirring, most welcome to a sailor's ear – the hollow rattle and rumble of the anchor-cable as it roared out of the hawse-pipe to end the voyage.

The huddled castaways raised a raucous cheer and ran to the water's edge, but Grant and Reuben stood, exchanging sharp, astonished looks, and Reuben said quietly: 'That "Let go!" – that didn't sound like no Yankee skipper to me.'

'No,' said Grant. You're damn right it didn't. If it wasn't so absolutely impossible I'd have said that voice belonged to… No, that's stupid…Couldn't possibly have been him.'

'Him?' said Reuben. 'Yes, I knows who you mean –

the young feller. But we're being bloody ridiculous, mun. How the hell could be him?'

'It's damned infuriating not to have glasses to give us a better look. But we'll know the truth - quite soon, too.' Grant's sharp eyes had caught sight of a figure running for'ard under the shaking sails to stand up on the heel of the bowsprit, grasping the fore-stay for support. He had a long speaking-trumpet in his other hand. Over the water, in an odd, tinny, hollow, but absolutely clear voice, came the most astonishing words that any of them would ever hear in their lives – ever! *'Bore da, bob un! Shwd ych chi bore'ma, te? Iawn?'*

There was an answering roar of amazement and laughter from the beach: *'Iesu Mawr!'* cried one man. 'I knows that voice! It's that cheeky bugger Jimmy Protheroe!'

Grant and bosun shared the amazement: Reuben gasped: 'We was right then, mister. After all, if Jimmy's for'ard, it's likely that young Raven's aft. But how come he's...?'

'What did Protheroe say then?'

'O, nothing much. Just his usual damn nonsense. Twas just as if he was meeting some of his neighbours on Fishguard Square, like. He just said "Good morning all. How are you today, then? All right?"'

'Typical! Still full of his cheek! But how come John Raven's not just aboard a Yankee whaler, but in charge of her too? It makes no sense to me. But still' - a sudden gust of doubtful joy swept him –'if Raven and Protheroe are aboard, surely that means that Eleanor and Carl may be safe too?'

'We'll know soon, mun. Now they've doused all

them stays'ls, they're lowering a boat and - *Iesu Mawr!* - that's our old quarter-boat! I can see the foredeck we put on it. And there's six, seven…no, eight of em piling into it, and – drop dead! - not a soul left on deck now! Let's just hope and pray, mister, that the *capten's* girl is one of em – and good old Carl too. But *eight* people to crew a barque like that on an ocean voyage? It's all mad!'

'Indeed. But I can't see Raven coming back without Eleanor - can you? And our precious Jimmy Protheroe – he's a card right enough, he is. They've been through one of the worst Southern Ocean storms I've ever seen, in an open boat, then they've somehow got command of an old whaler, and brought her back through another really bad blow these last two days – with a crew of just *eight,* apparently. Only themselves and four others, and God knows who they might be. And all he says is "Good morning all!" D'you know, bosun, I'm beginning to think we're seeing and hearing things – that this bloody awful island has driven us all barmy – clean barmy on the crumpet!'

*

The 'really bad blow' – a sailor's euphemism for a terrifying storm – of two days back, had, of course, struck the 'Bonito' as well, but aboard her there had been no harmony. The hands had watched as Lopez himself gave the two erring lookouts a merciless and bloody flogging, and now Connolly was every day more mutinous and more scornful of his captain.

For a whole day and a night the schooner, overcanvassed and heeling till her lee rail was awash, had struggled, staggered to windward against the westerly gale, close-hauled on her course to Bluff Harbour, her lookouts straining their eyes every moment for a sight of their slow, wallowing quarry. But still – nothing - nothing but the huge, grey, white-streaked flanks of the Southern Ocean seas.

On the second morning of the storm the schooner's captain and mate stood close by the helmsman on the steeply-sloping deck, Connolly clutching a shroud, Lopez the binnacle for support, each one a dull, glowing furnace of impotent frustration and rage. They hurled their sullen words of mutual hatred into the howling wind. 'It ain't no goddam use, Lopez,' bawled Connolly. "If she'd a been on this course we'd have caught sight of that old tub by now. We on'y lost one night and half the next day, so she couldn't have got that far ahead. Jeez, what kind of speed to windward could she do? Fact is, that old fat Tucker and his limey mate, they outsmarted you back then, and I'll lay my bottom dollar they've done it again. You ain't got no fucking idea where they've gone, and no more have I. We ain't never gonna see that ship no more. You screwed up when you had a good chance back there, and now it's too late. I told you, over and over, that they was just bullshitting you about their plague and all that malarkey, but would you listen?'

'Now you're talking bullshit yerself,' bellowed Lopez. 'You don't know nothing about her crew. How come, if they didn't have no plague, we never saw more'n eight of em, and only six of them proper sailors, eh? How come we saw em to and fro to the foc'sle all day with food and water and buckets and all?'

'Goddam it, they was play-acting to fool us, and

we'd a found that out if we'd boarded her, you lunkhead! We could a done that easy out there – but here? In this blow? Besides, if we was caught taking the ship over and ditching her crew, that'd be a swinging job for all of us. We're too close to the New Zealand shore now – you saw that coasting steamer passing us on'y an hour ago. D'you want a rope round yer neck and an eight-foot drop? I bloody don't!'

'You're so smart, ain't you, you dumb paddy, now it's all happened? You fell for that liquor trick they played on us. You wasn't so smart then, was you? You was pig-drunk down below, remember, with the rest of us.'

'Yeah, and more fool me. But for Christ's sake, *listen!* We had a chance; you screwed it up; now we might as well forget the whole thing, put about and head for Auckland Island and get ourselves some seal-pelts – do our proper job.'

'Jeez, I got an idiot for a mate! This ain't no time to give up! Somewhere – close now – there's forty-thousand bucks-worth of ship and cargo wallowing in the wind. That's worth more than a few stinking seal-skins, ain't it? Why don't we quit quarrelling and git ourselves some dough? Them bastards'll find I'm smarter than them in the long run. But I'll give you this: maybe they ain't on this course now. We gotter think: what would we do now if we was them? Well, now we got a gale from the west instead of that nice northerly breeze, I reckon in their place I'd give up on going to Bluff. I'd decide to dodge them damn sealers that's after me. I'd come off the wind and head up north for Otago – a nice easy reach in this blow. Right then – we'll foller em that way. No time like the present, Slim. Don't you worry, I'll get em in the end.'

He bawled to the watch on deck: 'Ease the sheets, boys!' and to the helmsman: 'Bring her round to nor-nor-west, Rasmussen, and watch your steering, boy, cos with this wind on the beam she'll go like a train. You watch she don't gripe up into the wind.' He raised his voice again: 'You boys for'ard, you keep your eyes skinned. Fifty bucks to the man who spots her first! Any time now, we gonna see our old friends aboard the "Pawtucket" whaler – and won't they just be pleased to see us! So come on, let's get this hooker going. We'll try her with the main tops'l.'

'The tops'l?' shouted Connolly. 'Now I *know* you're goddam raving mad, man! She can't hardly stand the sail she's carrying now! You'll have her flat on her ear! Then what if the cargo shifts? We got a whole lot a bales of skins in the hold. If they shift…'

'She'll stand it all right, so shut yer mouth, you dumb, yaller Irish nancy-boy! Come on, you bloody sojers, git that sail up!'

As she felt the huge leverage of the big, lofty sail, the schooner heeled over… over… over till her lee bulwark was buried. In this shallower part of the ocean the mountainous beam seas were rearing up, horrifyingly steep and high, with solid, breaking, bearded crests of foam. The hapless schooner was lurching, staggering and racing through the deep dark valleys and rising, almost submerged by foam, as the huge, speeding ridges of water passed under her, marching eastwards at a good twenty-five knots. Ignoring the appalling danger, Lopez stood, grasping the binnacle, eyes fixed ahead in a manic, obsessed stare of certainty. Any moment, any moment, his quarry would appear, labouring helplessly at his mercy! They might think themselves smart, but they'd find Charlie Lopez was one hell of a lot smarter!

But the mate had been right: the schooner couldn't stand it. Further, further, further over she heeled, till - the men on the deck staring at each other in blank horror at the sound – there was a deep rumbling thunder that shook the whole ship, as her cargo of tons of bales of seal-skins avalanched down to leeward.

Her end was as swift as it was savage: as she lay, heeled right over on her beam-ends in a deep trough, the helmsman yelled: 'Cain't hold her, cap'n! She's gonna gripe right up ...'

He never finished his last sentence. An immense, streaked cliff of water thundered down, filling the deck, brutally sweeping away the helmsman, the wheel and binnacle, the captain, mate and watch on deck, the galley and deckhouse, felling the over-strained mainmast, bursting in the foc'sle scuttle to drown the men off-watch in their bunks, and then, as the foremast too fell, rolling the 'Bonito' right over till only her weedy, barnacled bottom and keel showed above the dark-grey water.

She, her captain, mate and crew became mere statistics in the grim obituary lists of the Southern Ocean. A reckless lust for greenback dollars had finished them all.

CHAPTER TWENTY

Overhead, at Port Ross, the same old cold, whipping, Auckland wind, racing clouds and gloomy drizzle, but in the hearts of the gazing, longing crowd on the beach, the beginnings of a fierce joy – a joy that made them ignore the damp and the keen breeze on their hastily-clad bodies.

Standing side by side, Welly and Davey exchanged looks of desperate hope and astonishment, and the doctor echoed Grant's words: 'Tell you what, Davey: I can't believe my eyes nor my ears, man. None of this don't make sense, nor seem real.'

'It *is* real, mun! Look! In the stern-sheets! That's her! Look - next to Raven, and a funny old fat man in a big black hat on the other side of her. It's Miss Nelli – she's back! God be praised, He's brought her back to us! Now I'll ...I'll...I'll never swear again, and I'll go to chapel twice every bloody Sunday when I'm home. She's back!'

Joyous tumult, a hubbub of cheering, broke out as the quarter-boat's bow crunched on the shingle and her crew tumbled out. Wellington Jones and Davey jointly seized Eleanor, and would not let her go. Davey clung to her, sobbing uncontrollably. She stroked his damp wispy hair and tried to calm him by making him laugh: 'Davey *bach,* Davey *bach,* you're a strange boy! I come back all this way to you, and all you do is cry. Perhaps I'd better get back in the boat again, is it?'

The greeting of Grant and Raven was equally heartfelt but notably more 'English' and restrained. After a brief manly hug Grant drew back and said: 'God, it's good to see you – all of you – back again, old son! You brought that battered old hooker in a treat and rounded up to come to anchor like a real old harbour pilot. But there's still a hell of a lot I don't understand: you leave here in a lashed-up quarter-boat, in which you must have gone through one of the worst storms I've ever seen, and you and the others come back, with you apparently captain of a whaler, with no crew except Carl and Jim, a long-coated, large-hatted gentleman dressed like a Quaker and three black seamen.'

Raven did not at first respond to his eager curiosity, but instead drew Grant aside a little and said quietly, urgently: 'Where is Billy John? I don't want Eleanor to see him. She's still....'

'Don't worry, old boy. He's safe. None of the crowd would have him back among them, so we've had to build him his own wooden shack away from the galley. He's there now, with Tom Evans to guard him. He's become very docile and humble – never argues about anything.'

'I still don't trust him an inch. He's not like Jim Protheroe; he's deep, deep and cunning, and malicious beyond words. I will never trust him, Simon. However, I'm glad he's safely stowed, and, on a happier note, allow me to introduce you to my very good friend and ally, Nathaniel Tucker, purser of the "Pawtucket". He has played a very great part in our story.' The two men shook hands affably, Tucker first sweeping off his hat and bowing with an old-fashioned courtesy.

'Welcome to our somewhat wet and dreadful home, sir,' said Grant, 'and many thanks for your help to my comrades. I can guess there must be a story indeed to tell – a ship without a crew, and my young colleague now her captain. Extraordinary!'

'Indeed, sir. As we say in Massachusetts, you ain't

heard nothin yet. But perhaps there is too much joyful tumult here for the relation of it at present.'

The scene was indeed rowdy, as the hands pressed round Eleanor to greet her; Curly Kellock and Carl met in a bear-hug, and the former exclaimed: 'What cheer, me old china! Good to see your ugly old mug again!'

Pushing each other like eager puppies, the grinning brassbounders took it in turns to plant awkward brotherly kisses on Eleanor's cheeks.

The three black hands, Noah, Amos and George, stood a little apart, somewhat lost and bewildered by the commotion around them, until Welly strode over to them with a huge grin and both arms outstretched: 'Hey, it's real good to see you fellers! No wonder that Raven got back here safe with three good ole black guys in his crew. I'm from Jamaica, you from the South, I guess? Now we got a *real* mixture of folk here. We got you, me, your old Yankee, a Swede, half a dozen English and all the rest Welsh, and man, you never heard anything like the way these Welsh guys gabble away in their weird lingo. I don't unnerstand nothing of it yet, except that dinner is called something like *"kinny-oh"* and beans is *"ffahh!"*. He pronounced the last word explosively to suggest extreme flatulence, and the three blacks erupted in high, delighted African laughter.

'Right, then, everybody,' said Grant. 'Back for breakfast! Got anything special on the menu today, doctor?'

'Yes, *sir,* sure have. I can do you albatross egg omelettes and then put em with some beans on slices of a kinda bread I made yesterday. Mind, I ain't got no yeast, so that's mighty solid bread. That'll stick to your ribs all right!"

As the loud party tramped up to the clearing, the cloud began to shred on the mountain-tops, and a fitful sun streamed in at the door of the hut as the benches filled with hungry, happy diners. Jones and Davey sweated at the food, and only Isaac Hughes steward was sour-faced at his demotion to a mere waiter to mere seamen.

Grant sat at the head of the long table, Eleanor to his left, Raven and Tucker to his right. 'Now then, young Raven,' he said, 'you have a lot of explaining to do. What the devil have you been up to out there, all this time –three weeks at least? You leave here in a twenty-foot quarter-boat and arrive back here with that and a small matter of a four-hundred-ton Yankee whaler, of which you are captain. And you bring her into harbour under only umpteen stays'ls. How come, old boy?'

'That,' said Eleanor, smiling, 'is only the start of it. There was far more excitement than that. My only fear is that you won't believe any of it. I don't myself, really, although I was there.'

'Yes,' said Raven, 'and too much to tell in the midst of this racket here. I suggest you get your committee to join us four in the store, when it'll be a lot more peaceful. As for the stays'ls, I didn't have much choice, did I, with so few hands to go aloft? Anyway, Simon, how have you been getting on here since we left?'

'Well, as you see, the stores are getting a bit low, but the diet's a bit more varied. The hands have been scrambling about on the cliffs to get these eggs – not bad, are they? – but the best thing that's happened is that I sent Lewis, Parry and Davey down to Carnley Harbour, that big inlet about thirty miles south, during that fine spell, and they came back with a boat-load of potatoes. Luckily, we just caught the spuds before they started to sprout. There must have been quite a settlement there once. The potatoes have been a treat to eat, and good for the crowd's health too. Every now and then a party goes out on a seal-hunt, so we've had fresh meat – fishy-tasting, but fresh. And of course, we've gone on fishing, and the good Holy Parry has caught us some decent lobsters by making ingenious pots from twigs and twine. So we don't grumble, most of us.'

'Well done, all!'

'But just think back, Simon,' said Eleanor, flushing with pride in her man. 'If it hadn't been for this hero and his fellow-idiot brassbounders going back to the old ship's mast, Holy wouldn't have had that twine – never mind all the canvas and halyard rope. What would we do, all of us, without this paragon of maritime skill and virtue? *Chwarae teg,* now, what?'

'O, curl up and die, my dear, or jump off a cliff. What else?'

'Idiots, both of you,' said Raven, grinning. 'Idiots, but very kind ones.'

By contrast with this levity, the cabinet meeting in the forenoon was a sober, even grave occasion, for grim events had to be related, and big decisions reached. Tucker related, in sombre style, the massacre of the whaling crew on the island and the survivors' miraculous escape, followed by the chance meeting, on the vastness of the Southern Ocean, with the quarter-boat. Raven, Eleanor and Jimmy told of their preservation in the storm, the amicable take-over by Raven of the crippled 'Pawtucket', the laborious rigging repairs and the second –this time nearly disastrous – chance encounter with the 'Bonito', and their horribly dangerous escape from her clutches.

At the end of the tales there was a silence of astonishment among the cabinet members as Raven ended lamely, awkwardly: 'So....um... well, here we are, then.'

Grant let out his breath in a long, soft whistle: 'Well done, old son! Well done, all of you! But you, my lad, have missed out one very important bit: getting that poor old jury-rigged hooker back from God knows where to anchor her here in precisely the right spot in Port Ross.'

'Well, of course, when we first got away from those devils, escape was all I thought of. But the whaler had a decent sextant and log-tables and a patent log astern, so it wasn't too hard to find Port Ross again. We've been a long time because I hove her to every night while we listened for surf. I didn't want to find Enderby Island by hitting it.'

Even the grumpy and critical Reuben Mathias was deeply moved, and could only growl: *'Wel, da iawn, bob un ohonoch! Da iawn wir!'* (Well done, all of you.)

Grant changed the mood to one of business. 'I have been thinking: there are big legal and financial matters here. You four from the boat must now have an indisputable salvage claim for the value of both vessel and cargo. That will amount to a lot of dollars.'

'Indeed they have,' said Tucker, 'and by Heaven they shall get every last cent of it. Unhappily, since men in Texas have now discovered that they can pump what they call rock oil from wells in the ground, the prices for whale oil, and therefore the whale-ships themselves, are not what they were. But, as purser, I would estimate the total value of ship and cargo to be some forty thousand dollars. But that means that Mr Raven here, as captain, must himself deliver the ship safely back to harbour in New Bedford.'

'Which, in turn, means,' said Raven, 'that I must now have a proper crew – say, twenty-five hands at least. Will that many of this crew be willing to sign on for a long, slow trip round the Horn on biscuit and salt junk, when, by waiting, they would presumably have – one day – a leisurely trip home by steamer? Neither you, Simon, nor I can order them aboard. However, we four have decided on something which may help.'

'Good. Therefore we hold a general meeting this afternoon, where all can speak and decide collectively.'

'I would like to be there this afternoon, to meet everyone,' said Eleanor quietly, 'but in the meantime, Simon, I should like to return to the "Pawtucket". I'm sure you understand… this island…'

'I understand perfectly, my dear. In any case, I'm sure you are very tired.'

'Indeed,' she said, pulling a face at Raven. 'I have endured many very cold and long night watches, listening for surf-noise, watching for the glint of ice, under the command of this tyrannical captain.'

'Well,' said Raven defensively, 'that was only because you insisted, and your hearing's so good. And – you never know down here, Simon – there might be a berg or two, or some floes, drifting about.'

'Of course, Eleanor,' said Grant gravely, ignoring the banter, 'you realize that John Ffynnongroes will have to be delivered by me to the police at Bluff. Don't worry, you will be quite safe from him – we'll see to that. The legal business will no doubt detain us there for a while, but I don't think even he will be such an idiot as to plead "not guilty". He knows there are many witnesses only too pleased to testify against him, so it may be that you and Raven will only have to make written affidavits. Any sane defence lawyer will at once tell him that his case is hopeless, and that if he shows no remorse, and puts the law to the bother of a long jury trial, they'll give him a much longer stretch in jail. Very well, then, we'll have this meeting of the crowd this afternoon. I'll get no work out of any of them today, anyway.'

As they all left the meeting, Kellock came up to Raven, put a fatherly hand on his shoulders, beamed a large, red, round smile at him, and spoke from the heart, without deference or formality: 'You done good out there, me young cock-bird. I bin talking to Jac and Reuben and Carl and Welly: all of us old geezers'll sign on with yer, whatever the young uns do.'

Raven shook his hand warmly, and his eyes were moist: 'And that, Curly, is quite the best news I've heard today. Thank you; I promise you, you won't regret it – you'll see this afternoon.'

*

It was a rare fine Auckland afternoon, the breeze gentle and the spring sun warm on the backs of the crowd as they sat here and there on log-piles in the clearing, chatting and guffawing. Grant held up his hand for silence, but grinned at them: 'All right, all right, you idle sojers. You're like a crowd of school-kids on holiday, but now there's a lot to tell you – and ask you – so pipe down, for God's sake. I'm going to hand you over now to Mr Tucker purser and Mr Raven, who'll tell you the whole story of how they got together and then got back here, and if you don't think it's the rippingest and most unlikely yarn you've ever heard, I'm a Dutchman. I may say, gentlemen, that Mr Tucker himself played a leading part in this story.'

Tucker rose with dignity, happy and flushed by the warmth of the crowd's cheering, in which approval was mixed with just a dash of amusement at his solemnity and his quaint, antiquated attire. 'You are most kind, good people. But I am no dashing young hero. Indeed, as I observed to my young friends here at the time of our troubles, I had liked to think of myself as a religious man in my fashion, as a lifelong member of the Society of Friends, or Quakers, as you would call us. But I am saddened to say that my part in our success was almost wholly due to an unexpected talent in myself for smooth, inventive and – fortunately - convincing lying.'

There was laughter in the crowd at that, but it was silenced when, with the air of a particularly aggressive Old Testament prophet, Holy Parry rose to his feet and thundered: 'Do not trouble your soul too much with that, friend! Your lying was forced upon you no doubt by cruel necessity; but back in Wales, there are all too many men of the cloth of all sorts who lie professionally with fluency every Sunday from their pulpits!'

His neighbour pulled him down by his sleeve: 'Pipe down, Holy, for God's sake! Let's hear the yarn, mun.'

First, Raven told them of the quarter-boat's battle with the storm, and at the end Eleanor, with all her old confidence back, broke in with utter sincerity: 'God, you see, was good to us, but, as well as to Him, we owe our lives to those of you who worked so hard and skilfully, led – or perhaps I should say driven – by Reuben and Jac-y-Bont here, on the boat, the sails, and, most of all, the sea-anchor. It's hard to describe what a miracle you achieved with that contrivance of wood and canvas Thanks to you, a twenty-foot open boat lay safely at rest like a sea-bird among waves forty feet high and breaking. Mind you, I've absolutely no wish to experience that miracle again. But, friends' –and here she raised her hands as in a blessing – *'Diolch o galon i chi i gyd* - my heartfelt thanks to you all.'

The crowd cheered again, glowing this time with pride at her praise of their splicing, stitching and carpentry. The two old men shook their heads and gave rare smiles.

The crowd listened in a silence of astonishment and horror to Tucker's story of the massacre of the 'Pawtucket's' crew. 'Damn,' said Billy's jailer Eirian harshly. 'Them stupid bastards got what they deserved. Pity we couldn't a done the same with our Billy.'

Even greater was their amazement at Raven's story of the escape from the piratical sealer 'Bonito', and their laughing approval of the way it had been done. 'That was smart, sir,' said Yorry Splott, 'but damn, there was a pity to have to waste all that lovely booze on them miserable nasty *crwts,* though!'

'Smart? I don't know about that, Yorry. There was a lot of luck about it. When we were desperate to stop them coming aboard, Miss Roberts remembered that time when Billy John brought the typhus onto the "Figaro" from the jail; that plague could have spread through the whole crew, you know. And then later, when we urgently needed to get away, Jim just happened to say it would help if all the sealers got drunk; then Mr Tucker happened to say they wouldn't have any liquor on board, whereas we'd got barrels of the stuff, and then I thought to myself: "Suppose they woke up, not only with hellish hangovers, but also to find us missing and all their running rigging gone?" So Jim and I got our knives out.'

'And most unfortunately for them,' said Tucker smiling archly, 'none of the rascals had read his Virgil and the words of the wise Trojan: "*Timeo Danaos et dona ferentes.*"' He beamed complacently, but his classical allusion fell decidedly flat. Only Grant and Eleanor smiled and nodded, and Reuben muttered peevishly to Grant: 'Good God, mister: "Virgins....Timmy... Danny ... ferrets?" What the hell is he on about now?'

"Well, that was Latin, Reuben. Roughly, that Trojan chap was saying: "Don't trust your enemies, even if they bring you gifts." I think I'd say "especially if they bring you gifts".'

'Bloody toffs' schools! Why can't they teach boys something useful, like long-splicing?'

'Of course,' said Raven seriously, 'we've dodged them so far, but it's not impossible that they might turn up here, looking for seals. They were heading this way on the day we first sighted them.'

'Does dim blydi ots!' said the bosun ferociously. 'Doesn't matter, mun! There's a lot of us now. You got guns aboard, haven't you? I'll let some daylight into some of the buggers, I will!'

'Better than that,' cried old Jac. 'I've seen the way these old whalers were built, so they could go through the ice – iron bows, timbers four inches thick. *Duw,* in a breeze you could just steer straight at them swine! You'd crack a sealing schooner like an egg-shell Then they'd all go to Davy Jones' locker!'

'Yes,' said Raven. 'We'd see em off. But all that might happen and might not. What I want to talk to all of you about is this: what do you – and we – do now? We are all in a fix. You are stuck on a dreary island, with supplies running low, waiting for a steamer which doesn't turn up; we have to somehow sail a ship thousands of miles to New Bedford with no crew. There is an obvious way out of this, but you may not fancy it. For legal reasons – which I'll come to in a minute – I shall have to be captain of the "Pawtucket". If you were to sign on with me as crew, my problems would be over. On the other hand, you would be taking on a long and slow voyage – this old tub can just about do eight knots with a gale of wind astern – on the usual diet of salt junk and biscuit, instead of a quick warm passage on proper food on a liner – once the rescue ship turns up, of course. But there is, for all of us, a better side to this – a ray of sunshine, as you might say. Carl, Jim and I have now, we think, a legal salvage claim to the total value of the whaler herself and her cargo, because without us she would probably have become a total loss.'

There were whistles of surprise from the crew, and Raven continued: 'Now, I don't want to sound as if I'm driving a bargain with you, because I see you all as old friends, but we are up against it, so there has to be a bargain, and this is it: out of our salvage award we will guarantee to pay all of you signing on with me all the pay you have lost since the night "Figaro" went down. Then, once we are back at New Bedford, as what the law calls "distressed seamen", "Figaro's" owners will be obliged to provide you with a free passage back home.'

There was suddenly among the crowd a silence of astonishment, which the worried Raven took for one of doubt and disbelief. He went on anxiously: 'Of course, our money may be some time coming through – we all know what lawyers are like - but before God we swear that we will do this – and do it gladly. So.... what do you say?'

He need not have worried. A huge cheer went up, the crowd leaping to their feet and prancing at the sudden change of their fortunes. Pitiful as their wages were, they were the mainstay of the families of the married men. Stridently, from the back, Lewis AB from Milford, yelled (genially, gratefully, but disrespectfully): 'You're a dull bugger, Mister Raven, sir! We'd have all a-come with you anyhow, without the money!'

Amid the roar of assent and laughter, Eleanor stood up, elated, her eyes shining and moist: 'Thank you! Thank you all! I know this is what my father - God rest him – would have wanted, above all things. He would not have wanted your wives and children to go hungry or fall into crushing debt to callous money-lenders. As your new *capten* has said, it will take time, but you *shall* have it.'

Tears may have been in her eyes, but inside her soul there was happiness and even mischief: 'And who d'you think, gentlemen, who, out of the four of us, first realized that we had this legal claim? Who?'

There was a concerted roar of laughter, and a yell of: 'Jimmy Protheroe! *Da iawn* Jim, you bloody old sea-lawyer!'

Jim stood up and bawled back with a mixture of triumph and indignation: 'You see? You see? When everyone else is a bit *twp*, you *needs* a good sea-lawyer now and then.'

Eleanor, still carried away by her joy, cried: 'Yes, friends, we needed legal advice, and God sent us James

Protheroe, AB, Q.C.!'

'God?' called a joker from the back. 'Twasn't God that sent him, miss, twas the other chap – the one with the horns!'

Grant strove to restore a little order: 'I may tell you that all of us on the committee have decided to sign on as "Pawtucket" crew, but you don't have to. To make all this a bit more regular, I'm going to ask you to raise your hands if you are willing to join.'

There was an almost instant forest of waving hands, and Eleanor was touched to see that Davey's hand was the very first. There was an excited buzz, which fell away as the crowd turned, and with a shout of derisive laughter saw that Isaac Hughes steward still had his hand down, and now raised it only slowly and reluctantly, with his usual expression of sourness and disdain: 'All right, laugh your heads off, you jackasses! I've got a feeling that no good will come of this scheme. A steamer would be a lot safer and nicer.'

'Please yourself,' said Kellock scornfully. 'You can be another Robinson Crusoe for all we care. You can live here on yer own, nice and peaceful, fetching firewood, spuds and onions, hunting, killing, skinning and gutting seals.'

'No, no, I'll come, but it's against my better judgment.'

'Now, by the Lord, that a real comfort to me, Isaac, man' said Welly. 'Cos otherwise how we gonna keep cheerful without your happy smiles?'

Kellock now waved his hands, palms down, to quell the gust of scornful laughter at Hughes' discomfiture, and said: 'Right. Now, as senior lower-deck hand, I need to say a few words. No – don't groan, boys, it ain't gonna be none of my p'litical, revolutionary stuff. Jist the opposite, in fact. There's quite a lot of us, Mr Raven, and we bin without pay a good while, so what you've just promised will put a tidy hole in your salvage award. All the more credit to you, I say. So I want to thank you prop'ly, on behalf of all the crowd, for your generosity. You didn't have to make our pay up for us, but you're going to. You're going to rescue us from the cruel stinginess of a rotten system.' Involuntarily, his radical soul welled up, and had to be proclaimed rhetorically to his fellows: 'This is what I've always said to you, mates: if only them what has the world's goods, and money, and power would share some of those things with poor folk what work with their hands, this here world could be like a paradise. All of us – rich and poor – would be happier, cos there wouldn't be no hatred nor envy nor fear between us no more.' He paused and smiled at Grant and Raven almost apologetically, and said: 'It's all right, gents. I'll leave off now. Mustn't get started on one of my sermons.'

Grant returned his smile with affectionate warmth, and said: 'That was handsome of you, Curly, and I can't help agreeing with a lot of your gospel. Thank you.' He was delighted at the new state of the crowd's morale and their whole-hearted commitment to the whaler voyage. But there were more things to say: 'Very well then. We'll be off soon, and we'll be back in a ship under sail in stormy waters. So now you must see there can't be any more committees and long debates. You will have a captain, and you – and I – will have to do what he says. Well, as you know by now, once we are under way, Mr Raven will be our captain. He has asked me to be mate, and Reuben here will be second mate. Noah Brown will remain as bosun, and, according to Mr Raven, we could not find a better one. He knows that old tub like the back of his hand.'

'Great God alive!' muttered Isaac. 'A bloody darkie handing out orders to white men! I've never heard....'

He had not realized that he was standing right behind Carl Johanssen. The big, normally mild and placid Swede swung round, his face showing a rare disgust and fury: 'You don't like that, hey? Then fokkink stay on the fokkink island! That man worth ten of trash like you!'

*

Grant and Raven stood together, swaying under the wheel shelter as, on a fine morning with a good south-west breeze, the 'Pawtucket' drew clear of Enderby Island and began to lift, roll and pitch to the long Southern Ocean waves.

'H'm,' said Grant, 'you're lucky with your weather, captain. A nice leading wind to blow us clear of this whole dismal archipelago, which I never want to see again.'

'Yes. Don't suppose the weather will stay so friendly, though. The glass is dropping and the cloud's building up there astern. Never mind, we've got plenty of hands now to shorten sail, so we can crack on. That was our problem before – no way of furling square-sails in a hurry. The crowd have enjoyed themselves this morning, haven't they?'

They had. The rare sunshine, the feeling of release, and the pleasure of plying again their old craft had made them like schoolboys at end of term. With four lusty men on each handle of the antique winch, the anchor cable had come rattling up the hawsepipe; other hands, whistling and bawling, had shot up the ratlines to loose the sails. Eleanor, standing aft beside Raven, had laughed to see the speed and ease with which the anchor had been weighed, and the two courses and main topsail had been set: 'So fast, Jack! Remember how long all that took us?'

'Never mind, Nelli. We did pretty well, I reckon. Simon, I'm going to ask you to take the wheel for a good long trick now. You don't mind taking a rest, do you, Amos?'

The young man replied with a wide, white grin: 'No *sir!'* He stood aside as Grant took the spokes, and, with his usual cheerful impudence said to Grant: 'Course due north, and cap'n say to me, "No bloody shenanigans!"'

'Aye, aye,' said Grant, with remarkable tolerance: 'Due north and no bloody shenanigans. By the way, John, I've torn a page out of the log-book and left a nice polite letter of thanks to the rescue steamer captain, just in case he thinks the place has been looted. Come to think of it, we've left that refuge a lot better than we found it, haven't we?'

'Yes. I've asked you to take the wheel, Simon, because this hooker's so different from "Figaro". She's got the same beam with only a third of the length; she's higher out of the water and does less than half the speed. She bobs about like a cork and steers like one too. You have to watch her like a hawk. The slightest gust or slap from a sea makes her yaw six points. Well, if you haven't had a turn yourself you'd find it hard to help the "Figaro" hands to steer when you're on watch later. The black hands – they know the old girl through and through, of course, but it took me hours – all one night – to get the hang of it.

Mind you, half my mind was on murderous sealers at the time.'

'Phew!' said Grant. 'I see what you mean. She's like a nervous horse! Good idea to let me have a go; Reuben will need one too. Whoa there! Back you come, you spooky old mare!'

'This feels pretty weird you know, Simon – me ordering you about.'

'No, not a bit. You're the guvnor now, old son. Mind you, if I thought you were doing something completely barmy I'd drop a few hints. But so far, so good. By the way, about the money: when it comes to making up the crew's pay, you can leave me out. I live at home when I'm on leave; my old man's made a decent packet on the Baltic Exchange; he makes me an allowance, and he's built this big place in Berkshire. I'm an only child, and he's a widower, so that'll be mine one day, as well as all his cash. So spread my share out among the married lads. I don't need it.'

'Very decent of you. Yes, we will. Right now, to business, mister mate. The log's streamed and running, the North Cape of Enderby Island is abeam to port, distant – say – a mile and a half. I'll go below, check the chronometer and start the plot. Simon, there are two sextants on board. You'll take one, won't you, to confirm my sights?'

'Your wish, old boy, is my command. Hey, stop yawing and griping, you old Yankee cow! We'll finish up in Sydney!'

*

Hours later, deep down in a dark store-room, Billy John

sat on the edge of an improvised bunk. The caboosh where his jailers had put him was gloomy, the only light coming through a grating in the top of the door from a smoky whale-oil lantern in the passage. His cell smelt of fishy oil, Stockholm tar, paint and bilge-water. Well-fed rats scurried to and fro over its greasy deck.

Every day he was needing more and more of his iron will to stay quietly polite to his contemptuous and very bored jailers. A thousand times he had had to smother fits of blind lethal rage – the wild desire to batter their heads in with whatever crude weapon he could find. Only that final grim purpose held him back – revenge. Endlessly, images of his enemies plodded round in his mind –Grant, Raven, Eleanor, Jimmy Protheroe.

He had been rowed aboard at dusk the previous evening, and there had been no sign of any of them on deck – but they *must* be all on board now. Though he had been in the shack at the edge of the clearing while the meeting went on, he had heard enough of the racket and gossip to be able to glean what had happened. What had enraged him most, in his usual corrosive paranoid envy, was the fact that his treacherous accomplice, Jimmy, was one of the heroes of the hour, all his previous wrongs now, apparently, forgiven. And how the crawling, spineless rat was glorying in it!

Little by little, during his last hours in the camp and his first hours in the old whaler's bowels, the burning focus of his rage began to centre on Jimmy – his personal Judas. Grant was now a remote figure, with whom he had not spoken for weeks. Nelli Roberts would be stowed away somewhere aft and, he guessed, well guarded; Raven would be in the wheel-shelter aft when at work. Off duty he would be in his cabin, and that tart, for a bet, would be with him, giggling as she let him feel her up under the blankets. One day – God knew when – he'd be out of jail and back in Pembrokeshire. Then, by Christ, he'd settle with that pair! They'd have a house that could be set alight, maybe nippers that could be kidnapped; and nasty accidents might happen to either of them happy lovebirds. One day!

But Jimmy – he'd be working with the watch on deck, day and night. And he, Billy, was allowed on deck for exercise and to go to the heads. Even them bastard Evanses from the Parrog couldn't deny him a chance to have a crap. He gave himself a grim smile: And you've been such a good, quiet boy, Billy, that you've noticed that they don't bother too much about keeping such a sharp eye on you as they used to. Suppose you could get away from them for a while? A dark stormy night, a lot of hands on deck, setting or furling sails – that'd be the time! In the dark, one sailor looks much like another, so he wouldn't be noticed. Jimmy always made a lot of stupid noise at work, so there was a good chance of picking him out. Then, a quick, savage blow, a quick heave over the side – with a bit of luck it could be done! And, best of all, no bugger would know it wasn't an accident. Your arm still isn't quite right, where that damned bitch hit it, but it'll have to do!

The last time he'd been on deck he'd seen that the wind was in the south-west, on the port quarter, and getting stronger all the time; even in his miserable hutch below he could sense that the whaler was swooping and pounding her way north at about her top speed. He'd heard them say it was only three hundred miles to Bluff;

so that meant that he had tonight and tomorrow night – that was all the time he could be sure of. Come on then, Bill; don't think about it no more – just do it! Tonight's the night for Jimmy's nasty accident. Chuck him over the side! In the dark, with the ship going this speed, they'd never find him. Mind you, it's a bloody long shot, Billy, because the bugger might be down below, off watch, but you might be lucky. Anyway, things have gone so bad with you – who cares? Things couldn't get much worse than they are now, could they? Worth a shot! After all, if you couldn't find Jimmy you wouldn't have committed any crime. You could always make up some cock-and-bull story to explain why you was wandering about on deck. And if it worked, it would be worth it, by God! You're sure now to be stuck for years in some miserable cell anyway, so it'd be nice to think that that slimy bastard Protheroe had suffered worse: floundering in icy water, struggling, lungs choked, till a big breaker snuffed him out for ever, and the fishes picked his bones! But you got to do it quick, quiet, and clever, like, or else it's a swinging job for sure, and then you'll never be able to pay out all the other bastards that have dragged you down to this!

Hollowly, through the ship's wooden bones, he heard and felt the tramp of hasty feet, and felt too that the old ship was heeling further and further to leeward in the squalls. Good! It must be getting rough up there, and pretty dark too. Come on then, boy! Now or never!

He hammered on the door till he heard Eirian Evans' gruff voice in the passage: 'What's the matter with you, for Christ's sake? You've had your exercise.'

'Got to go to the heads, mun – honest.'

'No. *Cae dy ben!* (Shut your face) and piss in your

bucket.'

'Tain't that, Eirian, mun. My guts is shot to pieces. Must a been that bloody doctor's sea-birds' eggs. You don't want this place covered in shit, do you, and smelling worse than ever? Only up to the heads, please, mate. I won't be long, honest.'

'O, all right then, you bloody nuisance.'

The force of the cold wind and the splatter of spray over the rail hit Billy as he came up through the scuttle. Good! Pitch-dark too!

'Thanks, mate,' he said as he took two steps down the ladder to the foul-smelling crew's privy. 'Shan't be a minute.'

Evans grunted, then shuffled round to the starboard – the sheltered – side of the massive brick block of the try-works. He squatted down, shivering in the keen gale, took out his knife and his latest, much prized, acquisition, a plug of tobacco from the whaler's stock. Thank God for some backer at last! He'd almost forgotten the joy of the sweet, dark, chewy leaves, steeped in rum and molasses. He carved off thin slices and munched them blissfully. Let that swine be as long as he likes; he can't get up to no mischief down in the heads, can he?

Billy John, fully aroused now to his purpose, was a man who, despite his stocky, powerful build, could move with the silence and swiftness of a cat. In a second, he had seen Evans disappear behind the try-works, and darted round the weather side to crouch in darkness under the fife-rail of the foremast, where he could hide among the hanging rope-coils of the clewlines and buntlines.

Good, so far, but still a lot of luck needed! All the hands of the watch had been busy furling the massive main tops'l, and were now thankfully climbing back down the port shrouds for a little warmth and shelter. The old whaler had one aid to comfort they'd lacked on 'Figaro' – an after-shelter built over the wheel, open at the for'ard end, but its after-end closed, keeping out cold wind, rain and flying spray from astern. The watch was only nine in number, and the officers tolerantly allowed them in there in dirty weather, as long as they kept quiet and out of the way.

Billy ground his teeth in frustration and rage. All gone wrong already! He was pretty sure he could hear Jimmy's high voice, so he was one of the watch on duty, but that was no good if he was stuck among a whole crowd under the shelter. He needed him *alone,* out on deck.

Then he heard Raven's voice, crisp and urgent, coaching Curly at the wheel: 'Got to watch her like a hawk, man. She's a lubberly, beamy old thing, and in a quartering sea like this she'll gripe round on her ear before you know it. You've got to be ready to meet the swing – hard!'

Billy grimaced in the darkness: Bloody, jumped-up *Sais!* Full of himself now! Didn't even trust the old chaps like Curly with his precious old wreck! Good God, Curly was steering ships when Raven was a twinkle in his father's eye!

Then, of a sudden, Billy heard his luck change – change magically! Raven raised his voice, this time in anger: 'Which of you useless sojers fastened the gaskets on that tops'l? I can hear one of them now on the windward yardarm, thrashing around like buggery! It'll be in bits in a minute, and the sail pulling free. Get yourself aloft, one of you, and make it fast properly! If I knew who it was he'd have my boot up his arse to help him up!'

Then, to Billy, it was another miracle – as if all his bad luck had suddenly left him. He heard Jimmy's high, cocky voice cry: 'I'll go, skipper. Twasn't me who done it wrong, but I knows my way round this old packet better than them lubbers off the island.' Christ, he was still showing off and crawling round them bastards aft! Well, this was the last time he'd do that! Now was the time to get him!

'Very good,' said Raven. 'Only watch yourself. It's as black as your hat up there, and you know what those old ratlines are like.'

'Paid a becso, syr, paid a becso!' (Don't worry, sir.)

But climbing a sailing-ship's mast was no picnic at the best of times. The first climb up the shrouds, using the cross-tied rope ratlines as rungs, was straightforward enough, but as you reached the crosstrees – the first joint in the triple mast, you had, for a few rungs, to clamber out over the edge of the small platform on the so-called futtock shrouds, like a fly on a ceiling, your body sloping backwards and outwards diagonally. Experienced seamen were so used to it, they made little of it, but darkness, rain and gales made it harder, especially if, as now, the climber was hampered by wearing heavy sea-boots and a flapping oilskin coat.

Preoccupied with watching Kellock's uncertain steering, Raven hardly noticed Jimmy's departure into the pitch-darkness of the port rigging, and certainly did not see a second dark figure rise from the deck to follow him up. He was astonished, then, to hear, not two minutes later, a high scream of fear and rage from Protheroe:

'Naw! Naw! Let go, you bastard!' Billy's luck had soon run out. He'd wanted the murder to be quick, silent, so that it would seem like an accident, and he could hide in the dark in the upper rigging until there was a chance to get down unnoticed. Now that bloody Jimmy had raised the alarm and ruined everything. Never mind – get him anyway! What the hell now?

Instantly, on hearing that despairing yell, Raven's quick wits told him the worst: somehow, someone - Billy John for sure - had been able to swarm up after Jim, and was now trying to drag him to his death from sixty feet up above a raging sea or a hard deck – the finish, either way.

In two seconds he had ripped off his coat and was leaping for the main shrouds. As he shot up the ratlines he could see the horrible danger Protheroe was in. He had just begun to climb outwards over the top, but the dark shape below – Billy – had one arm looped through the shrouds, and was using both hands to grasp Jim's left leg to launch him to his death. Jim meanwhile was thrashing his other foot wildly about, trying to kick his enemy's head. But, of course, clinging desperately to the shrouds, he could see nothing to aim at.

But now it was Billy's turn to be alarmed at a similar attack from below, as he felt one of his legs being grasped, and heard Raven yell: 'Let go, you murdering bastard!'

Even in his fear and panic, Protheroe was relieved to hear Billy snarl: 'Fuck off, brassbounder, or you'll get it too!'

Such a violent, murderous struggle in such a horribly dangerous place could not go on long. Billy, secure in his grasp, was able to look down as soon as he felt Raven clutch his left leg, and with his other boot he caught Raven a heavy glancing blow which half-stunned him, but Raven ducked and hung on grimly. In the end, it was Jimmy's flailing boot that decided the battle; he had somehow struggled upwards to the point where he could now get a good hold on the lowest part of the topmast shrouds. Now it was Billy who was vulnerable, hanging backwards off the futtock shrouds, unable to protect his head.

Even in the roar of the gale, even though partly stunned, Raven below heard the sickening impact as Jimmy's swinging boot slammed into Billy's right cheek. Raven heard too Billy's wordless scream of despair as his hands lost their hold. An instant later, Raven himself had a moment of deadly peril as Billy's falling body bounced hard against him, back to back, nearly dislodging him. But Raven, who had been in his college days a formidable boxer, was quick and instinctive in a fight, and had time to pull himself in, flat against the shrouds.

He glanced quickly down; heard a final yell of agony; saw Billy land, from sixty feet up, clean on his back on the massive oak bulwark with an impact that must have split his spine in half; and then tilt, quite slowly, silently, to plunge into the ocean, his head soon a mere speck in the racing yeasty foam alongside.

Simon Grant, breathless from his rush from below, heard the cry of 'Man overboard!' and turned to Reuben, gasping: 'What do you think? Who's gone?'

The old man shook his head and shouted against the howling wind: 'Billy John – off the shrouds. Trying to kill Jimmy. No good, mister. It'll take us a mile to get her round, and it's black dark. Never find him. Too bloody dangerous for the rest of us, anyway. Besides, you didn't see him land on the rail on his back. *O, Iesu Mawr!* Horrible, that was! Reckon he was dead before he hit the water. I'll sign the log entry, as it's my watch, to say that nothing could have been done to save him. After all, we've both seen this happen, times before, isn't it? Hopeless! Billy's gone, and by God we know where to.'

Minutes later, on the heaving deck, in rain and wind, there was a bizarre reunion between Raven and Jim. Silently, they embraced in a clumsy male hug in which shock, relief from stabbing fear, and plain comradeship united them across the bounds of race and rank. At last, still breathless, Jimmy half-sobbed: 'Thank Christ! And thank God you was there with the guts to go after him quick! He'd a finished me off for sure. I didn't realize how much he hated me. I owes you my life, sir.'

'He's gone, Jim. Gone where he'll never trouble us again. You're a good man, Jim. How could I leave you to him? He's got his deserts, man, though mind' – he released his clasp and drew back a little – 'what'll come of it later, God alone knows. Some lawyer might say we just murdered him between us, which in a way, I suppose we did.'

Roused by the shouting from a deep sleep below, Eleanor suddenly appeared on deck, her loose coat flapping, her face a deadly white in the binnacle lamp's glow, mouth gaping, eyes staring. She grasped Raven's sleeve to pull him to her: 'Jack, Jack, what in God's name has happened to you? And to Jim too? Jack, your head is running with blood! Was it… *him?*'

'Yes,' said Raven, still breathless and shocked. Got away from Eirian. Tried to pull Jim off the shrouds. I went up after him, of course, as soon as I knew. He tried as hard as he could to kill us both. We might all have come off into the drink or been smashed to bits on deck. Luckily for us it was just him. Landed on his back on the top edge of the bulwark; smashed his spine for certain. Then over the side. Reuben decided there was no point, and a lot of risk to all of us, in trying to go back to find him.'

Protheroe whispered: 'He was a goner, miss, for sure, before he hit the water. Dead as mutton.'

She set her pale, glistening face in an iron mask of cold anger and triumph: 'Good! Thank God he's gone and that you're both safe! Perhaps it's wicked of me to say it, but thank God that we're rid of such a cruel, sly devil! Now let the Devil himself have him! I would never have felt safe anywhere as long as I knew he was still alive – never!'

Simon cut in, taking her hands in his: 'Nelli, my dear girl, it's over. You need never even think of him again. John, I'm going to deal with all this. At the time of his disgusting crimes and his punishment he was under my charge. His death will have to be reported to the coroner at Bluff or Invercargill. I will do that. I don't think there'll be any great stir about it. God knows many a decent honest sailor comes off the rigging in a storm – all too often. I'm feeling very angry with Eirian for letting Billy get away from him and roam about on deck, but he and Tom have done a lousy, boring job for a long time now, so I'll just give him a piece of my mind.. But there is much for us all to be careful about, and at eight bells tomorrow I would like you to get all the hands aft, please, so that I can put them straight about all this. In the meantime, you two chaps had better swallow a good tot of whatever old Tucker can find you, and get your heads down. You both did bloody well, but by God you were lucky too. Eleanor, off you go now, and sleep safe at last. Have a sip of Mr Tucker's laudanum if that would help.'

*

By eight the next morning the cloud and rain had cleared; the wind had veered westerly and 'Pawtucket' was reaching comfortably north under all plain sail. Simon Grant faced the crowd, who stood shoulder-to-shoulder and silent. 'Now then, lads: I don't often make speeches, but today I've got to, as there are extremely serious things to be settled amongst us. First of all, Mr Raven is, as you know, captain of this vessel, but, technically, Billy John Ffynnongroes was still a member of "Figaro's" old crew, and therefore my responsibility. I will, as you would say, have to carry the can for this. I, and I alone.

'Now, I know what ships are like for gossip; I'm quite sure that by now every man jack of you knows exactly what happened on the port mainmast shrouds late last night, so I don't need to tell you anything. My belief is that all of you feel that Billy got his deserts, and that none of you will shed many tears over him. He made a sudden murderous attack on a fellow crew-member. Mr Raven and Jimmy did nothing wrong. Jimmy had every right to defend himself, and as for Mr Raven – well, what would you have thought of him if he'd just stood by and watched? You'd have seen him for a pitiful coward. Nevertheless, three men fought, and one is now dead, and his death will have to be reported to the legal authorities ashore, and Kellock, as senior foc'sle hand, it'll be your job to gather up John's personal belongings and bring them to me for safe keeping, so that they can be returned to his next of kin.'

He paused, then continued with dramatic emphasis: 'Very well, all that knowledge of the true events is in your heads, and my guess is that you will never lose that memory. Well, in the weeks or months or years to come we shall all be scattered; you will all be right out of my control, so I cannot give you any *orders* about all this. All I can do is to beg you – to *beg* you – humbly – never to tell anyone, anywhere, in any language, what truly happened. Do not reveal it soon, or a year from now, or twenty years from now – not even to your wives and closest relations. Never…never… not even after several pints in Cardiff or Milford or Rio or Valparaiso. Never… anywhere. I will explain why in a moment, though you are all sensible chaps and will probably understand why.

'When we reach Bluff, the New Zealand coroner will hear from me that last night, in a south-westerly gale, William John AB, a member of the watch on deck, fell from the shrouds into the sea, suffering a probably lethal injury on the way. As is usual, the officers on deck at once conferred, and it was decided by the officer of the watch, Second Mate Reuben Mathias, that any attempt at turning back to rescue the seaman would have been futile, and dangerous to the ship itself and its crew. That much is the truth, but of course it is very far from the whole truth. I shall say that it was thought possible that his fall was caused by a loose or broken ratline, and I suggest, captain, that to prevent any further accidents of that kind, all ratlines on all three masts should be replaced today. The authorities may insist on an inspection of the rigging, and we do not want embarrassing questions.'

Raven nodded, and called to Noah: 'All hands to work at that today, bosun. Got enough cordage?'

'Got enough, sir. We do it straight.'

'Excellent,' said Grant. 'Now, I want you all to think – and think damned hard – about what might happen if the whole truth *did* become known - to lawyers here, or to people from your part of Wales, even if years from now. A serious question would be raised: why did William John so hate a fellow-Welshman and neighbour ashore that he wanted to kill him? To explain that, the whole story of his cruel and disgusting attacks on Miss Roberts and Mr Raven on the island might have to be dragged endlessly through some law-court, in public. Would you for one second wish that to happen to a young lady whom I know you like – love, indeed – and respect so much? Of course not. As for Jim and Mr Raven, the cold fact is that they, between them, killed Billy John. I can visualize a nightmare scene where a clever prosecutor, a feeble defence lawyer and a stupid jury might find them guilty of manslaughter – even murder. And where might that end, my friends? With the judge .... the black cap ...... the rope. Think, now, think very hard: how would you feel if a careless word from you – or you – or you had caused that to happen?' He punctuated this last sentence by stabbing his finger at random at men in the crowd. He went on 'That is what is now at stake. That is the heavy secret burden we must all now bear to our graves.'

Then, with a wry smile and a masterly lowering of the tense emotions flowing, he added: 'I mentioned just now the love I think you all feel for Eleanor Roberts. Well, I doubt if you feel quite like that about us English foreigners in the afterguard.' There was a rumble of amused and tolerant agreement. 'I thought so. But consider this: even if Jim and Mr Raven were to walk free from a court on those charges, Jim would live, in your district, under a lifelong shadow, and as for Mr Raven, his future career as a ship's officer would be ruined by his association with a scandal, a mystery, a trial. You know what people - Welsh or English - are like: "No smoke without fire" and all that nonsense. He'd find it damned hard to get on. And, *chwarae teg,* as you'd all say, you have to admit that for such a young chap – even if he is English – he's done brilliantly well on many occasions, showing real brains, leadership, seamanship, and, more important, real guts, and in the end he turned up at Port Ross with a decent, tight old ship to take us away. That alone, I can tell you, took some doing, never mind all the trouble and danger from the sealers. He's easily the best young officer I've ever met. And besides (this time his grin was openly playful) it's pretty obvious to all of us that his future is Eleanor Roberts' future too, so what do you say? Do we all solemnly swear to keep this secret for as long as we live, and to leave no written record of it?'

The previous tension was released in a roar of agreement, and cries of 'Aye, aye, he'll do, mister!' and from the back a yell: 'Well done, the bloody brass-bounder, and good riddance to that swine Billy! None of us won't say nothing – never!' Standing behind Simon and Reuben, Eleanor and Raven, pale and anxious till now, at last exchanged quiet smiles and twined their fingers together.

Elsewhere in the crowd there was a less friendly encounter. Wellington Jones shuffled up close to Isaac

Hughes and growled: 'If any of this gets out, I'll know it was along of you, man, cos you the biggest blabbermouth I ever see. I'd find you, man, and finish you off myself with these two big ole hands of mine. And by the holy God, you better believe me.'

Isaac replied with his usual disdainful sneer: 'Don't you worry about me, Jones. I just want to forget everything about that damned ship "Figaro" and her old ruffian of a *capten,* and his hoity-toity missis and that little baggage of theirs who's caused half this trouble, in my opinion.'

For a while the cook was silent, except for the sound of his deep breathing. Then he growled again, in a vicious fury: 'I starting to feel it better I finish you off right now. Then for sure you don't talk no more.'

With the air of a congregation recovering from a long chapel sermon, the hands were crowding for'ard for their long-overdue breakfasts, but Holy Parry could not let the occasion pass without an improving biblical parallel: 'You know, boys, if you thinks of Billy and Jimmy, both guilty men in their ways, you can't help remembering the bit from Luke, about the two thieves crucified with Our Lord. They went opposite ways too – one cursing, one confessing his sins and repenting. And it was the second who was promised paradise with Jesus. Makes you think, doesn't it, about your own sins?'

'Aye, maybe,' said the earthy and pragmatic Lewis from Milford. 'But at the moment my stomach's making me think I'm bliddy starving after all that jaw from old Grant. Not that I don't agree with him, mind. Forget it, isn't it? That's best.'

*

Unnoticed by them all in this daybreak drama, a few miles to the west, the old New Zealand rescue tug 'Hinemoa' plugged her way south, heaving sluggishly into the long swells.

'Hey! Look at them tops'ls, skipper,' said her mate. 'On the port beam there. Whaler, I'll bet, hull down on the horizon. Just coming away from the islands. What's she been up to, d'you reckon?'

'Gawd knows, but I'll lay good money she's been helping herself to all the stores. You know what them bloody whalers are like. Damned if I know why they keep sending us all down round these islands in dirty weather in an old rust-bucket like this. There's never any wrecks these days, only old sealers and old whalers thieving the stuff we've brought. And look at the time it's taken the yard to get this bloody old wreck of ours to float. Never mind, Tom, we'll just plough on, do what the flaming idiots in the government tell us to do, and collect our pay every month – for traipsing around piles of old, godforsaken rocks where sod-all ever happens.'

EPILOGUE

So much still to tell you, and there's so little time, for we have come far, in space and time, from where we began - those desolate, black, wave-lashed basalt cliffs, the forlorn yellow spike of mast, the grey seas and the little lifeboat flotilla seeking haven and shelter.

Much, then, must be told with ruthless brevity. First, the dry, humdrum coroner's court at Invercargill, where Grant, pale, stolid and laconic, spoke his half-truths, and a bored coroner mechanically registered the accidental death of yet another seaman, by the name of William John AB. Meanwhile over at Bluff, Raven and Reuben Mathias bosun yelled and swore and drove the focs'le crowd to heave and splice and grease and stitch to get the old whaler ready for a long, rough trip.

Then came the tedious, wallowing, rolling passage to the Horn, the stout old ship pushed ever eastwards, sometimes under only one close-reefed tops'l, by the helpful, if brutal, westerly gales of the Roaring Forties. Then a magical day of gentle breeze, high drifting clouds and sunshine, when at last the dark, snow-capped Cape, itself part of an island, slipped by only a mile off the port beam. Grant and Raven, the two navigators, exchanged grins of pardonable pride, for days of storm and low cloud had not made their task easy, and despite that, they had successfully guided the whaler to her home ocean, the Atlantic.

And then the blessing of at last turning north, so that each day felt a little warmer, and the ship ploughed on through tamer seas until, one sunny wonderful day, she felt the first benign push of the south-east trade wind. Then followed, for all hands, days of pleasantest ease; with the steady wind abaft the beam and all sail set, the old 'Pawtucket' swooped and rolled north at her best speed, the crowd free to spend every dog-watch smoking, loafing and singing, for no sheet or brace needed attention, and the spinning brass wheel of the patent log clocked up a run of over a hundred-and-fifty miles a day.

For a troublesome while, this easy progress was halted by the fluky breaths and flat calms of the doldrums, when often the ship lay like a dead log and the helmsman sat yawning on a grating, while the useless wheel turned idly this way and that and a fierce sun bubbled the pitch up from between the teak planks of her decks. Bad days for the crowd, these, as the bellowing mates drove them into sweating, laborious work at the braces, swinging the slatting sails to every brief, feeble catspaw of wind.

But as steadier winds returned, and every day took them further north, the hands became aware that it was now January in the northern hemisphere, and soon, in the chilly westerly breezes, thicker jerseys, sea-boots and smocks had to be hauled out and donned. It was bitter cold indeed on that last day as, in a light wind, they closed with the green shores of Massachusetts, Raven, with Tucker at his elbow, carefully tacking the 'Pawtucket' past Martha's Vineyard into New Bedford Sound and, at long last, making the signal for a pilot and a tug.

The latter, a strange little paddle-steamer, soon ranged alongside, her tall cigarette-like funnel belching wood-smoke, and once the towing hawser was fast, her paddle-wheels thrashed the water to foam as she dragged the whaler up the Acushnet River to her berth, while the crowd, whooping, joking, and whistling in high spirits, put a neat harbour furl on the sails.

In a small town like New Bedford, totally dedicated to the whaling industry, word had soon got around that, after two and a half years, the 'Pawtucket' was back home in the offing, so that by the time she made fast at the quay there was a happy crowd to greet her – her owners and the wives and children of the local members of her crew. But their joy was short-lived; both of these groups were silenced, horrified, by the sight of total strangers on her decks, and - once they had heard Tucker's account of the island disaster – by the terrible news of the slaughter of virtually all of her crew. Then, among the families, there was grief at the loss of loved ones, and fierce anger at the brutal stupidity and lack of authority of Captain Olsen in allowing such a calamity to happen. There was fury too against the owners for appointing such a worthless specimen to the captaincy. Among the more thoughtful there was also shame at the callous sensuality of many of the whaler hands themselves. As for the thrifty owners, who were, of course, also members of the New Bedford Shipowners' Mutual Insurance Society, there was horror at the prospect of a huge salvage claim. Whether this outweighed their sorrow at the loss of so many souls in the crew, only they could have said.

There followed next morning on the quayside a scene of heartfelt farewells, as all 'Figaro's' company but Raven, Eleanor and Grant left for Boston to embark for their return to England. Eleanor especially was moved by her gratitude to the crowd for their friendship, sympathy and support during her bitter suffering. She gave the warmest embrace to the ever-loyal and fatherly Wellington Jones, whom she was never likely to meet again. As for Davey, who clung tearfully to her, she said: 'You have not seen the last of me, my lad. We are both Newport born and bred, remember. Some day, when you are at home, I'll come trotting up Carn Ingli on my pony to see how you are behaving – and you can make me a nice cup of tea.'

Then, while the whaler's cargo was being discharged, for Eleanor there was a period of calm, rest and pleasant tedium. The solicitous Tucker had found a haven for her with a kindly cousin of his in a quiet street on the outskirts of the town, where she was well fed and housed, and happy beyond words to be able to dress once more in women's clothes, even though these were limited to a kind of Quaker uniform of a long, plain grey dress, decorated only by a white turned-down collar.

As for Tucker, Raven and Grant, they took the train to Boston, where they spent their nights in a grand, oppressively-formal hotel, conferring over dinner with the young, keen lawyer, Sam Goldberg, whom Tucker, with his apparently infinite network of contacts, had found to represent them. Grant and Raven had at last been able to shed the shabby, grubby seamen's clothes which they had worn ever since the wreck, and were now smartly suited and attired, hair and whiskers neatly trimmed, for the thoughtful Goldberg had confidently advanced Raven money against his claim, and lent Grant enough dollars to enable them to look like solid, respectable, reliable citizens in court, not roughly-dressed, hapless seamen in jerseys.

Their first days they passed in Goldberg's office, moving, a few days later, to the gloomy, stuffy Maritime Court where, for hours, gowned and be-wigged legal experts exchanged long, droning, incomprehensible arguments on procedural matters, for the insurers were fighting tooth and nail to save their dollars and grasped at every possible legal quibble. They had blanched white when the Chairman of the Assessors announced that the Court's valuers had established a total value of $42,800 for the ship and cargo, but, through their own attorney, held stoutly, desperately, to their defence - that the 'Pawtucket' had still been manned when 'Figaro's' boat arrived, and that the personnel of that boat – only one very junior officer, two seamen and a female (and, by implication, useless) passenger – had made little contribution to the whaler's eventual salvage, and could expect only a minor award. They produced so-called expert witnesses from among their many ex-whaling cronies to confirm their assertions.

As they took their places in the court on what was to be the last day, Grant murmured gloomily to Goldberg: 'Have you read Mr Dickens' novel "Bleak House"? This daily farce reminds me very forcibly of his account of the Jarndyce and Jarndyce case in the Chancery Court.'

'Everyone reads Mr Dickens, sir. But I assure you this case will end very differently. They have not a leg to stand on, and by God they will soon know it. Wait till I start on them!'

Coolly, laconically, his dark eyes glowing with righteous indignation (real, or assumed, who can say? He was a lawyer!), he spoke directly to the Chairman of the Court: 'Your Honour, you and your colleagues know far better than I that there is but one overarching principle in the settling of salvage claims: "No cure, no pay". Unless he saves a ship from probable destruction, it matters not how much time or money a would-be salvager has sacrificed. His reward is nil.

'On the other hand, it matters not either who he is or

how many men he has. The issues to be decided are starkly simple: was the vessel in question helpless and in danger, and did he bring it to safety? Gentlemen, in this case the answer to the latter question is very clear. The whaler "Pawtucket" is now alongside the quay at New Bedford, discharging an intact and undamaged cargo, having been efficiently jury-rigged on the foremast in very difficult circumstances. From Mr Nathaniel Tucker you have had a precise eyewitness account of what was achieved under the leadership of the admittedly young Mr John Raven. I may point out in passing that, only a few days before he encountered the "Pawtucket", Mr Raven had brought a twenty-foot half-open boat through an unusually violent storm in the most dangerous ocean in the world. Does that show seamanship or not? Does youth necessarily mean incompetence?

'As for the appellants' first plea – that the whaler was still manned at the time of Mr Raven's boat's arrival – that is technically true. She had a complement of four: a purser, who by his own testimony, is totally untrained in the many skills of the sea, and three foremast hands, only one of whom, Mr Noah Brown, could be said to be mature, experienced and responsible. You have heard from Mr Tucker, firstly, that at that time, literally tons of mast and tangled rigging lay over the side for'ard, where, had another gale sprung up, it might well have stove in the ship's side; secondly, that not even Brown had any clear idea of what their next step should be; and lastly – perhaps most vitally – that none of them had the least notion of how to navigate. They were hoping to sight New Zealand, but after their escape from the carnage on the island they had sailed several hundred miles, and by that time did not know whether New Zealand was north, south, east or west of their position. Could one regard that ship as being adequately "manned"?'

'Your honours will have seen, from the signatures in the "Pawtucket's" log-book, that, disabled, lost, and at the mercy of the next westerly storm, the "Pawtucket's" people at once – joyfully, Mr Tucker testifies – accepted Mr Raven as captain. Everything that happened afterwards was achieved by *his* leadership and vision – including, of course, the escape from the probably murderous and piratical intentions of the crew of the sealer "Bonito" – which vessel, incidentally, you may recollect, was listed as "missing, presumed lost with all hands" in the recent maritime journals.

'To conclude: Mr Raven jury-rigged the ship, navigated her to Port Ross in the Auckland Islands, enlisted his former shipmates, castaways from the wreck of the Cardiff barque "Figaro", and successfully docked her at New Bedford. In the light of the maxim "No cure, no pay" was that a "cure" or not?'

He paused, swung round to glare pitilessly at his opponents, then resumed: 'Your Honours, through you I should now like to ask the appellants to explain *exactly* how Mr Tucker and his fellow-survivors could have hoped to find safety, left to themselves. I should also like them to consider the illogicality of their position. For, if their whaler had been successfully assisted by the largest and finest liner in the Pacific, or, for that matter, by a man on a raft, they would still be facing this same claim. The "cure" is all.

'On a less nautical, but more immediate matter, I should like to remind them that the clock is ticking. We have already spent much fruitless time over this case; my firm's fees for my daily appearance here will be considerable, my three witnesses are being delayed from resuming their careers, and they are staying – as befits their status – at the Metropole Hotel, not noted for its cheapness. In the event of the Court's finding in our favour, all these expenses may well be added to the sum calculated by the assessor. Gentlemen, I will now resume my seat, and we may then await with interest the appellants' reply. I rest my case.' He shuffled his papers together and sat down, with a ghost of a furtive wink to Raven.

The outcome was all too predictable. The insurers' attorney asked for, and was granted, time for a withdrawal to consider their next step, and only half an hour later he and his clients returned and gloomily agreed to relinquish their appeal. Pronouncing the Court's official verdict, the chairman ended with a cold, severe judgement on the conduct of the whaling community generally: 'Most of your captains, we know, are decent men of skill and integrity, but there are some, like Captain Olsen, who are manifestly *not*. It is incumbent on whale-ship owners that they select their commanders much more carefully in future. We find in favour of Mr Raven's party for the whole of their claim, plus their costs. This Court will now rise.'

'Congratulations, old son,' said Grant, as he and Raven walked back through the snowy streets to their hotel. 'That will put a smile on Carl Johanssen's serious old face, and even Jimmy Protheroe won't argue about that verdict.'

*

And now, you and I, and the remaining trio of our wanderers, Raven, Eleanor and Grant, come to the last stage of their wanderings, and to a setting dramatically different from the savage bleakness and emptiness of our first sighting of them.

You now have to visualize the long, lamp-lit quay of the New York Ocean Terminal on the Hudson River on a late January afternoon. Yes, time has flown, and the calendar now shows '1897'. There is a black sky overhead, sprinkling down a thin fall of snow, but you do not notice the sky, for lying alongside the quay, every port-hole, window and doorway ablaze with bright electric light, is the finest, largest and fastest liner afloat, the White Star Line's flagship, the 'Teutonic' –ten thousand tons of her, over five hundred feet long, fifty-eight feet in the beam, and, with a speed of twenty knots, the holder of the Blue Riband for the Atlantic passage. Our trio will reach homeland in style, and – almost unbelievably - in less than a week.

There are crowds on her decks, exchanging shouted farewells to friends and relatives on the slushy quayside, but away from their noise you can hear, from deep in her massive hull, the sound of powerful generators and – faintly – the scrape of shovels as the stokers – the so-called 'black gang' – toil to get up steam. The ship will need two-hundred-and-fifty pounds of that to the square inch to move the huge pistons that will thrust the cranks, to turn the shafts, to turn her twin screws. Men whose fathers laid out along lofty yards, furling sails in bitter winds now sweat in hellish temperatures to feed the mouths of hungry furnaces with coal.

But our next scene is several decks above that clanging stoke-hold. Here, all is quiet, elegant, warm and well-lit, for we are in no less a place than the captain's cabin. At his desk sits Captain Charles Bruton, portly, impressively bearded, blunt, the doyen of the company's captains, and a man not to be trifled with. Opposite him, nervously shuffling papers, is his purser, Stanley Spinks, tall, gangling, permanently worried about some aspect of his difficult profession. He senses that his captain is not in the best of moods this afternoon.

'Well, Mr Spinks,' said Bruton, fidgeting with his high stiff collar, for he is in full fig – well-cut blue serge uniform, twinkling brass buttons – 'how is the passenger list looking? Full house?'

'Very nearly, sir. Third and second class full; a few vacant cabins in first, for it is late for the London winter season. However, we have many of our ... um ...more prosperous regular clients who will be travelling on to Switzerland for the skiing, I believe.'

'H'm. Lot of damned silly rich idiots with nothing better to do than slide down mountains on long bits of wood, breaking their legs, like as not! And I've got to dress up like a pox-doctor's clerk to preside at the captain's table tonight, where they like to be seen, and hear them drivelling on about who's marrying whom, and their new summer place on Long Island, and how many million dollars some rascal made out of real-estate or pork pies or barbed wire last year.'

Spinks was shocked: 'But sir, these wealthy regulars are the company's bread and butter – and ours too.'

'I know, Spinks, but you are lucky; you don't have to have a decent dinner spoilt every night by having to smile and butter them up and be gallant to dreadful rich hags, and pretend to be interested in their interminable, affected gabble. Do I give a fart for the doings of Mr and Mrs Hiram J. Huckster Junior or Mr and Mrs van der Popinjay and their frumpy daughters? Like hell I do! I came to sea to be a sailor, not some pansy, grinning society host. Heigh-ho! Anyway, let's have a look at the crowd we've got this time. I'll see the second-class list too.'

Scowling, he scanned the first-class list, groaning occasionally at the name of some familiar bore, but half-way through the second-class list he suddenly stopped and jabbed a finger at the paper. 'Just a minute, Spinks: I've seen some names here that ring a bell somewhere, but I can't for the life of me think where. "Captain Grant, Captain Raven and Miss Eleanor Roberts". Now I'm sure I've read or heard something about them. What was it, what was it? And anyway, what are captains doing in second-class, for Heaven's sake?'

'Ah, they are taking passage as distressed seamen. The New York agent of their company – a Cardiff concern, I believe – has booked them their cabins, and that of Miss Roberts. I understand that, in any case, both men are only acting, temporary captains. As for Miss Roberts, I can only assume that she was a passenger on whatever ship it was that was wrecked.'

'Got it! I heard about them when I was in Boston, visiting an old chum there. Yes! They were all survivors from a Welsh barque that was wrecked on Auckland Island, and was posted as "missing, presumed lost" weeks ago. The story I read in the Boston papers was about the exploits of a party from that crew in a lifeboat, who met a badly-damaged Yankee whaler. Yes... Raven was the chap in charge of the boat – young chap. There was a hearing at

the Maritime Salvage Court – the papers were full of it. "Young Limey Captain Saves Doomed Whaler" – headlines like that. Grant was a witness, and I think it hinted that the girl was Raven's fiancée. And they later got mixed up in some incredible affair with some villains on a Frisco sealer, too. Good God, they'll have a tale to tell! Right! I want them on my table, Spinks, every night, so that I can at last have some worthwhile conversation. See to it.'

'But sir, I cannot! Second-class passengers cannot dine in the first-class rest…'

'Of course they can't, Spinks! So obviously we make them first-class passengers. Up grade them. You said you had some vacant cabins.'

'Yes, sir, but the company's rules state clearly that….'

'Company's rules be buggered! I'll answer for any additional costs if necessary, man, so don't start wetting your pants about it! I'm sure you can arrange it, Spinks. If you can't, I'll see you washing dishes and cleaning out the heads on the company's Liverpool dredger! Oh, and one more thing: so that these folks and I can have a bit of peace to talk in, I will not be at my normal table tonight, on show to a lot of lounge lizards. I'll dine in my cabin with those three. Tell the Chief Restaurant Steward I want to see him with tonight's menu. Well, come on! Don't just sit there gaping! Chop-chop, man!'

'But I don't….'

'The dredger, Spinks! The dredger!'

*

One deck down, in second-class, Grant, Raven and Eleanor, well-wrapped against the piercing cold in smart new overcoats, stood at the rail, looking down on a snowy quay crowded with people bidding farewell to friends and relatives aboard the liner. Our travellers were standing in what amounted to a long, wood-decked street, also crowded, and brightly-lit by the ship's new-fangled electric lights.

'You're very quiet, Eleanor,' said Grant.

'Yes…. It's this amazing ship – so huge, like a town built on the water, and so…modern and smart.'

'Yes, she's only a few years old, the cabin steward told me. The White Star Line's newest and biggest and best.'

'So incredibly different from what we set out in!'

'Which ship d'you mean, Nelli?' said Raven. 'The liner that brought you out to Chile, the "Figaro" or the "Pawtucket"?'

'None of those, Jack. I mean the lifeboat "Susan". Twenty feet long, nearly all open; the cabin – a dark wet rabbit-hutch, the first-class lavatory – a bucket!'

'Never mind,' said Grant. 'She carried you safely – you survived. Hallo, something's happening down there. We're off soon, I reckon.' For, from the main deck below came shrill whistles and loud yells from the mates, as the thick hawsers mooring the liner to the quay were 'singled-up' with loud splashes, until only three remained. From out on the darkening Hudson River came siren-blasts from manoeuvring tugs. Shouts and the chattering of steam winches signalled that massive tow-ropes were being hauled aboard the liner.

The sounds – sounds that heralded the start of this journey - now brought joy, excitement and elation to all three, even to the normally controlled and sardonic Grant (though, it must be confessed, he had sampled some excellent Irish whiskey in the bar before coming on deck). He looked at the lovers, huddled together at the rail, with a burst of affection and boyish mischief.

He said casually: 'Raven, did you see that bit in the Boston newspapers about you two? I noticed that Eleanor here was referred to as your fiancée. But have you actually *asked* her to be your bride yet?'

'No,' said Raven, smiling at Eleanor. 'We understand each other well enough.'

'That's true, Simon,' said Eleanor. 'With all his many faults, I've decided he's the man for me.'

Raven hugged her. 'Yes, and she's the only girl for me – ever!'

Grant shook his head in disapproval: 'No! Won't do, old son, won't do. You're English, don't forget, and a stodgy, old-fashioned, conventional sort of chap at heart. There's a proper traditional code, a form to be observed in these matters, doncherknow? For instance, have you got an engagement ring for Eleanor? No, I thought not. You've got money now, and there are shops aboard this hooker, so damn well get one. But never mind, we can still do the ceremony now without that.'

'Ceremony? What the devil are you talking about?'

'Why, the official proposal, of course, you clown! You get down on one knee, you reach out your hand; Eleanor may or may not take it. You hold her hand, you kiss it, then you make an impassioned little speech of proposal, full of flowery compliments, of course, on her beauty, and then hope she's fool enough to agree to have you.'

'What! In front of all these people? You're mad! Or

have you got yourself plastered down in that bar? I will do no such thing! I'm not going to make a prize idiot of myself in public!'

'Right!' said Grant, smacking his hands together. 'Eleanor, you're a strong girl. Between us we can easily heave him over the rail, and then you can look for a better offer. I'll bet there's several young, handsome American millionaire bachelors in the first-class.'

Grant had not lowered his voice, and Raven was miserably aware that now there was a growing and attentive audience for what might transpire. Scarlet with embarrassment and rage, he allowed Simon to press him to his knees, a move which brought forth clapping from the spectators, which in turn greatly increased the audience's size and amusement.

'Well, go on, you mumbling idiot! D'you want me to dictate it to you?'

'All right! Give me a chance, for God's sake, and let's have done with this stupid nonsense! Um....Miss Roberts, will you marry me?'

Loud cheers and laughter broke out, and now the whole crowd was listening: 'Good sir,' said Eleanor, very clearly and crisply, 'I must thank you for your offer, but I shall need to think it over carefully (and here she grabbed his shoulders) for at least thirty seconds.' She hauled him to his feet and kissed him soundly to huge applause. Two cold faces and noses met in this forcible embrace.

Then Raven broke off, indignant and panting: 'I'll never forgive either of you for that! I've never been so bloody embarrassed and...and...and...humiliated in my life!'

'Oh dear, Simon,' said Eleanor. 'He does not love

me now! You have ruined all my matrimonial prospects with your drunken foolery.'

'Alas, I fear I have. We must start the hunt for the young handsome millionaires, then.'

There was a pause, as Grant and Eleanor shook their heads tragically. Then, after a sheepish grin, Raven burst out into involuntary laughter, in which they and the crowd joined. 'Oh, all right, you idiots, I'll forgive you this once, but don't you ever do anything like that again!'

The applause and laughter faded, as the passengers sensed that the comic scene was over, and turned their attention back to their farewells to the crowd ashore. Our trio of voyagers fell suddenly silent, as if simultaneously struck by an almost spiritual impulse – a jolt, an awakening. A deep emotion, the yearning hopes behind their foolish charade, had struck into their souls. They turned back to the ship's rail. Below them lay the quay, coated in dirty frozen slush, harshly-lit by street lamps, which palely illuminated the upturned faces of the farewell parties; there was a small sea of waving hands, from beneath which came a ragged chorus of 'goodbyes'. All three felt an overwhelming sense of a moment of change, of a shift in being, of dark things closing, fading, perhaps forever.

Eleanor, shivering in the raw cold, stood between the men and drew them gently to her. Their silence, amid the hubbub of farewells, yelled orders, mates' whistles, and the splash of released hawsers, stretched, lengthened into minutes, as each of them grappled with, tried to understand, the meaning of this abrupt blow of solemn, utter serenity.

Ironically, it was Raven, the bluntest, least intellectual, least articulate of the trio, who first found clumsy words to speak: 'It's odd....queer, isn't it – the way we all stopped messing about? Just as if something had suddenly hit us for six. As if, somehow, everything had changed, changed for good. I've never felt anything like it before.'

'That,' said Simon quietly, 'was, I think, what you religious people – and even heathens like me – would call an epiphany – a showing – a sudden insight into our own lives – a sign that they are going to be transformed – especially yours, my friends.'

Eleanor murmured: 'Yes, that's it. Like the moment when the three kings saw Christ in the manger. That must have changed their lives forever.'

'Well, to me,' said Raven, the least mystical of the three, 'it was like a huge great curtain coming down behind us – you know – shutting off all the troubles we've been through, and God knows we've had plenty of those.'

'Exactly,' said Grant. 'At the same instant, without a word, we were all struck by the same deep impact of feeling. Idiots one moment, silenced by a stunning impulse the next. By Jove, it was enough to make even a materialistic atheist like me remember what old Hamlet said: "There are more things in heaven and earth, Horatio, than are dreamt of in your philosophy".'

'Nothing could persuade me,' said Eleanor, 'that that epiphany was not sent into all our hearts by a merciful God, who has seen our suffering, and has ended it. Through that mercy I believe that we shall never experience such hideous darkness and fear again. Don't forget, Simon, that, though you may not believe there is a God – may scoff at the very idea of such a belief – He is real, and still loves and cares for you.'

Once again, they were all silent for long minutes; then Eleanor spoke in a lighter tone: 'But, by heaven, the old hymn was right: "God moves in a mysterious way, His wonders to perform". I cannot tell you how much I detested both of you fellows at first. To the silly, vain, unthinking creature I was then, you were snobbish, arrogant invaders from England.' She drew them even closer to her: 'Now I see you as strong, brave, loyal knights, who have for months stood between me and danger. I love you both most dearly – but of course I can marry only one of you.'

Grant chuckled, and turned to give her a peck on the cheek: 'Yes, and you won't catch me, old girl! I'm too fond of being a rootless, irresponsible bachelor. Funny, though – what you said about hating us at first. It was just the same between me and old Curly Kellock. Aboard the "Figaro" he seemed to me nothing but a jumped-up, half-baked, Marxist nuisance, but now I see him as the man who got me through a very difficult time, all those weeks on the island. Even when that specimen Billy John was put away, I could sense that there was still potential danger from the crowd. Idleness, short rations, monotony, isolation, despair – they were all possible sources of trouble. All the older men did their level best about the food and the idleness, but it was Kellock, with his gifts for quiet leadership, reason and common-sense – not to mention some useful cunning – who, I'm convinced, stood between me and anarchy. H'm – if only the country could find itself prime ministers with half his gifts!'

Piercing the freezing winter afternoon gloom came a shrill whistle and a yell: 'Let go bow-rope!' followed by a splash and the chatter of a steam winch reeling in the hawser. A huge, deep blast from the "Teutonic's" steam siren, just above their heads, made the whole air vibrate. Eleanor reached out her hand to the ship's rail, and said excitedly: 'Feel that! It's the change starting *here, now!* Can you feel the rail throbbing, trembling? The engines have come to life! At long last we're going home! But we don't seem to be moving yet.'

Simon peered professionally over the side and said: 'I thought so. You can see the wash from the screw going for'ard.' And then, like Eleanor, he adroitly eased the emotional tension by lapsing into flippant, absurd technicalities with Raven: 'Come on, then, mister hope-to-be-mate-someday: what's the captain doing? You have to know about steam handling as well as sail, you know.'

'He's held on to his spring and he's going slow astern.'

'On which engine?'

'Starboard, of course.'

'Very good! You're starting to get the hang.'

'Don't be so damned patronizing. I bought the manual for the First Mate's ticket exam in Boston. The Old Man's going astern on the spring to push the bow out, so as to help the tugs. In a minute it'll be "Stop engine, dead slow ahead both, let go stern-rope, let go spring".'

From the bridge above they could just hear the musical tinkle of the engine-room telegraph, then, after the yelled commands from the mate, the answering cries: 'All gone for'ard… all gone aft!' The great ship was free of the land. Then came a slow, solid beat as the two huge twenty-foot screws slid the liner forward and outwards, the gap between ship and shore rapidly widening.

'Very good, young man,' said Simon. 'There's hope for you yet. This captain seems to agree with you.'

'If you are going to start being so ridiculous again, Simon,' said Eleanor, 'I am going to my cabin to unpack. I'm beginning to freeze out here anyway. Dressed like a female again, I almost miss my thick trousers and jersey and so on.'

'I'll give you a hand if you like,' said Raven with a fond smile.

'No thank you, sir. I should prefer to concentrate on my unpacking without any …er …distractions.'

Entering her new abode, she paused in the doorway to savour the delicious warmth coming from the steam-heated radiator on the bulkhead, and the bright electric lights – all of it a great improvement on her tiny, stuffy hutch on the 'Pawtucket', with its flickering whale-oil lamp, coffin-like berth and pervading stink of fishy oil. Everything here was so neat, so compact – the berth, the wardrobe, the dressing-table in fine mahogany, the clever wash-basin that swivelled upwards, tipping used water into a drain. All so well thought-out for comfort!

She was about to start on her brief task when there was a tap at the door, and she heard Raven's voice: 'Can I come in?' She felt a small stab of irritation; couldn't she have a moment's peace on her own? Then she thought: No, I mustn't start getting impatient with him already! 'Yes, Jack,' she said, 'but I haven't started ….'

'Don't, then. I've just found this note on my table, from the purser. Listen: "Dear Captain Raven, will you and Miss Roberts please come to my office as soon as possible? If you ring the electric bell a steward will conduct you. S. Spinks, Purser".'

Stanley Spinks, a gaunt, harassed-looking man, dressed immaculately in his White Star uniform with its gleaming brass buttons, his dazzling white shirt-collar stranglingly high on his thin neck, rose from his desk as they entered, bowed and motioned them to chairs: 'Miss Roberts, Captain Raven, you are most welcome to the "Teutonic", the finest of the White Star Line's fleet, and therefore the finest and fastest ship on the Atlantic. I have good news for you. Our captain – Captain Bruton – has instructed me to invite you and Captain Grant to move to first-class cabins. He suggests that the Company (and here a flicker of pain and disapproval crossed his face) will be willing to waive the difference of fares, in view of your notable achievements. Furthermore, he cordially invites you and Captain Grant to take a private dinner with him in his cabin at eight o'clock. I will send a steward to conduct you, if you are willing to accept the invitation. Now, I trust, you will enjoy your voyage with us even more.'

'Phew!' said Raven, as they went back to their cabins. 'Nelli, darling, we're famous!'

Indeed, it seemed so, for the efficient Spinks had already sent two stewards, smart in their crisp white jackets, to shift our travellers' very meagre baggage up to the first-class deck, the abode of the great and the good. The stewards having unlocked for them the heavy door that separated the very rich from the merely prosperous, our lovers now met sleek, glossy-haired men escorting bevies of gorgeously-attired and elaborately coiffured girls and ladies. At one point Eleanor, still in her grey, white-collared Quaker dress, burned with fury as she heard quiet, catty female comments and half-suppressed giggles. She caught whispers: 'My dear – the hair! And that dress!' Eleanor had done her best at New Bedford, but that town was not a centre of feminine fashion. Her hair, its old sheen restored, was still too short for that era. It fitted her head like a neat cap, a small wave of it curling to cover her ears, in a way which you and I know would quite soon become a raging fashion in a later generation of flappers. 'And the complexion!' came another sneer. 'So rough and red, like a Minnesota farm-hand!'

Gritting her teeth, Nelli muttered: 'For two pins I'd go back and box their silly ears for them! They couldn't make an eye-splice to save their lives!'

'Please don't wallop anybody, old girl – not in first-class. They'd chuck us right down into the steerage for that. Ignore em. We're dining with the captain – they're not.'

Both were dumbstruck as, with a flourish, the stewards flung open their new cabin doors. 'Heavens above!' said Eleanor. 'Now we see how the other half lives! So big! Such a lovely carpet – and even wallpaper! Black marble wash-stand, easy chair, writing-desk – all the wood beautifully finished in bird's eye maple! It's like being in a superb hotel, Jack! And look how wide and roomy the berth is!'

'H'm,' said Raven thoughtfully. 'So it is!'

'All right, my boy. I can read you like a book – a not very desirable book, I'm sorry to say. Listen: I have decided to be a respectable woman – a reformed character – during this voyage. There is the small matter of a wedding ceremony at Ebeneser Chapel to be arranged, remember, before you can be let loose on me. So off you go and calm down and unpack. It'll soon be time for dinner with the captain.'

That dinner was memorable – like a gust of fresh breeze in a hothouse. Bruton was an affable, voluble host and greeted them as if they were already old friends. They had hardly seated themselves before he was busy lifting a bottle of champagne from a bedewed silver bucket and handing it to a waiting steward. 'There you are, Jenkins; open that and serve my guests. No, not me, you loon, I might be needed on the bridge any minute. You'll all understand, eh? I've got a damned good team up there, but they might need me. Getting a bit foggy, and lots of traffic in and out of the river. I've kept her to half speed – twelve knots – till we're in the clear. Then we'll wake her up a bit and you'll feel her go. Twenty knots – that's moving, eh? Don't want any accidents, though. D'you know how much this packet cost? Close on a *million* quid! Don't want that stopped out of my pay! Now then: a welcome aboard the finest ship afloat to the most distinguished company I've ever shipped! Your most excellent health, lady and gentlemen! *Iechyd da,* as Miss Roberts would say. (I was mate on a Welsh ship once, y'see). And while we drink and eat I want to hear all the details of your extraordinary boat-trip.'

'You shall hear chapter and verse from these young Argonauts,' said Grant. 'But first, on behalf of us all, I thank you heartily for your hospitality and kindness, and we raise our glasses in return to you and your beautiful ship: here's to Captain Bruton and the "Teutonic"!'

Heavens, thought Eleanor, a novice wine-drinker, as the delicious tingle of the quick, heady champagne struck her palate and a strange lightness of being followed the toasts. You must take smaller sips, not great gulps, or you'll have to be carried to bed!

'Hope y'don't mind,' said Bruton, 'but I've selected a dinner for you from the restaurant's main menu –

that's a yard long. Asparagus soup, grilled turbot and a breast of Maryland chicken in a supreme sauce. Desserts: well, Jenkins here has a list and will get you whatever you fancy when the time comes.'

Grant, warming every moment to their blunt, brusque host, said with an ironical smile: 'But captain, you make no mention of salt junk and cracker-hash – our staple diet.'

Bruton gave a gusty laugh: 'Many apologies! I will see that the head chef is dismissed at once.'

'Your menu sounds delicious, sir,' said Eleanor, emboldened by the wine, 'and I should warn you not to take too seriously anything Mr Grant says. It's just his way.' She realized, with some alarm, that she had had some difficulty in saying 'delicious,sir'.

As they ate and drank – a slim bottle of hock replacing the empty champagne bottle – Raven and Eleanor told the story of their eventful ocean voyage, Bruton now and then whistling in amazement. Eleanor later realized that she had omitted to relate her torturing fear of being captured alive by a crew of ruffianly sealers. That realization came as a balm, a relief. That nightmare, and the island nightmare too, had at last, after months of a peaceful life among friends, and the death of her chief tormentor, lost their power to haunt her. Now her mind, and her body too, were free, open. As Jack had said, a curtain had come down on past evils. That release, assisted, it must be said, by the excellent food and wine, in turn released a wave of urgent desire to be heedless, wild, naked in Jack's arms, as in her reckless nights aboard the 'Figaro'. But no – not quite yet. She would not torment him like that again. More importantly, her very soul and upbringing told her that fornication was a sin, and that love-making, the full joining of their bodies, must be preceded by the sacrament of marriage. She and Jack had waited long; they could surely wait just a little longer? Besides, despite her declared vow of respectability, there was no need to be totally cold towards him, was there? A little gentle fondling, perhaps, would do no harm, surely?

Mind you, said the less pious part of her mind, the part which always fought against her spirituality, it didn't say anything about fornication in the Ten Commandments, did it? Only adultery, and they were not planning that! And as for the 'lusts of the flesh' that ministers thundered on about, they themselves wouldn't be up in their pulpits preaching if it weren't for those, would they?

She came back, almost with a start, from her pleasant erotic musings to the splendid cabin and the contented chat of the three men when Bruton said 'You're very quiet, m'dear. Perhaps we are wearying you with our sailors' gossip?'

'I do beg your pardon, captain,' she said flushing, confused, somewhat tipsy and also guilty about her sensual train of thought. 'Er, yes, I... I am a little tired now. Thank you so much for your very kind welcome, and for the best meal I've had in years. Now I think I will turn in in my beautiful cabin.'

'Yes,' said Raven, jumping up abruptly. 'I'm the same. We've had a long day – on the train, and all that. And as Eleanor says, very many thanks, sir.'

As the door closed behind them, Bruton grinned at Grant and gave a conspiratorial wink: 'H'm! Exit lovers, stage left, in some very understandable haste! Phew! What a stunner she is! By Jove, I wish I was forty again!'

Grant shook his head: 'No, it's not quite like that, Charles. You're a little ahead of the game.'

*

The lovers, arms around each other, swayed, a little drunkenly, down the warm, empty corridors, feeling through their feet the comforting, steady rhythm of the massive turning screws far below them as, with a muffled triple drum-beat - *'Bud*-da-da, *bud*-da-da, *bud*-da-da' – they thrust ten thousand tons of steel through the long, slow Atlantic swells. They felt too the pressure of the deck beneath their feet grow and fade, grow and fade, as the huge ship pitched slowly into the long swells. At her door Eleanor gave Raven a brief kiss on the cheek and said: 'I'm not tired, really. I'd like to talk to you – on my lovely sofa, mind you – we'll have none of your funny business! Give me ten minutes, *cariad*.' As she closed the door on him, there floated into her head the words of one of the more detestable of Shakespeare's women, Lady Macbeth: 'That which hath made them drunk hath made me bold'.

Raven had sensed during their walk back that Nelli was a new woman – or rather her old self again – no longer tortured, tense, wary and withdrawn. The subtle, yielding closeness of her body as they walked had told him that.

When, a little later, he entered her cabin, having shed his tie, stiff collar and waistcoat, his own body was – despite her cautionary words - taut with sexual excitement, and he felt a slight twinge of disappointment to see her seated on the sofa, still in her chaste, plain grey Quaker dress. But then he caught sight, over her shoulder, of a crumpled, untidy heap of what looked very much like underwear that had been shed and flung hastily onto a chair. Whew! What a girl! The old mad Nelli again! Getting rid of some of those frilly obstacles to passion! But still, I'd better be careful – not too brash! Don't rush your fences, old chum!

She patted the sofa and said: 'Darling, come and sit here. Only be a good boy for a while, if you can, because there are practical things we need to discuss.'

'Yes, Nelli - our wedding. As soon as possible! I'll see about getting a special licence ....'

'Whoa there! Hold your horses, mister! You are forgetting something. Listen: in a few days' time we shall be in Liverpool. We are not short of money now, but there is no point in wasting it on train fares. I am an orphan now, but you are not. You have a family whom I'm sure you love, and I would dearly like to become a part of it. Loving me must not stop you from still loving them too. Why don't we first take the train to Oxford, for you to see your parents and for them to see me, and see what they think of me as a daughter-in-law, and then go on to Wales?'

'Oh, that's thoughtful of you, Nelli. Yes, I'll wire them from Liverpool. I haven't seen them for a long time, and I'd love to introduce them to my future wife. I know you'll get on famously with my Ma – she's just your sort of woman: feet on the ground, energetic, lively, funny quite often. As for Pa, well, he's quite a bit older than Ma; a nice kind man – a parson, you remember - but he's a bit...detached from the rest of the world. Got his head in a book, most of the time. Practically knows the Bible by heart, from Genesis to Revelations, as well as all the concordances and commentaries and the commentaries *on* the commentaries, and so on. He sits in his study for hours, cooking up really massive sermons out of all that.'

'He sounds,' she said, not quite sincerely, 'as if he would be a most interesting man to talk with. But if they allow you to throw yourself away on a wild Welsh girl from the wild west of Wales we shall need to go back to Newport. I'm so longing to see my homeland again, and to show you why I love it so much, and I'm so hoping that you will love it too, and want to live there.'

'Anything you say, *cariad*. Wherever you are is where I want to be. I can see there will be a lot to arrange: you will have to settle your parents' affairs with their solicitor, and we shall have to find a rented house where we can stay until we find a place of our own to buy. And d'you know, I really fancy getting ourselves a smart dog-cart and a good strong cob, so that we can…'

But she put her forefinger on his lips and whispered: 'Steady there, mister! We don't have to plan all the details of the rest of our lives tonight. We are alone, we are free, comfortable, safe, warm, at peace. We should enjoy the moment we have now.' And, deftly twitching a shirt button undone, she slid a hand through to the warmth of his chest, and whispered again: 'God in Heaven, but I do want you! *D'wi'n dy garu dy, capten bach!* I love you. That's the most important bit of Welsh you need to …Aah!' She gasped ecstatically and her whole body shivered with plain lust as, at last, after all those cold, dreary months of taut chastity, she felt his hand cup and fondle her breast and then sink smoothly, gently, slowly, down her body to rest on her thigh.

'No more talking then, Nelli,' Raven murmured,

and he sealed her open mouth with a long, breathless kiss, while she, quite lost now in a delicious trance, drew his hand upwards over her thinly-clad leg to the warm place where her now-parted thighs met, pressing it urgently into her flesh.

If Grant's epiphany on deck had been the end of the cold, harsh past, this long, slow, writhing, rapturous struggle was the start of another era.

'Ahead of the game, Simon? In what way?' said Bruton. 'In all my life I've never seen a pair so besotted with each other. By Jove, the look she has in her eyes for him! So longing to...you know! Phew!'

'Yes, but you see, to spare her feelings we didn't want to tell you the whole story in her presence. That girl has been through hell. I won't go into all the sordid details, but being beautiful, and the only woman on the island amongst all those men - mostly young focs'le hands – you can imagine it was a damned anxious time for her. We all knew there were one or two bad hats among them. She never felt really safe. In the end, the inevitable happened; she had one particularly dreadful experience, of which the less said the better. It was only by pure chance that she escaped being violently raped by one of the ABs. Raven was the one who saved her from that, and he got quite badly hurt in the process. You see how short her hair is? It wasn't like that before – it was long, wavy and very beautiful. But one day, soon after that attack, she took Raven's sheath-knife and hacked it all off, down to her scalp. It was an appalling, deliberate mutilation of her own beauty.'

Bruton gave a short grunt of disgust: 'Damn shame – for a nice girl like Eleanor, to be treated like that. Appalling! What's happened to the swine who did it?'

He saw Grant's face at once go dead, closed, at his question, and he shrewdly guessed that there were things in Grant's memory which were not going to be revealed.

There was a brief awkward pause, then Grant cleared his throat and said impassively: 'Dead. Accident.

Fell from the mainmast shrouds one night on the way to Bluff Cove. I was going to turn him over to the police there, of course. We were aboard a very old whaler, you see. Been at sea two years too. Some of the ratlines were rotten. You've been in sail, no doubt, so you know how it is. We were running pell-mell before a howling gale. There was no chance of going back for him. Anyway, the chaps on deck at the time reckoned he'd broken his back on the bulwark before he fell into the sea.'

'Rough justice, eh? Not many tears shed, I'd guess?'

'Exactly. Now look, old boy: I've only told you all this because you've been so deuced decent to her. But it's a horrible business that we all want to forget about. I'm sure I can trust you to keep everything I've told you entirely to yourself – for good, I mean. Believe me, there are very good reasons for that request. Sorry I can't say more.'

Bruton put out a hand and exchanged a solemn handshake with Grant: 'Don't you worry, captain, you have my word on that.' But as he settled himself back in his chair his private self said: Phew! there's a hell of a lot behind all this, and I'm never going to know what it is. Pretty serious stuff, for sure. Perhaps I shouldn't have asked that question.

'Thanks for that, Bruton,' said Grant. 'I know I can trust you. Some stones are better left unturned, eh? But as for Eleanor, just imagine – imagine her terror later at the thought of falling alive into the hands of that sealing crew! It could so easily have happened. Why, when Raven went to cut up the schooner's rigging, he even left her his loaded revolver – for herself if need be, you understand. That's how bad it was. She's needed a lot of time, and a hell of a lot of courage, to recover from those horrors.'

'Sealers! Aach! The scum of the earth, they can be. Bad luck to them, wherever they are.'

'Hear, hear! But in fact we heard in Boston that their schooner "Bonito" is listed as "missing, presumed foundered", so they may have had their bad luck already. If they have, I shan't shed many tears over those miserable bastards! But it's not just all that, Charles. She carries a burden of her own guilt too. Eleanor's Welsh, through and through, and, I'd bet, Nonconformist as well. Raven never refers to religion at all, so I expect he's Church of England. But Eleanor has obviously been brought up on the Bible. What's forbidden is forbidden. "Thou shalt not", and so on... That's caused another - perhaps to her more serious - reason, for her mental torment. When I arrived at the scene of the rape, a few minutes after Raven, the dirty swine who was trying to rape her had got Raven down, and was beating hell out of him, but she had got to her feet behind the rapist with a driftwood club – and she's a strong girl, you know. She broke his arm for him, and, given a few more minutes, would have smashed his skull to bits, I'm certain. I've never seen anything like it: In his attempt to rape her, he'd pulled her clothes off, so, in her rage, she'd become nothing but a naked, murderous savage. Being religious, she felt a terrible guilt about that for a long time. As you've seen, she's now a perfectly normal, high-spirited and highly intelligent girl, but she's been through so many horrors, and anyway her religion means so much to her that I don't think she'll make love – you know – fully, with him until she's properly married. It wouldn't seem right to her. But I think you're right – she'd jolly well like to!'

'Really? *Really?*' Bruton sprang to his feet and

pressed the bell-push on his desk. 'Well, I think we might be able to do something about that.' A steward appeared and Bruton barked: 'Ask the purser to come and see me.'

'What? *Now,* sir?'

'Yes, *now,* sir! Now! In his pyjamas if he's turned in. Away you go, man, chop-chop!'

Spinks, when he appeared in a hastily-dragged-on dressing gown, looked exhausted and cross, with the air of a doomed but indignant Christian martyr: 'Yes, captain. What is it now? It's very late, sir, and embarkation-day is always very wearing for...'

'Stop moaning, man. Think yourself lucky. You're off to bed. It's getting thick on top, so I'll be lucky if I get my head down at all tonight. What I'm asking for won't take you long. I want you *now* to read through the Company's rules for ships' captains - you've got that filed away somewhere, I take it – and find an answer to two simple questions: one, am I allowed to conduct a ceremony of civil marriage aboard this ship, and two: if not, may a member of the clergy do it in some suitable space in the ship? I want you back here by nine tomorrow with the answers – oh, and bring with you the full passenger list – third-class and all.'

'All fifteen hundred, sir? I really cannot see...'

'Nine tomorrow, Spinks, or the dredger!'

'Very good, sir.' And with a deep sigh of martyrdom, he stalked out, giving the door a petulant bang.

'Damned old woman!' said Bruton, grinning. 'One of the crosses I have to bear, but good at his...Hullo! Now what?' He had, half-unconsciously, heard and felt the pulse of the screws stopping. He jumped for the voice-pipe to the bridge and blew the whistle: 'Captain – bridge:

what's happening, Matthews?'

'Run into a fog-bank, sir – very thick. And there's still a lot of traffic on the opposite course to ours.'

'Very good. Start the fog-signal. Double up the lookouts. Put her dead slow ahead, both engines, so that you can keep to your course. I'll be up in a jiffy.' He shrugged on a heavy coat and grimaced: 'That's the end of our nice chat, Grant. Who'd be a skipper, eh, on a cold night like this?'

*

Next morning Bruton was awakened from a heavy slumber on his day-bed after a bare two hours of sleep by a brisk knock at his door. As he hauled himself out of the bunk, Spinks entered, glossy, smart, brass-buttoned and very cautious, though clearly still simmering with resentment at his treatment. He placed a thick file and a small booklet on the desk. 'I have been through the Company's regulations twice, sir, and can find no reference to civil marriage ceremonies, whether conducted by you or by anyone else.'

'Good. So they're not actually forbidden. We've got some sort of – what-d'ye-call – consecrated space amidships, haven't we?'

'Yes, we have a dedicated chapel of rest, sir, but of course that is normally used only for the mortal remains of elderly passengers who do not, as it were, quite last out the voyage. There is a suitable .... er... casket there, in which we can preserve the cadaver with ice from the galley.'

'Fine. No cadavers yet, I should hope? Well, get that blessed casket moved out of there, and let me see the passenger list. In over a thousand people there ought to be some kind of parson.'

'I have glanced through the first and second-class lists and found nobody, sir, of the clerical profession.'

'No, you wouldn't. First and second are respectively rich idlers and successful hucksters. Let's look at the third-class.'

'The steerage? Sir, it's hardly likely...'

But Bruton was paying no attention to his protests. Suddenly he gave a loud 'Aha!' and jabbed a stubby finger at the file. 'There you are! On the second page: "Reverend Obadiah Finch, Batesville, Arkansas". I thought so! Right, get below and see the Chief Steward in third-class – we don't call it "steerage" any more, remember – and tell him to locate this Reverend Obadiah Finch, and ask the gentleman if he will be so good as to come and see me as soon as possible.'

Less than ten minutes later Bruton called 'Come in!' to a polite knock, and in came a red-faced, round-faced, stoutish young countryman with a shock of curly black hair. He was dressed in a baggy, shabby black suit with a startlingly-white dog-collar. He was sweating from his haste, and anxious: 'Cap'n, you wanted to see me? Is sump'n wrong? A death, maybe?'

'No, no, sir, quite the contrary. And thank you for coming so quickly. Pray take a seat. Now then, my question is a simple one: are you licensed by your church to conduct a marriage ceremony in a suitable surrounding aboard this ship – today?'

'I surely am, sir. I'm a licentiate of the Little Rock Southern Baptist College. I've celebrated four – no, five – marriages of young folk in Batesville already, and one of those was in a hay-barn. In my church the place is not important. We believe God is everywhere.'

'Good. But you are a Baptist. Could you marry couples of another faith? Of the couple I have in mind, the girl is Welsh. I'm not sure of her precise persuasion, but I feel sure she is a Nonconformist. As for the man, I believe him to be nominally of the Church of England. What do you say, reverend?'

Finch gave a broad smile and reached out his arms as if to embrace the absent couple: 'Lordy, sir, I say I will be happy beyond words! Maybe in some dusty old Baptist book somewhere it says I shouldn't, but didn' the Apostle Paul himself say: "The letter killeth, but the spirit giveth life"? If'n I can launch these young folk into a Christian marriage, where they can raise a family of little ones to grow up in the praise of the Lord Jesus, what do I care about some goldarned old shibboleth I ain't heard of?'

Bruton leapt to his feet and impulsively grasped the preacher's hands: 'Mr Finch, you are a man after my own heart! I will be candid with you: I also am in the dark as to whether my company allows me to do this, but (pardon my language!) what the hell? If, between us, we can give these two – who I may say have for months shown incredible courage and endured many hardships and dangers – if we can give them, on my beautiful ship, a wonderful honeymoon – then, sir, why not, in God's name? I will send for them now.'

After dispatching the steward, Bruton said, more calmly: 'In the meantime, Mr Finch, I am not happy about a man of your position being in third-class. I know there are always some very undesirable roughnecks below there. My purser could find you a decent cabin a deck higher in second-class, more befitting to your status and calling, and, I think I can promise you, at no extra cost to yourself.'

'No indeed, cap'n. That's a kind thought, but I have the privilege and honour of being one of the Lord's missionaries to all men, rich, poor, black, white. I am on my way now, in fact, to spread His word among the freed slaves in Liberia – lest they fall back into their old heathen ways. But ours is a poor church, so I travel among the humblest. Besides that, I have already founded a small prayer- and bible-study group, and should be sorry to leave them now.'

'You're a good man, Mr Finch, and true to your calling. It is my fate to be sometimes merely the unctuous dinner-table host to the richest folk in the world, and I can tell you, that is a part of my job I do *not* esteem or relish.'

Finch shook his head and looked at him with a shrewd smile: 'I felt the ship stopping and starting during the night, sir, and woke sometimes to hear your steam siren boomin' away. I guess you were up there in the cold, losing your sleep? Fog, I dare say? So then you – and you alone - had the fate of this great ship and the lives of all of us on your shoulders, and you have brought us safely through that danger. Don't you undervalue your own calling, sir. The Lord made both of us to serve His great and manifold purposes – those who go down to the sea in ships, as well as the humble pastors of His flock.'

*

Raven and Eleanor were late for breakfast that morning, for their passionate, joyful, sensual re-discovery of each other's bodies had gone on long into the night. They were surprised and puzzled when, as they sipped their first cups of coffee, a smiling steward laid an envelope on their table: 'Sir, madam, a message from the captain.' The message from Bruton was characteristically brisk: 'Got an idea I'd like to put to you. Come and see me after breakfast.'

They were again surprised, when they entered the captain's cabin, to find, not only Bruton and Grant, but also a burly, curly-haired, black-suited young clergyman. They exchanged looks of wild surmise, and Eleanor, immediately aware of a totally new possibility, blushed to the deepest scarlet.

Bruton was laconic, as usual: 'Eleanor, Jack: what do you say to getting married today, eh? My ship has a consecrated space below, and Mr Finch here, from Arkansas, is a licenced minister of religion, who will be delighted to conduct the ceremony later today, if that will be suitable to you both.'

'Suitable?' said the astonished Eleanor. *'Suitable?* It would be our dearest, deepest wish, would it not, Jack?'

'By Jove, yes! But can it be done so soon? No licence, no banns or anything?'

Mentally crossing his fingers, Bruton said, with well-feigned confidence: 'The Reverend Finch and I are sure that this marriage will satisfy the civil law and the law of your churches, though no doubt you will want to hold a larger, more formal, ceremony when you arrive home, among your relatives and neighbours. Allow me to introduce you now to my new friend, the Reverend Obadiah Finch, from Batesville, Arkansas, who will, if you wish, launch you into the matrimonial state at – shall we say – two o'clock today?'

Still bewildered, Eleanor stuttered: 'But…but don't we need a best man, someone to give me away, witnesses, and a meal afterwards, and so on?'

Grant broke his silence: 'If Jack will have me, I'll be his best man. God knows he has been my best man for many a weary month of troubles.'

'And I,' said Bruton, 'would be delighted to give you away, if you will accept me as one of a suitably advanced age to deputize for your father, God rest him. I have never met a couple who so deserved, and so clearly longed for, happiness together. As for witnesses, Mr Finch will bring along some of his bible-study group to …Oh, my dear, whatever is the matter?'

For the volatile Eleanor had suddenly gone to him and laid her head on his shoulder, sobbing, her tears running down his smooth serge jacket. 'No, no, nothing is the matter – it's just that, after the horrors we've been through, suddenly we meet nothing but kindness and goodness from strangers. It is like another world. Captain, you are the kindest man alive!'

A little embarrassed, Bruton said: 'H'mph! Nice of you to say so, m'dear. Not sure all my crew would agree with you, though.'

Raven, at first too moved for words, shook his hand and the hands of Grant and Finch, and was at last able to say: 'Can't thank you enough – all of you. Jolly sporting of you! I'll never forget this.'

'Lordy, young feller,' said Finch, 'don't thank me. Thank Almighty God, who ordained that I should be here at your time of need. And miss, we ain't really strangers;

we are all fellow-pilgrims on the path to the same salvation.'

Bruton brought them back to earth from this spiritual solemnity: 'And after the happy occasion, you will all – your friends as well, Mr Finch – be my guests for a wedding breakfast at the for'ard end of the first-class restaurant. And, by Heaven, you will see what the chefs of the White Star Line can do. So make sure you come hungry! I'm going to get the purser to arrange all that now.'

So while, a little later, Bruton was telling an indignant and scandalized Spinks that six pious, but probably ill-clad, third-class passengers were to eat a special lunch in the first-class restaurant, back in Eleanor's cabin the lovers, hand-in-hand on the sofa, were at first too dazed by their luck to speak coherently. 'Can't believe it!' said Raven. 'That Bruton is a first-class chap. Fancy him bothering with all this when he's got a ten-thousand-ton ship to run and has been up all night, probably, because of that beastly fog! Grant says there's a westerly gale blowing up, too. Tell you what, though: you were wondering about my people accepting you as Mrs Raven. Well, they'll jolly well have to now, won't they? It'll be a …what-d'ye-call? A fate a… something.'

'A *fait accompli.* Didn't you learn *anything* in school? But listen, my boy: I have feminine problems that you haven't even thought about. You bought yourself that nice grey suit in Boston, so you're all right, but what in the world I'm going to wear, I don't know.'

'Darling, don't worry! If we love each other, what does it matter what you're wearing?'

'I do love you, Jack, dearly, but if you say that again, I shall hit you very hard indeed! Of *course* it matters a lot to me, on this day of all days! I've only got two of these very plain and dowdy Quaker dresses. I was wearing the better of the two last night, but I see it is very crumpled now – thanks to you and your disgraceful behaviour on my sofa.'

'We're in first-class now, Nelli. Ring for a stewardess and tell her to get it ironed.'

'Yes. Now that, for a man, is quite a sensible idea. So you go back to your own lair for a couple of hours, and let me try and arrange it.'

Half an hour later she was busy with her preparations when there was a tap at the door. Ah, she thought, that'll be the stewardess, come to collect my dress.

But it was not. Instead, a tall, fresh-faced girl, beautifully dressed, stood shyly in the doorway. 'Miss Roberts?' she said. 'May I come in? I'm Sophie van Houten. My parents and I are in the suite just down the corridor.'

Bewildered, Eleanor said: 'Why, yes, do come in, please. But what can I do for you?'

'Well, you know how all servants gossip. I've just been told by our stewardess – yours too, I guess – that you and your young captain are getting married today, so I wanted to wish you both well. All of us girls have been talking about you and your fine dark handsome sailor, and we wish you both all the happiness in the world.'

'O, but that is so kind of you, Sophie! Everybody has been so lovely.' She impulsively hugged the American girl, and noticed for the first time that she was carrying, doubled over her arm, a long parcel, clad in rustling tissue-paper.

'That's OK, honey. But listen – this is maybe the most awful nerve on my part, but as your marriage is, I guess, at pretty short notice, and you maybe haven't had a chance to prepare for it, would you like to borrow a white dress for this afternoon? We're about the same size, I reckon. Here, have a look at it.'

'Would I like a white dress? Now I know I've died and gone to heaven! Yes, yes! Why, Sophie, it's beautiful! But are you sure?' She had taken in the expensive elegance of her visitor's clothes. 'I mean, I might tear it, or stain it. That would be awful.'

'Honey, it's just a dress. It's not covered in diamonds. Actually, it's a ball-gown, so you may not think it's quite suitable for the daytime. It's cut a bit low in front, but I'm sure I could find something – a lace stole, maybe, to cover you up a little – though with a figure like yours, why worry? And look, I've brought along some pins, in case we need to take it in here and there. What say I help you put it on now?'

Eleanor swiftly slipped out of her sober dress, and after some brief struggles and a good deal of giggling, Sophie said: 'There! Look at yourself in that full-length mirror. It's a perfect fit, Eleanor. No need for pins. Hey, why are you laughing so much? You look just fine in it.'

'I'm laughing, partly because I'm so happy, and so very grateful to you, but also because I have never in my life worn a dress like this before. It's real silk, isn't it? But what is even funnier to me is the contrast between it and the clothes I've been wearing for months now – sailor's cap, tarry smock, thick blue jersey, thick man's striped flannel shirt under that, scratchy flannel drawers, heavy serge trousers, sea-boot stockings and sea-boots. It's so wonderful to look and feel like a woman again! But of course I needed all that sailor's rig-out to get round Cape

Horn in an old New Bedford whaler under sail – all the way from New Zealand, not to mention a week or so in an open lifeboat.'

'An open boat, and round Cape Horn in an old sail-boat! Honey, you are a heroine! No wonder you look so fresh and strong and healthy! But listen: right down the back of the ship on this deck there are a few shops for clothes and stuff. Quite nice too.'

'Yes, I'll take a look tomorrow. Since we came aboard I've been too .... um ...too...um..' blushing furiously, she came to a lame halt. Then they exchanged looks, and both burst into laughter, hugging each other tightly.

'Elly, darling, if I'd had that dark handsome fellow with me, I'd have been too... um..too..um too!'

'Ssh! Don't be so dreadfully naughty! You're making me blush! We are engaged, after all! D'you know, Sophie, I've only known you for a few minutes, but already you seem like my dearest friend. You will come to the wedding, and the wedding breakfast, won't you? I'm sure the captain won't mind one more - he's so kind. Dear, dear, I must be careful; I seem to be taking a shine to all the sailors, even middle-aged ones!'

When he tapped on the door a few moments later, Raven was surprised and amused to hear the high laughter and a cry from Eleanor: 'Jack, if that's you, go a-*way!* You're not supposed to see me now!'

*

The wedding was a cheerful affair, largely thanks to Finch's bible-class. One of their number had brought a battered concertina, and with that led the congregation in some hearty, bawling hymns. At one crucial point Eleanor panicked at a sudden thought: the ring! Jack hasn't got a ring to put on me! Then she saw Jack and Simon exchange small smiles, and the latter produced a bright gold ring, and coolly handed it to the groom.

Now, the wedding and the reception over, and back in her cabin, she turned the ring on her finger, glowing with pleasure and pride. 'Jack, it's beautiful…beautiful!'

'Glad you like it. And by gosh, you were stunning too, Nell, in that gorgeous white dress. What a wonderful piece of luck to find such a kind friend of the right size at just the right time!'

'Yes, as you can see, I've put the dress back in its tissue-paper wrap now. I was terrified to wear it any longer – it must have cost a fortune. Can you still love me, back in my old Quaker home-spun?'

'I will try very hard, Nelli.'

'You'd better, my boy. But this ring – where, when, did you get it?'

'Don't you remember? Simon said there were shops down aft. I went to a posh jeweller's there this morning.'

'But you were so clever, to get exactly the right size! And it must have cost an awful lot, surely?'

'We've got money now, *cariad*. It's useful stuff to have. As for size, they said they'd change it if it wasn't…'

'Change it? Never! Not as long as I live!' And, drawing him gently to her, her palms flat behind his broad, hard shoulders, she silenced him with a passionate, lingering, but gentle kiss. 'Now then,' she said, drawing back, 'I know you'll think I'm completely mad, but what I'd like us to do now is – go for a walk.'

'A *walk?* Now? On deck? It's cold, it's blowing a gale from astern, it's started to rain, and liners don't have sails to steady them, so, as you can see and feel, she's rolling a good thirty-five degrees each way in this following sea. So, yes, you are crazy – but then you always have been.'

'Of course, darling, and you know that I'm crazy most of all about you – not just the man you are – your soul – but also your body. More than anything else in the world I want to open myself to you joyfully, to feel that fine, long part of your body not in my hand any more, but moving deep, deep inside my body. But not just yet, *capten*. Night and darkness are right for love.' She ended, and patted his cheek: 'As for my general craziness, you will just have to get used to it, my lad. We've got nice warm coats now, there's a lovely long sheltered promenade deck just outside that door. We're high up, so the deck won't be three feet deep in water, as it was in "Figaro" sometimes. And it's so exciting to see and feel this huge, beautiful ship tearing through the waves at twenty knots. Besides, it's always so still, so warm in this cabin, and I'm too full of delicious food and wine to make love. I want to ... to savour this moment in time before we finally take that last step, and I want to feel some strong, cold blasts of fresh air. So come on, you goddam lazy sojer, as that awful Mr Crowe would say: all hands on deck!'

Not surprisingly, they had the promenade deck to themselves. As the winter twilight began, the following gale freshened; the steep, almost black, pursuing seas, fiercely crested with dull spikes of foam, rhythmically lifted the great ship's stern, causing her screws every now and then to race frantically and shake her whole hull. The waves, overtaking her slowly with a dull, deep, quiet roar, caused her to roll prodigiously, inexorably, till it seemed as if there was no reason why she should not turn completely turtle. They could hear the whole hull creaking in every plate and rivet; but she was a good ship, Belfast-built and well ballasted, so each slow swing gradually ceased, and up she came, all ten-thousand tons of her, see-sawing too, as bow and stern were rhythmically raised and lowered by the twenty-foot waves. Down below, in the galleys, the chefs shrewdly calculated that they would not need to cook many sumptuous dinners, for the huge, gilded, pillared restaurant would be scantily filled that evening.

Even our lovers, hardened sailors both now, felt the motion strange and queasy. They stood at the rail for a while. Raven said: 'Whew! If she were under sail now, you'd have to heave her to and….'

He was halted by a cold, firm finger on his lips: 'Don't you dare start talking shop, *capten!* I want to walk, to talk, to live in just this moment in time. Remember how we all felt at the quayside? Now we are on the brink of another change – a change for the rest of our lives. Besides, these seas are nothing much to us; are they? You must remember what it was like when we were in "Susan" and they were forty feet high or more. Now, come on.'

Arm in arm, leaning on each other, they strolled up and down the heaving deck for a long time in a contented silence, until Raven, who had been thinking of the night to come, said anxiously, with a note of sympathetic concern: 'You know, Nelli, I've read and heard that when a woman – a virgin – makes love for the first time, it is pretty painful for her. I shall need to be very gentle, I know, and you must tell me if I'm hurting you.'

But instead of echoing his fears, Eleanor giggled and drew him closer: 'O, you've been reading about the hymen, have you? What a nice, sensitive man you are, even if you have been a rake in your time! Listen: don't worry about that problem. It doesn't exist for me. Dai has seen to that.'

Raven halted abruptly and spluttered: *'What?* Dai! Who the hell is Dai, for God's sake?'

Eleanor laughed aloud now: 'Don't worry about that, either! No Newport lecher has preceded you, though a few have tried quite hard. No, Dai is Dai Bach, my beautiful wild Welsh mountain pony. I have spent many hours riding him bareback, tearing about on the slopes of the Preseli Hills. My mother kept warning me that I should lose that little bit of my anatomy by riding astride, instead of side-saddle, and I'm sure I have. So don't be jealous of a fourteen-two pony. And anyway, my lad, what sort of a virgin are you? I've heard Dadi telling Mam about your goings-on among the senoritas in Chile. So don't you make a fuss about my virginity. I've noticed that nobody even asks whether the groom is a virgin or not! Grooms don't have to wear white suits to demonstrate their purity.'

'Phew! I can see there's a devil of a lot I have to learn about females! But there is another serious thing I wanted to ask you: when we're making love, do you want me to "be careful", as they say? You know, to come out of you at the last minute, so that you don't...you know...'

For answer, she stopped their pacing and embraced him hard: 'No, no! I want to feel your seed flowing into me. I want to be your proper wife, a mother of your children, not a plaything. Jack, Jack, I don't care if I have triplets before we get to Liverpool!'

'H'm, can't promise that, old girl, though I'll do my best.'

'But seriously, Jack, I believe in my heart that God gave us our bodies, our organs, our passionate longings, so that we should beget children to follow us, to maintain His kingdom upon earth, and, upon their deaths, to follow us again into His heavenly kingdom. While we are young we should feel no shame, no guilt, about enjoying each other's bodies to the full. God Himself willed it that we should.'

'No more fig-leaves, then. And, by Heaven, *cariad*,' he said hoarsely, 'no more walking and talking either.' He suddenly seized her, thrust her hard against the ship's rail, and with his whole body taut, bent her head backwards over the racing foam with an almost savage kiss that brought forth a little cry of surprise, and then a soft whimper of pleasure.

'Yes,' she whispered, as he released her, 'It's time, Jack, it is more than time. There are other things I want to discuss with you, but certainly not now.'

The silence and warmth of the cabin were welcome after their long walk in the loud, boisterous gale. As she entered, Eleanor swiftly peeled off her new coat and flung it to the deck, then began to unfasten the neck of her sombre dress. But Jack took her hands gently and said: 'No, Nelli, that's not the way. Softly, softly, catchee monkey, as they say. Slow, slow, that's the way. We've all the time in the world. Let me undress you, and you can do the same for me.'

Swaying to the prodigious roll of the ship, each fiddling with unfamiliar fastenings, giggling and staggering sometimes as abrupt pitching and lurching caught them unawares, sometimes themselves interrupting their purposes by passionate kissing and fondling as each new, more intimate, piece of flesh was exposed, they were indeed slow, slow. When at last they went naked to Eleanor's bed, Jack murmured: 'The lights: shall I turn them off?'

'No, *cariad*, not all of them. Leave one on. Tonight I feel I want to see you, see myself, as well as feeling what real love is like. We both, thank God, have bodies to be proud of. Come then, and lie close to me.' She took his hand and raised it to cup one of her youthful, matchless breasts, and for a long time they exchanged deep, passionate kisses.

Then, with a touch like that of a feather, Raven drew his big, rough, sailor's hand up and down the sheer silk of her inner thigh, and gently toyed with the brisk curls of her mount, while, writhing and gasping as if in torment, she took a light, loving, finger-tip hold of his stiff erection. But their headlong mutual passion, thwarted and stifled for so many weary days, weeks, months, could not long brook the delay, even of the most exquisite foreplay, and soon, in a soft, hoarse voice, close in his ear, Eleanor gasped: 'Now, Jack, *now,* please, for God's sake! You're driving me mad!' And smoothly, expertly, he entered her, and they were true lovers, man and wife, at last.

Then ensued a night in their lives like no other before - or after, perhaps – a night which passed like an unending dream. They lost all sense of time, sleeping, exhausted by their fierce, joyous, love-making, slowly half-waking to murmur and fondle and explore, then, pricked, driven by happy lust, coupling yet again, each coupling more leisurely, assured and ecstatic than the last. Finally, they both sank into a profound sleep of several hours.

And all night, as they had twisted, writhed and thrust their bodies rhythmically together, far below them men with blackened faces had sweated with shovels, super-heated steam had blasted through pipes and, in the cathedral-like engine-room, long gleaming piston-rods had slid smoothly up and down above the cylinders, huge cranks had turned, to make the screws thump out their remorseless, rapid drumbeat, to urge the great ship and her fifteen hundred souls towards England.

It was nearly dawn when at last Eleanor sat up and, unwilling to wake Jack, began to slide her feet gently to the deck; but he did awake, yawning, and said: 'What's the matter, darling? Don't go.'

She laughed softly: 'I have had the most marvellous and magical night of my life, Jack, but nature is not always romantic. I just have to go to the bathroom. So sorry to break the spell so earthily, but Nature calls!'

When she returned she found him also wide-awake and sitting up. 'Me too,' he said. 'I'll follow you.' When he returned to the bedside he said: 'I'm feeling unromantic too, but in another way, because I'm absolutely starving. D'you realize it's six o'clock in the morning and we haven't eaten for twelve hours or more?'

'I'm starving as well, but we shall just have to wait for breakfast at eight o'clock, shan't we?'

He gave a complacent smile: 'Ah, now there you underestimate your new husband, Mrs Raven. He's an ignorant, semi-literate booby, compared with you and

Simon, and can't remember any quotations,but he's very practical in important matters.' He went naked to the wash-stand, and, with a showman's panache, pulled from under it a tray, on which were a glittering, bedewed ice-bucket, two tall glasses, and a plate covered with a spotless napkin. 'I went to the restaurant and ordered this to be brought to your cabin while we were busy getting married. What do you say, ma'am, to a coldish bottle of Chablis and a plate of smoked salmon sandwiches? And there is fruit to follow. Will that restore your vitality?'

'Vitality! Phew, what is that? I don't feel as if I shall ever have any of that again. Jack, you're wonderful, even if your waiter's uniform is a bit unusual. Whatever the poets say, love is not quite *all* that the body needs, is it?'

Reclining on their elbows, unclothed like a nymph and shepherd in a classical sculpture, they ate and drank, savouring the hedonistic luxury of their late supper – or early breakfast – call it what you will. When all the sandwiches had disappeared, Jack pulled out a fruit-bowl: 'Dessert, madam? Look, there's a nice bunch of bananas. Aren't they supposed to be nourishing?'

'I believe so, and, for you - ' she added with a lecherous grin, '- their shape could not be more appropriate.'

'No, I can't allow that comparison. That's libellous, in fact. They all have pronounced bends in the middle.'

When the fruit too had vanished Eleanor said: 'That was all delicious, Jack; you're a resourceful chap, aren't you? Now come back to bed, and for goodness'sake behave properly for a while, if you can. No more monkey business! I want to be sensible, even after all that wine. I said last evening that there was something we needed to discuss. It's very important, though it didn't seem so then.

Look: we need to come to an agreement about what will happen when we get home and settle down. We have money coming soon, but not enough to last us a lifetime. We have to have an income. My mother and father may have left me something in their wills, but it will not be a fortune. They owned no property that I know of.'

'Well, when I've got my mate's ticket...'

'No, hear me out, Jack. I know the sea is your calling, your life, your profession, and I'd hate to try and thwart you in that. But I've been a deep-sea captain's daughter, and I've seen how much my mother suffered from Dadi's interminable absences – two years at a time, quite often. Jack, I just can't bear the thought of all that lonely time without you, and having some money gives us choices my parents didn't have.'

'Maybe, Nell, but all the same, the only way I can make a decent living now is by going to sea. I'm no good at anything else, and we've got enough money to get by while I study for my ticket, and then...'

'And then, Jack, not every ship is a windjammer; there are other kinds of ships, which are not wandering the whole globe for years - steamers, for instance...'

'Steamers!' There was cool distaste in his voice. 'That's not proper sailoring! Too boring!'

'Calm down, my lad, and listen. I've been thinking hard about our future, but I don't think you have at all. Firstly, we need a house to live in; secondly' – she gave a playful grin – 'because of your quite disgraceful behaviour during the night it is highly possible that before long there will be more than the two of us in it. If and when we do have a little one – our own *baban bach* - to love and care for, I should so like you to be there, to share the joy, and give me support, not to mention changing dirty nappies. You can't do that if you're in Valparaiso loading nitrate, can you? And think what you would be missing!'

'Yes, but…'

'Hear me out, Jack. We shall not be living in some wild, remote desert. There is a railway station at Cardigan, only eleven miles from Newport; from there you could travel easily to New Milford, Llanelli, Swansea or Port Talbot. From all those places there are coastal ships and ferries making short voyages. Why, from New Milford there are regular ferries to Waterford and Cork.'

'That sounds boring beyond words – like running an omnibus.'

'Now you're being a bit tiresome and childish, Jack. We're going to be in a totally new situation, and we must cut our coat according to our cloth, and, *chwarae teg,* we've got to think of both, or all three - of us, not just you, Jack. Besides, nothing we arrange now needs to be forever. Whatever I said yesterday about children, I don't want to be like poor Mrs Dickens – landed with a herd of children, while her talented husband runs off (so they say) with a young actress. Two or three would be fine…'

'But you are talking about *years,* Nell.'

'Yes, a few years, during which you could earn good money as a mate, and have time to study for your master's ticket. And *then* there could be a whole new set of choices for us. And even if short steamer voyages in home waters sound boring to you now, there would surely be some compensations when you came home?'

'Oh Nelli, you know that I'd love to be with you, and with any new arrivals. Besides, if I'm realistic, I can see that in the long run, steam and coal and grease are the future, not sail. I'll have to get used to that situation.'

'Darling Jack, the wine and the food just now, besides a host of other actions, have shown how practical you are, but you don't see other, totally different, possibilities. You have got the fixed idea that you have to choose, in a way, between me and the sea. You're sure you couldn't have both ...'

'Well, of course I couldn't!'

'Yes, you could, Jack, you could! We have talked about *your* love of the sea; but what about mine? I have lived at its edge all my life; I spent time at sea, as I've told you, when I was little. I have spent the last year or so at sea, in two liners, a windjammer, an open boat, and an old whaler, and, despite everything – the grim weather, the cold, the danger, the awful food, the isolation – despite all that, I too have fallen in love with the adventure, the wandering life, the constant change, the wonderful beauty of sailing-ships, of the wind, waves, clouds and sun. In here, in my soul, there is a longing for a life at sea. And besides, I have learnt so much about the sea life by watching and listening to you and Simon, and old Jac-y-Bont and Reuben – so much! And I think, if we are together, I can, in return, show you much, too – about the countryside, animals, and other things like music and books and pictures – things that so far you seem to have missed. Once the "new arrivals", as you call them, have been safely delivered and can walk and run about, they and I could be with you at sea. How will they know and love their father if he is never with them?'

Raven turned in the berth and kissed her long and tenderly: 'Nelli, I've been a bit of cad – a rotter. I've only been thinking about myself – what I want from life - and not about what you want. Of course we need a home, a roof over our heads, and I'm happy for that to be in your beloved Newport. Oxford doesn't appeal to me much. Too far from the sea. Some poetic chap or other goes on about its "dreaming spires" and there are wonderful buildings there, but it's full of no doubt very clever coves draped in black gowns – like a lot of old crows.'

'Not ravens?'

'No, I could never be one of them, Nell. No brain, you see. But, being practical again, I can see a problem: I couldn't hope to be master of a large, deep-sea carrier for years, and only the master can have his wife and family aboard, as you know well.'

'I know, I know. But I also know that, with your deep-sea mate's ticket you could be master of a small ship – a brig, a tops'l schooner, or a ketch. I know about these things, Jack, from hearing my father and his friends talking. Just think, Jack: in quite a short time you could be master of your own vessel, and make good profits for us by your trading.'

'But listen, Nelli: we have to buy a house first. After that, how could we possibly afford to ...?'

'To buy a ship? Maybe we couldn't, by the time we've paid the hands from the "Figaro" what we promised, but then we don't have to. I don't think you realize that, all along the west coasts of Wales and England, there are lots of little companies – groups of shareholders in each little town or village - owning and running small trading ships, and making handsome profits too. The best of these ships - the Western Ocean yachts, they call them - ply sometimes as far as the Canary Isles in the south and west, to the Black Sea in the east, and all over the Mediterranean and the Baltic too. Why, the city of Hamburg is roofed with slates from Porthmadog, and much of the exotic fruit we eat at home has come to us in a Welsh schooner! That doesn't sound boring, does it, especially if we were together at sea?'

'No indeed. But it would be a hard life, Nelli: cramped quarters, sea-going food, wind, rain, snow, rough seas – and dangers too. You know all too well that sometimes it's not the sea that's dangerous and the land safe, but the other way round. After every bad storm you hear and read of coasting vessels driven ashore, and lives lost. I couldn't bear it if I thought you and our children were sacrificed to my choice of career.'

'Nor I, Jack, but there is no such thing as complete safety anywhere, and I would trust you, above all others that I know, to keep us safe from harm. I know that, as you say, in stormy weather small trading vessels are often wrecked. But that is often because the ships are poorly rigged, or through the sheer incompetence and folly and lack of sensible foresight of their masters. You will be captain of a first-rate, well-found ship, with decent captain's quarters, and we will find good sailors to man her. I'm certain that, once people in Pembrokeshire hear about your achievements, they will be eager to invest in, let's say, a smart tops'l schooner under your command. We could take, say, sixteen shares out of the sixty-four.'

'Sixty-four? That's a strange number to pick.'

'Come on, mister navigator, think of the mathematics: it's a good number, because you can easily factorize it down to one, two, four, eight, sixteen and so on, so that even quite poor people can invest something. It will mean quite a lot of book-keeping, but I will do that. Now then, skipper, what do you say?'

'I say it still sounds pretty mad. But then, I expect nothing else from my new, beautiful bride. So I say yes, but not for a while yet. I'll serve my time on the blessed steam-kettles first. I'll need the practice if I'm to finish up as skipper of a hooker like the one we're on now.'

'Excellent. That's the spirit – look ahead! But there is one other hurdle for you to surmount: if you are to take command one day of a Welsh ship and a Welsh crew, you will have to learn our language. You will have to be a *Cymro Cymraeg* – a Welsh-speaking Welshman.'

'Crikey, Nell, that's a tall order, on top of everything else! I was hopeless at French and Latin in school.'

'Yes, it will involve you in hours of mental torture, but then you didn't go to bed with your French and Latin tutors, I presume? Welsh is one of the hardest languages in Europe to master. Only Finnish, they say, is worse. Welsh has several kinds of mutations, declining prepositions, a different alphabet, and no words for either "yes" or "no", but you will manage, for I will be your tutor, by day and night, and, my lad' – here she took his hand and pressed it to the moist warmth of the exact geometrical centre of her body –'there will be wonderful rewards for good progress in grammar.'

'My God, Eleanor Roberts – sorry, Raven - I've never met anyone quite like you – totally mad and more than totally adorable. And, d'you know, after all that wine and food, and the long palaver we've had, I believe my …um …strength has come back. Shall we…'

She turned to press her body against his, gently stroking his thigh, and, gliding her hand upwards, said softly: 'Good Heavens, so it has, *capten!*'

'Well, then, shall we?'

She gave a sigh of deep pleasure, luxuriating in the warmth of their bed, the bounding vigour of their youth, the closeness of his hard body and the rapturous convulsions and moments of towering ecstasy that the night had brought her. She whispered, very close in his ear: 'Very well: your first Welsh lesson, then: *Pam lai?* Which is Welsh for "why *ever* not?"'